THE SPANISH GAME

ALSO BY CHARLES CUMMING

A Spy by Nature
Typhoon
The Hidden Man

THE
SPANISH
GAME

Charles Cumming

St. Martin's Press ≋ New York

THE SPANISH GAME. Copyright © 2006 by Charles Cumming. All rights reserved. Printed in the United States of America. For information, address St. Martin's Press, 175 Fifth Avenue, New York, N.Y. 10010.

www.stmartins.com

Excerpt from *The Talented Mr. Ripley* by Anthony Minghella (screenplay copyright © The Art Colony Ltd., 2000) at page 157 reproduced by kind permission of Methuen Publishing Ltd.

Library of Congress Cataloging-in-Publication Data

Cumming, Charles, 1971–
    The Spanish game / Charles Cumming. — 1st U.S. ed.
        p. cm.
    ISBN-13: 978-0-312-36639-1
    ISBN-10: 0-312-36639-6
    1. Intelligence officers—Fiction. 2. Terrorism—Spain—Fiction. 3. Madrid (Spain)—Fiction. I. Title.

PR6103.U484S67   2008
823'-92—dc22

                                  2008028749

First published in Great Britain by Michael Joseph,
an imprint of Penguin Books Ltd.

First U.S. Edition: December 2008

10 9 8 7 6 5 4 3 2 1

For my mother and Simon, my stepfather

Author's Note

The Spanish Game is a work of fiction inspired by real events. With one or two obvious exceptions, the characters depicted in the novel are products of my imagination. The book has been written with respect for opinions on both sides of the Basque conflict.

The story takes place in Madrid in the first half of 2003, many months before the events of March 11, 2004, which left 192 people dead and more than 1,700 injured. At the time of writing, no evidential link between the perpetrators of the Atocha bombings and Basque terrorist groups has ever been established.

London, June 2008

Madrid is a strange place anyway. I do not believe any one likes it much when he first goes there. It has none of the look that you expect of Spain . . . Yet when you get to know it, it is the most Spanish of all cities, the best to live in, the finest people, and month in and month out the finest climate and while other big cities are all very representative of the province they are in, they are either Andalucian, Catalan, Basque, Aragonese, or otherwise provincial. It is in Madrid only that you get the essence . . . It makes you feel very badly, all question of immortality aside, to know that you will have to die and never see it again.

—Ernest Hemingway

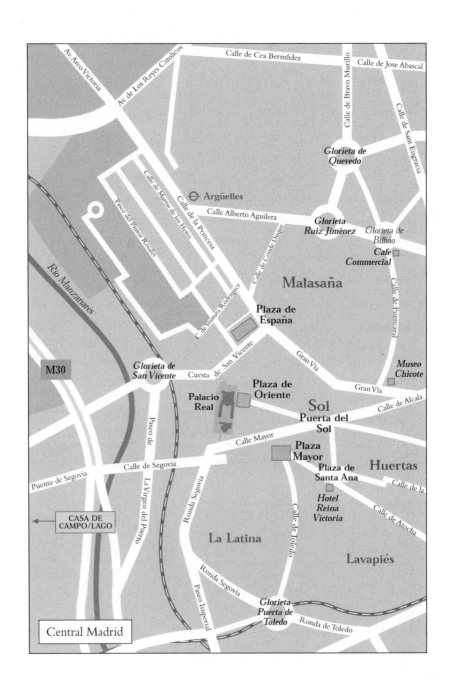

Central Madrid

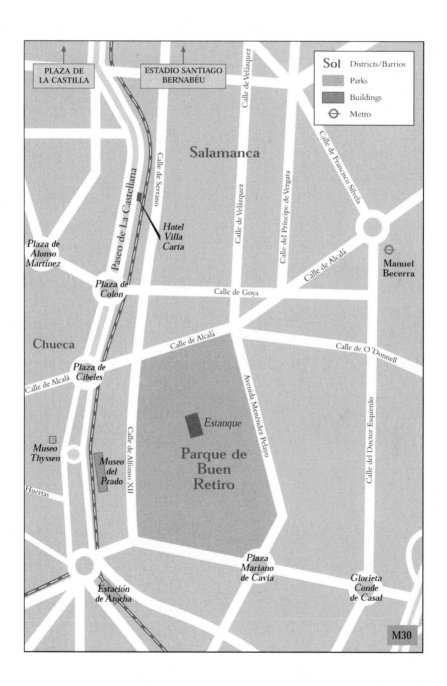

PLAZA DE
LA CASTILLA

ESTADIO SANTIAGO
BERNABÉU

Sol   Districts/Barrios
      Parks
      Buildings
      Metro

Calle de Velázquez

Salamanca

Calle de Serrano

Calle de Francisco Silvela

Paseo de La Castellana

Calle de Velázquez

Calle del Príncipe de Vergara

Hotel
Villa
Carta

Plaza de
Alonso
Martínez

Calle de Alcalá

Manuel
Becerra

Plaza de
Colon

Calle de Goya

Chueca

Calle de Alcalá

Calle de O'Donnell

Plaza de
Cibeles

Calle de Alcalá

Avenida Menéndez Pelayo

Calle del Doctor Esquerdo

Museo
Thyssen

Calle de Alfonso XII

Estanque

Museo
del
Prado

Parque de
Buen
Retiro

Huertas

Plaza
Mariano
de Cavia

Glorieta
Conde
de Casal

Estación
de Atocha

M30

THE SPANISH GAME

1

Exile

The door leading into the hotel is already open and I walk through it into a low, wide lobby. Two South American teenagers are playing Gameboys on a sofa near reception, kicking back in hundred-dollar trainers while Daddy picks up the bill. The older of them swears loudly in Spanish and then catches his brother square on the knot of his shoulder with a dead arm that makes him wince in pain. A passing waiter looks down, shrugs, and empties an ashtray at their table. There's a general atmosphere of listless indifference, of time passing by to no end, the prerush lull of late afternoons.

"Buenas tardes, señor."

The receptionist is wide shouldered and artificially blond and I play the part of a tourist, making no effort to speak to her in Spanish.

"Good afternoon. I have a reservation here today."

"The name, sir?"

"Alec Milius."

"Yes, sir."

She ducks down and taps something into a computer. Then there's a smile, a little nod of recognition, and she writes down my details on a small piece of card.

"The reservation was made over the Internet?"

"That's right."

"Could I see your passport please, sir?"

Five years ago, almost to the day, I spent my first night in Madrid at this same hotel; a twenty-eight-year-old industrial spy on the run from the UK with $189,000 lodged in five separate bank accounts, using three passports and a forged British driving licence for ID. On that occasion I handed a Lithuanian passport issued to me in Paris in August 1997 to the clerk behind the desk. The hotel may have a record of this on their system, so I'm using it again.

"You are from Vilnius?" the receptionist asks.

"My grandfather was born there."

"Well, breakfast is between seven thirty and eleven o'clock and you have it included as part of your rate." It is as if she has no recollection of having asked the question. "Is it just yourself staying with us?"

"Just myself."

My luggage consists of a suitcase filled with old newspapers and a leather briefcase containing some toiletries, a laptop computer, and two of my three mobile phones. We're not planning to stay in the room for more than a few hours. A porter is summoned from across the lobby and he escorts me to the lifts at the back of the hotel. He's short and tanned and genial in the manner of low-salaried employees badly in need of a tip. His English is rudimentary, and it's tempting to break into Spanish just to make the conversation more lively.

"This is being your first time in Madrid, yes?"

"Second, actually. I visited two years ago."

"For the bullfights?"

"On business."

"You don't like the corrida?"

"It's not that. I just didn't have the time."

The room is situated halfway down a long, Barton Fink corridor on the third floor. The porter uses a credit-card-sized pass key to open the door and places my suitcase on the ground. The lights are operated by inserting the key in a narrow horizontal slot outside the bathroom door, although I know from experience that a credit card works just as well; anything narrow enough to trigger the switch will do the trick. The room is a reasonable size, perfect for our needs, but as soon as I am inside I frown and make a show of looking disappointed and the porter duly asks if everything is all right.

"It's just that I asked for a room with a view over the square. Could you see at the desk if it would be possible to change?"

Back in 1998, as an overt target conscious of being watched by both American and British intelligence, I ran basic countersurveillance measures as soon as I arrived at the hotel, searching for microphones and hidden cameras. Five years later, I am either wiser or lazier; the simple last-minute switch of room negates any need to sweep. The porter has no choice but to return to reception and within ten minutes I have been assigned a new room on the fourth floor with a clear view over Plaza de Santa Ana. After a quick shower I put on a dressing gown, turn down the air-conditioning, and try to make the room look less functional by folding up the bedspread, placing it in a cupboard, and opening the net curtains so that the decent February light can flood in. It's cold outside, but I stand briefly on the balcony looking out over the square. A neat line of denuded chestnut trees runs east toward the Teatro de España where a young African man is selling counterfeit CDs from a white sheet spread out on the pavement. In the distance I can see the edge of the Parque Retiro and the roofs of the taller buildings on Calle de Alcalá. It's a typical midwinter afternoon in Madrid: high blue skies, a brisk wind whipping across the square, sunlight on my face. Turning back into the room I pick up one of the mobiles and dial her number from memory.

"Sofía?"

"*Hola,* Alec."

"I'm in."

"What is the number of the room?"

"*Cuatrocientos ocho.* Just walk straight through the lobby. There's nobody there and they won't stop you or ask any questions. Keep to the left. The elevators are at the back. Fourth floor."

"Is everything OK?"

"Everything's OK."

"*Vale,*" she says. Fine. "I'll be there in an hour."

2

Baggage

Sofía is the wife of another man. We have been seeing each other now for over a year. She is thirty years old, has no children, and has been married, unhappily, since 1999. To meet in the Reina Victoria hotel is something that she has always wanted us to do, and with her husband due back in Madrid on an 8 A.M. flight tomorrow, we can stay here until the early hours of the morning.

Sofía knows nothing about Alec Milius, or at least nothing of any hard fact or consequence. She does not know that at the age of twenty-four I was talent-spotted by MI6 in London and placed inside a British oil company with the purpose of befriending two employees of a rival American firm and selling them doctored research data on an oilfield in the Caspian Sea. Katharine and Fortner Simms, both of whom worked for the CIA, became my close friends over a two-year period, a relationship that ended when they discovered that I was working for British intelligence. Sofía is not aware that in the aftermath of the operation, my former girlfriend, Kate Allardyce, was murdered in a car accident engineered by the CIA, alongside another man, her new boyfriend, Will Griffin. Nor does she know that in the summer of 1997, I was dismissed by MI5 and MI6 and threatened with prosecution if I revealed anything about my work for the government.

As far as Sofía is concerned, Alec Milius is a typical footloose Englishman who turned up in Madrid in the spring of 1998 after working as a financial correspondent for Reuters in London and, latterly, St. Petersburg. He has lost touch with the friends he knew from school and university, and both his parents died when he was a teenager. The money they left him allows him to live in an expensive two-bedroom flat in downtown Madrid and drive an Audi A6 for work. The fact that my mother is still alive and that the last five years of my life have been largely funded by the proceeds of industrial espionage is not something that Sofía and I have ever discussed.

What is the truth? That I have blood on my hands? That I walk the streets with knowledge of a British plot against American business concerns that would blow George and Tony's special relationship out of the water? Sofía does not need to know about that. She has her own lies, her own secrets to conceal. What did Katharine say to me all those years ago? "The first thing you should know about people is that you don't know the first thing about them." So we leave it at that. That way we keep things simple.

And yet, and yet . . . five years of evasion and lies have taken their toll. At a time when my contemporaries are settling down, making their mark, breeding like locusts, I live alone in a foreign city, a man of thirty-three with no friends or roots, drifting, time-biding, waiting for something to happen. I came here exhausted by secrecy, desperate to wipe the slate clean, to be rid of all the half-truths and deceptions that had become the common currency of my life. And now what is left? An adultery. A part-time job working due diligence for a British private bank. A stained conscience. Even a young man lives with the mistakes of his past, and regret clings to me like a sweat that I cannot shift.

Above all, there is paranoia: the threat of vengeance, of payback. To escape Katharine and the CIA I have no Spanish bank accounts, no landline phone number at the apartment, two PO boxes, a Frankfurt-registered car, five e-mail addresses, timetables of every airline flying out of Madrid, the numbers of the four phone boxes thirty meters up my street, and a rented bedsit in the village of Alcalá de los Gazules within a forty-minute drive of the boat to Tangier. I have moved apartment four times in five years. When I see a tourist's camera pointed at me outside the Palacio Real, I fear that I am being photographed by an agent of SIS. And when the genial Segovian comes to my flat every three months to read the water meter, I follow him at a distance of no less than two meters to ensure that he has no opportunity to plant a bug. This is a tiring existence. It consumes me.

So there is booze, and a lot of it. Booze to alleviate the guilt, booze to soften the suspicion. Madrid is built for late nights, for bar crawling into the small hours, and four mornings out of five I wake with a hangover and then drink again to cure it. It was booze that brought Sofía and me together last year, a long evening of *caipirinhas* at a bar on Calle Moratín and then falling into bed together at 6 A.M. The sex we have is like the sex that everybody has, only heightened by the added frisson of adultery and ultimately rendered meaningless by an absence of love. Ours is not, in other words, a relationship to compare with the one that I had with Kate—and it is probably all the better for that. We know where we stand. We know that one of us is married, and that the other never confides. Try as she might, Sofía will never succeed in drawing me out of my shell. "You are closed, Alec," she says. *"Eres muy tuyo."* An amateur Freudian would say that I have had no serious relationship in eight years as a consequence of my guilt over Kate's death. We are all amateur Freudians now. And there is perhaps some truth in that. The reality is more mundane; it is simply that I have never met anyone to whom I have wanted to entrust my tawdry secrets, never met anyone whose life was worth destroying for the sake of my security and peace of mind.

Far below, in the square, a busker has started playing alto sax, a tone-deaf cover version of "Roxanne," loud enough for me to have to close the doors of the balcony and switch on the hotel TV. Here's what's on: a dubbed Brazilian soap opera starring a middle-aged actress with a bad nose job; a press conference with the government's interior minister, Félix Maldonado; a Spanish version of the British show *Trisha,* in which an audience of Franco-era *madrileños* are staring open-mouthed at a quartet of transvestite strippers lined up on stools along a bright orange stage; a rerun on Eurosport of Germany winning the 1990 World Cup; Christina Aguilera saying that she "really, *really*" respects one of her colleagues "as an artist" and is "just waiting for the right script to come along"; a CNN reporter standing on a balcony in Kuwait City being patronizing about "ordinary Iraqis"; and BBC World, where the anchorman looks about twenty-five and never fluffs a line. I stick with that, if only for a glimpse of the old country, for low gray skies and the stiff upper lip. At the same time I boot up the laptop and download some e-mails. There are seventeen in all, spread over four accounts, but only two that are of interest.

From: julianchurch@bankendiom.es
To: alecm@bankendiom.es

Subject: Basque visit

Dear Alec

Re: our conversation the other day. If any situation encapsulates the petty small-mindedness of the Basque problem, it's the controversy surrounding poor Ainhoa Cantalapiedra, the rather pretty pizza waitress who has won Operación Triunfo. Have you been watching it? Spain's answer to *Fame Academy.* The wife and I were addicted.

As you may or may not know, Miss Cantalapiedra is a Basque, which has led to accusations that the result was fixed. The (ex) leader of Batasuna has accused Aznar's lot of rigging the vote so that a Basque would represent Spain at the Eurovision Song Contest. Have you ever *heard* such nonsense? There's a rather good piece about it in today's *El Mundo.*

Speaking of the Basque country, would you be available to go to San Sebastián early next week to meet officials in various guises with a view to firming up the current state of affairs? Endiom has a new client, Spanish-based, looking into viability of a car operation, but rather cold feet politically.

Will explain more when I get back this w/e.

All the very best

Julian

I click "Reply":

From: alecm@bankendiom.es
To: julianchurch@bankendiom.es

Subject: Re: Basque visit

Dear Julian

No problem. I'll give you a call about this at the weekend. I'm off to the cinema now and then to dinner with friends.

I didn't watch Operación Triunfo. Would rather cook a five-course dinner for Osama bin Laden—with wines. But your e-mail reminded me of a similar story, equally ridiculous in terms of the stand-off between Madrid and the separatists. Apparently there's a former ETA commander languishing in prison taking a degree in psychology to help pass the time. His exam results—and those of several of his former comrades—have been off the charts, prompting Aznar to suggest that they've either been cheating or that the examiners are too scared to give them anything less than 90%.

All the best

Alec

The second e-mail comes through on AOL.

From: sricken1789@hotmail.com
To: almmlalam@aol.com

Subject: Coming to Madrid

Hi—

As expected, Heloise has now kicked me out of the house. The house that I paid for. Logic?

So I'm booked on the Friday easyJet. It lands at 5:15 in Madrid and I might have to stick around for a bit. Hope that's OK. I've taken three weeks off work to clear my head. Could go to Cádiz as well to stay with a mate down there.

Don't worry about picking me up, I'll get a cab. Just tell me your address. (And don't do the seven different e-mail/dead drop/is this line secure?/smoke signal bullshit.) Just hit "Reply" and tell me where you live. NOBODY'S WATCHING, ALEC. You're not Kim Philby.

Anyway, really looking forward to seeing you.

Saul

So he's finally coming. The keeper of the secrets. After six years, my oldest friend is on his way to Spain. Saul, who married a girl he barely knew just two summers ago and already lies on the brink of divorce. Saul, who holds a signed affidavit recounting in detail my relationship with MI5 and SIS, to be released to the press in the event of any "accident." Saul, who was so angry with me in the aftermath of what happened that we did not speak to each other for three and a half years.

There's a knock at the door, a soft, rapid tap. I switch off the TV, close the computer, quickly check my reflection in the mirror, and cross the room.

Sofía is wearing her hair up and has a sly, knowing look on her face. Giving off an air of mischief as she glances over my shoulder.

"*Hola,*" she says, touching my cheek. The tips of her fingers are soft and cold. She must have returned home after work, taken a shower, and then changed into a new set of clothes—the jeans she knows I like, a black turtleneck sweater, shoes with two-inch heels. She is holding a long winter coat in her left hand, and the smell of her as she passes me is intoxicating. "What a room," she says, dropping the coat on the bed and crossing to the balcony. "What a view." She turns and heads to the bathroom, mapping out the territory, touching the bottles of shower gel and tiny parcels of soap lining the sink. I come in behind her and kiss her neck. Both of us can see our reflections in the mirror, her eyes watching mine, my hand encircling her waist.

"You look beautiful," I tell her.

"You also."

I suppose these first heady moments are what it's all about: skin contact, reaction. She closes her eyes and turns her body into mine, kissing me, but just as soon she is breaking off. Moving back into the room she scans the bed, the armchairs, the fake Picasso prints on the wall, and seems to frown at something in the corner.

"Why have you brought a suitcase?"

The porter had put it near the window, half hidden by curtains and leaning up against the wall.

"Oh, that. It's just full of old newspapers."

"*Newspapers?*"

"I didn't want the receptionist to think that we were renting the room by the hour. So I brought some luggage. To make things look more normal."

Sofía's face is a picture of consternation. She is married to an Englishman, yet our behavior continues to baffle her.

"It's so sweet," she says, shaking her head, "so British and polite. You are always considerate, Alec. Always thinking of other people."

"You didn't feel awkward yourself? You didn't feel strange when you were crossing the lobby?"

The question clearly strikes her as absurd.

"Of course not. I felt wonderful."

"Vale."

Outside, in the corridor, a man shouts, *"Alejandro! Ven!"* as Sofía begins to undress. Slipping out of her shoes and coming toward me on bare feet, letting the sweater fall to the floor and nothing beneath it but the cool dark paradise of her skin. She starts to unbutton my shirt.

"So maybe you booked the room under a false name. And maybe my uncle is staying next door. And maybe somebody will see me when I go home across the lobby at 3 A.M. tonight. And maybe I don't care." She unclips her hair, letting it fall free, whispering, "Relax, Alec. *Tranquilo.* Nobody in the whole world cares about us. Nobody cares about us at all."

3

Taxi Driver

Saul's plane touches down at 5:55 P.M. the following Friday. He calls from the precustoms area using a local mobile phone: there's no international prefix on the readout, just a nine-digit number beginning with 625.

"Hi, mate. It's me."

"How are you?"

"The plane was late."

"It's normal."

The line is clear, no echo, although I can hear the thrum of baggage carousels revolving in the background.

"Our suitcases are coming out now," he says. "Shouldn't be long. Is it easy getting a cab?"

"Sure. Just say 'Calle Princesa,' like 'Ki-yay,' then 'Numero dee-ethy-sais.' That means sixteen."

"I know what it means. I did Spanish O level."

"You got a D."

"How much does it cost to get to your flat?"

"Shouldn't be more than thirty euros. If it is, I'll come down to the

13

street and tell the driver to go fuck himself. Just act like you live here and he won't rip you off."

"Great."

"Hey, Saul?"

"Yes?"

"How come you've got a Spanish mobile? What happened to your normal one?"

It is the extent of my paranoia that I have spent three days wondering if he has been sent here by MI5; if John Lithiby and Michael Hawkes, the controllers of my former life, have equipped him with bugs and a destructive agenda. Can I sense him hesitating over his reply?

"Trust you to notice that. Philip fucking Marlowe. Look, a mate of mine used to live in Barcelona. He had an old Spanish SIM that he no longer used. It has sixty euros of credit on it and I bought it off him for ten. So chill your boots. I'll be there in about an hour."

An inauspicious start. The line goes dead and I stand in the middle of my apartment, breathing too quickly, ripped out by nerves. *Relax, Alec. Tranquilo.* Saul hasn't been sent here by Five. Your friend is on the brink of getting divorced. He needed to get out of London and he needed somebody to talk to. He has been betrayed by the woman he loves. He stands to lose his house and half of everything he owns. In times of crisis we turn to our oldest friends and, in spite of everything that has happened, Saul has turned to you. That tells you something. That tells you that this is your chance to pay him back for everything that he has ever done for you.

Ten minutes later, Sofía calls and whispers sweet nothings down the phone and says how much she enjoyed our night at the hotel, but I can't concentrate on the conversation and make an excuse to cut it short. I have never had a guest in this apartment and I check Saul's room one last time: there's soap in the spare bathroom, a clean towel on the rail, bottled water if he needs it, magazines beside the bed. Saul likes to read comics and crime fiction, thrillers by Elmore Leonard and graphic novels from Japan, but all I have are spook biographies—Philby, Tomlinson—and a *Time Out* guide to Madrid.

Still, he might like those, and I arrange them in a tidy pile on the floor.

A drink now. Vodka with tonic to the brim of the glass. It's gone inside three minutes so I pour another, which is mostly ice by half past seven. How do I do this? How do I greet a friend whose life I placed in danger? MI5 used Saul to get to Katharine and Fortner. The four of us went to the movies together. Saul cooked dinner for them at his flat. At an oil-industry function in Piccadilly he unwittingly facilitated our initial introduction. And all without the slightest idea of what he was doing, just a decent, ordinary guy involved in something catastrophic, an eventually botched operation that cost people their careers, their lives. How do I arrange my face to greet him, given that he is aware of that?

4

The Keeper of the Secrets

At first it's all nervous silences and small talk. There's no big reunion speech, no hug or handshake. I fetch him from the taxi and we step into the narrow, cramped lift in my building and Saul says, "So *this* is where you live?" and I reply, "Yeah," and then we don't say anything for three floors. Once inside, there's twenty minutes of "Nice place, man" and "Can I get you a cup of tea?" and "It's really good of you to put me up, Alec," and then he sits there awkwardly on the sofa like a potential buyer who has come around to view the flat. I want to rip out all the decorum and the anxiety and say how sorry I am, face-to-face, for the pain that I have caused him, but we must first endure the initiation rite of British politesse.

"You've got a lot of DVDs."

"Yeah. Spanish TV sucks and I don't have satellite."

I am astonished by the weight he has put on, puffy fat slung round his neck and stomach. He looks worn out, barely the man I remember. At twenty-five, Saul Ricken was lean and lively, the friend everyone wanted to have. He had money in the bank, enough for him to write and to travel, and a medley of gorgeous, jealousy-inducing girlfriends.

Everything seemed possible in his future. And then what happened? His adulterous French wife? His best friend? Did Alec Milius happen to him? The man facing me is a burnt-out case, an early midlife crisis of exhaustion and excess fat. And it shames me that there is still a mean, competitive part of my nature that is glad about this; Saul is deeply troubled, and I am not the only one of us in decline.

"Anybody else been to stay?" he asks.

"Not here," I tell him. "Mum came to a different place. A flat I was renting in Chamberí. About three years ago."

"Does she know about everything?"

This is the first moment of frankness between us, an acknowledgment of our black secret. Saul looks at the floor as he asks the question.

"She knows nothing," I tell him.

"Right."

Maybe I should give him something else here, try to be a little more forthcoming.

"It's just that I didn't have the guts, you know? I didn't want to burst her bubble. She still thinks her son is a success story, a demographic miracle earning eighty grand a year. I'm not even sure she'd understand."

Saul is nodding slowly. "No," he says. "It's like having the drugs conversation with your parents. You think they'll empathize when you tell them that you've taken E. You think they'll be fascinated to learn that lines of charlie are regularly vacuumed up in the bathrooms of every designer restaurant in London. You think that bringing up the subject of smoking hash at university is in some way going to bring you closer together. But the truth is they'll never get it; in a fundamental way you always remain a child in your parents' eyes. You tell your mum that you worked for MI5 and MI6 and that Kate and Will were murdered as a direct result of that, she's not going to take it all that well."

To hear him talk of Kate's death like this is buckling. I had thought for some reason that Saul would let me off the hook. But that is not his style. He is direct and unambiguous and if you're guilty of something he will call you on it. The awful shiver of guilt, the fever, washes through me as we sit facing one another across the room. Saul is looking at me with a terrible, isolating indifference; I cannot tell if he is upset or merely laying down the facts. There was certainly no suggestion of anger in the way that he broached the subject; perhaps he just wants to let me know that he has not forgotten.

"You're right," I manage to tell him. "Of course you're right."

He stands now, opens the window, and steps out onto the narrow balcony that overlooks Princesa. Peering down at the street below, at the heavy traffic passing behind a line of mottled plane trees, he shouts out, "Noisy here," and frowns. What is he thinking? The characteristics of his face have been altered so much by age that I cannot even read his mood.

"Why don't you come inside, have a drink or something?" I suggest. "Maybe you'd like a bath."

"Maybe."

"There's not much hot water. Spaniards prefer showers. But then we could go out for dinner. I could show you around."

"Fine."

Another silence. Does he want an argument? Does he want to have it out *now*?

"Did you have any trouble with customs?" I ask.

"What do you mean?"

"Leaving England. Did they search your bag?"

If John Lithiby had wanted to find out if Saul was bringing anything to me, he would have alerted Customs and Excise at Luton and instructed them to search his luggage.

"Of course not. Why would they do that?"

He closes the balcony doors, muffling the sound of traffic, and begins pacing toward the kitchen. I follow him and try to seem relaxed, cloaking my paranoia in an easy, upbeat voice.

"It's just a possibility. If the cops want to check somebody's stuff without raising suspicion, they hold everybody up and go through all the bags, maybe put a plain clothes officer in the queue to plant a rumor about a drugs bust or a bomb threat . . ."

"What the fuck are you talking about? I went to HMV and Costa Coffee. Had an overpriced latte and nearly missed my flight."

"Right."

More silence. Saul has found his way into my bedroom and is peering at the framed photographs on the wall. There's one of Mum and Dad together in 1982, and a shot of Saul as a teenager with spiked hair. He stares at this for a long time but doesn't say anything about it. He probably thinks I hung it there this morning just to make him feel good.

"I'll tell you one thing about Luton airport," he says eventually. "Ann Summers. Don't you love that? Just the thought process behind putting a lingerie shop in the preflight area. Couples going on holiday, probably haven't had sex since 1996, then one of them spots the black garter belt in the window. The shop was *packed.* Every father of three handing over wads of cash for a soft lace teddy and a pair of jelly handcuffs. It's like announcing that you're planning to have sex on the Costa del Sol. You might as well use the PA system."

Taking advantage of his lighter mood, I fetch Saul a bottle of Mahou from the fridge and begin to think that everything is going to be OK. We make a plan to walk up to Bilbao metro to play chess at Café Comercial and he takes a shower after unpacking his bag. I notice that he has brought a laptop with him but assume that this is because of work. While waiting I wash up some mugs in the kitchen and then send a text to Sofía's work mobile.

Have friend staying from England. Will call you after the weekend. Agree about the hotel . . .

A minute later she responds:

A friend? I did not think alec milius had friends . . . xxxx

I don't bother replying. At 8:30, Saul emerges into the sitting room wearing a long coat and a pair of dark, slip-on Campers.

"We're off?" he asks.

"We're off."

5

Ruy Lopez

Café Comercial is located at the southern end of Glorieta de Bilbao, a junction of several main streets—Carranza, Fuencarral, Luchana—that converge on a roundabout dominated by a floodlit fountain. If you read the guidebooks, the café has been a favored haunt of poets, revolutionaries, students, and assorted dissidents for almost a hundred years, although on an average evening in 2003, it also boasts its fair share of tourists, civil servants, and mobile-clutching businessmen. Saul walks ahead of me through the heavy revolving doors and glances to his right at a crowded bar where bag-eyed *madrileños* are tucking into coffee and plates of microwave-heated tortilla. I indicate to him to keep walking into the main body of the café, where Comercial's famously grumpy white-jacketed waiters are bustling back and forth among the tables. For the first time he seems impressed by his surroundings, nodding approvingly at the high marbled columns and the smoked-glass mirrors, and it occurs to me that this is a foreign visitor's perfect idea of cultivated European living: café society in all its glory.

The upper story of the Comercial is used as a club on Tuesday and Thursday evenings by an eclectic array of chess-loving locals. Men, ranging in age from perhaps twenty-five to seventy, gather in an L-shaped room above the café cluttered with tables and green leather banquettes. Very occasionally a woman will look in on the action, although in four years of coming here twice a week I have never noticed one taking part in a game. This might be sexism—God knows, still a familiar feature of twenty-first-century Spain—but I prefer to think of it simply as a question of choice: while men battle it out at chess, the nearby tables will be occupied by groups of chattering middle-aged women, happier with the calmer arts of cards or dominoes.

Coming here on such a regular basis has been a risk, but chess at Comercial is a luxury that I will not deny myself; it is three hours of old-world charm and decency, uninterrupted by regret or solitude. I know most of the men here by name, and not an evening goes by when they do not seem pleased to see me, to welcome me into their lives and friendships, the game merely an instrument in the more vital ritual of camaraderie. Still, back in 1999, I introduced myself to the secretary using a false name, so it's necessary for me to stop Saul halfway up the stairs and explain why he cannot call me Alec.

"Come again?"

"All of the guys here know me as Patrick."

"Patrick."

"Just to be on the safe side."

Saul shakes his head with bewildered, slow-motion amusement, turns, and climbs the remaining few steps. You can already hear the snap and rattle of dominoes, the rapid punch of clocks. Through the doorway opposite the landing I spot Ramón and a couple of the other, younger, players who show up from time to time at the club. As if sensing me, Ramón looks up, raises his hand, and smiles through a faint mist of cigarette smoke. I fetch a board, a clock, and some pieces and we settle down at the back of the room, some way off from the main action. If Saul wants to talk about his marriage, or if I feel that the time is right to discuss what happened to Kate, I don't want any of the players listening in on our conversation. One or two of them speak better English than they let on, and gossip is an industry I can ill afford.

"You come here a lot?" he asks, lighting yet another Camel Light.

"Twice a week."

"Isn't that a bad idea?"

"I don't follow."

"From the point of view of the spooks." Saul exhales and smoke explodes off the surface of the board. "I mean, aren't they on the look-out for that sort of thing? Your pattern? Won't they find you if you keep coming here?"

"It's a risk," I tell him, but the question has shaken me. How does Saul know a tradecraft term like "pattern"? Why didn't he say "routine" or "habit"?

"But you keep a lookout for new faces?" he says. "Try to keep a low profile?"

"Something like that."

"And it's the same thing in your normal life? You never trust anybody? You think death is lurking just round the corner?"

"Well, that's putting it a bit melodramatically, but, yes, I watch my back."

He finishes arranging the white pieces and my hand shakes slightly as I set about black. Again the nonsensical idea arises that my friend has been turned, that the breakdown of his marriage to Heloise is just a fiction designed to win my sympathy, and that Saul has come here at the behest of Lithiby or Fortner to exercise a terrible revenge.

"What about girlfriends?" he asks.

"What about them?"

"Well, do you have one?"

"I do OK."

"But how do you meet someone if you don't trust her? What happens if a beautiful girl approaches you in a club and suggests the two of you go home together? Do you think about Katharine? Do you have to turn the woman down on the off chance she might be working for the CIA?"

Saul's tone here is just this side of sarcastic. I set the clock to a ten-minute game and nod at him to start.

"There's a basic rule," I reply, "that affects everyone I come into contact with. If a stranger walks up to me unprompted, no matter what the circumstances, I assume he's a threat and keep him at arm's length. But if by a normal process of introduction or flirtation or whatever I happen to get talking to somebody I like, well then that's OK. We might become friends."

Saul plays pawn to e4 and hits the clock. I play e5 and we're quickly into a Spanish Game.

"So do you have many friends out here?"

"More than I had in London."

"Who, for instance?"

Is this for Lithiby? Is this what Saul has been sent to find out?

"Why are you asking so many questions?"

"Jesus!" He looks at me with sudden despair, leaning back against his seat. "I'm just trying to find out how you are. You're my oldest friend. You don't have to tell me anything if you don't want to. You don't have to *trust* me."

There's genuine pain, even disgust in this single word. *Trust.* What am I doing? How could I possibly suspect that Saul has been sent here to damage me?

"I'm sorry," I tell him, "I'm sorry. Look, I'm just not used to conversations like this. I'm not used to people getting close. I've built up so many walls, you know?"

"Sure." He takes my knight on c6 and offers a sympathetic smile.

"The truth is I do have friends. A girlfriend even. She's in her early thirties. Spanish. Very smart, very sexy." It wouldn't, given the circumstances, be politic to tell Saul that Sofía is married. "But that's enough for me. I've never needed much more."

"No," he says, as if in sorrowful agreement. With my pawn on h6, he plays bishop b2 and I castle on the king's side. The clock sticks slightly as I push the button and both of us check that the small red timer is turning. "What about work?" he asks.

"That's also solitary."

For the past two years I have been employed by Endiom, a small British private bank with offices in Madrid, performing basic due diligence and trying to increase their portfolio of expat clients in

Spain. The bank also offers tax-planning services and investment advice to the many Russians who have settled on the south coast. My boss, a bumptious ex–public schoolboy named Julian Church, employed me after he heard me speaking Russian to a waiter at a restaurant in Chueca. Saul knows most of this from e-mails and telephone conversations, but he has little knowledge of financial institutions and precious little interest in acquiring any.

"You told me that you just drive around a lot, drumming up clients in Marbella. . . ."

"That's about right. It's mostly relationship-driven."

"And part-time?"

"Maybe ten days a month, but I get paid very well."

As people grow older they tend to display an almost total indifference to their friends' careers, and certainly Saul does not appear to be concentrating very intently on my replies. A few years back he would have wanted to know everything about the job at the bank: the car, the salary, the prospects for promotion. Now that sense of competition between us appears to have dissipated; he cares more about our game of chess. Stubbing out his cigarette he slides a pawn to c4 and nods approvingly at the move, muttering "here it comes, here it comes" under his breath. The opening has been played at speed and he now looks to have a slight advantage: the center is being squeezed up by white and there's not much I can do except defend deep and wait for the onslaught.

"I'll have that," he says, seizing one of my pawns, and before long a network of threats has built up against my king. The clock keeps sticking and I call for time.

"What are you doing?" he asks, looking at my hand as though it were diseased.

"I just need a drink," I tell him, balancing the timer buttons so that the mechanism stops working. "There's never a waiter up here when you need one."

"Let's just finish the game. . . ."

". . . Two minutes."

I spin round in my seat and spot Felipe serving a table of players.

Behind me Saul clicks alight another cigarette and exhales his first drag with moody frustration.

"You always do this, man," he mutters. "Always . . ."

"Hang on, hang on . . ."

Felipe catches my eye and comes ambling over with a tray full of empty coffee cups and glasses. "*Hola,* Patrick," he says, slapping me on the back. Saul sniffs. I order a beer for him and a red vermouth for me and then we reset the clock.

"Everything all right now?"

"Everything's fine."

But of course it's not. The position on the board has become hopeless, a phalanx of white rooks, bishops, and pawns bearing down on my defenses. I hate losing the first game; it's the only one that really matters. For an instant I consider moving one of my pieces when Saul is not looking, but there is no way that I could get away with it without risking being caught. Besides, my days of cheating him are supposed to be over. He was always the better player. Let him win.

"You're *resigning?*"

"Yeah," I tell him, laying down my king. "It doesn't look good. You did well. Been playing a lot?"

"But you could win on time," he says, indicating the clock. "That's the whole point. It's a speed game."

"Nah. You deserved it."

Saul looks bewildered and essays a series of lopsided frowns.

"That's not like you," he says. "I've never known you to resign." Then, with mock seriousness, "Maybe you *have* changed, Patrick. Maybe you *have* become a better person."

6

The Defense

Whenever I've thought about Saul in the last few years, the process has always begun with the same mental image: a precise memory of his face as I confessed to him the extent of my work for MI5. It was the morning of a summer's day in Cornwall, Kate and Will not twelve hours dead, and Saul drinking coffee from a chipped blue mug. By telling him, I was placing his life in danger in order to protect my own. It was that simple: my closest friend became the guardian of everything that had happened, and the Americans could not touch me as a result. To this day I do not know what he did with the disks that I gave him, with the lists of names and contact numbers, the Caspian oil data, and the sworn statement detailing my role in deceiving Katharine and Fortner. He may even have destroyed them. Perhaps he handed them immediately to Lithiby or Hawkes and then hatched a plot to destroy me. As for Kate, the grieving did not properly begin for days, and then it followed me ceaselessly, through Paris and St. Petersburg, from the apartment in Milan to the first years in Madrid. The loss of first love. The guilt of my role in her death. It was the one hard fact that I could never escape. Kate and Will were the ghosts that tied me to a corrupted past.

But I remember Saul's face at that moment. Quiet, watchful, gradually appalled. A young man of integrity, someone who knew his own mind, recognizing the limits of a friend's morality. It was perhaps naïve to expect him to be supportive, but then spies have a habit of overestimating their persuasive skills. Instead, having tacitly offered his support, he took a long walk while I packed up the car and then left for London. It was almost four years before he contacted me again.

"So, do you miss London?" he asks, pulling on his coat as we swing back out through the revolving doors, heading south down Calle de Fuencarral. It's approaching ten o'clock and time to find somewhere to eat.

"All the time," I reply, which is an approximation of the truth. I have come to love Madrid, to think of the city as my home, but the tug of England is nagging and constant.

"What do you miss about it?"

I feel like Guy Burgess being interviewed in *Another Country*. What does he tell the journalist? *I miss the cricket.*

"Everything. The weather. Mum. Having a pint with you. I miss not being *allowed* to be there. I miss feeling safe. It feels as though I'm living my life with the handbrake on."

Saul scuffs his shoes on the pavement, as if to kick this sentiment away. Two men are walking hand in hand in front of us and we skirt around them. It is becoming difficult to move. I know a good seafood restaurant within three blocks—the Ribeira do Miño—a cheap and atmospheric Galician *marisquería* where the owner will slap me on the back and make me look good in front of Saul. I suggest we eat there and get away from the crowds, and within a few minutes we have turned down Calle de Santa Brígida and settled at a table at the back of the restaurant. I take a seat facing out into the room, as I always do, in order to keep an eye on who comes in and out.

"They know you here?" he asks, lighting a cigarette. The manager wasn't around when we came in, but one of the waiters recognized me and produced an acrobatic nod.

"A little bit," I tell him.

"Gets busy."

"It's the weekend."

Resting his cigarette in an ashtray, Saul unfolds the napkin on his plate and tears off a slice of bread from a basket on the table. Crumbs fall on the cloth as he dips it into a small metal bowl filled with factory mayonnaise. Every table in the place is filled to capacity and an elderly couple are sitting directly beside us, tackling a platter of crab. The husband, who has a lined face and precisely combed hair, occasionally cracks into a chunky claw and sucks noisily on the flesh and the shells. There's a smell of garlic and fish and I think Saul likes it here. Using his menu Spanish he orders a bottle of house wine and shapes himself for a serious conversation.

"Out on the street, when you said you missed not being allowed to go home, what did you mean by that?"

"Just what I said. That it's not possible for me to go back to England. It's not safe."

"According to who?"

"According to the British government."

"You mean you've been threatened with arrest?"

"Not in so many words."

"But they've taken your passport away?"

"I have several passports."

The majority of *madrileños* do not speak English, so I am not too concerned about the couple sitting beside us who appear to be lost in an animated conversation about their grandchildren. But I am naturally averse to discussing my predicament, particularly in such a public place. Saul rips off another chunk of bread and inhales on his cigarette. "So what exactly's the problem?"

He may be looking for a fight.

"The problem?"

The waiter comes back. Slapping down a bottle of unlabeled white wine, he asks if we're ready to order and then spins away when I ask for more time. It is suddenly hot at our table and I take off my sweater, watching Saul as he pours out two glasses.

"The problem is straightforward." It is suddenly difficult to articulate, to defend, one of my deepest convictions. "I worked for the

British government in a highly secret operation designed to embarrass and undermine the Yanks. I was caught and I was fired. I threatened to spill the beans to the press and told two of my closest friends about it. In the corridors of Thames House and Vauxhall Cross, I'm not exactly Man of the Year."

"You think they still care?"

The question is like a slap in the face. I pretend to ignore it, but Saul looks pleased with himself, as if he knows he has landed a blow. Why the hostility? Why the cynicism? Short of something to say, I pick up the menu and decide, more or less at random, what both of us are going to eat. I don't consult Saul about this and gesture at the waiter with a wave of my hand. He comes over immediately and flicks open a pad.

"*Sí. Queremos pedir pimientos de padrón, una ración de jamón ibérico, ensalada mixta para dos, y el plato de gambas y cangrejos. Vale?*"

"*Vale.*"

"And don't forget the chips," Saul says, the sarcasm drifting away.

"Look." Suddenly the absurdity of my situation in a stranger's eyes has become worryingly clear. I need to get this right. "We're America's only friend in the world, for richer, for poorer, in sickness and in health. They do what they like, we do what they tell us. It's a one-way friendship that nevertheless needs to look rock solid or Europe will be singing the 'Marseillaise.' So having somebody like me at large is potentially a huge embarrassment."

Saul actually smirks. "You don't think you're slightly overestimating your importance?"

It's pure goading, poking around for a reaction. Don't rise to it. Don't bite.

"Meaning?"

"Meaning things have moved on since 1997, mate. Men have flown large planes into very tall buildings. The CIA is looking for anthrax in downtown Baghdad. They're not worrying about whether Alec Milius is getting cleared through customs at Gatwick airport. We're *days* away from invading Iraq, for Christ's sake. You think your average MI5 officer is concerned about a tiny operation that went wrong five years ago? You don't think he's got other things on his mind?"

I drain my glass and refill it without saying a word. Saul breathes a funnel of smoke at a fishing net tacked erratically to the wall and I am on the point of losing my temper.

"So you think I'm delusional? You think the fact that five years ago my apartment in Milan was ransacked by the CIA is just a product of a fertile imagination?"

"When were you living in Milan?"

"For six months in '98."

Saul looks stunned. "Jesus!"

"I couldn't tell you. I couldn't tell anyone."

He recovers almost immediately. "But that could have been just a burglary. How do you know it was the Yanks?"

I actually enjoy what comes next, wiping the smug look off his face. "I know because Katharine told me about it on the phone. She said that Fortner, the man who taught her everything, her mentor and father figure, had lost his job as a result of what I'd done and that he still hadn't found work two years later. A veteran CIA officer hoodwinked by a twenty-five-year-old rookie selling fake research data for hundreds of thousands of dollars. Both of them were made to look a laughing-stocks by what I did to them. She said that her own career was as good as over. Back to desk work in Washington, blown for all European operations. And all because of Alec Milius. Katharine spent two years after I disappeared trying to discover where I'd gone. I think she went a bit crazy. Eventually she tracked me to my apartment in Milan, got my phone number, address, everything. I'd been sloppy. The CIA broke in, took my computer, passport, even my fucking car that was parked outside. I had nine thousand dollars cash under a mattress. That went as well. Katharine said it was just payback for what I stole from her 'organization.' Hence the need to get the hell out of Italy. Hence the reason why I've been just a little bit paranoid ever since I got to Madrid."

"They don't know you're here?"

"Somebody knows I'm here."

"What do you mean, 'Somebody knows I'm here'?"

I am aware that what I'm about to tell Saul may sound over the top, but it's important to me that he should understand the seriousness of my predicament.

"My letters have been tampered with, my car has been followed, one of my mobile phones was tapped—"

Saul interrupts. "When did this happen?"

"It happens all the time. You haven't seen me since I moved here. You don't know what Spain is like. Just realize that they keep an eye on me, OK? That's all I'm saying."

"Even *now*? Nearly six years on?"

"Five years, two hundred, and thirty-eight days. Look. I have *five* bank accounts. When I call one of them and they put me on hold, I think it's because there's a note against my name and they're checking me out. I have to change my phone every three weeks. If someone is listening to a Walkman next to me on the metro, I make sure he's not wearing a wire. The other day I was driving to Granada and the same car followed me from Jaén for an hour."

"So? Maybe they were connected to Endiom. Maybe they were lost. You know how someone very high on coke will ask you the same question over and over again?"

"Yes."

"Well that's what you sound like. Somebody very high. Somebody very paranoid. Your e-mails, talking to you on the phone, listening to you now. OK, five years ago, as a one-off, Katharine tracked you down and gave you a scare. She was pissed off, she had a right to be. But she's a big girl, she would have got over it by now. The rest of this is not *happening,* Alec. You're living in cloud-cuckoo-land. For once in your life, try to see beyond your own ego. Christ, you wouldn't even come to my *wedding.* Believe me, if the CIA or Five or Six had really wanted to make your life difficult, they would have done it by now. Somebody could have planted drugs on you, got you thrown in jail. Not just turned over your flat. You get people on the run like Tomlinson or Shayler, and they make it *impossible* for them to move. No work, no residency, threats, and broken promises. You're a fucking footnote, Alec."

Food suddenly arrives in waves: a flat pink plate of *jamon* wedged in near my elbow; a deep metal bowl of salad tossed with carrot and canned tuna; the house speciality of prawns piled eight inches high on a rock of boiled crab and razor fish; a platter of *pimientos de padrón,* charred and salted to perfection.

Saul asks quietly what we're eating.

"They're grilled peppers. One in ten is supposed to be hot. As in spicy. You'll like them." He bites at one and nods approvingly. "Look, there's one thing you should understand."

"And what's that?"

"I am not delusional. I am not paranoid." I'm not a fucking footnote, either.

"Fine," he says.

"I'm just trying to live my life . . ."

". . . with the handbrake on."

Silence. It is as if the whole notion of my exile is a joke to him.

"Why are you being like this? Why are you trying to goad me?"

Saul has been piling salad onto his plate but he stops and fixes my gaze.

"*Why?* Because I no longer have any idea who you are, what you stand for. People change, of course they do, it's a natural process. They find work, they find something that fulfills them, they meet the right girl, blah blah blah. At least that's the idea. And as you get older you're supposed to work out what's important to you and dump what isn't. It's naïve to think that at thirty a person is going to be the same animal that they were at twenty. Life has an *impact.*"

I mutter, "Of course it does," as if to dilute what's coming, but Saul is shaking his head.

"Something *fundamental* shifted in you five years ago, man. You were my closest, my oldest friend. We went to school together, to university. But I had literally *no idea* that you were capable of doing what you did. One day you were just reticent, ironic, mildly ambitious Alec Milius; the next you're this creature of the state, a lying, manipulating, barely moral . . . *thing,* risking everything in your life for, what exactly? To this day I can't get my head round it. Personal fulfillment? Patriotism? And you used me in that, you used our friendship. Three straight years of lies. Every day it affected me, like the loss of someone, like mourning."

All of the shame and despair and regret that I have experienced since Kate's death is crystallized in this instant. Saul's face is as hard and as unforgiving as I can ever remember seeing it. It is the end of our friendship. With just a few stark sentences he has engendered a violent and sudden cutoff.

"So that's it?"

"That's what?"

"The end of things between us? That's what you came out here to tell me? That it's better if I don't contact you anymore?"

"What the fuck are you talking about?"

"You said it yourself. I'm a liar, a manipulator. I'm a *footnote*."

"That doesn't mean it's the end of our *friendship*." Saul looks at me in amazement, as if I have completely misjudged both him and the situation. "Jesus, we're not at school anymore, Alec. This isn't a playground." I stare down at the table and cradle the back of my neck, bewildered and embarrassed. "Short of you developing an all-new fixation with Catalan schoolboys, we're still going to be *mates*. Things don't end between people just because they betray them. In fact, that's probably when they start to get interesting." There is a long burst of applause from the next-door room. "Let's face it, we're always more grateful to the people who have hurt us in life than to the ones who just let things drift by. I learned from you, and that's what it's all about. I'm just not going to sit here and let you think that no harm came from what happened . . ."

"Believe me, I don't think that for a second."

"Let me finish. It's important for me to say this to you, face-to-face. I don't get the chance on e-mail. I don't get the chance on the phone."

"OK."

"What you did was wrong. You didn't kill Kate or Will, but your work and your lying led to their deaths. And I don't see you doing anything out here to put that right. I don't see you making amends."

Ordinarily I might challenge Saul on this. Make *amends*? Who is he to speak to me this way? I make amends with my solitude. I pay penance with exile. But he has always believed in the myth of self-improvement; any reasoning I might employ would only burn out in the fire of his moral authority. We find ourselves eating in silence, as if there is nothing left to be said. I could try to defend myself, but it would only feel like a tactic, a lie, and Saul would jump on it as quickly as he leaped on my earlier defense. At the next table the grandparents are standing up, with considerable effort, having paid their bill and left just a few small coins as a tip. At the base of their receipt it says "No A La Guerra" and the waiter has written "Gracias" in felt-tip pen. The husband helps his wife into a garish fur coat and casts both of us an inscrutable smile. Perhaps he understood English after all. For once, I do not care.

"Jesus!"

Saul has bitten into a hot *padrón* and downs an entire glass of wine to kill the heat.

"You OK?"

"Fine," he says, pursing his cheeks. "We need more booze."

And this small incident seems to break the spell of his disquiet. A second bottle comes and we spend the rest of the meal talking about Chelsea and Saddam Hussein, about Saul's grandfather—who has lung cancer—and even Heloise, whom he is inclined to forgive in spite of her blatant adultery. I note the double standard in his attitude to the two of us and wonder if there is something saintly in Saul that actually encourages people to betray him. There has certainly always been an element of masochism in his personality.

With coffee, the waiter brings us two small shots of lemon liqueur—on the house—and we down them in a gulp. Saul is keen to pay ("as a present, for putting me up") and I feel mildly drunk as we make our way out past the kitchen and into the bustle of Chueca. It is past midnight and the nightlife is well under way.

"You know a decent bar?" he asks.

I know plenty.

7

Churches

Spaniards dedicate so much of their lives to enjoying themselves that a word actually exists to describe the span of time between midnight and 6 A.M., when ordinary European mortals are safely tucked up in bed. *La madrugada.* The hours before dawn.

"It's a good word," Saul says, though he thinks he'll be too drunk to remember it.

We leave Chueca and walk west into Malasaña, one of the older *barrios* in Madrid, still a haunt of drug dealers and penniless students, though, by reputation, neither as violent nor as rundown as it was twenty years ago. The narrow streets are teeming and dense with crowds that gradually thin out as we head south in the direction of Gran Vía.

"Haven't we just been here?" Saul asks.

"Same neighborhood. Farther south," I explain. "We're going in a circle, looping back toward the flat."

A steep hill leads down to Pez Gordo, a bar I love in the neighborhood, favored by a relaxed, unostentatious crowd. There's standing room only and the windows are fogged up with posters and condensation, but inside the atmosphere is typically rousing, and flamenco music rolls and strums on the air. I get two *cañas* within a minute of reaching the bar and walk back to Saul, who has found us a spot a few feet from the door.

"Do you want to hear my other theory?" he says, jostled by a customer with dreadlocked hair.

"What's that?"

"I know the real reason you like living out here."

"You do?"

"You thought that moving overseas would give you a chance to wipe the slate clean, but all you've done is transfer your problems to a different time zone. They've followed you."

Here we go again.

"Can't we talk about something else? It's getting a little tedious, all this constant self-analysis."

"Just hear me out. I think that some days you wake up and you want to believe that you've changed, that you're not the person you were six years ago. And other times you miss the excitement of spying so much that it's all you can do not to ring SIS direct and all but *beg* them to take you back. That's your conflict. Is Alec Milius a good guy or a bad guy? All this paranoia you talk about is just window dressing. You *love* the fact that you can't go home. You *love* the fact that you're living in exile. It makes you feel significant."

It amazes me that he should know me so well, but I disguise my surprise with a look of impatience.

"Let's just change the subject."

"No. Not yet. It makes perfect sense." He's toying with me again. A girl with a French accent asks Saul for a light, and I see that his nails are bitten to the quick as she takes it. He's grinning. "People have always been intrigued by you, right? And you're playing on that in this new environment. You're a mysterious person, no roots, no past. You're a topic of conversation."

"And you're pissed."

"It's the classic expat trap. Can't cope with life back home, make a splash overseas. *El inglés misterioso.* Alec Milius and his amazing mountain of money."

Why is Saul thinking about the money?

"What did you say?"

A momentary hesitation, then, "Forget it."

"No. I won't forget it. Just keep your voice down and explain what you meant."

Saul grins lopsidedly and takes off his coat. "All I'm saying is that you came here to get away from your troubles and now they've passed you by. It's time for you to move on. Time for you to *do* something."

For a wild moment, undoubtedly reinforced by alcohol, it crosses my mind that Saul has been sent here to *recruit* me, to lure me back into Five. Like Elliott sent to Philby in Lebanon, the best friend dispatched at the state's request. His angle certainly sounds like a pitch, although the notion is ridiculous. More likely Saul is simply adhering to that part of his nature that has always annoyed me and that I had somehow allowed myself to forget, namely, the moralizing do-gooder, the self-righteous evangelist busily saving others while incapable of saving himself.

"So what do you suggest I do?"

"Just come home. Just put an end to this phase of your life."

The idea is certainly appealing. Saul is right, that there are times when I look back on what happened in London with nostalgia, when I regret that it all came to an end. But for Kate's death and the exhaustions of secrecy, I would probably do it all again. For the thrill of it, for the sense of being *pivotal.* But I can't state that directly without appearing insensitive.

"No. I like it here. The lifestyle. The climate."

"Seriously?"

"Seriously."

"Well then, at least don't change your mobile phone every three weeks. And just get one e-mail address. *Please.* It pisses me off and annoys your mum. She says she still doesn't know why you're out here, why you don't just come home."

"You've talked to my mother?"

"Now and again."

"What about Lithiby?"

"Who's Lithiby?"

If Saul is working for them, they have certainly taught him how to lie. He runs his finger along the wall and inspects it for dust.

"My case officer at Five," I explain. "The guy behind everything."

"Oh, him. No, of course not."

"He's never been to see you?"

"Never."

Someone turns the music up beyond a level at which we can comfortably speak, and I have to shout at Saul to be heard.

"So where did you put the disks?"

He smiles. "In a safe place."

"Where?"

Another grin. "Somewhere safe. Look, nobody's ever been to see me. Nobody's ever been to see your mum. It's not as if . . . Alec?"

Julian Church has walked into the bar. Six inches taller than anyone else in the room and dressed like a Royal Fusilier on weekend leave. There are certain things that cannot be controlled, and this is one of them. He spots me immediately and does a little electric shock of surprise.

"Alec!"

"Hello, Julian."

"Fancy seeing you here."

"Indeed."

"Night on the town?"

"Apparently. And you?"

"The very same. My beloved wife fancied a drink, and who was I to argue?"

Julian, as ever, is delighted to see me, but I can feel Saul physically withdrawing, the cool of Shoreditch and Notting Hill reacting with violent distaste to Julian's tasseled loafers and bottle-green cords. I should introduce them.

"Saul, this is Julian Church, my boss at Endiom. Julian, this is Saul Ricken, a friend of mine from England."

"Ah, the old country," Julian says.

"The old country," Saul repeats.

Think. How to deal with this? How do I get us away? A chill wind comes barreling in through the open door, drawing irritated looks from nearby tables. Julian hops to it like a bellboy, muttering *"Perdón, perdón,"* as he shuts out the cold. "That's a bit better. Bloody chilly in here. Bloody noisy, too. Señora Church won't be far behind me. She's parking the car."

"Your wife?" Saul asks.

"My wife." Julian's pale skin is flushed and pink, his widow's peak down to a few fine strands. "Madness to drive into town on a Friday night, but she insisted, like most of her countrymen, and who was I to argue? You staying the weekend?"

"A bit longer," Saul replies.

"I see, I see."

This is clearly going to happen and there's nothing I can do about it. The four of us locked into two or three rounds of drinks, then awkward questions later. I try to keep my eyes away from the door as Julian takes off his coat and hangs it on top of Saul's. Do I have an exit strategy? We could lie about meeting friends at a club, but I don't want to arouse Julian's suspicion or risk a contradiction from Saul. Best just to ride it out.

"Did you get my e-mail?" Julian asks, and I am on the point of responding when Sofía walks in behind him. She does well to disguise her reaction: just a flat smile, a clever look of feigned recognition, then fixing her gaze on Julian.

"Darling, you remember Alec Milius, don't you?"

"Of course." It doesn't look like she does. "You work with my husband, yes?"

"And this is his friend, Saul . . . *Ricken,* was it? They were here quite by chance. A coincidence."

"Ah, *una casualidad.*" Sofía looks beautiful tonight, her perfume a lovely sense memory of our long night together at the hotel. She uncurls a black scarf, takes off her coat, kisses me lightly on the cheek, and gently squeezes Julian at the elbow.

"We've met before," I tell her.

"*Sí*. At the office, yes?"

"I think so."

Once, when Julian was away on business, Sofía came down to the Endiom building in Retiro and we fucked on his desk.

"I thought you two met at the Christmas party."

"I forget," Sofía replies.

She places her scarf on the surface of the cigarette machine and affords me the briefest of glances. Saul appears to be humming along to the music. He may even be bored.

"So what's everybody drinking?"

Julian has taken a confident stride forward to coincide with his question, breaking up the huddle around us by dint of his sheer size. Saul and I want *cañas,* Sofía a Diet Coke.

"I'm driving," she explains, directing her attention at Saul. *"Hablas español?"*

"Sí, un poco," he says, suddenly looking pleased with himself. That was clever of her. She wants to know how much she can get away with saying.

"Y te gusta Madrid?"

"Sí. Mucho. Mucho." He gives up. "I just arrived tonight."

And what follows is a pitch-perfect, five-minute exchange about nothing at all: Sofía conducting a conversation about the Prado, about tourists at the Thyssen museum, the week she spent recently in Gloucestershire with Julian's aging parents. Just enough chat to cover the span of time before her husband returns from the bar. When he does, all of his attention is focused on me.

"Actually, Alec, it's a good job we've bumped into each other." He clutches me around the shoulder. "Saul, can I leave you with my wife for five minutes? Need to talk shop."

Dispensing the drinks, he steers me into a cramped space beside the cigarette machine and assumes a graver tone. The need for secrecy is unclear, although I should still be able to eavesdrop on Saul's conversation. I don't want him leaking information to Sofía about my past. Things are nicely compartmentalized there. They are under control.

"Look, as I said, I need you to go to San Sebastián early next week. Is that going to be a problem?"

"Shouldn't be."

"We can pay your expenses, normal form. It's no different from your usual work. Just diligence. Need you to look into something."

"Your e-mail said it was about cars."

"Yes. Client wants to build a factory making parts near the border with Navarra. Don't ask. Blindingly dull small town. But the work-force will be mostly Basque, so there might be union trouble. I need you to put together a document, interviews with local councilors, real estate bigwigs, lawyers, and so forth. Something to impress potential investors, calm any nerves. Sections about the tax position, the impact on exports of the strengthening euro, that sort of thing. Most impor-tant, what effect would Basque independence have on the project?"

"Basque independence? They think that's likely?"

"Well, that's what we need you to find out."

I'm tempted to tell Julian that Endiom would be better off buying a crystal ball and a subscription to *The Economist,* but if he wants to pay me €300 a day to stay in San Sebastián as a glorified journalist, I'm not going to argue. Saul has already mentioned that he wants to go to Cádiz to see a friend, so I'll kick him out on Tuesday and take the car.

"You want to fly there?"

"I'll drive."

"Up to you. There's a file at the office. Why don't you pick it up on Monday and we can go through all the bumph? Might have a spot of lunch."

"Done."

But Julian won't let me go. Rather than return to Sofía and Saul, he lingers in the corner, engaging me in a mind-numbing conver-sation about Manchester United's chances in this year's Champions League.

"If we can just see our way past Juventus in the second group phase, there's every chance we'll draw Madrid in the quarter finals."

This goes on for ten minutes. Perhaps he is enjoying the male ca-maraderie, a chance to talk to somebody other than Sofía. Julian has always held me in the highest esteem, valuing my opinion on anything from Iraq to Nasser Hussain, and is strangely deferential in approach.

Behind me, Saul is sounding enamored of Sofía, laughing at her jokes and doing his best to talk me down.

"Yeah, we were just saying how friends change in their twenties. It's tough staying loyal to some of them." This is all very pointedly within my earshot. "I think people used to think I was a bit of an idiot for hanging out with Alec, you know, but I felt sorry for him. There was a time when he really tested me, when I felt like cutting the rope, only I didn't want to be the sort of person who bailed out on his mates when they were in trouble, know what I mean?"

I can't hear Sofía's response. Her voice is naturally quieter than Saul's and she is speaking out into the room, with Julian in full flow leaning into me for greater emphasis.

"I mean, most people would now agree that Roy Keane is not the player he was. Injuries have taken their toll—hip surgery, knee ligaments—he simply can't get up and down like he used to. I wouldn't be surprised if he goes to Celtic next season."

"Really? You think so?" It's a struggle to remember the name of Manchester United's manager. "Alex Ferguson would be prepared to sell him?"

"Well, that's the million-dollar question. With Becks almost certainly off, would he want to lose Keano as well?"

Saul has started talking again and I try to pivot my body against the cigarette machine so that I can still hear his conversation. He's saying that he's known me since childhood, that he has no idea what I'm doing out here in Spain. "One day he just upped and left and none of us have seen him since."

Sofía sounds understandably inquisitive, although it's still impossible to hear what she's saying. Now Julian is asking me if I want a couple of spare tickets to the Bernabéu. Was that a question about London? Saul's answer contains the phrase "oil business" and now I really start to worry. Somehow I have to break away from Julian and intrude to stop their conversation.

"Do you have a cigarette?"

I have turned and stepped up to them, my weight shifted awkwardly onto one leg, looking unguardedly at Saul as an instruction to make him shut up. He pauses midsentence, extracts a Camel Light, and passes it to me saying, "Sure." Sofía looks startled—she has never seen me smoking—but Julian is too busy offering me a light to notice.

"I thought you gave up?" he asks.

"I did. I just like having one every now and again. Late nights and weekends. What were you two talking about? My ears were burning."

"Your past," Sofía says, fanning smoke away from her face. "Saul says you're a man of mystery, Alec. Did you know that, darling?"

Julian, checking messages on his mobile phone, says, "*Sí,* yup," and heads outside in search of better reception.

"He also said you worked in the oil business?"

"Briefly. Very briefly. Then I got a job at Reuters and they shipped me out to Russia. What do you do, Sofía?"

She grins and looks up at the ceiling.

"I'm a clothes designer, Alec. For women. Didn't you ask me that at the Christmas party?"

The tone of the question is unambiguously flirtatious. She needs to cool it or Saul will cotton on. In an attempt to change the subject, I say that I once saw Pedro Almodóvar drinking in the bar, sitting at a table not too far from where we are standing. It's a lie—a friend saw him—but enough to interest Saul.

"Really? That's like going to London and seeing the queen."

"*Qué?*" Sofía says, her English momentarily confused. "You saw the *queen* here?"

And, thankfully, the misunderstanding engenders the conversation I had hoped for: Saul's lifelong distaste for Almodóvar's movies perfectly at odds with Sofía's loyal *madrileñian* obsession.

"My favorite I think is *Todo Sobre Mi Madre,*" she says, summoning a wistful look more appropriate to a lovestruck teenager. "How would you translate in English? *Everything About My Mother.* It's so generous, so . . ." she looks at me and produces the word "inventive."

"Total bullshit," Saul says, and Sofía looks startled. He's more

43

drunk than I had realized and may have misjudged the wonders of the Ricken charm. "Worst movie I've seen in the last five years. Facile, adolescent, piss-poor."

Silence. Sofía slides me a look.

"You get—what?—transvestites and pregnant nuns and benign hookers, and what does it all add up to? *Nothing.* AIDS is just co-opted for cheap emotional impact. Or the new one, *Talk to Her.* I'm supposed to feel sympathetic toward a retarded necrophiliac? None of it makes any *sense.* There's no recognizable human emotion in Almodóvar's movies, and I'll tell you why—because he's too *juvenile* to cope with real suffering. The whole thing's a camp pantomime. But his films are shot so beautifully you're tricked into thinking you're in the presence of an artist."

The outburst allows me to speak to Sofía in Spanish, as if to apologize for Saul getting out of hand.

"I'm going to make an excuse and get us out of here," I tell her, speaking quickly and employing as much slang as I can. Then, looking at Saul as if to laugh him off, "Don't believe everything my friend has told you. He's drunk. And he's in a difficult mood."

"What are you saying?"

"Alec was just telling me that you love the cinema," Sofía tells him quickly. "But I don't think this can be true. How can you love cinema if you don't love Pedro Almodóvar?"

"It's a Madrid thing," I explain. Saul makes a sucking noise with his teeth. "Almodóvar came onto the scene after Franco, made a lot of risqué comedies; they associate him with freedom and excess. He's a cultural icon."

"Exactly." Sofía nods. "It is very English of you not to embrace him. The films are crazy, of course they are, but you mustn't be so literal about it."

Saul looks contrite. "Well, we don't have anyone comparable in England," he says, which may be his way of apologizing. "Maybe Hitchcock, maybe Chaplin, that's about it."

"Judi Dench?" I suggest, trying to make a joke of it, but neither of them laughs. Julian has come back in from the street and he seems flustered.

"Look, I'm afraid we've got to bugger off." He pinches Sofía's neck in a way that annoys me. "Just had a message from our friends. We were supposed to meet them in Santa Ana."

Is this an excuse? When Julian arrived he said nothing about meeting anyone for a drink.

"Santa Ana?" Sofía drains her Diet Coke. "*Joder*. Are you sure?"

"Quite sure." Julian brandishes his mobile phone as if producing evidence in a court of law. "And we're late. So we'd better hit the road."

There are rapid apologies and farewells—Sofía and I very pointedly do not kiss—and then they are gone. Saul drains his *caña* and places the glass on a nearby table.

"That was a bit sudden." He is as suspicious as I am. "You think they just wanted to be alone?"

"Probably. Not much fun bumping into an employee on your night off."

"They seemed nice, though."

"Yeah, Julian's OK. Comes on a bit strong. Gale force Sloane Ranger, but he pays my wages."

"How do you know he's not SIS?"

I look around to ensure that nobody has overheard the question.

"What?"

"You heard."

"Because I just do."

"How?"

Saul is smiling. There's no chance that he will drop the subject. I try to look irritated and say, "Let's just chat about something else, OK?" but he keeps going.

"I mean, surely you must have had your doubts? Or was the job at Endiom too important to sacrifice for the sake of a paranoid hunch?" My expression must give something away here because he looks at me, knowing that he has struck a nerve. "After all, you didn't seek

45

him out. He approached *you*. So, according to the Laws of Alec Milius, he's a threat." A big grin with this. "You said he heard you speaking Russian in a restaurant and offered you a job."

"That's right. And then I ran basic background checks on Endiom, on Julian and his wife, and everything came up clean. So it's cool. He's fine."

Saul laughs, rapping his knuckles against the wall. In an attempt to move off the subject, I say that it's his round and he goes to the bar, buys two more *cañas,* coming back with his mood completely unchanged.

"So you ran background checks?"

"That's right."

"And what came up about Sofía?"

"Sofía?"

"Yes, the woman he was with. Julian's wife. Didn't you catch her name?"

The sarcasm has deepened. There is mischief in his eyes.

"I hardly know her."

"She's good-looking," he says.

"Do you think?"

"Don't you?"

"It's not that. I've just never thought of her that way. She's not my type."

"Not your type." A small silence, then Saul says, "What age would you say she was? Early thirties?"

"Probably. Yes."

"Very smart? Very sexy?" It takes me a moment to realize that he is quoting from our earlier conversation. He stares directly into my eyes. "You're fucking her, aren't you?"

Yet again he has seen right through me. I use the noise of the bar and the low light to try to disguise my reaction.

"Don't be ridiculous."

He ignores this.

"Does Julian know?"

"What are you talking about? I met her for the second time tonight."

"Oh come on, mate. It's *me*." Why am I bothering to lie, and to Saul of all people? What possible harm could come from him knowing? "Your little exchange in Spanish? That was about Pedro Almodóvar? It wasn't about both of you saying how much you missed each other and how awkward things were getting with me and Julian hanging around?"

"Of course not. Where's this coming from?"

I seem to possess a default personality set to perfidy and misinformation. Not for one moment has it occurred to me to tell Saul the truth, but my relationship with Sofía is one of the few things out here that give me any pleasure, and I don't want him trampling on it with his decency and his common sense.

"You remember Mr. Wayne," he says, "our Spanish teacher at school—the one with the BO problem?"

"I think so. . . ."

"Well, it turns out he was pretty good. I understood what you were saying. . . ."

"And what was that?" I raise my voice above the music. "Seriously, Saul, you can't have understood. I was apologizing to Julian's wife because you'd turned into Barry Norman. It was getting embarrassing. Just because you thought she was fit doesn't mean I'm fucking her. Christ, the way your mind works . . ."

"Fine," he says, "fine," waving his hand through the air, and for a moment it appears that he might have believed me. I would actually relish the opportunity to talk to Saul about Sofía, but I do not want him to judge me. The adultery is my sole concession to the darker side of my nature and I want to show him that I have changed.

"Look, what about a different bar?" I suggest.

"No, I'm tired."

"But it's only one o'clock."

"One o'clock is late in London." He looks deflated. "I was up early. Let's call it a night."

"You sure?"

"I'm sure." He has withdrawn into disappointment. "There's always tomorrow."

We finish our drinks, with scarcely another word spoken and head out onto the street. I feel as if I am in the company of a favorite schoolmaster who has discovered that I have deceived him. We are waiting in his study, the clock ticking by, just killing time until Milius can find it in himself to come clean. But it is too late. The lie has been told. I have to stick to my tale or risk humiliation. So nothing has really changed in six years. It's pitiful.

8

Another Country

Perhaps as a consequence of this argument—and several others that occur over the course of the weekend—I allow Saul to stay in the flat while I am working in San Sebastián. He was clearly not ready to go to Cádiz, and I did not have the heart, or the nerve, to ask him to move into a hotel. He played so cleverly on my sense of guilt on Friday night, and ridiculed my paranoid behavior to such an extent, that forcing him to leave was out of the question. He would, in all probability, have simply hopped on the next plane back to London, never to be seen again. Besides, I told myself—unable to sleep on Sunday night—what harm could come from allowing my best friend to stay in my house? What was Saul going to do? *Bug* the place?

Nevertheless, before leaving for the coast I take several precautions. Details of the safe house in Alcalá de los Gazules are removed and placed in my PO box at the post office in Moncloa, ditto coded reminders of e-mail addresses, computer passwords, and bank accounts. I have €14,500 in cash concealed behind the fridge in a plastic container, which I place in a black trash bag to stow beneath the spare wheel of the Audi. Safes are pointless; most can be cracked in the time it takes to boil a kettle. It is also necessary to disable my desktop computer by removing the hard drive and telling Saul that the system is clogged by a virus. Everything is password protected, but an expert could vacuum up most of the information on the system using a modified PDA. If Saul wants to check his e-mail, he can dial up from his own laptop using a mobile phone or, better still, go to an Internet café down the road.

I wake at seven on Tuesday morning and open the windows of the sitting room, letting the flat air for five minutes as coffee bubbles on the stove. Saul's bedroom door is closed and I leave a note, with keys, saying that I will be back on Friday evening "in time for chess and dinner." He already knows the neighborhood fairly well and will be able to buy milk and booze and British newspapers at the various shops I have pointed out over the last three days. Nevertheless, closing the door behind me feels like an act of the grossest negligence, every instinct I possess for privacy recklessly ignored. But for the impact on my Endiom career, I would immediately telephone Julian at home, explain that there has been a problem, and cancel the trip.

At my regular breakfast café on Calle de Ventura Rodríguez I eat a croissant, with a copy of *The Times* for company. The Kuwaiti desert is gradually filling with troops and tanks and the prospects for war look bleak: a long, drawn-out campaign and months to take Baghdad. Beside me at the bar a construction worker has ordered a balloon of Pacharán, iced Navarran liqueur, at 8 A.M. I content myself with a vodka and orange juice and head outside to the car.

For €250 per month I keep the Audi on the second floor of an underground car park beneath Plaza de España, the vast square at the western end of Gran Vía dominated by a monument to Cervantes. It has been some time since I was last down here and a thin film of dust has formed on the bonnet and across the roof. I lift the spare wheel out of the boot, conceal the bag of money in the molded recess, remove several CDs from my suitcase for the journey ahead, and lay two suits flat along the backseat. A woman passes within ten feet of the car but walks by without so much as a glance. Then it's just a question of finding the ticket and driving out into rush-hour Madrid. Cars have double-parked along the length of Calle de Ferraz, reducing a three-lane street to traffic that can only bump along in single file. The aggression of horns at this hour of the morning is jarring and I regret not having left an hour earlier. It takes twenty minutes to reach Moncloa and a further ten until we are at last loose on the motorway, bunched traffic moving clockwise on the inner orbital, heading north for Burgos and the N1. Low clouds have settled on the flat outer plains of Madrid, industrial plants and office blocks broken up by thin, dew-rich mists, but otherwise there is little to look at but endless furniture superstores, German technology companies, and blinking roadside brothels. Living in the center of Madrid, I forget the extent to which the city sprawls out this far, blocks of flats deposited on the featureless plain, built with no greater purpose than proximity to the capital. These could be the outskirts of any major city in the American Midwest. It does not feel like Spain.

The driving, on the other hand, is as Spanish as flamenco and *jamón*. Cars whipping past at over 160 kph, sliding lane to lane oblivious of sense or reason. It is my habit to copy them, if only because the alternative is a snail-slow crawl in the slipstream of an aging lorry. Thus I take the Audi well beyond the speed limit, sit on the bumper of the car in front, wait for it to pull to one side, and then surge off into the distance. Traffic police are not a problem. The Guardia Civil tend not to patrol in the long stretches between major towns, and one glimpse of my (counterfeit) German driving license, accompanied by an inability to communicate in Spanish, is usually enough to encourage them to wave me on.

As the weather closes in, however, I am forced to slow down. What had seemed at first like the beginning of a decent, sunny day becomes fogbound and wet, hard rain falling in patches and glistening the road. At this rate it will be four or five hours before I cross the border into the Basque country. A preliminary meeting scheduled in the capital, Vitoria, for one o'clock may have to be postponed or even canceled. Climbing into the Sierras, I get stuck behind two articulated lorries driving parallel in a macho overtake and decide to pull over for a coffee rather than sit in the funk of their exhaust. Thankfully, the rain has stopped and the traffic thinned out by the time I rejoin the road, and just after eleven I am passing Burgos. This is where the landscape really comes into its own: rolling, patched fields of green and brown and the distant Cantabrian mountains smashed by a biblical sunlight. At the side of the road, little patches of undecided snow are gradually melting as winter draws to an end. To be away from Madrid, from the pressure and anxiety of Saul, is suddenly liberating.

When the road signs begin to change I know that we have crossed the border. Every town is announced in translation: Vitoria/Gasteiz; San Sebastián/Donostia; Arrasate/Mondragón: government concessions to the demands of Basque nationalism. This is not País Vasco; this is Euskal Herria. Spain is divided into a number of regions with far greater political and social autonomy than, say, devolved Scotland. Under the terms of the constitution hammered out in the aftermath of Franco's death, the Basques—and the Catalans—were granted the right to form their own regional governments with a president, legislature, and supreme court. Everything from housing to agriculture, from education to social security, is organized at a local level. The Basques levy their own taxes, run their own health service—the best in Spain—and even operate an independent police force. As Julian exclaimed over lunch, "What *more* do they fucking want? Explain *that* in your magnum opus."

The "magnum opus," as he put it, will probably run to several thousand words, a blend of conjecture, facts, and business jargon designed to impress Endiom's investors and provide a broad overview of the political-financial consequences of investing in the Basque region. "Still," Julian disclosed, polishing off his second glass of cognac, "the idea is to encourage our clients into parting with the readies, yes? No sense in putting them off. No sense at all."

So, what more *do* they want? I stop in Vitoria, late for the first of many meetings, and come no closer to an answer. Two hours of employment law and social security benefits with a bespectacled union representative struggling to rein in a bad case of dandruff. It takes twenty-five minutes to find his office and another fifteen for the two of us to walk the damp city streets in search of an eventually mediocre restaurant serving thin soup and stodgy beans. I begin to regret coming. But this is only my second visit to the Basque country and I had forgotten the striking transformation in the landscape as you drive northwest toward the sea, the flat plains of Castilla suddenly soaring into magnificent, bulbous mountains dense with trees and lush grass, the motorway winding frantically along narrow valley floors. This is another country. At half past four I have reached the outskirts of San Sebastián, rain starting to fall and obscuring the hillsides in mist. Every now and again the silhouette of a typical *casería*, low alpine houses with obtuse angular roofs, will punch through the fog, but otherwise little is visible from the road. So nothing prepares me for the beauty of the city itself, for the long graceful stretch of the Concha, the grandeur of the bridges spanning the Urumea River and the elegance of the broad city streets. Julian's secretary, Natalia, has booked me into the Londres y de Inglaterra, perhaps the best hotel in town, situated on the seafront looking out over a wide promenade dotted with benches and old men wearing black Basque berets. The promenade is lined by a white iron balustrade and there is no traffic in sight. It would not seem strange for a woman carrying a parasol to pass on the arm of a Spanish gentleman, or for a child bowling a hoop along the seafront to scurry past in a pair of salmon-pink culottes. I seem to have emerged into a time warp of the fin-de-siècle bourgeoisie, as if the heart of San Sebastián has not changed in over a hundred years, and all of the grim political sparring of the Franco years and beyond has been a myth now happily exploded.

Natalia has reserved a room with a view looking out into the center of the bay, a perfect natural harbor crowned by a bowl of pristine sand that sweeps in a precise crescent along its southern edge. Even in the cold of February, brave swimmers are inching gingerly out to sea, shivering in the soft breakers rolling in off the Bay of Biscay. I take a shower, write down some notes from the meeting at lunch, and fall asleep in front of CNN.

I am woken just after seven by the shrill of the telephone, a call from Julian in Madrid.

"Forgot something," he says, as if we had been in midconversation. "Meant to say at lunch yesterday, completely slipped my mind."

"And what's that?"

"I think you should look up an old acquaintance of mine, useful for the magnum opus. Chap by the name of Mikel Arenaza. Belongs to Batasuna. Or, at least he *did*."

"To *Batasuna*? Since when did you start making friends with them?"

Herri Batasuna was the political wing of ETA until the party was banned in the late summer of 2002. For an unreconstructed blue blood like Julian Church to have an "acquaintance" within its ranks seems as unlikely to me as Saul getting a Christmas card from Gerry Adams.

"I'm a man of mystery," Julian says, as if that explains it. He is tapping something on his desk. "Truth is, Mikel approached us a few years back with an investment proposal we were obliged to turn down on ethical grounds. Hugely entertaining individual, however, and somebody you should definitely look up. *Bon viveur*, ladies' man, speaks immaculate English. You'll like him."

Why does Julian think that I would like a ladies' man? Because of suspicions he has about Sofía? As a consequence of Saul's interventions over the weekend I am trying to suppress my wilder flights of paranoia, but there is something I don't like about this. It feels like a setup.

"So you stayed friends? You and this Mikel? A representative of a terrorist organization in cahoots with the boss of a British private bank?"

"Well, I wouldn't say 'cahoots,' Alec. Not 'cahoots.' Look, if it makes you uneasy, God knows I understand . . ."

"No, it doesn't make me uneasy. I'm just surprised, that's all."

"Well then, fine, why not give him a call? Natalia will e-mail you his details. No sense in spending all of your time up there lunching with lawyers and car salesmen. You might as well *enjoy* yourself."

9

Arenaza

Mikel Arenaza, politician and friend of terror, is a lively, engaging man—I could tell as much by his manner on the phone—but the full extent of his ebullient self-confidence becomes apparent only upon meeting him. We arrange to have a drink in the old town of San Sebastián, not in an *herriko taberna*—the type of down-at-heel pub favored by the radical left-wing nationalist *abertzale*—but in an upmarket bar where waves of tapas and uncooked mushrooms and peppers cover every conceivable surface, two barmen and a young female chef working frantically in sight of the customers. It is my final evening in the city, after three solid days of meetings, and Arenaza arrives late, picking me out of the crowd within an instant of walking through the door, at least six feet of heavy good looks pulling off a charming smile beneath an unbrushed explosion of wild black hair. The fact that he is wearing a suit surprises me; the average Batasuna councilor might view that as a sop to Madrid. On television, in the Spanish parliament, for example, they are often to be seen dressed as if for a football match, in sartorial defiance of the state. Nevertheless, a single studded earring in his right lobe goes some way toward conveying the sense of a subversive personality.

"It is Alec, yes?"

A big handshake, eyes that gleam on contact. The ladies' man.

"That's right. And you must be Mikel."

"Yes indeed I am. Indeed."

He moves forcefully, all muscle-massed shoulders and bulky arms, wit and cunning coexistent in the arrangement of his face. Was it my imagination, or did time stand still for a split second, the bar falling quiet as he came in? He is known here, a public figure. Arenaza nods without words at the older of the two barmen, and a *caña doble* appears with the speed of a magic trick. His eyes are inquisitive, sizing me up, a persistent grin at one edge of his mouth.

"You've found a table. This is not always easy here, it's a triumph. So we can talk. We can get to know each other."

His English is heavily accented and delivered with great confidence and fluidity. I do not bother to ask whether he would rather speak in Spanish; in the absence of Basque, English will be his preferred second language.

"And you work for Julian?" The question appears to amuse him. "He is the typical English banker, no? Eton school and Oxford?"

"I guess so. That's the stereotype." Only Julian went to Winchester, not Eton. "How do you know him?"

There is a fractional pause. "Well, we tried to do some business together a long time ago but it did not come off. However, it was an interesting time, and now whenever I go to Madrid I always try to have a dinner with him. He has become my friend. And Sofía, of course, such a beautiful woman. The British always taking our best wives." A laugh here of Falstaffian dimensions. Arenaza, who must be about Julian's age, has sat down with his back to the room on a low stool that does nothing to diminish his sheer physical impact. He offers his glass in a toast. "To Mr. and Mrs. Church, and to bringing us together." *Clink.* "What is it that you think I can do for you?"

He may be in a hurry, the man-about-town with fifty better things to do. It occurs to me that whatever information he might usefully impart for my report will have to be extracted within the next half hour. It is the challenge of spies to win the confidence of a stranger, and I would like to know more about Mikel Arenaza, yet charisma of his sort usually denotes a distracted and restless personality. Time is of the essence.

"What would be most useful for Endiom to know is your view on the question of separatism. What has become of your party in the wake of the ban? Do you think the Basque people would vote for independence in a referendum? That kind of thing."

Arenaza bounces his eyebrows and puffs out his cheeks in a well-rehearsed attempt at looking taken aback. I note that he is wearing a very strong aftershave.

"Well, it's not unusual to meet an Englishman who arrives straight to the point. I assume you are English, no?"

I take a chance here, going with an arranged plan based on Arenaza's ideological convictions.

"Actually, my father was Lithuanian and my mother is Irish." Two sets of suitably oppressed peoples for a Basque to mull over. "They settled in England when my father found work."

"Really?" He looks gratifyingly intrigued. "Your mother is from Ireland?"

"That's right. County Wicklow. A farm near Bray. Do you know the area at all?"

Mum is actually Cornish, born and bred, but ETA and the IRA have always had very close ties, shared networks, collective goals. About a year ago a general in the Spanish army was killed by a bicycle bomb, a technique ETA were believed to have acquired from the Irish.

"Only Dublin," Arenaza replies, offering me a cigarette, which I decline. It's a South American brand—Belmont—which I have seen only once before. He lights one and smiles through the initial smoke. "I have been to several conferences there, also once to Belfast."

"And you're just back from South America?"

He looks taken aback. "From Bogotá, yes. How did you know this?"

"Your cigarettes. You're smoking a local brand."

"Well, well." He mutters something to himself in Basque. "You're a very observant person, Mr. Milius. Julian makes a good decision in hiring you, I think."

It is a politician's flattery but welcome nonetheless. I say, *"Esker-rik asko"*—Basque for thank you—and lead him back into the conversation.

"So you want to know what has become of Herri Batasuna?"

"That's right. To hear it from someone so close to the center would be very useful."

"Well, it is a complicated situation, as you can probably be guessing. It is not only my party that is affected. I am sure you have already been informed about what happened last week?"

"With *Egunkaria?*" At dawn on February 20, a Thursday, masked members of the Guardia Civil burst into the offices of the Basque newspaper *Egunkaria* and arrested ten of its executives, accusing them of supporting ETA. "I heard the police were a bit heavy-handed. Didn't they go in wearing bulletproof vests?"

"That's right. That's right. It was ridiculous. These are newspaper offices. What are the staff going to shoot them with? *Ink?*" I laugh encouragingly as Arenaza spends fifteen minutes telling me things I already know: that more than a hundred men were ordered to search and board up *Egunkaria* offices throughout the Basque country and Navarra; that they confiscated documents and computer records; that several Basque publishers offered temporary offices and printing facilities to enable the paper to go to press. "It was a direct attack on our culture," he says finally. "This was the only newspaper in the region to publish entirely in Euskera."

"And what about the accusation that it was funded by ETA?"

Arenaza tilts his head very slightly to one side so that his eyes momentarily lose their sheen. This may be a sign of irritation or simply a warning to me to be more discreet.

"I cannot speak for E-T-A," he says, spelling out each letter to disguise the acronym, "but these accusations were also directed at another newspaper, *Egin,* during 1998, before it was also banned by Madrid. They say that the armed struggle wanted a Basque-language newspaper, that they moved shares from *Egin* to *Egunkaria* to pay for this, and that they nominated certain journalists to be editors. And this is bullshit, of course. Total bullshit." Arenaza takes a relaxed drag on his cigarette. His mood is one of nonchalance bordering on conceit. "If you want to talk about funding, let's talk about funding. *Egunkaria* was given six million euros by the state government, and still the People's Party accuses them of 'political responsibility' in the spread of terrorism. These people are just fascists, Alec. Ignorant fascists."

I have noticed over the last few days that parties on either side of the Basque conflict use exactly the same terminology when attacking one another. Thus, Aznar is "a fascist," Ibarretxe, the president of the Basque region, is "a fascist," ETA are "a bunch of fascists," and so on. A useful way of polarizing the debate for those with no interest in resolving it. Still, I nod approvingly, careful to remain on the right side of Arenaza's prejudices. He suggests we have another drink. Within a few moments he has returned from the bar armed with more *cañas* and two large plates covered in *pintxos*.

"The best tapas in the Parte Vieja," he says, an arm falling on my shoulder, and I know now that he is warming to me. Arenaza is a man's man and, for some reason, his sort always likes me. We talk for a long time about the superiority of Basque cuisine over all others, which is at least a subject about which I can speak with real sincerity. But in due course he is keen to return to *Egunkaria*. There is now a powerful smell of alcohol on his breath and I wonder if he was drinking over lunch.

"If I could just tell you, Alec, that the editor in chief of the paper was tortured in Madrid this week by the Interior Ministry police. OK? This is fact, no matter what anybody tells you. An all-night interrogation in the cells of the Guardia Civil between midday on Monday and Tuesday morning. They strip him naked, place a plastic bag over his eyes, and put a gun to his head." For the purposes of illustration, Arenaza presses two fingers to his temple and pulls an imaginary trigger. I notice that the ladies' man is wearing a wedding band on his ring finger. "And all the time pouring insults about Basque culture and politicians into his ears. They are animals."

I knew about this. It was covered in yesterday's *Independent*.

"Jesus, I had no idea."

"Well, of course. And why should you? It is in the interests of the state media not to report these things. And then five of the ten journalists arrested in connection with *Egunkaria* have been denied bail on the basis that they are terrorists. Excuse me? Men of *sixty* years old who write about football and education policy. *Terrorists?*"

For the first time, Arenaza has raised his voice to a level at which it might be understood by anybody at the bar who speaks English. Sensing this, he bites into a canapé of blood sausage and launches a self-deprecating smile: for some reason, he doesn't want me to think that he takes any of this too seriously. I make a start on my second beer, eating a tortilla canapé and directing the conversation back toward Batasuna.

"So can you tell me, as a former councilor, about the consequences of the ban? Your reaction to it and that of your colleagues?"

"My reaction to it? OK." He leans forward. A tiny speck of *morcilla* has caught on his chin. "The truth is, Alec, that support for the party was falling away all the time because of the violence. That is not something that I, or anybody else, can deny. From maximum twenty percent of the region down to less than ten when the cease-fire began. Voters do not like seeing people being killed. That is not to say that armed struggle is ineffective. On the contrary, if you look at any revolutionary group in an international context—Hamas, IRA, Chechen fighters, bin Laden—all of these have been undoubtedly effective, with the possible exception of al-Qaeda, who to me do not seem to have any ideological objective other than pure rage. Violence is the only way to get politicians to come to the table, to make them give concessions, and people recognize this. The suicide bombs on the buses of Tel Aviv will one day pay dividends, just as the war fought by E-T-A has borne fruit. You only have to look at what the IRA extracted from your government and from Tony Brair."

"Who never banned Sinn Fein."

"Exactly!" Arenaza seizes on this point with obvious delight, as if he has found a kindred spirit. "The British were very clever," he says, strumming his fingers on the table. "They never banned the party. They knew that it would be undemocratic to do this. And when the time came to negotiate the peace process, these talks were able to go ahead in a civilized fashion. The IRA had a respectable political face to invite into the drawing rooms of England and everybody could proceed with British dignity. But Señor Aznar has banned Herri Batasuna and now he has nothing. He means to drive the nationalist movement, in your expression, 'into the sea.' But he will not succeed."

"Well, you can't really blame him."

It is as if Arenaza has not heard me. His eyes narrow considerably and there is even a slight pouting of the lips, as if I have failed to laugh at one of his favorite jokes. "I am sorry. I do not follow." Very skillfully, he maintains the politician's charm.

"It's just that a few years ago E-T-A tried to blow Aznar up with a car bomb. That kind of thing tends to leave an impression, no? You can sympathize with the Palestinians all you like, but if one day your daughter is on that bus and she's the one who gets her arms blown off, your perspective is going to change on the subject."

For once, perhaps as a result of being contradicted, Arenaza's superb English fails him and he asks me to repeat what I have said. For the sake of clarity I abandon the Israeli parallel and remind him about ETA's attempt on Aznar's life.

"You think Aznar's motivation is a revenge?"

"I don't think you can discount it."

Mikel Arenaza appears to consider this thesis for some time—looking up at one point to scope an attractive woman who walks in on the far side of the bar—and lights another cigarette before responding.

"You are an interesting man, Alec Milius." The flattery is accompanied by the sort of winning grin I suspect he might ordinarily reserve for the ladies. "How does a politician make his name? By putting more books in schools? By making the buses run on time? Of course not. He does it by the big gesture. So Mr. Bush will bring democracy to Iraq, Mr. Aznar will win the war against ETA. This is how they want to be remembered. And of course it is delusional. We are being led by weak men, and we will pay. All that fucking tax inspector in Madrid has done is anger a lot of moderate nationalists and turned them against his government. Herri Batasuna never killed anybody. You must remember this. We were a democratic institution. Either you believe in freedom of expression, in one person and one vote, or you do not. Do you believe in this, Mr. Alec Milius of Endiom Bank?"

"Of course I do."

"Well, I do not!"

Arenaza looks at me with an expression of unguarded triumph, as if delighted to have pulled the rug out from under my feet. He actually lifts both hands off the table and appears to look around for applause. I lean forward on my stool and pick up another canapé.

"You don't believe in freedom of speech?"

"Not anymore."

"In democracy?"

"I have concluded after a lot of thinking that it is wasted on people."

This might be interesting. "You want to explain why?"

"Of course." Another trademark grin, prompting the thought that Mikel Arenaza has a fatal weakness—a desire to be liked. He will say or do anything to achieve that end. What is seduction, after all, if not the constant pursuit of another's approbation? I would be prepared to make a substantial bet that he has no firm convictions to speak of, only the desire to strip people of theirs.

"Look at what is happening with the war in the Gulf," he exclaims, staring out of the window as if members of Iraq's elite Republican Guard were suddenly massing in the Parte Vieja. "Millions of people, all around the world, protesting to their governments about the invasion of Iraq, and who listens to them? Nobody. Not Mr. Blair, not the PP, certainly not the Americans and Bush. But they will do it anyway, they will go into Baghdad. And you know what makes me laugh? It is this same so-called democracy that they wish to impose on the Middle East. The same corruption. The same lies. Do you see? The people do not *matter*."

"But that's not *their* fault." I don't like hearing this from a politician, conviction or no conviction. "Democracy isn't wasted on the public just because they don't have a voice. It's wasted on the politicians who take advantage of them."

"Exactly, exactly." Arenaza appears to agree wholeheartedly and drains his drink. "But the idea that governments listen to the public, that they are accountable to the men and women who voted for them, is a notion from the nineteenth century, in your country from the beginnings of socialism when people finally had a voice and a way of communicating with one another. Before that politics was about the special interests of elites. People forget this, and now we are back at this point. Your British government pursues a policy based on one simple ideology: follow America. That is the extent of their imagination. And in the long run it is easier for Mr. Blair to say no to hundreds of thousands of British voters, even to ignore the voice of his own conscience, than it is for the Foreign Office of the United Kingdom to say no to George Bush. Now, follow my logic. Once the prime ministers of Spain and of the UK have a decision of this kind forced upon them, that is to say, they have no choice in what they do because of America, then they start to see themselves as men of destiny. Good Europeans against bad, friends of democracy against friends of terror. The ego takes over."

I've lost the thread here but find a question. "So why are you still involved in politics?"

"I am not. We have been banned."

"Yes, but—"

"Listen to me. I have sat in on these meetings, even at the level of local politics, and none of my superiors ever cared for anything but his own personal and political advancement. They are all little Dick Cheneys, all the same. Politics is the vanity of individual men. Policy is shaped by flaws in the character."

Why is he telling me this? Because he is drunk? "You're saying that you disapprove of your colleagues?"

A heavy pause. Arenaza runs his hand through a thick clump of hair.

"Not exactly, no. Not disapprove." I suppose he doesn't want to overstep the mark. "It is more a question of human nature, of reality. Listen, you have somewhere else you have to go tonight?"

"No."

"Then come with me. I will explain everything to you. We go to another bar and I will show you exactly what it is that I mean."

10

Level Three

A light drizzle has started to fall by the time we leave the bar, the dark, narrow streets of the old quarter coated in black rain. The sea air is damp, Atlantic, quite different from the dry and dusty atmosphere of Madrid, and to take it in deep breaths is a welcome relief after the fug of the bar. Moving quickly beside Arenaza as we walk along the street, I try to anticipate what the next few hours might hold. Anything could happen. The evening may disappear in a mulch of booze and ideology, or it could acquire a completely different character. Unless I have read the situation wrongly, Arenaza appears to have undergone some sort of political epiphany, criticizing his former masters in the armed struggle and happily articulating that revelation to strangers such as myself. It is the airplane phenomenon: the most sensitive information is often disclosed to the passenger sitting by our side whom we expect to never see again. As Arenaza spoke to me in the bar, confidence seemed to ebb away from him with each passing drink, as if a mask were slipping from his face. On the basis of a shared acquaintance with Julian, a former councilor with Batasuna was taking me into his confidence, and yet it somehow made perfect sense. I charmed him back there. I worked him around.

"First we have to go to my car," he says. "I have to take off this jacket, Alec, to change out of my suit and shoes. You OK if I do this?"

"No problem."

Most of the better bars and restaurants in San Sebastián are clustered around the Parte Vieja, but I have spent very little time here, largely because Julian's contacts preferred to meet in the lounge bar of the Hotel Inglaterra, where the comfortable sofas and armchairs offer views out onto the promenade and the ocean beyond. As a result, I don't know my way around, and Arenaza's frequent switches of direction along the grid of streets are disorientating. It feels as though we are heading west toward the Concha, but it is impossible to take a bearing. Arenaza is holding a copy of the *Gara* newspaper over his head to protect it from rain, using his other hand to talk into a mobile phone. He is speaking to someone rapidly in Basque:

"Denak ondo dago. Gaueko hamabietan egongo maizetxean. Afari egin behar dut Ingles bankari honekin."

Who is he talking to? His wife? A colleague? Halfway through the conversation he breaks off and gestures at a poster tacked to the window of a nearby bar. It is a cartoon depicting a caricature of Aznar, the prime minister's tongue curling deep into the ass of President George W. Bush. The caption is written in Basque and I cannot understand it. Through the window I can see two men playing chess on stools. Arenaza mouths the word "Truth" and continues speaking into the phone. *"Ez arduratu,"* he says. *"Esan dizut dagoenekoz. Gaueko hamabiak. Bale ba, ikusi ordu arte."*

Then the conversation ends and we emerge into a pedestrianized area immediately behind the town hall. It is past nine o'clock and the streets are teeming with people. Arenaza explains that his car is parked in an underground garage about fifty meters away. Putting his hand on my back, he steers me across a set of blinking pedestrian lights and we walk toward the entrance.

"Down here," he says. "Down here."

The staircase is poorly lit and I hold on to the banister, pushed aside at one point by a pensioner coming the other way wearing a fake mink coat. The car park is on three subterranean levels, each one increasingly damp. Arenaza's car, a tiny, door-dented Fiat, is parked in the far corner of the bottom floor, squeezed in between a brand-new Mini Cooper with British plates and a dark blue Renault Espace. This must be the long-term car park, because the area is completely devoid of people. It is very dark now, and for the first time it occurs to me that I may have completely misread the situation. Why did Arenaza need me to come all the way down here? Why is he changing his clothes?

"You know what, Mikel, I think I might wait upstairs." This could be a kidnap attempt, a robbery, anything. "I'll see you at the entrance to the town hall."

I should never have come here of my own volition. I'm letting things slip.

"What are you saying?" He sounds relaxed, fishing around in the boot of the Fiat, his face is out of sight. "Alec?"

"Just that I need to make a phone call. From the entrance. To a friend in Madrid. She's trying to call me. I'll see you at the top, Mikel, OK? I'll see you at the top."

"Wait, wait." He emerges between the Fiat and the Mini, dressed in an old sweater worn over a clean white T-shirt. "You're going upstairs? Can you wait just for two minutes please?"

I back away from the car and spin slowly through a complete turn, trying to read his eyes. In the distance, something metal drops to the ground. It is dark and very quiet. Just the concrete chill of basements and a pervasive smell of spilled petrol. Then, thirty feet away, two men emerge quickly from a van and start moving toward me. Immediately I turn and run back toward the exit staircase, with no thought other than to get out as quickly as possible. Behind me, Arenaza shouts out "Hey!" but I do not respond, sprinting hard up three flights of stairs and into the blessed relief of rain and fresh air.

At street level I bend down and double up in the crowds, resting my hands on my knees in an attempt to catch my breath. Why did Julian set me up with this guy? My head aches and the backs of my legs are shaking. Then, behind me, the two men emerge onto the street, walking at a steady pace. With a sense of relief that quickly changes to shame, I see that they are Chinese. Not Basque nationalists, not errand boys for ETA, but two tourists wearing denim jeans and raincoats. One of them is telling a story, the other laughing while consulting a map. It is humiliating. Seconds later Arenaza himself emerges, looking around with an expression of complete bewilderment. How do I get out of this one? I take out my mobile phone, press it to my ear, and say the words "Two three four five, two twos are four, two threes are six" in an attempt to give an impression of urgent conversation. Arenaza spots this and frowns. I wave happily back, gesturing to the phone, and then snap it shut as he comes toward me.

"Sorry, Mikel, sorry." My breathing is fast and irregular. "My phone started ringing down there and I wanted to take it. There's this girl I've been seeing and the signal was weak. . . ."

He doesn't believe me. "What happened?" he says gently.

"Like I was just telling you. A girl . . ."

"No, come on. What? You become scared by something?"

He is not angry. In fact he is being surprisingly sympathetic.

"Scared?" I produce an absurd burst of laughter. "No, of course not."

"You suffer claustrophobia, Alec?"

It's an idea. I might as well play along rather than try to pretend that I received a mobile phone signal under fifty feet of concrete.

"OK, to be honest, yes. I do. I got a bit freaked out. Call it claustrophobia."

"My brother has this as well." God bless Mikel Arenaza's brother. "I am sorry, very sorry to hear about it." He shakes his head and puts a hand on the lower part of my neck, giving it a little squeeze. "You should have said something before we go."

"Well, I thought I'd outgrown it, Mikel, I really did. I haven't had an episode like that for years. We bankers aren't very tough, you know?"

He doesn't laugh. "No, this is not funny. I know because of Julio. It ruins his life." Opening a wide-brimmed umbrella, Arenaza shields me from the rain and assumes an almost avuncular air. "You want to rest? You want to go back to your hotel?"

"No, of course not." He has applied a fresh layer of aftershave in the car park and I wish that we were not standing so close together. "Let's carry on. Let's have a drink. I'd like to, I really would."

And he accepts, talking all the way about his own fears—of heights, of spiders—purely to lessen my own sense of embarrassment. It is an unarguably kind thing to do and I feel an unexpected sense of shame that I should have suspected him of anything but openness and decency.

"This is where I want to take you," he says as we arrive outside an *herriko taberna,* back in the depths of the Parte Vieja. "Inside you will see the problems with the *abertzale.* Then it will all become clear."

The small bar is jammed and thumps with the cacophonic roar of Basque heavy metal. A smell of marijuana hits me like a memory of Malasaña, and Arenaza looks back as we drift past its source: two Goths sucking on a joint the size of a Magic Marker. He is greeted, though not warmly, by several of the customers, yet he stops to talk to no one. At the bar we turn to face one another and I insist that it's my round.

"We pay at the end," he says. "You're not too uncomfortable here? Not too much crowd?"

He is harping back to the claustrophobia.

"No, I'm fine. It's more a fear of the dark, Mikel. Generally I'm all right in crowds."

A woman is serving behind the bar with the sides of her head shaved and the hair grown out long at the back. It is a Basque style. Looking around, I can see half a dozen young men with similar cuts, and another three or four with what can only be described as mullets. The idea, according to a journalist I had lunch with in Villabona on Wednesday, is to present a stark contrast to the primped rugs of Madrid's young conservative elite, who tend to favor neat side partings or waves of sculpted gel. Arenaza leans over and kisses the barmaid on both cheeks, though again he is greeted coolly.

"Let's drink something," he says, ordering two large whiskeys— Irish, of course—with plenty of ice in mine. There is a small blueblack pot on the bar, like an Inca urn, and I ask what it is.

"That is a collection box," he replies quietly. "Money for our prisoners."

"For prisoners of E-T-A?"

"Exactly."

This catches me off guard.

"That's legal?"

Arenaza shrugs. I can see now that there are photographs of ETA prisoners all over the bar, hidden in corners next to aging stickers promoting Batasuna, mug shots of "freedom fighters" with self-conscious stares gazing out in defiance at the insult of devolved power. About one in every five is a woman, and none of them can be much older than thirty. What must it be like to live with the day-to-day conviction of political violence, to take a human life in the name of a cause? Epiphany or no epiphany, Arenaza must have some experience of this; you do not work for Batasuna for sixteen years without drops of blood accumulating on your hands. It is in *herriko tabernas* like this one, all over the Basque country, that ETA firebrands will do a lot of their recruiting, pouring nationalist propaganda into the ears of susceptible young men who will later go off to bomb the hotels of British tourists in Alicante, or to blow up the cars of a politician or judge brave enough to have taken a stand against the "armed struggle." Is that how he started out? Was Arenaza talent-spotted as a teenage terrorist, later to send out acolytes of his own on the path to an ignorant martyrdom?

"Would you like something to eat?" he asks.

"I'm not hungry."

As if on cue my mobile phone trills and a text message comes through from Sofía:

Miss u tonight. Hope u are being careful in the north. Be aware of the basques. They are fascists. xxx

"Is everything all right?"

I switch off the phone.

"Everything's fine. Still feeling a bit strange from the car park."

He picks up our drinks and finds a corner in which to stand and talk.

"Tell me something," I ask him, feeling like I want to have this out. "Are these bars used for money laundering? If I buy you a whiskey or a *bocadillo,* am I helping to pay for a detonator on E-T-A's next car bomb?"

He appears to admire my frankness.

"Well, it is true, up to a point. What is the reason for denying this? A lot of people are engaged in the war, Alec. A lot of people want to see an independent Basque state."

"And a lot of people just want to be left in peace. Most people want to have nothing whatsoever to do with politics. You said so yourself, just half an hour ago."

"It's true, it's true." He looks suddenly disgusted by his cigarette and extinguishes it in an ashtray. "Politics is over for the great majority. We have talked about this. The complete irrelevance of political discourse of any kind. This is why an event like 9/11 comes as such a shock to the average American. 'Who are these people?' they ask themselves. 'What have we done to them that they can do this to us?' People are ignorant of the facts. They are misinformed by journalists on the television and in the newspapers, and anyway they do not care. If they did, they would seek answers. If they did, they would take to the streets."

"But Spanish people never *stop* taking to the streets. There are protests in Madrid all the time. I can't hear myself think in Calle Princesa at the moment. Every time I look out of the window there are ten thousand people protesting against the war in Iraq."

He smirks. "And they will not be heard. It is only a story that fills news programs, something to give people a subject to talk about over lunch. This protest makes them feel good, as if they have done something. But it is just the orgasm of the collective act, a masturbation." Arenaza mispronounces this word and I almost laugh. "Take away that person's television, their car, their house, *then* you will see them commit to a cause."

"But that's the position here in Euskal Herria. You insist, in spite of all the freedoms enjoyed by modern Basques, that Spain has stolen something from you. Your country. And yet you've given up—on yourself and on the people. You think democracy and freedom of speech are wasted on them."

This gives Arenaza pause, as if I have locked him in a contradiction, and again I begin to wonder whether he really believes anything he says. It all seems so cynical, so reductionist, so completely at odds with the confident Madrid-bashing nationalist of first acquaintance. Has he been *told* to say it?

"I will explain." Moving only his eyes, he gestures toward a spidery figure standing about ten feet away in the bar. A stooped, aging man, bald and bearded, is jabbering with electric conviction at a teenager wearing jeans and leathers. "What do you see over there?"

"I see somebody trying to make a point. And I see an impressionable young man."

When I have explained the word "impressionable," Arenaza says, "Exactly!" and reproduces an earlier smile of triumph. "This man was one of my former colleagues. We work together in the same office. Do not worry, he does not speak English. He will not be able to understand what we are saying. He is a man filled with hate. Once a true patriot, now extreme in all of his views. Just as I was telling you—a person of conviction who allowed personal vanity and weakness to cloud his judgment. And this boy you see, this is the first time that I have seen him in the bar. He is just a child, there are hundreds like him, and my colleague will be instructing him in the good sense of the armed struggle, letting him pick up the street slang of our language, giving him a purpose, a direction. See the way he looks at him, as if in the presence of greatness."

It is indeed obvious that the teenager is eager and suggestible, to the point of caricature: the tilted head, the careful gestures, the respect and deference of his gaze. Blond threads of adolescent beard coat the sides of his face and his forehead is pockmarked by acne. Here is a person at the dawn of adult life engaged in a search for meaning, a young man of undecided character pounced upon by opportunists. Just as I was when Hawkes and Lithiby sucked me into the secrecy of Five and Six back in 1995. It is the first rule of recruitment: get them before the cynicism sets in. Get them while they're young.

"So your colleague is recruiting for E-T-A?" I ask.

"Who knows?" Arenaza shrugs and drinks his whiskey and of course there will be no certain answer. I steal a second glance at the man and suppress an urge to confront him. Is there anything more dangerous than the ideologue, the fanatic with his bitterness and his cause? I feel a profound and urgent desire to protect this young man from his innocence, from all the pain and anguish that will visit him in his future.

"Personally I have lost all belief," Arenaza says, interrupting this thought. "My colleague—his name is Juan—certainly believes that E-T-A will triumph. But I know now that armed struggle is wrong."

"But you said it could work. You said bombs will bring politicians to the table."

"To the table, yes. After that, everything is consensus. Just look at what has happened in Ireland. So what were we fighting for? It was as pointless as putting on sunglasses in the dark."

Even if Arenaza is spinning a line, I would like to hear how this plays out. "What happened to you?" I ask.

He repeats my question, possibly for melodramatic effect, and sinks the whiskey in a single gulp.

"Two things happened. The first is that they set off a car bomb in Santa Pola, a bomb that killed a six-year-old girl. She was playing with toys in her bedroom. You were probably in Madrid when it happened. You probably took part in the manifestations that followed." "Manifestations" is a mistranslation of the Spanish word for "protest." "The E-T-A did not think to find out if the young girl was there. She was just a child, innocent of politics, of frontiers. And the day after the bombing I was very shaken, it surprised me to feel this way. I could not work, I could not sleep. For the first time I could not even talk to my wife or to my colleagues. It was as if all of my doubts about the direction of my life had been brought together by this single incident. They had printed the girl's photograph in the newspaper. She looked like my own daughter, almost a copy. The same eyes, the same hair, the same clothes. And I thought, 'This is madness, this cannot go on.' And to make it worse, a few hours after the bombing I was forced to issue a statement on behalf of the party, saying that we would be happy to 'analyze' the situation. Not condemning the accidental murder of an innocent child, but 'analysis.' A nothing word, a word that Rumsfeld might use, even the fucking tax inspector Aznar. The prime minister called us 'human trash,' and for once he was right. Then, one week later, another bomb, and I thought, 'Now the ban will go through,' and of course it did. The electricity was ordered to be shut off. No water came to any of the Batasuna offices across the whole of Euskal Herria. And in private I criticized the leadership, I told them they could not see what was going on, although of course nobody knew the extent of my dissatisfaction. Then I marched through the streets of the city with everyone else in protest against what the government was doing, because it was undemocratic, because it was stupid of the judge, Garzón, but the situation was hopeless. My heart had gone."

Across the room, Juan emits a tight, rasping cough, like a dog with something caught in its throat. I hope he chokes. Arenaza leans on the shelf and lights another cigarette. There are dried balls of chewing gum, like little pieces of brain, lying at the bottom of his ashtray.

"But the killing hasn't stopped," I tell him. "Two weeks ago a police chief was shot dead. . . ."

"Yes, in Andoain. Eating his breakfast in a bar." Mikel's face almost collapses with the pointlessness of it all. If this is an act, it is Oscar winning. He is now in the throes of a full confession. "So I wanted to get out of it anyway. The ban came at the right time."

"Why are you telling me this?"

He laughs halfheartedly. "Well, we confide in strangers, don't we? I am drunk. I am not careful." He leans toward me. "This is not the sort of thing that I can tell my friends, Alec. A man does not leave the party. There are those who would take revenge."

"You mean E-T-A?"

"Of course I mean E-T-A." He tries to drink more whiskey, forgetting that it is finished. "There is a younger leadership now, more brutal. And then there is the fear that we all lived with, of reprisals from the families of the victims. We were the spokesmen of the armed struggle, we appeared on television, and that always made us a target for revenge."

"And now you're caught in the middle?"

Upon reflection, very quietly, Arenaza agrees. "Yes, in the middle." U2 pounds on the stereo—a track from *The Unforgettable Fire*—while Arenaza stares despondently at the ground. When he stoops, the muscles in his shoulders swell and stretch the fabric of his sweater.

"And the second thing?"

"What?"

"You said two things happened. The bomb and something else."

"Oh." His head rears up, as if regaled by memory, and for a moment all of the pain and the doubt and the sadness seems to leave him. He looks suddenly happy. "The second thing that happened was that I fall in love."

"With your wife?"

It is a stupid question and Arenaza laughs in a way that opens up his face, gives it light. "No, not with my wife. Not my wife. With Señorita Rosalía Dieste. A young woman. From Madrid, in fact. We meet two months ago, at a conference on new energies here in Donostia, at the Hotel Amara Plaza. She is an industrial engineer, very beautiful. Ever since—how can I say?—we enjoy ourselves."

He is grinning manically. The ladies' man.

"She's your mistress?"

"My mistress," he says proudly, as if the description pleases him. I feel like giving him advice on not getting caught. *Get an e-mail account that your wife knows nothing about. Keep any presents that she gives you in a drawer at work. If you go to her house, leave the loo seat down after using the bathroom.*

"So you've been to see her? She comes up here and you try to get away from your wife?"

"It is not this easy. She also has a man she lives with. A boyfriend. But next week I am coming to Madrid to be with her. On Thursday.

74

So we spend the weekend together at my hotel." As an afterthought, he adds, "Maybe we should meet for an evening, no? You show me around Madrid, Alec?"

Is this part of the grand plan? Is this what Julian wants?

"With Julian and Sofía?"

"Sure. But the two of us as well. Rosalía has to go home at night so I have a lot of time on my hands. We go to Huertas, we go to La Latina. I know a wonderful Basque restaurant in Madrid, the best cooking in the city. Two men with no cares in the world. I would like to leave all of my problems behind. I have no responsibilities for five days. And we find you a girl, Alec. You have a girl?"

His hand slaps onto my biceps as I reply, "Nothing regular," and shake my head. "Julian doesn't know anything about this?"

"Julian?" The idea seemed to take him by surprise.

"Julian. Julian Church."

"I know who you mean. No, he must know nothing. Nobody knows anything, and you must speak to nobody about it." He starts grinning again, wagging his finger. "Can you imagine telling Julian this, anything that I have told you? He would not understand. He would be English about it and wave his hands in the air, trying to make it all go away. They do not understand sex or politics in your country. You do, Alec, I can see that. Maybe it is because of your family's history, the suffering in Ireland and the Baltics."

"What? That helps me to understand sex?"

He laughs. "Of course, of course. But I tell you this. I once shared a room with Julian and he was asleep as soon as he turned out the light. No dialogue in his brain, no conscience or worry. Just a flick of the switch and *boom!*"—Arenaza chops his hand through the air— "Julian Church snores. Can you imagine such a person? So peaceful. No struggle in his soul."

Why were Julian and Mikel sharing a room?

"That does sound like him, yes. Yes it does."

"But of course it was not always this way. Like all of us, he has also had troubles in his relations."

"Yes." He obviously thinks that I know Julian far better than I do.

"For example when he was living in Colombia."

"Colombia."

"All the problems with his wife."

"Oh yes."

Sofía has never mentioned anything about living in Colombia. Arenaza looks at me doubtfully, but he's too drunk to make the connection.

"You know about his time in South America? You know about Nicole?"

"Of course." I have never heard Julian speak of any woman of that name, nor of any time spent in South America. It certainly didn't come up when I ran checks on him three years ago. "He told me over lunch one day. It must have been difficult for him."

"Of course, of course. Your wife runs off with your best friend, this is more than 'difficult.' I think it nearly killed him."

I am grateful for the low light and the din of the *taberna,* because they help to smother my reaction. Julian had a wife before *Sofía?*

"You obviously know him a lot better than I do," I respond. "You and Julian have a history. I don't think he would reveal something as personal as that to an employee, no matter how close we are. It's very private."

I try to work out the implications. Has Arenaza spoken out of turn? I need to put the pieces together without appearing ignorant of the facts. Yet I cannot even work out whether Sofía knows the truth about her husband's past. Is she an innocent party in this, or has she been playing me all this time?

"Another whiskey?" I ask, assuming that alcohol will help to lower Arenaza's defences.

"Sure."

And the brief respite at the bar allows me time to conceive a strategy, a question designed to discover what Julian was doing in Colombia.

"I forget," I ask, returning with two tumblers of Jameson. "What was Julian's job title out in South America?"

"In Bogotá? His job title?" He looks perplexed. "I think he was just teaching English. That was the whole problem."

"The whole problem."

"Well, Nicole is the reason they are there, yes?"

"Yes."

"I mean, she works at the embassy all day and Julian has nothing to do but teach English to businessmen and students. . . ."

I experience a thump of shock, a tightening through the upper part of my body. "The embassy."

"That's right."

"Yes. For some reason I thought Julian was connected to that."

But which embassy? US or UK?

"Are you all right, Alec? You look worried."

"I'm fine. Why?"

"You sure?"

"It must be the drink. We've had quite a bit."

He shrugs. "Yes I think so."

"So where did they meet?"

"Julian and Nicole?"

"Yes."

He is starting to look uninterested. "In the United States. Julian was working for a bank in Washington and they meet through work." Does that make Nicole a Yank? "But he gives it all up for love. Follows his new wife to Colombia where she falls for this other man. Why?"

"Well, maybe that's why Julian prefers marrying foreign girls," I suggest, adopting an ambiguity in the hope of discovering Nicole's nationality. Arenaza duly obliges.

"Sure. But I don't think he will marry any more Americans, no? I think one is enough for a lifetime."

Maybe it's all coincidence, but at the very least Julian's wife worked for the State Department. Yet in what capacity? The fact that neither Sofía nor Julian has ever mentioned her would surely suggest a connection with the Pentagon or the CIA—and that means a link to Katharine and Fortner. But why would Julian put me in touch with someone who had access to that information? Is it because he knows that I will not be able to prevent myself from investigating?

"I'd forgotten all this," I tell him. "I'd always assumed that Julian had been with Sofía for longer. I guess that explains why they don't have any children."

"I suppose." He is starting to look tired, glancing at his watch. I try to keep the conversation going, but his answers about Julian's past are either evasive or ill informed. Only when questioned directly about Nicole's adultery does he become animated.

"Look, the infidelity is not so rare, yes? We are all guilty of it. I was like Nicole. I get married very young and we make mistakes. Both of us."

But this is surely self-serving, words designed to lessen his feelings of guilt over Rosalía. Within moments, Arenaza is looking at his watch again, finishing his whiskey, and announcing that he has to leave. I invite him to stay for one more drink, but his mind is made up and he is determined to head for home.

"It was my wife I was speaking to before," he explains. "She likes me to be home by midnight. The women, they keep their claws in us, no? But I give you my card, Alec. We call each other when I come to Madrid."

And that's it. Any further information will have to wait for a week, when I can ply Arenaza with drink over dinner and tour him around the bars of Madrid. At the edge of the Parte Vieja he waves me off, sinking into the backseat of a cab, and half an hour later I am back in the hotel running through three years of encounters with Sofía and Julian, trying to piece them all together. There's a bad American movie on TV and I have five miniatures of Scotch for company, but nothing makes any sense. In the end, I get into bed, resign myself to a night without sleep, and switch off the light.

11

California Dreaming

I check out of the hotel at seven the following morning and leave San Sebastián in darkness, heading south to Madrid on roads blurred by fog. Stopping for breakfast in a motorway café north of Vitoria, I send Arenaza a text message thanking him for the meeting and we arrange to have dinner next Saturday in Madrid. That should give him a couple of days of unbridled passion with Rosalía, after which he might feel like opening up. Then Saul calls when I am an hour south of Burgos, sounding oddly nervous about my return. On the basis that he is probably hiding something, I tell him that it will be at least three o'clock by the time I make it back. This is a lie. Given decent traffic, I should be home by midday.

I park the Audi in its reserved space below Plaza de España, remove the bag of money from the boot, and carry my luggage the short distance up Calle de la Princesa to the apartment. A woman's voice, American with a Hispanic lilt, is audible as soon as I step out of the lift.

"You're *serious*?" she says, rising on the question with Californian surprise. "People pay that much money for an apartment in London?" It is not possible to hear any answer.

I press my ear to the door but there is now no sound. Three or four seconds pass and all talking has stopped. Have they realized I am outside? I turn the key in the lock and expect—what? A team of American operatives planting bugs in light fittings? Instead I am confronted by a sight both strange and wonderful: a stunning black girl walking out of the spare bedroom wearing nothing but a pair of bright yellow panties. She stops dead in her tracks when she sees me.

"Who are you?"

Saul comes rushing out of the bedroom, wrapped in a crumpled sheet.

"Alec!"

"Hello, mate."

I ought to be angry, but it's a bedroom farce.

"You said you weren't coming back until three. What happened?"

"I wasn't hungry. Didn't stop for lunch. Been having fun?"

The girl has disappeared.

"Almost, almost," he says, a considered response given the circumstances. "You don't mind, do you?"

He's worried that I'll think she's a spook. Nothing could be farther from my mind, but I'll play along just to give him a fright.

"Who is she?"

"Just a girl I met last night." He struggles to remember her name, frowning with frustration. "Sasha? Sammy? Siri? Something like that. She's cool, man."

"Really? You sure?"

Saul shakes his head. "Don't go paranoid on me."

"Who said anything about going paranoid?"

We have drifted out of earshot of the spare bedroom, moving toward the kitchen.

"Look, she's not here to steal stuff. She's not here to plant bugs. I went up to her in a club. We came back and watched a DVD."

"Yeah? Which one?"

"*Ronin.*"

"Sounds exciting. Glad to see you haven't lost your touch with the ladies."

Saul rubs his eyes. There's a twist of amusement in his face. "Look, she's an art student from Columbia. Studying Cubism."

"Analytic or synthetic?"

And now he's on to me. "Oh, fuck off."

I turn away, grinning, and walk back toward my bedroom. "See to your guest. Make her feel at home." If anything, I am relieved by what Saul has done; it helps to balance out my own moral failings. Does adultery still count if your estranged wife is sleeping with another man? "Would she like some coffee? A daily newspaper? A glass of freshly squeezed orange juice?"

"I'm going to get dressed," he replies.

Yet once Saul has disappeared back into the bedroom I experience a strange mixture of contradictory emotions: mild panic, assuaged by his insistence that the girl is just a student; relief that he will no longer occupy the moral high ground when it comes to criticizing my own behavior; and jealousy, if only because the sounds of giggling coming from the spare bedroom would be enough to make any man feel lonely.

I text Sofía:

Home now. Thinking of you. Can we meet? x

The next half hour is spent unpacking and stowing the money behind the fridge. There's no sign of Saul or the girl so I leave a note and head outside. I want to get some background on Arenaza and look into Nicole in more detail. At the post office I retrieve my computer hard drive and the various coded reminders of passwords and contact addresses, then head down to the Internet café at the foot of Calle de Ventura Rodríguez.

According to articles I find in nexis.com, over the past five years there have been 127 Spanish newspaper stories linked to Mikel Arenaza. I print out those in which his name appears in the first two paragraphs and then run a separate search through Google. Mostly this leads to generic information about Batasuna, although something pops up from Bilbao University concerning a lecture Arenaza gave in 1999, and that is soon spooling out of the printer. Predictably, any combination of Arenaza/Bogotá, Batasuna/Colombia, or Church/Arenaza produces either garbage or irrelevant material. A Julio Arenaza from Argentina, for example, stayed at an obscure mountain hostel in Chile in 2001, and left a note in the online guest book saying how much he had enjoyed visiting the local church. Typing Batasuna/FARC into Nexis produces two interesting articles on the US wires about ETA's relationship with the Italian Mafia (from whom they have purchased Balkan weapons in exchange for drugs) and their links with FARC, the Colombian guerrilla movement. The US embassy in Bogotá also provides a detailed Web site, although a thorough check of e-mail addresses listed on the various pages fails to turn up anyone named Nicole or Nicki or Church. There's an "nrodriguez" working in the human resources section, but unless Nicole has married someone of Hispanic descent and taken his name, it seems unlikely that this could be her. I take a note of the main switchboard number and begin again.

Arenaza said that Julian and Nicole met in Washington, DC, several years ago, while Julian was working in a bank. There are more than seventy financial institutions listed on the Web for the DC metropolitan area, although I know that Endiom has only one office on the eastern seaboard, in lower Manhattan. At first I check private banks and British-owned institutions in Washington, later widening the net to American-owned organizations, or those with any kind of Hispanic connection. The list grows and grows and mostly it's just a question of writing down phone numbers in order to check with the banks directly at a later stage. The Foreign Office Web site, unlike that of its American counterpart, contains woefully little information about Bogotá. The page takes about six minutes to load and contains little more than a few tidbits about visa requirements and Jack Straw. Eyes stinging with screenache, I head off for lunch and resolve to start again in an hour.

Saul calls just as I am about to tuck into a tortilla.

"Sasha's gone," he says.

"So you remembered her name . . ."

"Hope you didn't mind her being here. Maybe I should have asked."

"Don't worry about it."

I am too caught up in Arenaza's revelations to care. Besides, I'd like to have a hold over Saul, so there's no point in giving him a hard time about the girl.

"Listen," he says, "Andy's back in Cádiz. I thought I might head down there for a few days."

"This afternoon?"

"Maybe tomorrow. You want to come?"

It is the last thing I feel like doing.

"I'd love to, but I have to write up this report for Julian. It's going to take days."

He sounds disappointed. There is a long pause. It is as if we have no more to say to one another.

"How was the trip?"

"Fine."

And the rest of the conversation is inconsequential. I ask him if he liked the car chases in *Ronin*. Is he going to see the girl again? Then I hang up and see that Sofía has left a message.

Not this weekend. Must be with Julian. Lo siento. S x

And suddenly the paranoia returns. Why would she turn me down? Has Arenaza spoken to them? Has their plan unraveled? This will be the aftermath of San Sebastián: not concerns over Saul's sex life but other mistrusts and suspicions. I finish the tortilla—almost breaking a tooth on a diamond-hard chunk of *jamón*—and ring Julian in an effort to establish what's going on.

"So! You're back. How was it?"

He is at his desk, chipper as ever, no suggestion of concern.

"Terrific, thanks. Just need the weekend to write up the magnum opus. How are things with you?"

"As ever, but who am I to complain?"

Indeed.

"Manchester United still winning?"

"Oh yes, oh yes."

The question, as I might have anticipated, instigates a five-minute monologue about United's chances of "stealing the title" from Arsenal. ("If we can just put a string of results together, I reckon Wenger will really eat his words.") Then a call comes through on Julian's other line and he is forced to cut the conversation short.

"Doing anything this weekend?" I ask, trying to establish Sofía's motive before he rings off.

"Nothing," he says. "Nothing. Bloody parents coming into town."

This, at least, reassures me that she was telling the truth.

"Well, maybe we can have lunch on Wednesday," I suggest. "Go through my report."

"Good idea," he says. "I'd like that." But he hangs up without saying good-bye.

To disguise any pattern, I choose a different Internet café, on Calle de Amaniel, and work until six tracing language schools in Bogotá. If Colombia is anything like Spain, companies offering language tuition will go out of business every few weeks, but most of the old stalwarts, including Berlitz, are listed on the Web. I take down a series of numbers and realize that most of next week will be taken up making phone calls to Washington and Colombia. I also find a Basque translation service on the Web that quotes me just under €800 for converting several Arenaza articles from *Gara* and *Ahotsa* into English. They promise that the results will be ready inside five working days, although it angers me that I'll have to shell out the equivalent of almost £500 just to read what, in all likelihood, will be ill-disguised nationalist propaganda.

Finally, I access a site for marriage license information at the Superior Court of the District of Columbia and call the number listed using the Amena SIM card. For at least two minutes I'm trapped in a maze of automated voices, until a spirited receptionist eventually puts me through to "Leah" in "our executive office."

"Who shall I say is calling, sir?"

"My name is Simon Eastwood."

"Just a moment, please."

At the next-door computer terminal, a thickset teenager wearing headphones is busy shooting up a gang of armed drug smugglers, pounding on his mouse to reload. His forehead sweats as blood decorates the screen. I have to sit through thirty seconds of synthesized Mozart before Leah picks up. Her voice is clipped and machine efficient.

"Mr. Eastwood. What can I do for you today?"

I move away from the banks of computers and find a quieter spot at the back of the room.

"Yes, I wonder if you would be kind enough to assist me with a small problem." Outside of New York City and Los Angeles, Americans can still be charmed by Limeys who sound like David Niven. "I'm trying to discover whether a person of my acquaintance was married in the District of Columbia at some point between 1991 and the present day."

"May I ask the nature of your inquiry, sir?"

"I'm a genealogist."

Judging by the surprised tone of her voice, Leah doesn't get too many of those phoning her up. "I see," she says. "And you just want to know if they were *married*?"

"Not exactly. I'm fairly sure about that side of things, but there's a geographical discrepancy in my records between Maryland and DC. I'm also unsure of the date. It's a question of trying to verify the location and tracking down the actual license."

"For a family tree?"

"Precisely."

A tiny pause. She sounds relaxed, so I'm not at all worried.

"What was the groom's surname, sir?"

"His name was Church. A Mr. Julian Church."

"And the bride?"

Nicole's surname was always going to be the sticking point. Before making the call I decided to make something up.

"The bride's maiden name was Harper, Nicole Harper." And there's a long silence, almost as if Leah has a note beside her telephone instructing her to contact a supervisor immediately if nosy Englishmen start asking questions about Julian Church. "Are you still there?"

"Sure, I'm still here." She laughs. "I have a Julian Church marrying a Nicole *Law* in March of 1995."

"You do?"

"Could that be the one?"

For the sake of credibility I persevere with the lie.

"No. I'm looking for a Nicole Harper. But the coincidence does seem odd. You're sure there isn't another listing?"

Leah takes her time. She really wants to help me out on this one.

"I'm sorry, sir . . ."

"Mr. Church was British. Perhaps that might help."

And at this, her voice leaps an octave. "But that's what it says *here*. Julian Anthony Charles Church, British national, married Nicole Donovan Law, US citizen, March 18th, 1995. That's *gotta* be him."

"Sadly not," I reply, stooping to write "Donovan Law 1995" on a scrap of paper. "The marriage must have taken place in Maryland. But thank you for your assistance."

"Well, you're welcome, Mr. Eastwood. I'm just sorry I couldn't be of more help."

12

Pillow Talk

Saul leaves at eleven o'clock on Sunday morning, traveling on the AVE train to Córdoba where he plans to visit the Mezquita and pick up a hire car en route for Cádiz. I suggest he spend three nights in Seville and another two in Ronda, in the hope that it might be at least a fortnight before he returns.

"You can even go to Morocco by ferry," I tell him, his cab pulling away on Princesa. "Spend a few days in Fez, man. I've heard it's really nice."

There is a lot to do. I spend the rest of Sunday and most of Monday morning writing up the Endiom report and sending it via e-mail to Julian. Work feels irrelevant in the current situation, but Julian is a perfectionist and will doubtless want several alterations before committing the document to the printers. Finally, at four in the afternoon—10 A.M. in Colombia—I call the US embassy in Bogotá. I am sitting in the kitchen of my flat, a cup of tea on the table beside a notepad and two ballpoint pens, in case one of them runs out.

"This is the American embassy of Colombia." Another automated system. *"Press one for English, dos para Español."*

I press one and connect to a sleepy-sounding receptionist with a local accent who asks how she can direct my call.

"I'm trying to track down a friend of mine from the United States. I think she works at the embassy."

"What was the name, sir?"

"Well, it used to be Nicole Law, but I'm fairly sure she got married."

There is a listless recognition. "Oh sure. I know Nicki." I feel a skip and thump of excitement. "But she no longer works here. I can connect you to somebody who might be able to assist. Would you hold the line please, sir?"

"Of course."

Obtaining confidential information by telephone is usually fairly straightforward. There is the great advantage that one cannot be seen by the person at the other end of the line; it is necessary to lie only with the voice. On Friday, speaking to Washington, I attempted to convey the sense of a slightly dotty Brit adrift in unanswered questions. It's the same on this occasion; I am easygoing and polite, and persistently grateful to the staff for taking the time to help me out.

There's a ten-second delay before a sound comes on the line, like a metal chain falling on concrete. Then a confident-sounding American male picks up the phone.

"Hi, this is Dave Creighton. I understand you're lookin' for Nicki?"

I've already worked out my plan of attack. "That's right."

"And it's a personal call?"

"Yes. We're old friends."

Dave makes a noise at the back of his throat. "Well, you're kind of in the right area."

"I am? Oh that's fantastic."

"Nicki actually hasn't worked here in a while. She's running a day-care center out at the Granahorrar for expat families. You want me to dig you out the number?"

"That would be wonderful. A day-care center?"

"Yeah. Lotta kids here. Lotta busy people."

"Well, Nicki always loved children."

Dave agrees wholeheartedly with this sentiment and taps something into a keyboard, keeping the conversation lively as he does so out of sheer American politeness.

"So you and Nicki are old college buddies?"

"Not really. I always wanted to go to university in the States, but we actually met in London a few years ago and became friends that way. Now I've got the opportunity to come to South America with my wife and son and we wanted to look Nicki up for a spot of lunch. Is she still with her husband?"

"Felipe? Sure." Dave sounds surprised. "You know him?"

"*Felipe?* I thought she married an English banker?"

"Oh no. No." Laughter now. He's buying the strategy. "You really haven't seen her in a while, huh? That was a long time ago. It's Felipe now."

"She's no longer Nicole Church?"

I want to find out if the new surname is Rodríguez, which would tally with the e-mail address on the embassy Web site.

"No. Never was. Kept her name as Law, far as I know. Now it's definitely Palacios. Señor y Señora. Let me see if I can find her. Where you calling from, sir?"

"Barcelona."

"Wow. OK. How's the weather there?"

"Really nice. Sunny."

"Great." He has found the number and I write it down, splashing black tea on the surface of the table when the mug rocks. "That about all I can do for you?"

"That's about it. Thank you, Dave, you've been very helpful." The conversation has gone so smoothly that I risk one more question. "So what happened to the English husband?"

"Well, I'd better let you ask Nicki that. Complicated situation, right? You take care now. Have a nice evening."

I hang up, trying to work out how I feel. If Nicole is just a glorified nanny, then there's nothing to worry about. Her job at the embassy can have involved only clerical or commercial work: a former colleague would never speak so candidly about someone who had been in the agency. But why was he reluctant to discuss Julian? Purely to protect a colleague's privacy, or because the relationship ended in scandal? Now my mind really starts to turn over. Who was I talking to? Did the receptionist follow protocol and connect me to a CIA officer who used the day-care center as routine cover? And why did he ask where I was calling from? They could be running checks on the SIM card right now, warning Nicole and Julian, doing anything to protect the plan. Yet he gave up the number without hesitation and never even asked my name. The conversation was surely just as it appeared. Either way, there's no sense in dialing the center. If Nicole is there, I will have to talk to her and pretend to be a parent inquiring about fees and facilities. If she isn't, the possibilities are endless: that she never works there; that she took the day off; that she has been instructed to avoid my call. I need some air.

Out on Princesa I consider throwing the Amena card in a bin but decide against it and go for a coffee in Plaza de Comendadoras. I walk up Calle del Conde Duque and turn right into Guardias de Corps, following more or less the same route that Saul and I took on the way to Café Comercial. There are young children playing on swings in the small, fenced-off area at the western end of the square, watched by listless parents and a tramp lying flat out on a bench. Beyond them, on the far side of the square, three older boys wearing torn T-shirts are kicking a burst football against the wall of the old convent. The slap of the punctured leather is oddly relaxing. I come to a decision: in order to obtain conclusive answers about Julian's true identity, it will be necessary to question Sofía. This will be a considerably more difficult task than phoning bored officials in Bogotá and Washington, but they always say that the best information is pillow talk. To that end, at around five o'clock I call her at work and encourage her to come around. Sofía sounds excited and says that she can be at my apartment by 6:30. This gives me time to sink a *café solo* in a bar at the far end of the square, to head home for a shower, and to buy her an expensive box of chocolates at VIPS. Then it's just a question of waiting.

She is three-quarters of an hour late and arrives wearing a fur-trimmed coat, high-heeled leather boots, a knee-length tweed skirt, and the white Donna Karan shirt I bought her in Marbella after my last trip in November. Adultery clothes. In the hall I slip the coat to the floor and we guide one another wordlessly into the bedroom, underwear leaving a cinematic trail all the way to the headboard. We say virtually nothing to one another for the next hour, rediscovering the passion of our very first weeks together. It is almost as if the threat of Sofía's betrayal has brought us closer together. Only toward eight o'clock, showered and padding around the flat, does she unwind and begin to talk.

"You looked exhausted when I came in," she says. "The trip north tired you?"

"A little," I reply. "But it was more having Saul to stay. We went out drinking until six on Saturday."

"Six!" There is nothing unusual about this in Madrid, but Sofía sounds surprised. "He stayed a long time, your friend."

"Too long," I reply, and now we speak in Spanish. "I don't particularly like myself when he's around. I can't explain it. And his wife has just left him, so he was tetchy. He needs a break. He went to Córdoba on Sunday, might come back next week."

I am lying wrapped in a cotton sheet in the bedroom, unable to keep an eye on Sofía as she wanders around the apartment, audibly picking up odd bits of paper and magazines, making no secret of her nosy fascination for my closed, obscure existence. In the sitting room she switches a CD from Mozart to Radiohead and then returns to give me a kiss. It surprises me that she has not picked up on what I said about Saul.

"What time do you have to go home?" I ask.

"You want me to leave?"

"Of course not. I want you to stay. I want you to stay forever."

"Ten o'clock," she says, ignoring the flattery. "Julian thinks I have yoga with María."

She has left the room again. From the kitchen she asks if I would like some water and I hear her pour two glasses from a bottle in the rack. I put on a T-shirt, pull the duvet across me for warmth, and catch Sofía's perfume on the pillow.

"Your friend said that you used to work in oil," she calls out. "How come you never told me about this?"

"Does that upset you?"

"That you didn't tell me?"

"Yes."

She comes back into the bedroom, hands me the glass of water, and appears to give the question some serious thought.

"It doesn't upset me that you didn't tell me," she says eventually. "It upsets me that you have things to hide."

"Well, that's my problem, my past," I reply, with more candor than intended. "We all have secrets, Sofía. We all have things we conceal."

"I don't."

This might be a way into the Julian situation, a chance to begin asking awkward questions. She is wearing one of my business shirts and a pair of thick winter socks, leaning up beautifully against the wall at the foot of the bed next to a Habitat Matisse.

"You don't have secrets? You don't have things you hide from me?"

"Nothing," she says with melodramatic conviction. Lifting her foot onto the bed she begins stroking my leg through the duvet. I adore the shape of her thighs. "I show everything to you, *cariño*. I trust you with my marriage. There is nothing I wouldn't tell you."

"And Julian?"

Her face falls. "What about Julian?"

She doesn't like it when we talk about him. It is a sour subject, guilt gathering. She fucks me wearing his wedding ring but flinches if I ever touch it.

"Does he keep things from me?"

"What do you mean?"

Fearing that I have been clumsy, I adjust the pronoun in Spanish to alter the meaning of the sentence.

"You misunderstood me. I said, 'Does he keep things from *you?*' "

"I don't think so." Sofía looks nonplussed.

"You don't *think* so?"

"No." She pulls away, no longer touching my leg. I have played it badly. She walks up to the window, seems to pick a piece of dust off the wall, and then flicks it out of her fingers like an insect. She turns to face me. "Why are you asking me these questions?"

"I'm just interested." I'm also beginning to wish we had had this conversation on the telephone. "Don't you like it when we talk? I don't want us just to fuck and not speak. I want us to mean more to each other than that."

This turns out to be an effective if unpremeditated tactic. Sofía returns to the bed, touches my arm, and looks at me with a mixture of surprise and delight. "Of course, of course. I don't want that either. We make love, Alec, we have some time together, I like to talk."

"I just wanted to know more about Julian."

"Of course."

She kisses my forehead.

"It's just that Mikel Arenaza told me something. In San Sebastián. Something about him."

That stops her. Dead in her tracks. She sits up. "What?"

"That he was married before you. That he had another life."

If Sofía and Arenaza are part of a conspiracy against me, they will have expected me to bring this up. Equally, if she has no inkling about Julian's past, that may help to expose his true motivation. But she begins to smile.

"You didn't know about that? Julian never told you he was married?"

"Never. And neither did you."

She begins to caress my palm with her thumb. "Well, that is *his* secret."

"Of course."

"And he is ashamed by it, I think. A part of his life that went wrong. Julian is a very proud man."

"Very."

"And Mikel told you this?"

"He was drunk."

"Mikel is a fascist."

She curls her bare legs up onto the bed so that her knees are almost tucked under my chin. This is how I wanted the conversation to progress. I would like to run my mouth along the bliss of her soft thigh, but need to stick to the task at hand.

"He told me that Julian's wife left him for another man. His best friend."

"Felipe, yes. An engineer."

"Where was he from?"

"Colombia."

"Julian's wife was *Colombian?*"

It doesn't feel good to be feigning surprise like this, but it is necessary in the circumstances.

"No. American. An East Coast family, lots of money. But they moved there because she was working for the government."

"The American government?"

"Yes. She was some kind of banking or finance specialist. So *boring.*" Sofía uses a great Spanish expression here. *Que coñazo!* What a *drag.* I feel a great sense of relief.

"And that's how she met Felipe?"

"I suppose, sweetheart, I suppose."

For the sake of seeming disinterested I break off now and spend a wordless ten minutes exploring her naked body. Eventually we make love again, have a shower, and then head back to bed.

"So what was Julian doing all day?" By now it is as if I am making light of the whole thing, a joke of it. Both of us have a glass of wine in our hands and my skin is damp from the shower. "Was he working at the American embassy as well? Was he working for Endiom?"

"Oh no." She laughs. "This is why he keeps it a secret. He was teaching English, like all good British people when they live away from home. In the old days Julian wasn't the successful private banker. He was just following Nicole around the world."

"Nicole was her name?"

"*Sí.*"

"Did you ever meet her?" This elicits a brief look of Hispanic disgust, sour as old milk, which effectively provides me with an answer. "OK, but how come Julian's best friend was Colombian?"

Sofía spins on the bed and places her head next to mine. She has finally grown tired of all the questions.

"Felipe was not his best friend. Julian does not have friends. Only silly people from his school in England." She starts to imitate them, adopting a clipped British accent, arching her neck so that she is kissing me as she speaks. "*'Sofía, darling! How charming to meet you! I don't know how you put up with old Jules.'* They are such idiots, these English. But not you, *cariño*. Not you."

I reach for her stomach and walk my fingers up to her nipples.

"*So?*" she says, sighing. "You have no more questions? The little interrogation session is over?"

"It's over," I tell her. "It's over," and I take the glass of wine out of her hand and place it on the floor.

13

Development

Late on Thursday morning the Nokia mobile shrills beside my bed.

"Alec?" It's Arenaza.

"Mikel, hi. Sorry, I was asleep. How are you?"

"You *sleep*? At eleven o'clock? Are you sick, Milius?"

"I was up late last night."

"OK. I am ringing to tell you that I'm going to the airport now. I fly into Madrid this afternoon. We still going to have dinner, right? You want to meet up on Saturday?"

"That sounds great." I twist a crick out of my neck and sit up against the headboard. "Is Julian coming?"

"No, I don't call him this time. Who knows? Maybe I'll see him for lunch on Sunday."

"What about your friend?"

"You mean Rosalía?" He must be calling from a public place because he says her name very quietly. "She meet me at Barajas this afternoon. We will be together tonight and tomorrow, but I will be free at the weekend. Let's meet for a cocktail at Museo Chicote, yes? You know it?"

"On Gran Vía? Sure."

Chicote is probably the most famous and certainly one of the most expensive bars in Madrid. A haunt of Hemingway and Buñuel. A haunt of tourists.

"Good. I will see you there at ten. Take it easy, my friend."

"You too, Mikel. You have a good flight."

Interesting that he should go cold on Julian. Is Sofía the problem? Does she refuse to have fascists in the house? I get dressed, make some coffee, and head down the road to check e-mails at the Internet café on Ventura Rodríguez. Julian has read the Endiom report and sounds happy. "Bloody good job," he writes. "Really chuffed with the magnum opus." So at least that's out of the way. The Basque translations have also come through and I print them out, asking the bearded attendant for a large plastic bag in which to carry them. While I am waiting, an e-mail comes through from Saul:

From: sricken1789@hotmail.com
To: almmlalam@aol.com

Subject: On the road

Hi mate

Thought I'd drop you a line from sunny Cadiz. Andy's had to go out of town until tomorrow but he has a nice apartment near the beach that doubled for Havana in *Die Another Day.* Have you ever been here? It's on a peninsula that sticks out into the Atlantic. This morning an aircraft carrier the size of the Empire State Building sailed across the horizon en route for Iraq. Apparently there's a US naval base five miles up the coast. Franco handed over the land in the 50s in exchange for economic aid and now there are thousands of Yank sailors in shorts eating Oreos and drinking "Bud" and really making a big effort to blend in with the local culture. These are the kind of things that a man learns on holiday.

Cordoba was great. I didn't stay long. Met a girl from Bristol in the Mezquita and impressed her with my knowledge of mihrabs and caliphs culled from your *Rough Guide to Spain* (thanks). She was a bit shocked that Charles V had built a Catholic cathedral bang in the middle of a mosque and said something about "the whole building being, like, a metaphor for what's going on right now in the Middle East" and I said: "You know what? You're right" and then lied about being late for a train.

One bit of bad news. You remember Kate's friend, Hesther? She's apparently got cancer. Had just met a really nice bloke, they were probably going to settle down and get married, and now she's got to deal with this. Anyway, she asked after you and I told her you were fine and she said to say hi.

Don't know when I'll be back. Might well take you up on the idea of going to Fez/Morocco.

Have heard nothing from Heloise.

Take it easy pal—

Saul

Hesther. Someone I haven't thought about for years. She was one of Kate's friends from acting school who used to flirt with me and fall asleep after two glasses of wine. The random strike of incurable disease. It occurs to me that statistically my own chances of avoiding cancer have probably improved as a result of her illness: if one of my peers has it, then I should be OK. Sadly it no longer appalls me that I am capable of such thoughts. I pay the attendant and leave.

There's a busy restaurant with a decent *menú del día* on Calle de Serrano Jover, just opposite the big Corte Inglés supermarket in Argüelles. I go there for an early lunch at 1:30. The articles have been badly translated into barely comprehensible Spanish and I feel like registering a complaint with the Web site. However, it's still possible to get the gist of their meaning and I quickly conclude that there is little about Arenaza that I did not already know. Mostly he is a rent-a-quote spokesman for Batasuna on any number of issues. I find the story in which he pledges to "analyze" ETA's murder of the six-year-old girl in Santa Pola, and discover that he was arrested for *un alterador del orden público*—basically a breach of the peace—during a Batasuna rally in 1998. Even the lecture at Bilbao University was on nothing more significant than voting patterns. Trying a different tack—and to give me something to talk about at Chicote—I cross the street after lunch and buy a paperback about ETA by an Irish journalist, heading home to read it on the sofa.

According to the book, Basque nationalism as a political movement stretches back more than a hundred years, to the foundation of the PNV in 1895. Its founding father, Sabino Arana, who would nowadays be called an out-and-out racist, was concerned that Basque ethnicity was being diluted by peasant laborers flooding into the northeast from impoverished Andalucía and Extremadura. Arana, who is still regarded with almost saintly reverence in the region, essentially made eugenics a cornerstone of the party's manifesto. Hardline nationalists to this day will tell you that the blood types of "pure" Basques are different from those of Europeans from other regions; indeed, in its early years, the PNV would accept only those members who could prove that they had four ethnically Basque grandparents.

Until the Civil War, the PNV was the dominant party of nationalism across the region, convinced that Euskal Herria was a country under occupation by Spain. That occupation became a reality in the Civil War when Bilbao fell to fascist troops in 1937. In the ensuing years the PNV banked everything on the fall of Hitler and was dangerously isolated when the Allies failed to kick Franco out in the aftermath of World War II. Instead, as the Cold War took hold, the West lifted a series of economic and diplomatic sanctions against Franco, forgave him his dalliance with Nazism, and embraced him as a loyal anticommunist. It comes as no surprise to learn that the CIA worked briefly alongside members of the PNV with the idea of toppling Franco. For a while, the nationalists believed they might be part of a US-backed coup d'état, until Eisenhower cut the rope and swung behind the general.

The roots of the armed struggle can be traced back to Franco's brutal thirty-year suppression of Basque culture and identity. The general, motivated by a profound political and ideological contempt for Euskal Herria, and keen to punish the region for supporting the Republicans during the Civil War, banned all nationalist movements, forbade parents from giving their children Basque names, and made it illegal to speak Euskera in the streets. ETA was forged in this atmosphere—a country of checkpoints and police brutality, of torture and abuse—though at first the organization was little more than a small group of nonviolent Catholic students who met in conditions of almost total secrecy in the 1950s. Dedicated to outright independence for all seven provinces in the region, ETA drew inspiration from anticolonial struggles all over the world and had developed a military wing, inspired by the examples of Mao and Che Guevara, by the early 1960s. The organization claimed its first victim by accident, in the summer of 1968, but thereafter the killings became more discriminate. When they blew up Franco's right-hand man and heir apparent, the deeply unpopular Admiral Luis Carrero Blanco, ETA suddenly found itself on the world stage.

The plan was stunning. In 1973, a *comando* unit led by José Miguel Beñarán Ordeñana dug a tunnel under a street in central Madrid along the route that Blanco passed every morning on his way to celebrate Mass. On December 20, in an operation code-named "Ogre," the *comando* detonated three dynamite charges, killing Blanco and two of his bodyguards instantly, and blowing their car over an entire city apartment block into a neighboring street. Committed today, such an act would be considered an outrage; thirty years ago, sympathy for ETA was running high, and Blanco's murder was welcomed, even in international circles. Until recently you could still see the remains of the vehicle in the Museo del Ejército on Calle de Méndez Núñez. It was just a short walk from the Prado.

14

Chicote

When it rains in Madrid, it rains for days on end, driving people from the streets and changing the character of the city. These aren't the thin, bloodless showers of England; these are subtropical storms accompanied by punchy, umbrella-inverting winds. When I step outside the flat at half past nine on Saturday night, en route to meet Arenaza at Chicote, gusts of rain are sweeping down Princesa so hard that it is an effort to cross the street in search of a cab. I wait in vain under the ineffective shelter of the bus stop and then make a run uphill to the metro at Ventura Rodríguez, shoes and trousers already soaked by the time I make it to the station.

Seven high-school students—two girls and five boys—are smoking cigarettes and listening to music on a concrete bench beside the Legazpi platform, cartons of cheap red wine and liter bottles of Coke littering the ground around them. There is nothing unusual about this: smoking on the metro in Madrid takes place right up to the point at which passengers step onto the trains, and underage weekend drinking—known as the *botellón*—is a norm. Until they reach an age when they can afford to drink in bars, Spaniards will inebriate themselves on cheap alcohol and then pool their money for entry into a late-night *discoteca*. On a (dry) Friday or Saturday night, particularly in summer, Plaza de España comes to resemble the location for a small, informal music festival, as vast numbers of students armed with stereos and bottles of J&B converge around the statue of Cervantes, drinking and snogging themselves into oblivion. Tonight they have been driven underground, and it will be only a matter of time before some jumped-up station attendant barrels along the platform and orders them to move on.

It's a short walk from Gran Vía metro to the entrance of Museo Chicote. The bar is relatively quiet—it's dinnertime—and there's no sign of Mikel. I take a small leather-lined booth at the back and order a Rob Roy from a pretty waitress who hangs around for a chat after she has brought my drink. Her name is Marta. She has bobbed black hair and a gentle, possibly mischievous nature.

"What are you reading?" she asks.

I brought the ETA book in case Mikel was late and feel awkward showing her the cover. You never know how Spaniards are going to react to the Basque issue.

"It's a book about ETA," I tell her. "A book about terrorism."

She nods, giving nothing away. "You're a journalist?"

"No, I'm just interested in Spain."

"Vale."

To change the subject, Marta asks if I live in Madrid and I lie, for no good reason, telling her that I'm just visiting for a few days. The deceit, as always, is instinctive, although it encourages her to start recommending bars and clubs in the area that she thinks I might enjoy. We are flirting by now—she keeps flattering me with fixed, tickled stares—but in due course her boss gets itchy and calls her back to the bar.

"See you later," she says, and her waist is so supple and lithe as she sways away that I consider cheating on Sofía for only the second time. I had the definite sense that she wanted me to invite her out for a drink after work. Maybe I deserve a steady girlfriend. Maybe it's time to cast adultery aside and think about having a normal relationship.

Fifteen minutes go by. Gradually the place fills up and a group of German weekenders settle into the booth next to mine, ordering *jar-*

ras of lager for the boys and margaritas for the girls. Marta makes occasional eye contact from the bar, but it's increasingly difficult to see her as the crowd swells. By 10:45 Mikel has still not shown and I walk briefly back to the entrance, checking the tables that look out on Gran Vía in case he has sat down in a less discreet section of the bar. I try his mobile phone, but it has been switched off. Perhaps he is ignoring my calls. Either way, it seems unlikely that Arenaza is ever going to come. Toward eleven I have another brief conversation with Marta and order a third and final Rob Roy, at last beginning to feel the effects of the alcohol. Chicote is now crammed and jazz has given way to the tedious electric thump of house music. Twenty minutes later, without saying good-bye to her, I take my coat down from the chrome rack above the table and head out onto the street. The rain, at least, has stopped, and I walk north into Chueca to find something to eat.

Right up to two o'clock in the morning I keep trying Arenaza's phone. It's strange, but I develop a growing sense that something has happened to him, an accident or crisis. He did not strike me as the sort of person who would stand up an appointment, particularly one that he himself had been keen to organize; at the very least he would have exercised some charm and gone to the trouble of inventing an excuse. Late on Sunday, Julian happens to ring and in the course of an otherwise mundane conversation about Endiom, I manage to ask him if he has heard from Arenaza. It's clear that he had no idea he was even coming to town and we hang up shortly afterward. Eventually I go to bed, convinced that he will either call first thing in the morning, or that I'll never hear from him again.

15

The Disappeared

The police call late on Tuesday afternoon.

"*Buenos días. Podría hablar con Alec Milius, por favor?*"

I immediately know that it's a cop and feel an instantaneous dread of the law. The voice is nicotine rich and official, speaking from an office where telephones ring incessantly in the background.

"*Soy yo.* This is Alec Milius."

I am sitting alone in a tapas bar just south of the Bernabéu. To order a cup of coffee I spoke Spanish to the waiter but make a decision now to stall the policeman by feigning an inability to communicate in any language but English.

"*Soy el Inspector Baltasar Goena. Llamo de la comandancia de la Guardia Civil en San Sebastián.*"

"I'm sorry?"

"*Quisiera hacerle unas preguntas sobre la desaparición de Mikel Arenaza.*"

The revelation does not surprise me as much as it might. Arenaza has disappeared. Nevertheless, I pretend not to have understood.

"You'll have to excuse me, sir. I don't speak very good Spanish."

There is an annoyed pause. I'm hoping that Goena will simply lose patience and pursue another line of inquiry. That would be ideal. The last thing I need is a member of the Guardia Civil coming around to my apartment asking awkward questions.

"I speak English a little," he replies. "I am a police. My name is Baltasar Goena. I ring you with the concern of the disappearing of Mikel Arenaza."

"Mikel *who*?"

"Arenaza. You are knowing him?"

I take an appropriate beat, always trying to stay one step ahead of the conversation, and say, "Yes, yes." There's no point in denying my association with Mikel at this stage, not at least until I know exactly what's going on. Goena has tracked down my number, so it's a decent assumption that he has conclusive proof of our meeting. "I met Mr. Arenaza for the first time two weeks ago. You said he has *disappeared*? Is everything all right?"

Goena clears his throat. "I have questions."

"Of course. Of course." The waiter comes over with my coffee. "What can I do for you?"

"I explain this. I am explaining." Goena says something in Basque to a colleague. "You meet with Señor Arenaza for a meeting ten days before I am calling you. *Febrero día vientesiete.* A Thursday. Can you tell me about this please, Mr. Milius?"

"Señor Goena, it's terribly difficult for me to understand what you're saying. Is there somebody in your office who speaks English?"

The waiter looks down at my table, registering with a flick of his eyes that he has caught the lie. Goena coughs like a cat with something stuck in its throat.

"No, no, there is not that here. Only I can speak English. I have just these questions, very quick now on your time. Your meeting with Señor Arenaza . . ."

". . . Señor Arenaza, yes . . ."

"Can you be giving me details please?" I pour two packs of sugar into the coffee. "Does he speak to you that he is going away?"

"Oh no, not at all." I wonder if the police know about Rosalía.

"We had dinner in San Sebastián, we discussed some business. I haven't seen him since." Goena may have a record of the phone call Arenaza made to me from the airport, so I add, "We did speak briefly on the telephone a few days later, but he was only calling to verify some details."

"I am sorry. You speak to him?"

Damn.

"Yes. Last Thursday. At least I think it was. I'd have to check my diary. Why? What has happened exactly?"

Goena ignores my question. "And what time was this?"

"To be honest, I can't remember. In the morning, I think."

"And did he say that he is to go to someplace when you speak to him?"

"I'm sorry. Could you repeat the question?"

"Qué?"

"I said, 'Could you repeat the question?'"

"Sí, sí. I repeat. Does Señor Arenaza say that he is doing a travel to another city?"

If Mikel was booked onto a Madrid flight, the San Sebastián police will have that information as a first line of inquiry, but there is no reason why I should have known about it. "No," I reply, "he said nothing to me about going away. Why? Where did he go?"

Goena is writing things down. There's a long pause before his next question and I can't tell whether I am aiding or obstructing the investigation.

"We believe he fly in an airplane to Madrid. He arrive and disappear. So you did not intend to meet Señor Arenaza when he was coming to your city?"

"No. No. What do you mean, he arrived and disappeared?" It's easy to sound worried; I just put my voice at a slightly tighter pitch. "Like I said, we didn't know each other. We had a meeting in San Sebastián. Otherwise nothing. I'm sorry I can't be more helpful."

This final remark does the trick. Goena asks a couple of supplementary questions but seems to believe in my innocence. I drain the coffee in two mouthfuls, praying that the conversation will now end.

Purely for reasons of bureaucracy Goena asks for my home address and passport number, but the interrogation goes no farther. As soon as we have hung up I leave two euros on the table and run outside to the nearest newsstand, buying a copy of *El País*. Sure enough, prominently set out on page five, is the following story:

LEADING BATASUNA POLITICIAN VANISHES

One of the key figures in Herri Batasuna, the banned political wing of the terrorist organization ETA, has disappeared.

Mikel Arenaza, a councilor based in San Sebastián, boarded an Iberia flight bound for Madrid on Thursday. He later checked into the Hotel Casón del Tormes, but staff became suspicious when he did not return to his room for 48 hours.

Señor Arenaza's wife filed a missing person report with Guipúzcoa police at the weekend. Señora Izaskun Arenaza told police that her husband, 43, left home at around 9:20 A.M. on March 6 and was planning to be away on business for several days.

The article goes on to describe Mikel's career with Batasuna but says very little about the details surrounding the case. With the exception of his luggage at the Hotel Casón del Tormes, no personal belongings have yet been found. I call Julian from the Endiom mobile and discover that he too has spoken to Goena and was able to offer little in the way of helpful information. He did not know, for example, that Arenaza was planning to come to Madrid, nor had he seen the article in *El País*. Indeed, he sounds curiously uninterested in the whole episode and even makes a joke to lighten the mood of our conversation.

"What did you do, Alec? Pack him in cement boots and drop him in the Atlantic? You got him hiding in your cellar, boot-of-the-car job, drowned in the attic water tank?"

In the circumstances I don't find this funny but summon a boss-flattering laugh. "Actually I never saw him after San Sebastián." Then Julian asserts, with baseless confidence, that "old Mikel will surface in a day or two" and we bid each other farewell.

But things go from bad to worse.

The following morning, the Nokia rings at 8:05, shaking me from a deep sleep. An assertive-sounding Spaniard, this time with impeccable English, asks to speak—"immediately please"—to "Mr. Alexander Milius."

"I'm Alec Milius. What time is it?"

"It is eight o'clock." The voice is young and humorless and offers only a scant apology for calling so early. "My name is Patxo Zulaika. I am a reporter with the *Ahotsa* newspaper in Euskal Herria. I need to ask you some questions concerning the disappearance of Mikel Arenaza."

I look at the clock again. It's going to be harder to think my way around any questions before at least having a shower and a cup of coffee.

"Couldn't we do this later?"

"We could, yes, we could, but a man's life is at stake." This baffling overstatement is delivered without a hint of irony. "It is my understanding that you have already spoken to the police. I am currently in Madrid and would like to arrange to meet you this morning."

Zulaika must have gotten my number from Goena. I sit up out of bed, clear my throat, and try to stall him.

"Look, could you call back? I have company."

"Company?"

"Somebody here."

He sounds suspicious. "Fine."

"Thank you. Maybe in an hour or two? I'll be at my desk."

But there's scarcely enough time in which to think clearly. On the stroke of nine o'clock, Zulaika rings back, tenacious as a dog with a bone. I've had a quick shower, answering the phone in my dressing gown.

"Mr. Milius?" Still pushy, still overfamiliar. "As I explained earlier, I would like to meet you to discuss the disappearance of the Batasuna councilor Mikel Arenaza. It is a matter of great importance to the Basque region. What time would you be free today?"

There's no point in stalling him. His sort never give up. "What about later this morning?"

"Perfect. I understand that you work for Endiom."

"That's right." Perhaps he has already spoken to Julian.

"Would their offices be suitable, or do you have a different location that you prefer?"

I tell him it would be better to meet nearer my house and set a time at Cáscaras, the *tortilleria* where I eat breakfast on Ventura Rodríguez. He takes down the address and we arrange to meet at eleven.

In the intervening period I buy most of the Spanish dailies. No new information has emerged about Arenaza. The story continues to feature prominently in the news pages and I find Zulaika's byline in *Ahotsa*. A Basque waiter I know in the *barrio* is able to translate the main points of his story, but it would still appear that the police have very few leads. At no point do any of the journalists reporting the disappearance mention Rosalía Dieste. I make a decision not to mention her name to Zulaika. However, our initial telephone conversations may have been interpreted as evasive, so it will be important to seem cooperative. To that end I get to Cáscaras fifteen minutes early, find a quiet table near the back, and offer him a wide, diplomatic smile when he walks in.

"You must be Patxo."

"You must be Alec."

I have stood up, coming out from behind the table to shake his hand. Zulaika is wearing ironed jeans, cheap shoes, and a scruffy tweed jacket, the clothes of a boy at boarding school on weekend leave.

"How did you recognize me?" he asks.

"I didn't. It just seemed likely that it was you. Your face fits your voice."

In truth, Zulaika is even younger than he sounded on the phone. I would put his age at no more than twenty-five, although he is wearing a wedding ring and going bald around the widow's peak. He has the still, humorless face of a zealot and makes a point of continually meeting my eye. Something close to a deranged sense of entitlement is apparent in these initial moments. He tries to take control of the meeting by asserting a need to sit nearer the window, questioning the bright yellow decor with his eyes and squinting at the reproduction Mirós and Kandinskys. Now that he's got me where he wants me, he's not even going to bother thanking me for giving up my time.

"So, you're in town investigating the disappearance?"

"I am *Ahotsa*'s senior correspondent in Madrid," he replies, as if I should have known this already. "This is the story that I'm working on at present. How did you meet Mr. Arenaza?"

No preliminaries, no pause before what will almost certainly be a long and detailed interview. Zulaika has a spiral-bound notebook in front of him, two ballpoint pens, and a shopping list of questions, in Basque, written in a neat hand on three pieces of lined paper. He also came in carrying a battered laptop briefcase, which is currently leaning against my leg beneath the table. At some point I might move my foot, just so that it falls to the floor.

"Well, I was introduced to him by my manager, Julian Church, at Endiom. They're old friends. I was up in San Sebastián on business a couple of weeks ago and he put me in touch."

Zulaika doesn't write down Julian's name, which would suggest that he has already heard about him from Goena, or perhaps even conducted an interview. Diego, one of the waiters whom I see most days, approaches our table, greets me with a warm *"Hola,* Alec," and asks what we'd like to order. Zulaika doesn't look up. Sullenly he says, *"Café con leche y un vaso de agua,"* and then scratches his ear. You can tell a lot about people by the way they treat waiters.

"Dos cafés con leche," I add, putting an emphasis on the *"dos."* Diego asks me how things are and, to create a good impression, I tell him that they've rarely been better.

"And how many times did you speak to Arenaza before your meeting?" Zulaika talks right over us. "Once? Twice?"

"Just the once. I got his number from Julian's secretary and called him from my hotel."

"And where were you staying?"

"The Londres y de Inglaterra."

A pulse of contempt. "The big hotel on the Concha?"

"That's correct."

Any number of miserable prejudices flicker behind Zulaika's eyes. The Londres y de Inglaterra is a bourgeois indulgence, a place of Castilian excess. Only a rich foreigner would stay there, a *pijo*, a *guiri*.

"And did you communicate with him using e-mail at any time?"

Why ask that?

"No. Just on the phone."

He writes this down and lights up a cigarette, blowing smoke across the table.

"Tell me, Alec, how much did you know about Herri Batasuna before you met Mr. Arenaza?"

"Very little. We spoke of the ban on the party and the prospects of a cease-fire in the future. That was the purpose of my visit—to assess the viability of the Basque region for investment."

"Why would a person not want to invest in Euskal Herria?"

I had forgotten, of course, that Zulaika writes for a left-wing nationalist newspaper that often carries ETA declarations. To imply any criticism of the Basque region to such a person is tantamount to insult.

"We actually concluded that people should invest there."

That shuts him up. Diego comes back and places two coffees and a glass of water on the table. Zulaika nods at him this time but returns immediately to the list of questions.

"Could you describe what happened during your meeting?"

His cigarette has been resting in the ashtray, untouched, for about a minute, and is now blowing a curl of smoke into my eyes. Against my better judgment, I say, "Do you mind if we move that?"

"What?"

"It's just that I don't particularly like cigarettes, especially this early in the morning."

"I don't understand."

"I said, would you mind moving your cigarette? It's blowing smoke in my face."

I might as well have asked Zulaika to spit-shine my shoes. He looks at the cigarette, back at me, and slowly grinds it out in the ashtray. The transformation from his earlier civility on the telephone is now complete.

"Is that all right?"

"There was no need to put it out."

He sniffs and goes back to his notes. "Well?"

"Well what?"

"The meeting. Could you describe the meeting?"

"Sure." I would love just to stand up and walk out on this jumped-up little shit. If there's one thing I can't stand, it's being pushed around or patronized by people younger than I am. Bland as possible, I reconstruct a half-baked account of the evening with Arenaza, deliberately avoiding any mention of the fact that he had seemingly lost faith with the armed struggle and was clearly at a juncture in his life. Zulaika can find that out for himself. As it is, he takes very few notes and perks up only when I mention the car park.

"Why did you go with him?"

"I had nothing better to do. He wanted to take me to a different bar."

"So you would say that by this stage in the evening you were getting on well?"

"Not particularly. I think Mr. Arenaza was just being a typically generous Basque host."

"But why the car park?"

"He wanted to change out of his suit."

"He was wearing a suit?"

As I had thought at the time, it was strange for a councilor from Batasuna to be dressed so smartly. "We were going to an *herriko taberna*," I explain. "I think Mikel had been in meetings all day and wanted to feel more comfortable."

Zulaika stares directly into my eyes, as if by referring to Arenaza as "Mikel" I have implied a closer relationship.

"You seem troubled by something."

"What?" he says.

"You're looking at me as if there's some sort of problem."

"I am?"

"You are. Perhaps it's just your manner."

It is now requiring a great effort of will on my behalf not to snap and react, not to let the interview escalate into a full-scale row.

"My manner?" he says. "I don't understand this word."

"Forget it. What was your next question?"

Zulaika takes his time, holding off the confrontation, shifting backward in his seat and glancing briefly around the room. If anything, he looks pleased. I move my foot now and let the computer drop to the ground. Don't be childish, Alec, don't be dumb. Zulaika leans over, makes a noise through his teeth, and places the briefcase on the seat beside him.

"I want to know about the *herriko taberna*," he says. You can hear the lilt of Basque in the term's correct pronunciation. "How long did you stay there?"

"About three-quarters of an hour."

"And after that?" He lifts his *café con leche* and finishes it in a single gulp.

"After that I went home."

"Back to your hotel?"

"Back to my hotel."

"And what did you talk about during this time?"

"The same things as before. Politics. Investments."

"And he said nothing about coming to Madrid, nothing about going away?"

"Nothing at all."

Outside on the street, a driver trapped by a double-parked car sounds his horn and then leans on it incessantly, a noise that fills Cáscaras through the open door. The office workers gathered in clutches around the bar seem oblivious to this, continuing with their conversations and snacking on *churros*. An elderly woman perched on a stool makes a show of blocking her ears, attracting a shrug from Diego.

"And you didn't speak to him the next day?" It is difficult to hear Zulaika's question above the noise of the horn.

"I'm sorry?"

He speaks slightly louder. "I said, you didn't speak to him again after your meeting?"

"No. But we spoke on the day he disappeared. He called to confirm a fact for my report."

"What fact?"

That was careless of me. Never volunteer information unless it has been specifically requested. I may have told Goena about the call on Thursday, but there was no need to enlighten Zulaika.

"I just wanted to know the likely result of a referendum on Basque independence. If it went to a vote immediately, Arenaza said that Madrid would probably win."

"He did?" Zulaika looks doubtful. "I disagree. It is *Ahotsa*'s view that this would not happen. We have conducted our own independent research and, if trends continue, the likelihood of both Basque and Catalan independence within the next five years is considerable."

"Well, I'll be sure to put that in my report," I reply, grateful for the diversion. The horn finally stops and, by twisting around in my seat, I can see a white van out of the window pulling into the street, freeing the trapped car. Zulaika appears to have run out of questions, because he flips over two sheets of paper, revealing nothing but blank pages underneath. When he closes the notebook, he takes a sip of water and finds a new line of inquiry.

"How would you have characterized Mr. Arenaza's mood on the night of your meeting?"

"Friendly. Affable. Helpful. I liked him. I would have liked to meet him again. What do the police think has happened?"

The question is ignored.

"Helpful in what way?"

"In the sense that he wanted me to enjoy his city. Helpful in the sense that he answered my questions. He was charismatic. He was sociable. I was expecting somebody more . . . aggressive."

"Why?"

"Well, let's just leave that in the realm of speculation."

Zulaika doesn't like the inference here, the terrorist prejudice. He lights another cigarette, probably to annoy me. "Don't worry, I'll blow it away from your face," he says, and makes a point of moving the ashtray onto the laptop briefcase. "Why are you here in Madrid, Alec?"

"Is that relevant?"

"It's just background."

"I've been living here for about five years."

"And all that time working for Endiom?"

"No. About half."

"What is the company's link to Mikel Arenaza?"

"There isn't one, as far as I'm aware. Julian Church is a personal friend, that's it. You'd have to ask him that."

"And you don't know why Mr. Arenaza was coming to Madrid?"

"Like I said, I really don't know."

"He calls you two hours before he's due to get on a plane and doesn't mention that he's on his way here?"

"It would seem so."

Where is Zulaika getting such precise information? From Goena? Does he have a contact at the phone company? I need to find a way of deflecting his questions.

"And you didn't know where he was planning to stay?"

"Look. You must understand that by asking me these questions again and again, you're essentially accusing me of lying. And I don't like being accused of lying, Mr. Zulaika. I've told you that I met the guy for tapas two weeks ago. It's just a grim coincidence that he should have telephoned me on the day he disappeared. I didn't know he was coming to Madrid, so I didn't know what hotel he was booked into. And I have absolutely no idea where the fuck he is."

"Of course."

"Fine."

Was that an apology?

"So I have no more questions."

"Good. Because I have to get back to work."

16

Peñagrande

Over the next few days I experience an odd transformation in temperament, as if—like Zulaika, like the police—I cannot rest until I find out what happened to Mikel. Call it boredom, call it the smell of a conspiracy, but I can't just sit at home, forever guarding my privacy, while his family and friends go nuts over the disappearance. If Mikel is shacked up with Rosalía, so be it. But something tells me that that is not the case. Something tells me that Arenaza is in deep, possibly unrecoverable, trouble. And I am in a unique position to be able to help him.

Tracing Rosalía proves surprisingly easy. Mikel said that she was attending a conference on renewable energies at the Hotel Amara Plaza in San Sebastián when they met, so I simply call the hotel reception desk, pretend to be an employee of the Institute of Industrial Engineers putting together a newsletter for a Web site, and ask for a list of all the delegates who attended the conference to be faxed to me in Madrid. I give the number of a Mail Boxes Etc. outlet on Calle de Juan Alvarez Mendizábal, and within forty-five minutes a six-page document has been spooled through to the shop. I didn't even need to speak to the hotel's PR department; the concierge did the whole thing for me without the slightest hesitation. On the third page of the fax, the name "Dieste, Rosalía Cristina" appears next to her job description (research scientist), a list of qualifications (including a five-year *licenciatura* from the Universidad Politécnica de Madrid) and the name of the company that employs her: Plettix S.L. A quick flick through the telephone directory locates their offices in Peña-grande, a godforsaken suburb in northwest Madrid. I call to arrange an appointment just after five o'clock on Thursday.

"Good afternoon, could I speak to Rosalía Dieste, please?"

"I'm afraid she's left for the afternoon." The receptionist sounds chirpy and speaks with a heavy Extremaduran accent. "It was actually her last day here. Is there somebody else who might be able to help?"

I was going to pretend to be the science correspondent from an obscure British quarterly seeking an interview, but this changes the strategy considerably.

"I'm not sure." Somehow I have to find a way of getting to Rosalía before she leaves the company for good. Thankfully the girl produces a little laugh, acknowledging that I have stumbled on a coincidence, and offers up a possible solution.

"She had to go home early because we're all meeting for a drink," she says. "Rosalía wanted to get ready."

And I think quickly now.

"Well, that's actually why I was calling. I'm an old colleague of Rosalía's from the Universidad Politécnica. I was supposed to be coming to the party but I wasn't sure if it was today or tomorrow. She's not answering her mobile. Do you happen to know where the bar is?"

And the receptionist, thank God, is the gullible, uninquisitive sort. "Sure. It's just across the street. The Sierra y Mar, in the basement of the Edificio Santiago de Compostela. Do you know our offices?"

"Of course. Of course." The thrill of the lie is like an old friend. "I can find it no problem."

But there's not much time. As soon as I have hung up, I grab a book, my coat, and keys and head straight to the garage under Plaza de España. The Audi is low on petrol, but there's enough fuel to get me twenty minutes north to Peñagrande, where I park beside the entrance to the metro station on a street devoid of people. The *barrio* is just like any other postnuclear suburb in twenty-first-century Spain: a dusty wasteland of towering concrete apartment blocks, down-at-heel corner shops, and tatty bars. Roads come at you from all directions. Across an abandoned lot strewn with litter and dead plants, the incongruously smart offices of Plettix S.L. rise up in a gleam of steel and glass. I walk down a wide, featureless avenue and cross a bridge spanning the M30 motorway. The Edificio Santiago de Compostela is one hundred meters downhill to the left, situated immediately alongside the Plettix headquarters and set back from the road by about thirty feet. The Sierra y Mar looks smart and clean and obviously serves as a meeting point for employees working in both buildings: a place to eat lunch, a place to drink coffee. I walk in and settle at the bar, just a few paces from the door, ordering a *caña,* which comes with two gherkins and a pickled onion skewered onto a cocktail stick. There are four other customers on the premises: a construction worker sitting on a tall stool beside me; a courting couple unabashedly kissing at a table near the door; and an old man drinking coffee on the other side of the bar, which breaks at a 90-degree angle to my right. This is where the book comes in handy; with any luck, Rosalía's colleagues will start pitching up for the party within about half an hour, and I will need something to occupy myself in the intervening period.

At a quarter to seven, two men wearing suits and chunky watches walk in and it's obvious they're the first guests to arrive. The owner has sectioned off about eight tables in the corner of the restaurant, decking them out with bowls of olives and crisps and several bottles of *cava.* This is my first problem: the tables are behind me and it will therefore be difficult to keep an eye on Rosalía from my position at the bar. The men shake the owner's hand, order two beers, and carry them over to the nearest of the tables. It's possible to watch them in the reflection provided by a mirror hanging above the coffee machine, although the field of vision is small. Three minutes later, a half dozen pack of Plettix employees comes surging through the door, laughter encircling them like smoke. Two of them are women, though neither strikes me as Arenaza's type: he described Rosalía as "young" and "very beautiful," but the two giggling *mujeres* bringing up the rear are puffy and premenopausal. She'll doubtless be along in a minute.

Sure enough, at five past seven Rosalía Dieste walks in with a group of five colleagues. A small roar goes up, followed by clapping and even a whoop. The two men who had settled in the corner stand up and walk back toward the bar, and both of them kiss Rosalía on the cheek. She is standing right beside me now, about five feet five, about 110 pounds, a light tan, and blond hair—both out of a bottle—with clear skin, large breasts, and wide, tired eyes. I was half expecting Arenaza to walk in with her, but one of the women says, "Where's Gael?" and I assume that's the name of her regular boyfriend. Her voice is quiet and intelligent and she seems genuinely affectionate toward colleagues who have clearly grown fond of her. Is she leaving to start a new life with Mikel? Has she any idea what mysteries she has left in her wake? On instinct, I would say that she looks troubled, but it is always best—particularly where attractive women are concerned—to take nothing on gut reaction. Glass in hand, she accompanies the group to the back of the room and calls out *"Joder!"* when she sees the bottles of *cava* on the table. After that, it's hard to hear what anybody is saying. The tables are at least fifteen feet away and obscured by a large pillar with a fire extinguisher bolted to it. Rosalía is rarely visible in the mirror and all conversation is lost in the general din of the party. To make matters worse, a diarrhea of Spanish pop music is continually pouring out of the speakers, song after song about *"amor"* and *"mi corazón,"* the sound track of Benidorm and Marbella. Now and again I will turn round and check my watch, as if frustrated and waiting to meet someone, but my surveillance becomes increasingly pointless. If I am going to follow Rosalía this weekend, she cannot become aware of me, nor suspicious of the fact that I am sitting alone at the bar. So, having settled the bill, I walk back to the Audi and drive it to a parking space immediately in front of the building. Through the rearview mirror I have clear sight of the entrance to the restaurant and, with any luck, will be able to follow Rosalía as soon as she leaves to go home.

It's a long wait. Toward nine o'clock the first of the guests begin to leave, but they're mostly senior management, gray-haired men with mink-comforted wives not young enough to stay on and party. Sitting becomes increasingly uncomfortable and my back starts to ache in the lower part of the spine. It's another hour and a half before people begin to come out in droves, and I have to concentrate hard on the entrance to make sure that Rosalía, who is comparatively small, doesn't slip away in the crowd. Then a car pulls up behind the Audi and the driver makes a phone call. Hazard lights come on, and it's clear that he will block me if Rosalía leaves. I am on the point of opening the door and asking him to move when she comes out of the restaurant and walks directly toward him. This must be Gael, come to pick her up. Sure enough he leans across, unlocks the passenger door, and she slides in beside him. They kiss briefly on the lips, but she is too busy waving good-bye to a weeping colleague to engage him properly in conversation. Nevertheless, on instinct I would say that the two of them look comfortable together and I feel a lurch of dread for Mikel; Rosalía seems *unaffected* by his disappearance. I start the engine, reverse out behind them, and follow the car down the hill. Gael is driving a dark blue Citroën Xsara, license plate M 6002 GK, and I scribble this down on the inside back page of the book as soon as we reach the first set of traffic lights. He heads directly for the M30 orbital, looping northeast onto the Autovía de Colmenar Viejo and from there directly onto the Castellana, the eight-lane spine of Madrid that runs as far south as Gran Vía. We pass beneath the leaning Kia towers at Plaza de Castilla, sticking to the Castellana until the roundabout at Santiago Bernabéu. The great stadium looms like an ark in the darkness as Gael makes a left along its southern face, accelerating up the hill toward the Hospital de San Rafael. Just beyond the summit of Concha Espina he turns left into a quiet residential road and I slow down in order to make the pursuit less obvious.

I have only just made the turn myself when I see them ahead making a second left into a narrow, car-crowded street. Without knowing the neighborhood, I would guess that this is where they live. If Gael is taking a shortcut, the chances are that I will lose them. Pausing a car's length from the turn, I switch off both engine and headlights and try to spot where they have gone. About fifty meters on the right, a car is reversing into a space beside a line of silver birches. Another tree is partially blocking my view, but it has been recently pruned and I can clearly see Rosalía's head as she steps out of the car. Gael appears now—dark hair, around five feet ten, a good-looking man of about thirty-five—and bends to lock the door. Then he follows her across the street. They are going into the first building on the corner, the one immediately to my left.

Now I move quickly. Leaving the Audi double-parked, I walk to a point where I have an unobstructed view of the front of their building, which is a comparatively small apartment block covered in creeping ivy, with six floors of flats on either side of a central staircase. There are lights on in seven of the two dozen visible windows and, with any luck, I should be able to tell where Rosalía lives once they get inside. I pull out a mobile phone and press it to my ear, pretending to hold a conversation while staring at the building ahead.

Bingo. Sixth-floor window, right-hand side. A light has been switched on. Gael appears briefly, tugs at the curtains, and then draws them shut.

So now I have her address. Calle de Jiloca 16/6 Izq.

17

The Lost Weekend

The next morning at five I pick up the car from the garage and drive back to Jiloca to be certain of following Rosalía if she leaves before dawn. Like some washed-up private eye in Hammett or Chandler, I buy a cup of polystyrene garage coffee and drink it in a freezing front seat, cursing the pain in my back. That's why all the experts recommend surveillance from a van: you can walk around, you can stretch your legs, you can piss without having to do it in a bottle.

Gael finally comes out at 7:25, wearing a badly cut suit and shouldering a small red backpack. He is only the second person to have left the building all morning. He walks directly across the street, opens up the Xsara, throws his jacket on the backseat, and drives off to work. This is now the crucial time. If Arenaza is still in Madrid, the chances are that Rosalía will leave to meet him within the next thirty minutes. He may even show up at the apartment. That's what I have to hope for. Otherwise this is going to be a very long day.

In the end, it's three hours before she shows. Three hours of hunger, three hours of back pain, three hours of inconsolable boredom. What the hell am I doing? Why not just go straight to the police, tell them what I know about Mikel and Rosalía, and let the cops sort everything out? Yet there is something thrilling about being privy to Arenaza's dark secret, and if there is more to his disappearance than a mere adultery, perhaps that will lead me back into some of the excitement of '96 and '97. I am still buoyant from the initial lie to Plettix, from the stakeout at Sierra y Mar and the interview with Zulaika. Somehow all the kick and buzz of the old days has come flooding back; it's a relief to have something with which to lift the everyday tedium of exile.

Rosalía is wearing a denim jacket over a thick woolen turtleneck and carrying a handbag about the size of a large hardback book. She has makeup on, although not as much as last night, and still looks somewhat withdrawn and tired. She may be on her way to meet Arenaza, although her appearance would suggest otherwise. It strikes me that this does not look like the mistress of a married man who has dolled herself up for a day of romance and passion; on the contrary, this looks like an ordinary woman with the day off work, on her way to go shopping or to meet a friend for coffee.

I looked at a map of the area last night and memorized every street within a three-block radius, and it's immediately clear that she isn't going to hail a taxi. Instead, she turns away from Concha Espina—where they drive past all the time—and walks north along Calle de Rodríguez Marín toward the metro station on Príncipe de Vergara. Risking a ticket on the Audi, I decide to follow her on foot, and it's bliss to be moving again, my spine stretching out, pursuing at a distance of between thirty and forty meters, sometimes walking along the opposite side of the street, sometimes not. In the cluster of shops at the north end of Marín she buys a copy of *El Mundo* and then heads into a café for breakfast. I have a clear view of her table from the plastic bench at a bus stop just across the street, but she speaks to no one—not even on a mobile phone—in all the time that she is inside. Afterward she heads home and doesn't come out again until 3:15, when she lunches alone in a restaurant four blocks from her apartment. The highlight of my day comes at 5:05 when Rosalía does a series of aerobic stretches in the sitting room and I get to feel like Jimmy Stewart watching the ballerina in *Rear Window.* Otherwise it's a pointless day. Gael comes home at 7:40, by which time I am dizzy with boredom and hunger. In thirteen hours I have eaten just two *magdalena* sponges and a cheese *bocadillo,* bought quickly from a corner shop when I was sure that Rosalía was safely settled in for lunch. The two of them stay at home all night, and by 11:30 I cut my losses and leave. There must be an easier way of doing this. There must be a *reason* Arenaza hasn't shown.

The next day—Saturday—it's the same routine: up at five, in place by a quarter to six, nothing going on until eleven. I organize myself a little better this time, bringing sandwiches, a bottle of water, a Walkman, and several CDs. Still, the time creeps by as slowly as the last hour of a train journey, and I am increasingly nervous about being spotted, either by Rosalía or—more likely—by an alert, curtain-twitching neighbor. If only I had access to a disused apartment, to a neighborhood shop or café with clear sight of her flat. It might be a good idea to take the Audi out of circulation on Monday and to switch it for a different vehicle, a rental from Hertz, say, maybe even a van. In fact, it would be sensible to hire a professional investigator. What, after all, do I manage to deduce by the time the weekend is over? That Rosalía likes going to the gym on Saturday mornings. That she seems happy and physically intimate with Gael. That she visited an elderly relative in the suburb of Tres Cantos on Saturday afternoon and went for a brief walk in the park. Rosalía and Gael met friends for drinks in La Latina that evening but were home by one o'clock. This allowed me to grab three hours of much-needed sleep but left me with the overwhelming sensation that I was wasting my time. On Sunday they woke up late and took the metro to Callao and I followed Rosalía into FNAC, a department store selling music, books and DVDs. Gael left her at the entrance and I was briefly concerned that he might have spotted me and was going to double back in order to watch her tail, but he walked south toward Sol and didn't return for twenty minutes. By that time Rosalía had bought two CDs (Dido, Alejandro Sanz) and—as ever—was seemingly oblivious to any threat of observation. Later they went for coffee near the Reina

Sofía museum but were home by 8:15. They seem to spend a worrying amount of time sitting on the sofa.

All of which raises the inevitable question: where the hell is Arenaza? *ABC, El Mundo,* and *El País* are still reporting on the disappearance, but every journalist working on the story—including Zulaika—appears to have run out of leads. According to reports published on Friday, closed-circuit cameras at Barajas airport picked up Mikel getting into a taxi at Terminal One on the day of his disappearance. The driver, who has now been questioned by police, recalled dropping him off at the Hotel Casón del Tormes in Calle del Río, but he wasn't able to provide any information on his mood. That would appear to tally with earlier reports in which a receptionist said that she could not recall anything unusual about Arenaza's behavior. He wasn't anxious or nervous or making a song and dance; he was just a businessman with a wedding ring on his finger who left the hotel at seven o'clock in the evening, never to be seen again. So it is with an odd mixture of dread and exhilaration that I begin to accept the reality of his murder. What else could have happened? Unless I have the wrong Rosalía Dieste, why hasn't he come forward to declare himself?

I follow Rosalía for a fourth consecutive day, on Monday, March 24, using a rented Renault Clio. She goes back to the gym, to Plettix to pick up a box of odds and ends, and attends a doctor's appointment at half past four. Otherwise, nothing. Based on the lack of progress I decide to hire somebody to look into her background in the hope of establishing a connection with Mikel. If nothing has turned up within a week, I will go to Goena.

18

Atocha

Toward the back of every daily edition of *El País,* just after the six-page section dedicated entirely to classified adverts for prostitution, six numbers are listed for private investigators operating in Madrid. First thing on Tuesday I ring each of them in turn and settle for the one who sounds most professional and efficient—a Chilean from Detectives Cetro calling himself Eduardo Bonilla.

"I'll send one of my assistants to meet you as soon as possible," Bonilla says, picking out my accent and opting to speak in convoluted, if fluent, English. "Do you know the main *cafetería* at Atocha station?"

"The one in the conservatory? Next to all the plants?"

"That is *exactly* right. We say twelve o'clock?"

The café is squared off at the southern end of a vast barnlike structure more akin to a garden center than the terminus of a main-line railway station. A jungle of tropical plants, sprayed at heights of ten or fifteen meters by the frequent mists of an automatic watering system, completely dominates the center of the conservatory. It is one of the strangest sights in all Madrid. I take a corner seat beside a wooden railing and order freshly squeezed orange juice from a young waiter who seems nervous and out of control. Maybe it's his first day.

Bonilla's assistant is a respectable-looking woman in early middle age wearing a neat navy blue suit and plenty of mascara. She might be a single mother with a sideline in encyclopedia sales; it's hard to imagine her tracing a missing person or snooping around in an extramarital affair.

"Señor Thompson?"

I gave Bonilla a false name, of course. "I'll be wearing a brown leather jacket," I told him. "Look for a man with short, dark hair, reading a copy of yesterday's *Financial Times*." That was just my little private joke.

"Yes. Chris Thompson. And you must be . . . ?"

"Mar," she replies. "I work for Mr. Bonilla. What is it you think we can be doing for you?"

The conversation takes place in Spanish and I lie right from the start. I'm not going to mention Arenaza. I'm not going to tell them about Zulaika or the cops. This is just a matter of finding out a little about Rosalía's life: why she left Plettix, how she met Gael.

"I need you to conduct some research into a woman named Rosalía Dieste."

"For what purpose?"

"I'm not really at liberty to discuss that."

Mar shakes out a vaguely suspicious look and writes something in shorthand on a pad. "So where does Señora Dieste live?"

A small boy runs past the table, colliding blindly with a passenger trolley piled high with luggage and plastic bags. There are tears and screams. Then his mother appears and whisks him off.

I give the address, fill in Mar about Gael, but don't admit to watching the apartment over the last few days. All I need are phone records, I tell her, some family background, previous relationship history, any pseudonyms she might employ—and twenty-four-hour surveillance for at least the next ten days.

"Twenty-four-hour surveillance?" The question is asked in a suitably impassive fashion, but there might as well be dollar signs spinning behind her eyes. "That will require a team of between six and eight operatives working around the clock. What's your budget on the investigation, Mr. Thompson?"

"What do you charge?"

"Per day, per employee, 115 euros, with expenses. Over ten days, with eight staff, you'd be looking to pay around . . ."

I do it for her.

"Nine thousand two hundred euros."

"Your arithmetic is good."

"Well, in that case we may need to think again. How much would it cost just for doing the research into her background?"

"Depending on the amount of time involved, probably not more than 1,000 euros."

"Fine. Then I'd like to start right away."

And the remainder of the meeting is purely logistical. How would I like to pay? Cash, with half in advance. Do I have a fixed address in Madrid? Yes, but use my PO box in Moncloa. How often would I like to receive a report? Every two days. We arrange for the enquiry to begin as soon as Mar has returned to Bonilla's office and I agree to meet her again in forty-eight hours.

19

Middlegame

In the old days, working against Katharine and Fortner, I didn't have to do any snooping around. The relationship was stable; I knew what to expect. They wanted something out of me and I wanted something out of them. There was the odd nose around their bedroom—a time I almost got caught—but otherwise the work was mainly psychological. It was purely about trust and lying. And the longer I spend following Rosalía in Madrid, the more I realize that I am not cut out for the legwork of surveillance, for the patience and the wait. There's too little excitement in it, no buzz.

She's at home by the time I make it north in a new hire car on Tuesday afternoon. Hertz at Atocha had a Citroën Xsara going for forty-four euros a day, and I picked it up as soon as the meeting with Mar had ended. Though clearly something could have happened in the past eight hours, it's now the same old story as the weekend—gym visits and meals, coffee and Gael. Doesn't this woman do *anything* with her life? Surely there must be *something* going on?

I track her for three more days, waiting for a report from Bonilla. Now and again Mar will call up, wondering if I know Rosalía's e-mail address, her phone number, or DNI? None of these questions exactly fills me with confidence—if she can't find out that kind of information, what hope is there of her uncovering anything useful?—but no other option appears to exist. Access to a Spanish intelligence database would, of course, dramatically accelerate the investigation, but I have long grown used to the frustrations of private citizenship.

So Rosalía goes swimming. Rosalía buys herself a nice new pair of shoes. Rosalía meets the same girlfriend twice for lunch and reads Pérez-Reverte thrillers on the metro. She is shy and physically inexpressive but clearly very fond of Gael and noticeably attentive to the older members of her family. On Wednesday afternoon, for example, she took the train back to Tres Cantos and spent most of the time with the same elderly woman whom she visited at the weekend. I assume that this is her mother—a widow, dressed head to toe in black—because they hugged for a long time on the doorstep when Rosalía finally left. In spite of all the frustration and the boredom, I begin to understand what Arenaza saw in her, besides an obvious physical appeal. There is something melancholy about Rosalía, an absence, as if to break down the defense of her self-possession would yield access to a full and tender spirit.

The second meeting with Cetro, scheduled for Thursday afternoon, is canceled on the basis that Bonilla (who has now taken "personal responsibility" for the investigation) is waiting to hear back from two "extremely important" contacts. Instead I spend the afternoon trailing Rosalía around the Retiro, where she goes to an exhibition and buys an ice cream near the lake. At one point, twisting her head out of a sudden gust of wind, she turns and looks directly at me, our eyes meeting for the first time. This is over a distance of perhaps eighty or ninety feet, but there is something in it, a momentary flicker of surprise. It is the worst possible outcome, and in normal circumstances would be sufficient to pull me off the case. A watcher who has been observed by the subject is considered ineffective and blown. But I am working alone and can only take off my jacket and put on a baseball cap in a feeble attempt to effect a short-term change in my appearance. She does not appear to look for me again, but until Rosalía leaves the park I follow her using parallel paths, tracking her progress through screens of buildings and trees. It's a mug's game.

Then Friday comes. Somehow I always knew something was going to happen on Friday.

Gael leaves on what looks like a business trip at 6:55 A.M. He's carrying the same red rucksack and a large suitcase and they wave good-bye to one another with the quiet sadness of parted lovers. Standing at the sixth-floor window as he drives off, Rosalía looks lost and appears to wipe tears—or is it sleep?—out of her eyes. How long is he going for? The suitcase looked big enough for at least a week. Is this the moment? Is this when Arenaza comes?

Nothing happens until the early evening. Rosalía doesn't go anywhere, not even to buy a newspaper. It feels like the longest day of the week and I break a golden rule of surveillance by going for a five-minute walk to lessen the searing pain in my back. Her front door was never out of sight, but it's becoming clear to me that I can cope with only two or three more days of sandwiches and observation. I'm becoming sloppy and will soon have to hand things over to the police.

Rosalía finally leaves the apartment at 7:10 P.M. wearing a pair of thick-rimmed Anna Wintour sunglasses. I haven't seen them before and it has been a dull, overcast day. She has never struck me as the vain, fashion-conscious type, so I can only assume that she has an allergy or has been crying. She walks quickly out of the front door onto Rodríguez Marín and turns right toward Concha Espina. When she is twenty meters from the corner I switch on the Audi engine in anticipation of her catching a cab. Only she doesn't stop. Instead she turns right and I lose sight of her for about thirty seconds until I have caught up, on foot, and spotted her fifty meters downhill moving briskly west in the direction of the Bernabéu.

She keeps on walking, crossing Serrano, then the southern end of Paseo de la Habana, past the bank of ticket windows built into the lower section of the stadium. I keep about sixty meters behind her, farther than usual, but wary of being sighted a second time after the incident in the Retiro. In any case, it's fairly certain that this is just a trip to the metro. We've been here before: Rosalía hops on Line 10, changes at Tribunal, and then goes late-night shopping in Sol.

Only she keeps on walking. She waits for the pedestrian lights on the Castellana and crosses over to the far side of the road. She's moving more quickly than normal; she's in a hurry. I hide behind a turquoise bus with German license plates in the stadium car park and watch as she shrinks into the distance. This is risky. If Rosalía heads immediately into the grid of streets beyond the Castellana, I might lose her for the first time in eight days. We are separated by twelve busy lanes of traffic moving quickly in both directions. It was stupid of me to let her get this far ahead. I should have tucked in close behind and not allowed a gap of such size to open up.

Where has she gone?

Up to the right, about 150 meters away at two o'clock, I spot her on the pavement. Pale jeans, denim jacket, still walking quickly, still alone. There's a flashing green man at the pedestrian crossing and I take it, sprinting over to the far side of the road and then jogging north to follow her.

I can't see her anymore. She must have turned left at the next street. I take the corner of Calle de Pedro Teixeira at a wide angle, as the pavement artists advise. That way, if Rosalía has stopped for any reason—to double back, to check her tail—there is no danger of us colliding and I can continue in a straight line, as if intending to cross the road. But I can see that she has made the turn. Seventy meters west she is walking hurriedly along Teixeira. I follow from the opposite side of the street. After about forty seconds she makes a second left-hand turn onto a road running parallel to the Castellana. It dawns on me now that I have been here before, for a drink with Sofía about a year ago. There's a bar on the next block called Moby Dick with an area directly in front of it reserved solely for cars. We had a pint next door, in a prefab Irish pub the size of Dublin. Is that where she's going? Is that where she and Arenaza are planning to meet? He was always talking about Ireland. Basques love the *craic*.

She walks inside, so I wait across the street with clear sight of the entrance. It's a safe bet that she is meeting somebody and will therefore be at the location for at least another fifteen or twenty minutes. To follow immediately behind her would run the risk of being spotted, particularly if she doubles back at the door or pauses in the entrance to take her bearings. Better to wait until she is static at a table. Then I can move more freely and try to ascertain what is going on.

From memory, the Irish Rover is laid out in three sections on the ground floor. You walk into a foyer where tall wrought-iron street lamps and mocked-up storefronts are meant to give the impression of an Irish village. The bar is thus "The Village Pub," a second structure within the building with its own windows and doors. At the back of the bar are two pool tables and there's also a cloakroom selling T-shirts. To the right is a raised area large enough to accommodate a live band, with a staircase behind it leading up to a second story. Rosalía could be anywhere. My best option may be to wait for the next large group of people heading into the building and to make conversation with them as cover. If Rosalía is sitting near the front door she will be less likely to notice me entering in a cluster of five or six people.

Here they come. Spaniards from the business district heading for preweekend drinks. Three guys, two girls, all under thirty and coming in from the right. I walk through the cluster of cars and time my arrival at the door to coincide with theirs. One of the girls notices me and I take my chance, directing a general greeting at the five of them.

"*Hola.*"

"*Hola. Buenas tardes.*"

It's something I probably couldn't get away with in the UK, but Spaniards are generally more affable and easygoing.

"*Parece que tenemos la misma idea,*" I tell them. It looks like we have the same idea.

One of the guys, good-looking and threatened, gives me a slightly puzzled look, but the other girl picks up on my remark and says, "*Sí, sí,*" with enthusiasm.

"*Una pinta antes del fin de semana. Un partido de billar, y a relajarnos.*"

"*Claro.*"

We have walked through the door now and into a small, poster-covered vestibule about the size of a garden shed. A meter in front, the other girl has opened the main door into the pub and is making her way inside. It's loud and smoky and Van Morrison is blaring out on a music system.

"*Eres americano?*" I make a point of getting ahead of her and turning round as she asks the question.

"*No, irlandés,*" I reply.

"*Sí? Sí?*" The good-looking one loves this. There's no sign of Rosalía at any of the tables nearby. "*Oye, Xavi,*" he calls ahead to his mate. "*Fíjate! Este chico es un irlandés de verdad. Cómo te llamas?*"

"Paddy."

"*Hola, Paddy. Soy Julio. Encantado.*"

"*Encantado.*"

And job done. Rosalía is either upstairs, gone to the bathroom, or seated at the back near the pool tables. I make conversation with Julio for another couple of minutes and then break off, explaining that I have to look around for a friend.

"No problems," he says, adopting nursery-level English. "Very—nice—to—meet—you—Mr.—Irishman."

I check the back area, but it's standing-room only and filled to capacity with smoke and students. A teenager with smug eyes and a bad shirt is holding court on the nearest table. I'd like to take him on. Back in the "village," a member of staff is coming down from the second floor carrying a tray of dirty plates. He has pale, spot-strewn skin and red hair and I assume—incorrectly—that he's Irish.

"Could you help me please?"

"What's that?"

Scottish.

"I'm looking for a friend of mine. Wonder if you've seen her. A Spanish woman of about thirty, dark glasses, blond hair, denim jacket . . ."

"No idea, pal," he says, moving past me. "Try up the top."

I don't appear to have any choice. When I came here with Sofía neither of us went upstairs, so I will be walking blind into an unknown location. Employing the same technique as before, I wait for a small group of people to make their way upstairs and fall in behind them. This at least gives me the chance to scope the upper level at the least risk of being observed. The pub is very full, both downstairs and up, and all the tables near the top of the staircase appear to be occupied. Directly ahead there's a smaller room containing a mock fireplace and some faked-up dusty bookshelves, but the bar is off to the right, beyond a narrow corridor leading into an open area decorated in a maritime theme. There are furled sails on booms suspended from the ceiling and a fat black anchor bolted to one wall. On a hunch, I assume that Rosalía is seated in the smaller room because there's no sign of her at the bar and she has had enough time by now to go to the ladies. I make my way to the bar, order a pint of lager, and then look for a mirror or reflective surface with which to observe what's going on behind me.

No such luck. Instead I have to turn around, discovering that I can see directly into the smaller room through a narrow doorway. Rosalía is seated with her back to me, about twenty-five feet away at a table beyond the fireplace, talking to a man whom I do not recognize. He is at least fifty years old with combed jet-black hair, a dark woolen sweater, and eyes like stewed tea bags. Not her type, in other words: a tough working-class hombre, maybe a cousin or an uncle. Only she appears upset. Rosalía seems stressed. And there isn't a trace of sympathy or kindness in the man's washed-out eyes. Merely irritation. He actually seems drunk with contempt.

This is self-evidently a vital time. There are developments here, links to Arenaza. Somehow I have to maneuver myself into a position from which it will be possible to overhear their conversation. But the room in which they are sitting is not as crowded as the rest of the pub, and if I stand or sit anywhere near their table, Rosalía will be bound to notice. A man standing next to me at the bar sways onto one leg and I have to catch him to hold his balance.

"Sorry, mate," he says, a Midlands accent, grabbing my arm. One of his friends lets out a hearty laugh.

That's when I see my opportunity. Beyond Rosalía's table is a second doorway leading out onto a balcony overlooking the chaos of the ground floor. If there's a chair there, even space in which to stand, I would be concealed and possibly within earshot of the conversation.

Having picked up a discarded newspaper from the bar, I take the pint, make my way back through the crowds, and find a narrow bench at which to sit and listen. The music is very loud but I can see the base of the man's chair and Rosalía's left hand resting on the table. Both of them are smoking cigarettes. Rosalía never smokes. Ahead of me, built into the cinder-block walls, is a badly fitted window smudged by fingerprints. Through it I can see the fireplace and most of the other tables in the smaller room, as well as the obligatory portraits of Yeats and Beckett and George Bernard Shaw. The man says something, in Spanish, about *guilt*. I pick up the specific Spanish word. *La culpabilidad*. Rosalía's response is very quiet, or at least inaudible from where I am sitting. Maddeningly, the DJ operating from a booth directly behind me has chosen to play "Living on a Prayer" at deafening volume. Five women on a hen night at the next-door table blare out the chorus, making it impossible to hear.

I have to get closer.

Attempting to look as natural as possible, I pick up the pint and lean against the wall beside the door. If Rosalía leaves through this entrance there is every possibility that she will recognize me, but it is surely worth the risk. I can now hear snippets of their conversation more clearly, and a new Spanish song is fractionally quieter. Words such as *time* and *patience*. At one point the man mutters something about *loyalty*.

"I don't care about loyalty," Rosalía snaps back. *No me importa la lealtad.* She is audibly upset. But what about? If only I had a general clue as to the subject under discussion.

"You don't have to worry," the man replies. *Usted no tiene que preocuparse.* I heard that very clearly. Then: "Just go home for the weekend, relax, and wait for your boyfriend." Rosalía coughs and her answer is again smothered by the music. But I obtain one vital piece of information. The man's name. Abel.

A chair scrapes back. It sounds as though one of them is standing up. I pivot away from the door, take the newspaper out of my back pocket, and quickly sit down on the bench. Fogged by drink, the other customers on the narrow balcony seem oblivious to my strange behavior. Looking up through the window I see Abel walking away from the table and out toward the stairs. Rosalía is not going with him. He turns left, perhaps to go to the bathroom, but he is already wearing an outdoor coat. One of the girls on the hen night catches my eye, but I ignore her.

Three minutes later Abel reappears and heads down to the ground floor. Rosalía, as far as I can tell, is staying where she is. I make a split-second decision to follow her companion. Whoever he is, he must know *something* about Arenaza. Far better to take a chance on an instinct like this, to seize the opportunity, than to waste even more time at Jiloca.

It is raining outside, the shower that had been threatening all afternoon. Two bouncers are huddled in the vestibule and they bid me good night. Abel turns right toward Moby Dick, yet something catches my eye. When I was waiting across the street before entering the pub I saw a bottle-green Seat Ibiza pull up in front of the entrance. It parked a few meters away from me, but the two men inside did not get out. Instead, one of them lit a cigarette and started talking. I thought nothing of this at the time, but it seems unusual that they should still be there. Spanish couples—many of whom live with their parents until they are ready to marry—will use cars as one of the few places in which they can have any kind of physical intimacy, but these are two guys and they are certainly not lovers. Furthermore, although it has clearly been raining for some time, the windshield of their car is absolutely clear, as if it has been recently swept by wiper blades to give an unobstructed view of the pub. The clincher might be the two cans of Fanta Limón resting on the dashboard. These guys are on a stakeout. But who are they following?

Meanwhile Abel walks down the road as it narrows off into a lane leading into a second car park dotted with pine trees. There's an empty playground on one side and more bars on the other. The rain has kicked up a smell of dogshit and people have started to run for cover. Rosalía's contact seems oblivious to it, as if pressed for time, and I cover my head with the newspaper and try to stay in sight of him. Then another strange thing: a woman, without an umbrella, standing off to the right beside a garage selling tires. She's talking into a mobile phone but turned toward the wall as if to shield her face from strangers. Am I being paranoid? Why doesn't she come out of the rain? Is she part of a team assigned to follow Abel? Or has Rosalía finally cottoned on to my surveillance and hired a team to check me out?

Abel, for his part, may be employing antisurveillance as he reaches a two-way cross street perpendicular to the Castellana, starting to look around for a cab. This presents me with two problems. If he finds one, it will be virtually impossible in this weather to hail another quickly enough to track his progress. Second, by turning constantly through 360 degrees, he is giving himself every opportunity to watch his back for a tail. Is this guy a pro? Who the hell is Rosalía dealing with? He crosses to the opposite side of the road and I follow him as discreetly as possible, the rain letting up only slightly. Within two minutes he has reached the Castellana and immediately spots a taxi heading in a southbound direction. Up goes an arm, in goes Abel. Shit. I jog the last twenty meters to the intersection and look north in desperation. Nothing. The cab is stuck in traffic just a few meters away, but it only requires the lights to change for Abel to disappear forever. *Remember the number plate, Alec. At least remember that.*

Then—and every spy needs a bit of luck—a taxi comes shooting across from the southern end of the stadium, hazard lights on, halting immediately beside me. A gray-haired woman breaks from the pavement to hail it, but I step in front of her as the door opens and the passenger steps out. *Hurry. Pay the driver. Leave.* The lights have changed and Abel's cab has started to move south. The passenger is Japanese—young and city quick, thank God—and as he bends to thank the driver, I dive in behind him and slam the door.

"Vaya al sur! Deprisa, por favor!" Ahead, at twelve o'clock, I can still see the roof light of Abel's cab as it disappears down the Castellana. The gray-haired woman raps on the window with her knuckle but I just ignore her. "My wife is in a taxi with another man," I tell the driver. "He's my business partner. You have to follow that cab."

"*Claro*," says the driver. "*Claro*," as if this sort of thing happens to him all the time. Engaging first gear, he sets his clipboard to one side and just catches the lights as they turn red.

"Get closer," I tell him. "*Más cerca*," and he obliges with a nod and a shrug. Surely Abel is now aware that he is being followed? Will he try to lose me, either by making a series of unnecessary turns, or exit his cab early and continue by bus or on foot?

"You're going to have to get nearer," I keep telling the driver. "It's very important we don't lose them."

"*Muy importante, sí*," he replies, hacking phlegm in the back of his throat.

And that's when I see the green Seat Ibiza. Three cars back in the outer lane. Can it be the same vehicle? Using the wing mirror on the passenger side I try to ascertain who is driving, but it's impossible to tell through the traffic and the drizzle. A moped buzzes past close to my door and the cabbie swears. Up ahead, near Nuevos Ministerios, Abel's car is already through a set of traffic lights that are switching from green to amber.

"Quickly," I tell the driver again, "quickly," and thankfully he obliges by shooting through on red.

"Your *business* partner?" he asks, finally taking an interest in my predicament. A horn sounds long and hard behind us.

"My business partner," I reply, trying to look suitably distraught. The Seat didn't come through the lights, but the traffic ahead is moving slowly. There's every chance it will catch us.

"*Joder*," he mutters.

We continue another half mile south to Rubén Darío, where Abel turns off to the right in the direction of Alonso Martínez. But it's a U-turn: taking up a position in the left-hand lane, his cab sweeps back across the Castellana as if heading into Barrio Salamanca. We are following at a three-car distance as he makes a second left-hand turn, heading north again, perhaps in an effort to lose us. Very quickly, however, he pulls over to the side of the road and turns into the forecourt of the Hotel Villa Carta. This can't be where he is staying; Abel dresses like a two-star pimp and the Carta is one of the finest hotels in Madrid.

I instruct the driver to pull over to the side of the road, hand him a ten-euro note, and walk the short distance up the ramp toward the entrance. A porter dressed in gray tails and a top hat opens the door and ushers Abel inside. They've clearly met before because words are exchanged and Abel puts his hand briefly on the porter's shoulder.

"Alfonso," I hear him say.

"Buenas tardes, señor." Alfonso jokes that he is tired but will be finishing work in half an hour. Abel then shakes his hand, steps past him into the hotel, and walks toward a bank of lifts on the left of the lobby. I wait a few seconds behind a group of American tourists before following him inside, approaching the reception desk just as the lift doors are closing. It's almost certain that he has taken a room in the hotel; if he were meeting somebody, he would have waited in the foyer, or turned to the right in the direction of the bar. Abel's familiarity with the porter would also suggest that he has built up a relationship with the staff over a number of days.

To give legitimacy to my own presence in the hotel, I leave the lobby and walk toward the bar, passing illuminated glass boxes advertising products by Chopard, Gucci, and Mont Blanc. Most of the tables are occupied by businessmen and older couples enjoying an evening drink and I effect a brief scan of the room before turning and heading back toward the entrance. A security guard of roughly the same age and appearance as Bob Hope has appeared near the main door wearing an earpiece and looking self-important. To avoid his eye I take the back exit out past a Chinese restaurant attached to the hotel and head into a passageway running directly behind the building. There's a branch of El Corte Inglés to one side and an Aeroflot shop to the other. I need a bank for the plan I have in mind.

Five minutes later I have withdrawn €400 from the Paris account and located the hotel's staff entrance on the corner of Calle de José Ortega y Gasset. Positioning myself across the street, away from the gaze of a fixed security camera bolted to the wall, I wait for Alfonso to leave work. At first it's hard to recognize him, but the snub nose and slightly bowed legs that were in evidence beneath top hat and tails gradually become apparent in the physical characteristics of a man who emerges shortly after 9:15. He is wearing dark chinos and a black coat and walks slowly south, probably toward one of the two metro stations near Plaza de Colón. It has stopped raining and after 400 meters I make my pitch.

The discussion goes predictably well. Most of the concierges at Europe's leading hotels are susceptible to bribes from intelligence officials, and there was no reason to suspect that this one would be any different. Henry Paul, after all, was almost certainly an informer for SIS, and Alfonso is small beer by comparison. Having initiated a conversation on the pavement by asking for a light, I quickly persuade him into a nearby bar—in case we are under surveillance—discovering that he is biddable to the point of blatant corruption. Giving a false name, I explain that I work for a private technology company, based in Geneva, that will amply remunerate him for any information he might be able to provide about the identity and purpose of the individual who engaged him briefly in conversation at the entrance of the hotel at 8:35 this evening. To speed things along, I hand Alfonso four fifty-euro notes folded inside a small piece of paper on which I have written my name—Chris Thompson—and a Telefónica mobile telephone number. Should he feel like talking, he should call me within the next twenty-four hours with details of the individual's surname ("He invariably uses a pseudonym"), home address, passport origin and number, credit card details, car make and license, if applicable, as well as any other information that he might consider useful to my enquiries.

"What's Mr. Sellini done?" Alfonso asks, already giving up Abel's surname.

"I'm afraid I'm not at liberty to divulge that information," I explain, hinting at something shady involving children on the Internet. Alfonso looks suitably appalled, but I'm in a position to treble his weekly salary so he won't be losing any sleep over it. We shake hands and I insist only that he keep our conversation private. Alfonso agrees and looks pleased as he leaves the bar. At Plaza de Colón, he crosses to the Barclays Bank building and disappears into the metro. I then call Bonilla from a phone booth around the corner, pass on Sellini's name and ask for an update on Rosalía.

"It has been very difficult," he insists, adopting the evasive style that has become increasingly common in our conversations, "not easy to obtain answers, not simple at all." Having listened to his excuses for the best part of five minutes, I insist on a full progress report by Monday evening and arrange for a small team of four surveillance operatives to watch Rosalía over the weekend. Bonilla cuts me a deal—€1,600 for three days, with nobody in place, barring exceptional circumstances, between 2 A.M. and 6 A.M. After that I hail a cab, go for dinner in Malasaña, and get to bed before midnight for the first time in ten days.

20

Dry Cleaning

The banging starts at half past five in the morning, very quietly at first, but gradually increasing in volume until I am almost shaken out of bed. The sound is initially like hammering, a spot of dawn DIY, but slowly I become convinced that somebody is deliberately dropping a large metal ball on the ceiling directly above my bed. At about ten to six the noise finally stops, only to be replaced within minutes by what sound like giant marbles being rolled en masse across a parquet floor. There is the sound of a young child laughing, then heavy footsteps and, finally, a crash.

My neighbors upstairs, a Danish couple from Copenhagen, gave birth to their first child around eight months ago. I see him in the lift every now and again, a sweet blond-haired baby being taken for a walk in his stroller by a pretty Venezuelan au pair. He has now reached an age where he can crawl, thumping around on his hands and knees, doubtless with a box full of Lego bricks, while his parents clear up the mess behind him. Why don't they take him into another room? Don't they have soft toys in Copenhagen?

It's pointless trying to go back to sleep. As though a mosquito were persistently dive-bombing my ear I wait, semiconscious, for the next thump on the ceiling, the next floor-shattering bang of the ball. At half past six I get out of bed, make myself a cup of coffee, and stand under the shower for ten minutes trying to work out the link between Rosalía and Sellini. Then I walk down to the newsagent on Plaza de España and buy all the British broadsheets, with *The Economist* thrown in for my conscience. Jaded clubbers are still drifting down Gran Vía in the dawn light and it occurs to me that Saul is due back any day now. Having walked through Plaza de los Cubos, I take a window table at Cáscaras, order coffee, tortilla, and orange juice, and sit for two hours reading the papers from front page to back.

Sofía calls me at home at half past ten, just as I am beginning to make headway through a ten-day pile of fetid washing-up.

"How was your visit to England?" she asks.

In order to get away for the week of surveillance, I told Sofía that I had to go to London for a wedding. She has no idea that I haven't been home for six years.

"It was fine, thanks. Fine. Saw a lot of old friends. Ate some good food. Christ, London's expensive."

"You sound like Julian," she says.

"I sound like anybody who spends five minutes in England."

Sofía laughs at this and asks what the bride was wearing and whether I danced with any pretty girls, but I grow tired of making things up and suggest we meet if Julian is out of town.

"He's in Cádiz," she says.

Cádiz? Where Saul has been staying. I experience that old familiar thump of paranoid dread but try to dismiss it as mere coincidence. "Well, why don't I take you shopping?" I suggest. "We could go to the Vermeer exhibition at the Prado."

"You don't want me just to come over?"

"No. I want us to behave like a normal couple. Meet me at the main entrance to El Corte Inglés in Argüelles at midday."

I have a hidden agenda, of course. Two or three times a week I follow a short countersurveillance routine from the flat to El Corte Inglés via the post office off Calle de Quintana. The ten-minute route

144

provides several opportunities to observe for a tail, while the department store itself is an ideal location in which to flush out a hostile team. In tradecraft terms, this process is called "dry cleaning."

If I lived on a quieter street, one of my first actions would be to step out onto the balcony in order to check for operatives in "trigger" positions, that is to say, anybody keeping an eye on my front door. But Princesa is far too busy to make an effective assessment of outside surveillance, so I set out down Ventura Rodríguez and make a right just beyond Cáscaras. At the next block, on the corner of Martín de los Heros and Calle de Luisa Fernanda, there's a branch of the Banco Popular with a broad glass façade set at a perfect angle with which to observe the pavements behind. Still, I have only about one and a half seconds to notice the teenage girl with her hair in pigtails walking twenty meters behind me, and a middle-aged man on the opposite side of the street holding a carrier bag and scratching his nose. The trick is to memorize faces in order to be able to recognize them if they reappear at a later date. Were I, for example, to see the woman who was talking on her mobile phone yesterday outside the tire shop, that would conclusively prove that I have a surveillance problem.

The post office is also ideal, particularly for watchers who may not know the interior layout and might therefore lack the nerve to wait outside. My PO box is on the first floor, up a narrow flight of stairs inside a small room that's usually deserted. If an operative were careless enough to follow me, I could get a good look at his face simply by nodding to greet him. Downstairs, the post office itself is usually crammed with customers, providing a convenient choke point in which to flush out a tail. Again, the trick is to remember faces without making eye contact. You don't want them to know that they've been spotted, and they certainly don't want to be seen.

After the post office I double back onto Quintana and walk up the hill toward El Corte Inglés. There are two zebra crossings en route and I always pause to make a phone call at the second of them, dialling just as the pedestrian lights are turning green. This is a useful technique, and one facilitated by mobile phone technology, because it allows me to turn through a complete circle without drawing attention to myself. Furthermore, anyone following me on foot is obliged to pass and cross the street, or to walk on toward the next corner. Today I call Saul, who says he left Cádiz a few days ago and drove back via Ronda to Seville. He sounds jaded, perhaps depressed, and has a ticket on the AVE leaving for Madrid at four o'clock this afternoon.

"Should be back by eight," he says wearily. "Looking forward to seeing you."

Sofía, as ever, is twenty minutes late. It's annoying to have to wait for her, standing around in plain sight of the entrance to Corte Inglés with nobody to speak to and nothing to pass the time. She is wearing sunglasses, not unlike Rosalía's, and looks around nervously before greeting me with an abrupt kiss.

"Let's go inside," she says, anxious not to be spotted by one of Julian's friends. "You look terrible, *cariño*. Didn't you sleep in London?"

"I was on a camp bed," I tell her, a lie so instantaneous that I have no sense of its origin. "Kept waking up every two hours, couldn't get back to sleep."

"Then you should have stayed in a hotel," she says, as if I have been both stupid and unreasonable, and not for the first time it occurs to me that we are entering into a discussion entirely without basis in fact.

"Well, I thought about it," I tell her, "but my friend would have been offended. I hadn't seen her in years."

"You were staying with a *girl?*"

Now why did I say that?

"Sure. Not a girlfriend. An old flatmate from university. She's engaged. She has a boyfriend."

"I'm *married*," Sofía replies curtly, and it will now be at least ten minutes before the clouds of her jealousy subside.

We begin on the ground floor, ostensibly shopping for handbags and makeup. There are a few small reflective surfaces in the department but nothing to compare with the full-length mirrors upstairs in men's and women's fashions. I keep a constant lookout for faces and try to recall as many of them as I can before suggesting to Sofía that we take the switchback escalators up to Level One. These are perhaps the best surveillance traps in the entire *barrio*. For a start, they are mirrored all the way up, allowing any number of opportunities to observe customers moving up or down on parallel stairs. Better still, they are situated in the center of the building. It is therefore possible between floors to make an apparently wrong turn into a department, to spin around, briefly check the escalator for a tail, and then continue in the opposite direction. That's exactly what happens on Level One, where Sofía even adds a note of unwitting authenticity by grabbing my arm and saying, "No, not that way," as I turn left, rather than right, into women's fashions. She picks out several dresses and I buy two for her with the cash left over from Alfonso. At this point her mood visibly improves. Then we go up to Level Two where Sofía insists that I try on an array of Eurotrash jackets, most of which, she agrees, make me look like an Albanian pimp. Still, she's determined to buy me something and it is with a sense of foreboding that we head toward Ralph Lauren. In Spain, the *pijo* look—Polo shirts, pressed chinos, tank tops—is considered the height of fashion among the more conservative classes, and Sofía finds no irony in recommending outfits that would have me beaten up in Notting Hill.

"What are you trying to do, turn me into your husband?" I ask as she passes yet another striped shirt through the changing-room curtains.

"Just try it on," she says. "Don't be so *trendy*, Alec."

Eventually I settle for a sweater, endlessly checked in a full-length mirror providing almost total coverage of the men's department. There's no sign of the girl in pigtails, nor of the man with the carrier bags. Laden with shopping, we then leave via the exit on Alberto Aguilera, looping back toward the main entrance at Argüelles metro before proceeding east down Princesa. The walk offers conclusive proof that I don't have a surveillance problem; in almost an hour of dry cleaning I haven't noticed anything to arouse my suspicion.

Back at the apartment, Sofía makes lunch but shows no interest in going to bed. I am secretly glad of this but irritated nonetheless by the sock to my vanity. Although she has never mentioned it directly, her sex life with Julian is clearly abysmal and I relish my role as the handsome young buck, Pyle to his Thomas Fowler. Instead we take a cab to the Prado, Sofía bombarding me with a series of uncharacteristically aggressive questions en route.

"How come you didn't answer your phone when you were away? For ten days you haven't talked to me. Is it because you were sleeping with this girl?"

I respond as calmly as possible, sensing that she is picking a fight for the sake of it, yet the presence of the taxi driver is unnerving. I am naturally reticent and loathe holding potentially embarrassing conversations in the presence of strangers. Perhaps on this occasion, however, it is a blessing in disguise; were we back at the flat I would certainly accuse Sofía of hypocrisy and encourage the conversation to escalate into a full-scale row. Who is she, after all, to accuse me of infidelity when she shares Julian's bed, night after night?

"Can we talk about this later?"

"No. I would like to talk about it now."

"You're worried about me going to bed with another woman? You think I'm seeing somebody else?"

"I don't care who you see," she says, unconvincingly. The cab slides across two empty lanes in bright sunshine. "I just care that you don't lie to me."

"Well, that's reassuring. Thank you. This is turning out to be a terrific afternoon, just what I had in mind."

Perhaps we have arrived at adultery's inevitable final reel: it can go no farther than mild escapism. Sofía cannot respect me for what I have done to Julian, and I cannot respect her for betraying her husband. She wants nothing more from the relationship, and I have nothing left to give. It has all gone on for far too long. We have absorbed one another's lies.

"What is this about, Sofía? What is it that you want?"

A withering look. *"Qué?"*

"If it's not worth it, if you're not having a good time, then why did you agree to meet me today? Just to have an argument?"

Silence. The driver swings the taxi around the fountain at Cibeles and it's obvious he has one ear on our conversation. I switch to English.

148

"If you want to end it, then end it. Don't make me do it, don't make me into the scapegoat."

"The *what?*"

"The fall guy. *El cabeza de turco.* It's an expression."

"I do not want this to end. Who said that it was ending?"

"Then let's not fight. Let's go to Vermeer. Let's enjoy the afternoon together."

"I'm just tired of all your stories, Alec," she says. "I don't believe them. I don't believe you went to England. I don't know who you are."

It is like being with Kate again, a hideous sense memory of the last time we saw one another at her house. Stupidly I say, "I can be whatever you want me to be," and Sofía looks at me with utter contempt. "I don't mean it like that. I mean this is supposed to be fun, otherwise why are we doing it?"

"Fun?" she says, and it appears as though she might laugh. "You think that's all this is for me? Fun?"

"Well, what more can I ask for? I am faithful to you. I went to London for a wedding. I didn't sleep with Anne. You're married. I don't know what else to say."

The cab stops at a set of traffic lights beside the Museo Thyssen-Bournemisza, about 500 meters short of the Prado. We'll be there in under a minute, but time might as well have stood still. Very quietly, in English, Sofía says, "I love you, Alec," the first time she has spoken these words. The mixture of dread and exhilaration they engender, the flattery and the panic, leaves me speechless. I take her hand gently in mine as she turns away and looks out of the window. I touch her neck, her hair, and wonder what to say.

"How much is it?" The driver pulls over to the side of the road. "We'll get out here."

I hand him a fistful of change and we emerge in silence. Gallery tourists are taking up most of the pavement, with their money belts and their liter bottles of water. Sofía follows me, her face flushed red, eyes brimming with sadness. I want to hug her but cannot do so for fear of being seen.

149

"Just forget it," she says. "Forget what I have said."

"How can I forget it? I don't want to. You just surprised me, that's all."

"I surprise myself."

To reach the Prado we have to cross the road at a zebra crossing. Years and years ago, Kate and I took this exact route on a long romantic weekend in Madrid, holding hands and laughing. I spent an hour inside looking at exquisite portraits by Titian and Coello; she went for late Goya and Hieronymous Bosch, and I thought at the time that this said something worrying about our relationship. Sofía walks about five feet ahead of me, passing a line of stalls selling trinkets and bullfight posters, and folds her arms across her body.

"Look, why don't we go back to the apartment?" I suggest, quickening my pace to catch her. "Let's just go back and talk."

"No. It's OK." She sneezes. "I want to see the exhibition. I want to see Vermeer. We won't get another chance." Recovering some of her earlier composure, she adds, "It's best if we go in separately. If anybody sees us inside we can tell them we meet in the queue."

"Are you sure?"

"Why not?"

"Not about that. About us. Are you sure you don't want to go home? Are you sure you don't want to go for a coffee or something?"

"I am certain."

So we have to wait in line for fifteen excruciating minutes. Sofía stands several places in front of me and only rarely catches my eye. At one point she is chatted up by an Italian man carrying a brown leather handbag. Inside, she goes to the bathroom and rents a headset at the information desk, almost certainly as a conscious means of avoiding me during the exhibition. The paintings are extraordinary, but the temporary rooms are crowded and smaller than is usual in the Prado and I feel claustrophobic.

Afterward, outside in the main hall on the first floor, Sofía turns to me. "This exhibition is all about living with moderation."

An Englishman in a pin-striped suit passes us, calling out, "Lead on, Macduff."

"That's what your guide said?"

"No. It's what I *feel.*" A brief pause. "I think Julian would like it."

It isn't clear if this is a joke at her husband's expense or a veiled threat. I merely nod and say, "So you found it interesting?"

"Of course. And you?"

"Very much. Twenty-five paintings about moral instruction and suppressed sexual desire. What more could a man want on a Saturday afternoon?"

And this, at last, brings a little grin to Sofía's face and her mood begins to lighten. As if our earlier argument had never taken place, she proceeds to talk at length about the exhibition, about her job, about plans she has for buying a clothes shop in Barrio Salamanca and striking out on her own. We walk back through Chueca side streets in the general direction of my apartment, arriving home just as the mass peace march against the war is beginning on the other side of the city. Sofía wanted to take part, but I changed her mind with an expensive bottle of *cava* and a brief speech about the pointlessness of political rallies.

"If you think Bush and Blair and Aznar give a monkey fuck what the public thinks about Iraq, you've got another think coming."

After that, she became a little drunk and we finally went to bed. Perhaps I should have told her that I love her, but her eyes would not have believed me. Best to wait on that; best not to complicate things.

21

Ricken Redux

"Fuck me, this flat stinks of perfume. You been dressing up as a woman again, Alec?"

Saul comes back from Cádiz at ten wearing a three-week beard and a brand-new pair of Campers. From his bag he pulls out a half-finished carton of cigarettes and hands me a bottle of whiskey.

"Sorry it took so long to get back. Tube was packed at Atocha. Peace march. A present," he says. "You drink this stuff?"

"All the time," I tell him. "How was your trip?"

"Good. Really good. You look knackered, mate."

"I haven't been sleeping much."

"No?"

"No."

"Still fucking the boss's wife?"

I look up at the ceiling. "Ha ha. No. There's this baby upstairs. Wakes me at five every morning."

"Doing what?"

"I don't know. Building a dam. Tearing down support walls. I think he wears clogs." Saul takes a piece of chewing gum out of his mouth and throws it in the bin. "There's something different about you."

"Yeah? Maybe it's the beard. Makes me look like the Unabomber."

"No. You look happier, more relaxed."

"Well, that's good to know. I did a lot of thinking down there."

We carry his bags back into the spare room and keep on talking. He has decided to fly back to London tomorrow morning and to ask Heloise for a divorce. I don't feel it's my place to say that he has made the right decision, but it's good to be free of lies for once, just chatting with my mate about things that are important to him. It's also significant that he is leaving Madrid so soon. If there were any connection with Julian or Arenaza, he would surely be sticking around. Nevertheless I check out the Julian coincidence, just to be sure.

"So you know who was down in Cádiz while you were there?"

Saul is in the spare bathroom washing his hands. I can watch his face in the mirror as he says, "Who?"

"My boss, Julian. The guy you met at the bar. The one with the wife."

"Really?" He turns around. The tops of his cheeks have flushed slightly red.

"You didn't see him?"

"No."

"Well, maybe you'd left before he got there."

"Or maybe in a town the size of Coventry, Alec, we didn't bump into each other."

"Good point."

I go into the kitchen, find a cigarette, and pour both of us a glass of Rueda. When I come back to the room Saul has unzipped his laptop computer and powered it up on the bed.

"Want to see some photos?"

There are dozens of pictures from his trip downloaded onto the hard drive: shots of the Mezquita, of the bullring in Ronda, the beach at Cádiz. One has Saul eating *boquerones* in a crowded restaurant sitting next to a pretty girl.

"Who's she?"

"Just some bird. Yank. A lot of them down there. She was going out with the guy who took the picture."

I'd like to have five minutes alone with Saul's PC, just to check his e-mails, browser history, and cookies for any sign of a connection to Julian. Just to put my mind at rest.

"And what about your friend, the one with the flat?"

"Who, Andy? Refuses to have his photo taken. Says it steals his soul."

This sounds unconvincing and I get my chance half an hour later. Saul goes for a shower before dinner and while he's locked in the bathroom I scroll through his Outlook Express package looking for anything that seems out of place. I have the door of the room wide open and there is a lot of traffic passing by outside, but it should still be possible to hear the lock snap on the bathroom door if he comes out prematurely. I recognize some of the names in the "Sent" folder as friends of Saul's from London, but check several others in case Julian is using an e-mail account of which I am not aware. There is a brief exchange with Andy about handing over keys in Cádiz, but otherwise the messages are a mixture of business and pleasure: inquiries about Saul's availability for work; round-robin jokes; the latest updates on Chelsea players.

Internet Explorer is also simple to access. His history of Web sites is a straightforward mix of soft porn and Google, information about traveling in Andalucía, and advice to prospective divorcés. Nothing for me to worry about. I go into the C: Drive Windows directory and look at deleted temporary files, but it's all legitimate. With characteristic concern for his fellow man, Saul has accessed a medical Web site about cancer in an effort to understand more about Hesther's condition. There are also numerous charities that he has visited in order to donate money online, and a portal for games where he has played a lot of chess. The cookies seem innocent, too, simply hundreds of links to sites already listed in the browser. Leaving the computer as I found it, I head back toward the kitchen and knock on the bathroom door.

"You all right in there?"

It opens ajar. Saul's face is smothered in shaving foam and the mirror is completely fogged up with steam. He's going to be at least another five minutes.

"I'm losing the beard," he says, coughing. "What's for dinner?"

"Wine."

Using the extra time I find Saul's mobile, take it out of his jacket pocket, and check the address book, the list of numbers called and received, writing down any with a Spanish prefix. None, from memory, match numbers associated with Julian or Arenaza, but I may be able to find a link once Saul has gone back to London. Then I send Sofía a brief message and make spaghetti in the kitchen. Saul emerges ten minutes later wearing a pair of jeans and a white T-shirt bearing the slogan "Passive Aggression Rules (as long as that's OK with you)." His newly shaved cheeks are pink and smooth.

"That feels a lot better," he says, tapping his face. "Now I can actually eat without storing up food for the winter."

Neither of us feels much like going out, so we eat dinner on our knees and take out *The Talented Mr. Ripley* from the rack to watch on DVD. Just as I'm putting the disc into the machine, the Telefónica mobile rings in my bedroom.

"Do you have to answer it?" Saul is mopping up sauce with a hunk of bread and wants to watch the movie.

"Just give me two minutes. Hang on."

It's almost certainly Alfonso, the concierge at the Hotel Carta. Very few people have this number.

"Señor Chris?"

"Alfonso. Qué tal?"

He sounds relaxed, calling from a phone booth. I make sure that we speak in rapid Spanish in order to prevent Saul understanding.

"I have the information that you ask for. Do you have a pen?"

"Yes. Just one moment." I reach for the pad beside my bed and retrieve a ballpoint from my trouser pocket. "OK, go ahead."

"The guest staying in room 306 is registered as Abel Sellini. He has stayed at the hotel with us on many occasions. The license number of his car is M 3432 GH, a gray Opel Corsa. I check with previous entries and this is always different."

"Meaning that it's rented?"

"Almost certainly sir, yes." Alfonso's voice is very steady and I am surprised by his lack of anxiety. "He has a mobile telephone, Señor Chris, and I can also give you this number."

"Great. How did you get that?"

I close the bedroom door.

"Señor Sellini asks me for information about *puticlubs*. He likes to take girls back to the room. So he told me to ring him with information on the first night he arrived. The number is 625 218 521."

"A Spanish phone."

"I suppose. He is traveling under an Irish passport."

"Are you sure?"

"I am sure." This almost condescending. Perhaps the money has gone to his head. "The passport number is 450912826. But Mr. Sellini does not appear to me to be Irish. I have met many people in the course of my work and he is South American. His place of birth was Bogotá, Colombia, and his accent tells me this."

"Did you get a look at the passport?" From the sound of it, Saul is watching a trailer from the DVD extras. "Any visas? Any customs stamps?"

"No. It was handed back after registration. This is just information from our computer. He was born on December 28, 1949, if that is any help to you."

"Perhaps." I don't want to sound too grateful in case Alfonso puts his prices up. "Is there anything else you can tell me?"

There is the sound of more change being pumped into the pay phone, then a brief pause. The booth must be on a quiet street because I'm not picking up much in the way of background noise.

"Well, of course Mr. Sellini also left a credit-card imprint to confirm his reservation. A Visa card. But the information is in a part of our computer system that I am not permitted to access. Maybe you can find another way?"

"Maybe."

"The only other thing I can tell you is that he asked to switch rooms last Wednesday night because he thought it was too noisy. That's all, Señor Chris."

It wouldn't necessarily have occurred to the hotel management that Sellini might have been worried about audio surveillance.

"That's interesting. What room was he in before?"

"I do not know. I would have to check this."

I open the door as Saul walks past in the corridor carrying the empty plates from dinner. He looks at me, I smile back at him, and then indicate with my hand that the conversation will soon be over.

"If anything else comes up you can reach me at this number. And of course we can discuss the financial arrangements at our next meeting. I'd like to make them more permanent."

"*Vale,*" he says, without much enthusiasm. "*Adiós.*"

When I come back into the sitting room Saul has opened a second bottle of Ribera del Duero and rolled himself a joint. The picture on the television is frozen on the logo of Miramax International.

"Who was that?" he asks.

"Just business. Just a thing about Endiom."

"Julian?"

"No. Somebody else."

I sit on the floor.

"You all right down there?"

"Fine."

The opening credits start to roll. We probably won't speak any more because both of us hate it when people talk during movies. A woman is singing a slow lament set to piano on the sound track. Graphics slice through Matt Damon's head, revealing eyes, lips, mouth, and hair until finally we see him sitting on a bed alone in a small room. Then he begins to talk:

If I could just go back. If I could rub everything out, starting with myself.

And Saul says, "I know the feeling."

22

Barajas

He is touched that I go all the way to the airport with him, but I want to make sure that Saul boards a plane. His flight is delayed, so we drink coffee for an hour in the arrivals lounge and he buys me a paperback of *Ripley's Game,* in Spanish, at the newsagent. Later I see that Ripley's wife is called Heloise.

At the security checks we embrace briefly, but he continues to hold my arms when we break off.

"It's been good to see you, mate. Really good. I'm glad things have worked out. So just look after yourself, OK? Don't do anything stupid."

"I won't."

"You know what I mean. You're missed in London. Don't stay here for the rest of your life. This is not where you should be."

"I like it here."

"I know you do. It's a great country. And Madrid is a great city. But it's not home."

He releases my arms and picks up his bags one by one from the trolley.

"Saul?"

"Yes?"

I am about to apologize for all my suspicion, all my tricks and paranoia, but I don't have the guts. Instead I just say, "Good luck with everything," and he nods.

"Everything will be fine. We're still young, Alec. We can start again." He is grinning as he says this. "Don't you think that everyone deserves a second chance?"

"Absolutely. Have a good flight."

And as soon as he is gone, waving just once before passing through into departures, I feel a great sense of loss. How long will it be before we see one another again? How long before I can go home? I have to find a bar and order a whiskey to lift the gloom of sudden solitude. It feels as if I wasted his visit to Madrid, as if I misjudged Saul's intentions and kept him constantly at arm's length. He didn't leave just one day after getting back from Andalucía because of Heloise. He didn't leave because there was no connection with Julian or Arenaza. He left because something elementary in our relationship had shifted: what was once there is lost, and there was nothing Saul could do to get it back. The Alec he knew as a younger man is now a different creature, a creature whose true nature has been revealed. And if a friendship no longer gives you pleasure, then why remain loyal to that friend? Getting a cab back home I conclude that Saul will now move into a different phase of his life, just as I have done in mine. It's ridiculous, really, speeding along the motorway in the taxi and thinking that, in all probability, I will never see my oldest friend ever again.

23

Bonilla

When Bonilla cancels yet another scheduled meeting I begin to think that I may have been ripped off. Five hundred euros in cash, handed to Mar at Atocha station almost a week ago, and not a single piece of useful information to show for it. Cetro's entire weekend of surveillance turns up the following breathtaking facts: that Rosalía went to a party on Saturday evening dressed as a Bunny Girl; that she spoke to Gael for forty-five minutes on the telephone from the Delic café in Plaza de la Paja on Sunday morning; that she visited "a widow— almost certainly her mother" in Tres Cantos that same afternoon. Neither has Bonilla been able to find out anything about Abel Sellini. Instead he is cloyingly apologetic on the telephone as he explains that he must attend a funeral in Oviedo ("My wife's brother, he has died suddenly") before returning to Madrid on Thursday.

"But let's meet in person, Señor Thompson," he says. "I will take you to lunch at the Urogallo restaurant in Casa de Campo. This has been an interesting case. I always like the opportunity to meet a client in person."

Once a hunting ground for the Spanish royal family, the Casa de

Campo is now a vast area of protected land southwest of the old city overrun with prostitutes and mountain bikers. On an average evening in spring and summer, virtually every road running through the park from Pozuelo to downtown Madrid is jammed with curb-crawling Pedros looking for a backseat hand job or a fumble in the woods. It's a depressing sight: line after line of illegal immigrant girls from Africa, South America, and Eastern Europe, wandering into the headlights of oncoming cars, flashing their underwear, and then banging on the roofs of the vehicles as they pass them by. Urogallo is at the more respectable end of the park, one of several outdoor restaurants lining the southern edge of a lake where rowboats can be rented all year-round.

Bonilla calls to confirm the lunch early on Thursday morning and I know that he's not going to cancel again when he reminds me that I still owe him €1,600 for the weekend's surveillance.

"A check will be fine," he says, "although of course we prefer cash."

A two-stop metro ride takes me from Plaza de España to Lago station, from where it's just a short walk downhill to the restaurant. Urogallo has a large eating area set among a grove of plane trees looking out onto the lake, the jet fountain at its center bisecting a magnificent view of the city beyond. Bonilla has picked a table at the far side of a white marquee with flaps that can be raised and lowered according to the weather. It's a bright afternoon, the first sign of spring, so the tent is open to the elements. He recognizes me from a description provided by Mar but doesn't bother removing his €200 sunglasses as he shakes my hand.

"Señor Thompson. I'm finally happy to meet you."

Bonilla is younger than I expected, about thirty-eight, and in impressive physical condition, with inflated pectoral muscles visible through a black nylon T-shirt. Gym-honed biceps roam through his light white jacket and he has tightly cropped black hair, long narrow sideburns, and a very thin strip of beard that runs in a plumb line from the center of his lower lip to a tanned cleft chin. Looking at him for a split second, you might be reminded of a bar code.

"Let me start by apologizing for any of the inconvenience my organization may have caused you in terms of any canceled meetings," he says. "Maybe I can start by ordering you something from the bar, Mr. Thompson, a cocktail of some sort?"

It's two o'clock in the afternoon and we're sitting next to a polluted municipal lake, so there's something faintly ridiculous about the offer. Nevertheless I ask for a *fino manzanilla* and make small talk about the weather.

"Yes," Bonilla replies, gazing up at the sky as if dazzled by God's munificence. "It is a beautiful day, isn't it? Tell me, how long have you lived in Madrid?"

"About five years."

"And you plan to stay?"

"I plan to stay."

His manner is forced and oleaginous, not a single thing about him that one would trust or believe. He sports an artificial tan and enough cheap jewelry to stock a small flea market. I can hardly comprehend that I'm about to hand this guy a check for €1,600. He looks like an extra in *Carlito's Way*.

"I was sorry to hear about your brother-in-law. How was Oviedo?"

"Oh fine." Again, the polished white smile, the grin. Let's not allow a little death to stand in the way of lunch. "I did not particularly know him, but my wife of course is very upset."

"How long have you been married?"

"About three years. But there's still time for life, yes?"

Bonilla might as well have winked here. One side of his mouth curls into a reptilian sneer and he pops an olive onto his tongue. The waiter comes back with my sherry and we open up the menus. Both of us order *gazpacho* in honor of the decent weather, and I opt for *merluza a la plancha* as a main course. Bonilla is a red-meat man and wants his *solomillo* cooked *poco hecho* with an *ensalada mixta* on the side.

"Just kill the cow, wipe its ass, and bring it to the table," he says, laughing energetically at a joke I've heard before. Without consultation he then orders a bottle of red wine—in spite of the fact that I'm eating fish—before treating me to some of his opinions about border controls and immigration.

"These whores are disgusting," he says, gesturing behind him in the vague direction of the park. "Animals from Africa bringing AIDS to Spain."

"Wasn't AIDS here before?" I ask. He doesn't pick up on the sarcasm.

"Aznar lets in thousands of *putas* from Romania, from Hungary, from Russia. What are they good for but to ruin this country? They pay no tax, they steal, they are bad for the tourists."

"But you're Chilean."

The right pectoral appears to twitch.

"Of course."

"Well, a lot of these girls are from South America. . . ."

"Sure," he says, "but not from Chile, not from *Chile*." Bonilla leans back in his chair and actually wags a finger at me. All of this is perfectly normal behavior for a business lunch in Spain; just two hombres sizing each other up. His technique is to impose his personality as quickly as possible; mine is to sit there and watch him get on with it. "These girls are from Brazil, Mr. Thompson, from Argentina and Colombia, not from my country. We don't have the same economic difficulties in Chile."

"Of course not. When did you emigrate?"

"My parents were forced to leave after the coup that removed Allende."

"So you were educated over here?"

"In the south of Spain, yes."

We then spend the next quarter of an hour talking about Nixon and Kissinger ("Chile had her own 9/11, you know. A benign Communist state fucked up the arse by the Republican Party"), a period which allows Bonilla to exercise his vigorous contempt for all things American. I hear him out, aware that my sole purpose today is to discover the truth about Rosalía's link to Arenaza without revealing anything of my relationship with Mikel. To that end, I need to encourage a candor in Bonilla, a candor that would be snuffed out by seeming argumentative or asking too many awkward questions. It is always best to flatter the vain man.

"And what do you do, Mr. Thompson?"

"I'm a screenwriter. In actual fact I'm currently working on a story about al-Qaeda. But enough about me. How did you become a detective?"

And this leads to twenty minutes of tall tales about Bonilla's past as a member of the Guardia Civil in Alicante.

"Of course, I knew a lot of girls," he says, the waiter spooning croutons and chopped onion into his flesh-pink bowl of gazpacho. "The uniform, it gets them wet, yes?"

I laugh in all the right places, nod when the conversation becomes more serious, appear dazzled by the sophistication of his work as a private eye. It is what might best be described as a feminine approach to the task at hand, a means of withdrawing into the shadows as Bonilla strides out into the light. A pattern emerges in his conversation, a habit of telling stories in which third-party players are routinely criticized with the intention of portraying himself in the most flattering possible light. Men who have lived alone for some time often display the same characteristic, and I begin to wonder if Bonilla is either profoundly insecure and unhappy or perhaps even lying about having a wife and children. Some of his stories don't add up and there are strange discrepancies in his descriptions of home. Eventually I manage to steer the conversation toward the subject of Rosalía Dieste. By this point the main course plates have been stacked and hauled away and for the first time he looks unsure of what to say. Two paramedics wearing orange jackets have settled at the table next to ours and he says, "You're happy talking about this here?"

It's obvious that he has nothing to tell me. That's why there's been a two-course delay. Now he wants to use the paramedics as an excuse not to carry on with the briefing.

"I'm happy," I tell him. "I don't see a problem."

There is a large, visible intake of breath. Leaning over, Bonilla lifts a battered briefcase from the ground and extracts a worryingly slim file. The sunglasses come off, a pen appears from his jacket pocket, and he rolls up the sleeves of his jacket like Tubbs in *Miami Vice*.

"Rosalía Dieste . . . Rosalía Dieste."

"Yes."

"Well, we must confess that she was not an easy assignment for us. Not easy at all."

So effortless the slip into the plural. Collective rather than personal responsibility.

"I see."

"We were constricted by not knowing the exact nature of your inquiry."

"I don't understand. I explained to Mar—"

"Yes of course you did, of course you did." A pause. "But the exact *nature.*"

A teenage girl strolls past the restaurant and, like a tracking shot, Bonilla scopes her nodding breasts all the way to the edge of the lake.

"Eduardo?"

"*Sí?*"

"I explained to Mar what I wanted. Deep background. Previous relationships. Some information about Plettix and Gael. I thought I made it clear."

Thick lips bulge in thought. There is a moment of reflection before some of the poise and self-assurance returns to his face. He taps the file, mutters the word "Gael," and begins searching for a piece of paper. There cannot be more than twenty pages contained within the folder's narrow cardboard flaps, but it is some time before he has found it.

"Gael and Rosalía met on holiday two years ago," he announces finally. "At the Parador in Cáceres." The waiter comes back and takes an order for coffee. I ask for a cigar to buy more time. "He was away on a business trip to Lyons this weekend."

"I knew that. What's his job?"

"Gael Marchena works for a small French pharmaceutical company called Marionne. The headquarters are based near Tours. He trained as a chemist at a university in Paris and was recruited after graduation."

"He's French?"

Bonilla has to look that one up.

"Spanish."

One of the paramedics looks over and I wonder if I have underestimated the surveillance threat. Bonilla scratches his neck.

"Rosalía and Gael have lived together at an apartment in Calle de Jiloca for under one year now." He is still reading from the file. "The rent is shared, they pay by a regular monthly *transferencia* from Gael's bank account with the BBVA. He is under a lot of pressure from his family to be married." A strangled laugh.

"You listen to his telephone conversations?"

"I cannot necessarily reveal the source of my information." This appears to be a small moment of triumph for Bonilla and he celebrates by putting his sunglasses back on. "I have a telephone record of all calls made from Señorita Dieste's landline at Calle Jiloca." He passes a Telefónica bill across the table. The paramedics are making a lot of noise, laughing and joking and raising glasses over the table. "If you were concerned about an infidelity, Señor Thompson, my experience tells me people are using a secret mobile telephone that their partner knows nothing about. We have been able to trace only one mobile belonging to Rosalía, and the results were completely normal."

"Just calls to friends, calls to Plettix?"

"Exactly."

"And e-mail?"

"Nothing."

"No strange Internet activity? No private accounts with Yahoo, Hotmail, Wanadoo?"

He shakes his head. An insect lands on my arm and I flick it away.

"No."

"And what about her past? Her education, previous relationships?"

The coffee comes, with a tubed Romeo y Julieta cigar proffered on a small white plate. It may be simply my characteristic paranoia, but I have a developing sense of anxiety that Bonilla is about to mention Mikel by name. Either that, or his whole approach is a charade designed to lure me into confession. If he reads the papers or watches the television news, he will know about Arenaza's disappearance. Any evidential link with Rosalía and there's a significant chance that he will have already alerted the police.

"Again you asked us to look into this for you and we discovered nothing of consequence. Miss Dieste had a boyfriend for three years at the Universidad Politécnica de Madrid . . ."

". . . Called?"

Bonilla checks his notes. "Javier Arjona. But he moved to the US in 1999."

"And no pseudonyms?"

"No pseudonyms."

"Dieste took one year in the United States at the University of Illinois. After that, she returned to Madrid, completed her degree, and went directly to France to complete postgraduate study in *energía nuclear*."

"Nuclear energy? Where?"

"The *tesis* was at the INSTN. That lasted for two years. Then more postdoctorate work at the Argonne Laboratoire Nationale. I have to say that my impression of her is as a very focused, very hardworking, and ambitious person, what we sometimes call in Spanish *una empollona*."

It's a word I have not heard before, which Bonilla loosely translates as a "geek." Three South American musicians hove into view and start to set up operations about ten feet away from our table. The tallest of them, a battered-looking accordion slung over his embroidered white shirt, steps forward to greet the assembled diners with an accent that sounds Peruvian. Across the restaurant, a lone balding businessman looks down into his plate and groans. He knows what's coming. Now the drum machine starts up, attached to a powerful battery-powered amplifier, and before long we are treated to the first bars of "My Way" played at astonishing volume.

"Oh Christ."

"You don't like this music?" Bonilla is grinning.

"I was just enjoying the peace and quiet." I drop the head of the cigar onto the ground and light the end very slowly. "What else have you found out? Nothing from the weekend? Just this Bunny Girl party? Just brunch at Delic?"

"I am afraid so, Señor Thompson. I am afraid so. Why you want to know about her? What is your interest?"

I have to give him something. It's becoming a problem.

"She may have been having an affair behind Gael's back. With the husband of a friend of mine. It's a delicate situation."

"Really? Who? What was his name?"

Bonilla seems excited.

"I would rather not say. He's from a well-known family in Spain and he doesn't want any scandal."

"So it is the husband who hired you?"

"That's right."

Bonilla is bound to see through this, but it's the best I've got. "He wants to know how serious she is. Whether she intends to leave Gael or if she's just after his money."

"He is rich, your friend?"

"Very."

"I see. And where does he live?"

"In the Basque country."

Bonilla almost splits his jacket. "In the Basque country? *Joder*."

"You look shocked."

"No. It's just not something we were able to discover. Mar I think checked all the numbers for source and not one of them originated in San Sebastián."

I feel an awful lurch of shock, oddly close to betrayal. Bonilla has slipped up. He knows something.

"Why did you say San Sebastián? How do you know where my friend lives?"

He looks baffled.

"I didn't. Is that his home?" A consummate impression of innocence registers across his face, no blushing, no telltale covering of the nose or mouth. A man suspected of lying who has done no wrong. "I just mention it by coincidence. It's the city I associate with the Basque country. I have been there and I do not like Bilbao. Too much industry. San Sebastián is beautiful, no?"

For a moment I do not know whether to carry on. I should have gone to the police weeks ago and saved myself all this trouble and money. If Arenaza is dead and Bonilla knows about his relationship with Rosalía, I could be accused of conspiring to pervert the course of justice. But if the slip really was just coincidence, I have €1,600 riding on the rest of this conversation.

"There was just one other thing," Bonilla says, so calm and relaxed it seems impossible to believe that he might be setting me up.

"And what's that?"

"We are assuming that you know about Rosalía's family? About her stepfather?"

"No."

He is looking at my cigar, following the smoke as it drifts in thick puffs toward the roof of the marquee.

"It cannot probably be important because it was very long ago, but it was the only thing of significance in the investigation. I found out this morning."

"Yes?"

"When Rosalía was six, her father died from liver failure. He was apparently a *borracho,* a drunk." This seems to amuse Bonilla, who finishes the last of the red wine before leaning back in his chair. "Her mother, the woman she visited in Tres Cantos at the weekend, went on to marry a member of the Guardia Civil in Madrid. His name was Pasqual Vicente. He became—how would you say it?—a substitute father to Rosalía, and to her brother, Adolfo. But he was particularly close to the girl."

"How do you know this?"

"I find the interviews. The police reports."

"Police reports? I'm not following."

"Vicente was blown up by an ETA car bomb in 1983. Close to the Chamartín station. Killed alongside a colleague in the Guardia Civil. You look surprised, Mr. Thompson. You start to look pale. Is everything all right?"

24

El Cochinillo

It was a honey trap. I allowed the simplicity of Rosalía's deceit to obscure the truth about Arenaza's disappearance. She posed as his lover, lured him to Madrid, and—most probably—Sellini did the rest. Walking in the Casa de Campo after Bonilla has paid the bill, taken my check, and left, I put the pieces together with ease. Mikel's death was revenge for the stepfather's murder, pure and simple. It's time the police knew about that. It's time to call Patxo Zulaika.

Back at the flat I find his phone number and dial it just after five o'clock in the afternoon. A full confession to Goena is not an option: instead, I will tell Zulaika that Mikel briefly mentioned he had a mistress called Natalia or Rosalía in Madrid who worked as a lawyer or industrial engineer. It was something he said over dinner that completely slipped my mind. A guy as professional as Patxo should be able to put the pieces together based on these simple clues. Unless Bonilla already knows the whole story. Unless he has already gone to the cops.

But Zulaika isn't answering his phone. According to a message in crackled Basque and Spanish, he will be out of the office until Monday. He doesn't leave a contact number but suggests calling one of his colleagues at *Ahotsa* "in the event of an emergency."

Hello, Mr. Zulaika. This is Alec Milius. You may recall that we spoke about Mikel Arenaza's disappearance when you were in Madrid a couple of weeks ago. It may not be important, but I've remembered something that could be interesting for you. Would you give me a call when you get this message? *Gracias.*

Sure enough, the Internet is choked with stories about the Chamartín bomb. Pasqual Vicente was a thirty-four-year-old Guardia Civil, respected and well liked by his colleagues, intelligent and ambitious and clearly going places with his career. He was called to the railway station on the morning of June 6, 1983, to investigate a petty theft. He arrived in a squad car with his partner, Pablo Aguirre, and spent about an hour interviewing a woman who claimed that her bag had been stolen from a café on the station concourse. It later transpired that the woman—who disappeared—had given a false name and that no such theft had occurred. Instead, the absence of the two police officers from their car gave three ETA operatives time to attach an explosive device to the chassis. When Vicente turned the key in the ignition, the entire vehicle was blown apart, killing both of them instantly and injuring a number of passers-by. Rosalía Dieste was eleven. Her brother was eight. Their mother, already widowed once, had to bury a second husband before she was forty years old.

The next day, to clear my thoughts, I take a drive out to Segovia and eat *cochinillo* for lunch at Mesón de Cándido, the city's best-known restaurant, situated below the aqueduct at Plaza de Azoguejo. It's about an hour's drive northwest of Madrid, quicker than it used to be now that they've extended the motorway, and it feels good to be free of the city, just strolling around the cathedral, the Plaza Mayor, and the Alcázar. Zulaika must be away on holiday because he hasn't rung back. Once he returns my call on Monday I can begin to put the whole Arenaza episode behind me and maybe think about going home to London. I can't afford to become associated with a murder inquiry, particularly one with links to an organization like ETA. It was stupid of me to get sucked back into this world. As if unable to escape from a drug whose effects first ensnared me as long ago as 1995, I could not see a way of ignoring what had happened to Mikel. The possibilities seemed too great, the chances for excitement too much for me to resist. And now, for the second time in my life, I have blood on my hands. First Kate, now Arenaza. The secret world betrays me. To hold out any hope of salvation I have to cut myself off from it entirely.

But then Alfonso, the concierge at the Hotel Carta, rings the Telefónica mobile with a piece of information that immediately tests my resolve.

"Señor Thompson?"

"Sí, Alfonso. Qué tal?"

"Abel Sellini is checking out."

"Checking out?"

"Sí. Five minutes ago he stopped to talk to me in the lobby and asked for a taxi to take him to Barajas airport at five fifteen."

That's in just under two hours.

"OK. Thanks for letting me know."

In truth, I don't even consider the consequences of not continuing my surveillance. You might as well ask me to cut off an arm. I am designed for this.

"Did he say where he was going?"

"No, sir. I just thought you might want to know."

At the very least I can tail Sellini to the airport, find out what flight he's on, try to work out a final destination. That is the sort of information that would be useful to the police. This is the individual, after all, who most probably murdered Mikel Arenaza. I have a responsibility to follow him. A duty.

So I sprint in bright sunshine from the cathedral all the way down the eastern edge of Segovia to the space where I parked the car off Plaza de Azoguejo. It's about a half-mile run, and by the time I have unlocked the doors and thrown my coat in the back of the Audi my body is drenched in sweat. There are lines of traffic at every set of lights leading out of the city, but I horn and barge and cut my way to the front of the queues and make it out onto the *carretera* by ten to four. By five, having driven at a steady 170 kph all the way home, I'm passing through Moncloa. With luck I should be outside the Carta within a quarter of an hour.

"Has he left yet?" I ask Alfonso in Spanish, dialing his mobile from a set of lights on Gran Vía.

"Sí, Señor Chris," he says, sounding rushed and anxious. "He came downstairs five minutes ago to pay his bill. He asked me to have the taxi waiting and I don't know what to do. There's a rank directly outside. There are always cars there. I will have to go down and flag one."

"Well, at least get me the license plate. At least try and stall him. Have a chat before he leaves and ask where he's going. I'll be there in less than ten minutes."

As it turns out, I'm there in five and park the Audi in a slot immediately behind the taxi rank, about fifty meters short of the slope leading up to the hotel. Alfonso isn't answering his phone and there's no sign of Sellini. I walk slowly up toward the lobby doors, prepared at any moment for either one of them to emerge. A second porter, whom I don't recognize, is operating the main door and I walk past him into the lobby. Sellini and Alfonso are engaged in conversation near reception. Alfonso looks up, registers my presence with a shift in the eyes, and then proceeds to drag a trolley laden with luggage out through the main entrance. Turning away from them, I walk back outside and down the slope toward the Audi. There are two cabs on the rank and the chances are that Sellini will get the first of them. Then it will just be a simple question of following him out to Barajas.

But there's a problem. Looking back down the street I see that a silver-gray Citroën C5 has double-parked beside my Audi, completely boxing it in. The hazard lights on the Citroën are flashing but there is no sign of the driver. If Sellini leaves now, I will not be able to follow him. Alfonso is coming down the ramp behind me and he hails the first of the two cabs, which leaves its station and drives quickly up the slope toward the entrance of the hotel. Then, just as I have made the decision to abandon my car and follow by cab, a man wearing a pin-striped suit steps into the back of the second taxi and drives off.

Why did I think I recognized him?

This is now serious. Turning to face the oncoming traffic I begin a desperate search for another taxi. Two come past, both occupied. If the driver of the Citroën doesn't appear in the next thirty seconds I will lose Sellini. He may not even be going to Barajas; he may have told that to Alfonso simply to set a false trail. His cab is coming down the slope from the entrance of the hotel and preparing to make a right-hand turn north along the Castellana. Sunlight reflects off the back windows but I can still make out his slumped silhouette. As he pulls out, I open the driver's door of the Audi and press on the horn, more in anger than in expectation, but still the driver of the Citroën does not appear. Another full cab whips past as Sellini's disappears into the distance. The sound of my horn is deafening, long blasts followed by short, incensed bursts that begin to draw stares from passers-by.

At last a pedestrian comes ambling up the pavement dangling a set of car keys in his left hand. Relaxed and oblivious. This must be him. I release the horn and stare as he makes guilty eye contact and quickens his step. He's about my age, with brown hair and puffy, freckled skin, wearing jeans and a white cotton shirt. At first glance I would say that he is a British tourist but I speak to him initially in Spanish.

"*Ese es tu coche?*"

He doesn't respond.

"Hey. I said is this your car?"

Now he looks up and it's clear from his expression that he failed to understand what I was saying. To avoid a confrontation he may walk past and pretend that the Citroën does not belong to him. I won't let him get away with that.

"Do you speak English?"

"Yes I do." The accent takes me by surprise. British public school with the privilege stripped out of it. BBC. Foreign Office.

"I think this is your car. I think you blocked me in." We are facing one another on the pavement just a few feet apart, and something about the man's level gaze and apparent lack of concern for my predicament serves only to deepen my sense of anger.

"What seems to be the problem?" he says. The question is just this side of sarcastic.

"The problem is that you blocked me in. The problem is that you prevented me from doing my job."

"Your *job*?"

He says the word with a slight edge of ridicule, as if he knows that it's a lie.

"That's right. My job. So do you want to move? Can you get your car the fuck out of my way? What you did was illegal and stupid and I need to get going."

"Why don't you calm down, Alec?"

He might as well have dropped a low punch into my stomach. I feel winded. I look into the man's face for some distant trigger of recognition—Was he a student at LSE? Did we go to school together?—but I have never seen this person before in my life.

"How do you know that? How do you know who I am?"

"I know a lot of things about you. I know about JUSTIFY, I know about Abnex. I know about Fortner, I know about Katharine. What I don't know is what the hell Alec Milius is doing in Madrid. So why don't we hop in the back of my car, go for a little drive, and you can tell me all about it."

25

Our Man in Madrid

"Before I get into anybody's car, I want to know who the hell I'm talking to."

"Let's just say that you're talking to a Friend," he says, employing a standard SIS euphemism. A woman walks past us and looks at me with a twist of worry in her face. "Better if you keep your voice down, no? Now let's get in the car and head off."

Once inside he frisks me—shins, calves, back of the waist—and seems to take a perverse pleasure in asking me to fasten my seat belt. I try to summon a suitably hostile look to meet this request, but the heat of sweat and panic I can feel in my face has stripped me of any authority. I drag the seat belt down and clunk it into place.

"My name is Richard Kitson." On closer inspection he looks nearer to forty than thirty, with a face that I would struggle to describe: neither ugly nor good-looking, neither smart nor stupid. A vanishing Englishman. "Why don't we head up to the M30 and drive around in circles while you tell me what's on your mind?"

For the first couple of minutes I say nothing. Occasionally Kitson's eyes will slide toward mine, a sudden glance in traffic, a more steady gaze at lights. I try to stare back, to meet these looks man to man, but the shock of what has happened appears to have robbed me of even the most basic defensive reflexes. After six years on the run, it has finally come to this. I am shaking. But why was Sellini involved? What did he have to do with it?

"What's your interest in Abel Sellini?" Kitson asks, as if reading my mind. "You buying drugs, Alec? Acquiring some weapons?"

"Excuse me?"

"You don't know who he is?"

"I know that he probably killed a friend of mine."

"Well, you see, that's exactly the sort of thing you and I need to talk about."

"You first. What are you doing here? How do you know who I am? How do you know about JUSTIFY?"

"One thing at a time, one thing at a time." A black BMW overtakes us on the blind side, gliding past my window. Kitson mutters, "Bloody Spanish drivers."

"OK. One: how do you know my name?"

"Took a photo. Pinged it back to London. You were recognized by a colleague."

Jesus. So I was right about the surveillance. In a simultaneous instant of horrifying clarity I recall exactly where I saw the man in the pinstriped suit who got into the cab. At the Prado. With Sofía. *Lead on, Macduff.*

"How long have you been following me?"

"Since Friday last week."

The night I tailed Rosalía to the Irish Rover.

"And this colleague who recognized me, what was his name?"

If Kitson doesn't come up with something I recognize, I can assume he's an impostor.

"Christopher Sinclair. Chris to his friends. Happened to be passing a desk in Legoland when your photo popped up. Nearly dropped his cappuccino. Sends his regards, by the way. Sounded very fond of you."

Sinclair was Lithiby's stooge. The one who drove me to the final meeting at the safe house in London on the night they killed Kate.

Said that he admired me. Said that he thought I was going to be all right.

"So you've read my file? That's how you know about JUSTIFY?"

"Of course. Ran your name through the system and got *War and Peace*. Well, *Crime and Punishment,* anyway." Kitson has an irritatingly supercilious sense of humor, as if he would be incapable of taking anyone, or anything, too seriously. "Quite a story, hadn't heard it before. You had them in knots for a while, Alec, and then you did the runner. Nobody knew where the hell you'd gone. There were rumors of Paris, rumors of Petersburg and Milan. Nobody pinned you to Madrid until last Tuesday."

I do not know whether to be offended that Kitson had never heard of me or delighted that six years of antisurveillance has paid off. I am generally too shaken and confused. "And that's why you're here? To bring me in?"

Kitson frowns and glances in the rearview mirror. "What?"

"I said, is that why you're here? To bring me in?"

"Bring you in?" He takes the first exit onto the M30, heading clockwise toward Valencia, looking at the road ahead as if I am delusional. "Alec, that was all a long, long time ago. Water under the bridge. You haven't made any waves, you haven't been a problem. You kept your end of the bargain, we kept ours."

"You mean you had Kate Allardyce murdered?"

There is a moment of silence as he weighs his options. He must know about Kate, unless they covered it up. It occurs to me that our conversation is almost certainly being recorded.

"You were wrong about that," he says finally. His voice is very quiet, very firm. "Quite wrong. John Lithiby wanted me to make it clear. What happened to your girlfriend was an accident, end of story. The driver was drunk. The Office, the Cousins, neither one of us had anything to do with it."

"Total bullshit." I stare outside as an endless sequence of concrete apartment blocks, road bridges, and trees flick past. Someone has hung a banner over the motorway scrawled with the black slogan ETA—NON! "You don't know the full story. They don't *want* you to know the full story. The Yanks had her killed and Elworthy was told to cover it up."

"Peter Elworthy is dead."

"*Dead?* How?"

"Liver cancer. Two years ago."

I have been away so long.

"Then ask Chris Sinclair. He knows what really went on."

"I don't need to. I have the proof." Kitson's response here is quick and well rehearsed. He moves into a slower lane of traffic as if to emphasize the seriousness of what he is about to tell me. "When we have the opportunity I can show you the accident report. There were people at the party who urged Kate not to get into the car. Her friend— William, was it?—had done a lot of Colombian marching powder and drunk his way through the best part of two bottles of wine. He was a twenty-three-year-old idiot, pure and simple, and he got the girl killed."

"Don't talk about Kate like that, OK? Don't even begin. If there was alcohol or drugs in Will's bloodstream, they were put there by the CIA. It was a standard cover-up operation to protect the special fucking relationship. They tampered with the brakes and a car drove Kate and Will off the road. End of story."

Kitson remains silent for a long time. He knows that what he has said has both angered and upset me. He probably knows, too, that I want to believe him. Alec Milius was once a patriot who thought that his government didn't kill people for political convenience. Alec Milius wants to be brought back in.

"So why are you interested in Sellini?" We are south of Las Ventas by now, the sky beginning to darken and headlights coming on all around us. I don't want the conversation to founder on Kate's death. Not yet. "What's this about him selling drugs and weapons?"

"Abel Sellini doesn't exist." Kitson takes a cigarette from a packet of Lucky Strikes on the dashboard and invites me to help myself, lighting his own as I decline. "It's a nom de guerre. Sellini's real name is Luis Felipe Buscon. He was a former fighter for the Portuguese Secret Service, served in Angola, now an international hired hand with more pies than fingers. Mr. Big of no fixed address, operates as a middleman for any criminal or terrorist organization that can afford to put him up in nice hotels like the Villa Carta. We've been tracking him ever since we were tipped off about a consignment of illegal arms he'd purchased from an organized crime group operating out of Croatia."

For Six to be involved, that consignment must be on its way to the British Isles. But how does Rosalía fit in?

"Tipped off by whom?"

Kitson glances across at me and says, "That information was brought to us by a protected source. Now, what's your interest in him?"

"Not yet. I need to know more. I need to know why I was being followed and why you've pulled me in."

It is hard to tell if Kitson is impressed by this show of stubbornness, but he answers the question with a candor that would suggest he trusts me and knows that I'm instinctively on the side of the angels.

"I'm here as part of an undeclared SIS op tracking Buscon. Local liaison knows nothing about it, so if they find out, I'll know who to blame." I get a scolding, smoke-exhaling stare with this remark, a switch in Kitson's demeanor that is actually frightening. "The Mick and the Croat get along like a house on fire. Always have. Call it a shared antipathy toward their neighbors. For the Irish, the bloody Brits; for the Croats, the murdering Serbs. So they have lots in common, lots to talk about over a pint of Guinness. We had a tip-off that Buscon had become involved in what was euphemistically described as a humanitarian project in Split. Only Luis wasn't interested in feeding the poor. What he *was* interested in was the consignment of weapons sitting in a hay shed in the ultranationalist hinterland that wasn't being put to suitably romantic use. So, on behalf of the Real IRA, he ordered a takeaway."

"And now the weapons are here in Spain? In Madrid? They've gone missing?"

"Again, I'm not at liberty to discuss that. All I can say is that Buscon has contacts in organized crime groups with structures all over Europe. These weapons could be on their way to the Albanian Mafia, the Turks in London, the Russians, the Chinese. Worst-case scenario, we're talking about an Islamist cell with enough high explosive to blow the door of 10 Downing Street into Berkshire."

"Fuck."

"Quite. Which is why we need to know what you were doing listening in on Mr. Buscon's conversation with Rosalía Dieste at the Irish Rover last Friday."

"You were there?"

"We were there. Had command of Buscon and couldn't tell if you were liaison or just a lonely tourist who liked Bon Jovi."

"Where were you sitting?"

"Not too far away. We had ears at the table, hours of prep, but the mike failed at the last minute. I was actually rather jealous of your proximity. Not to mention anxious to find out who the hell you were."

"And the two guys outside in the green Seat Ibiza? They were A4?"

Kitson accidentally swerves the car here and has to check his steering. "Very good, Alec," he says. "Very good. You've done this before."

"And the older man who took the second cab at the hotel? Gray hair, pin-striped suit. He was tailing me at the Prado last weekend."

"Quite possibly. Quite possibly."

Kitson likes me. I can sense it. He hadn't expected such a level of expertise. My file is most probably wretched, Shayleresque, but this is pedigree.

"So what were you doing there? What's your relationship with the girl?"

"I think she might be involved in the murder of a politician from the Basque country. Mikel Arenaza. A member of Herri Batasuna."

"The political wing of ETA?"

"Exactly."

"Never heard of him." Kitson's reply is blunt, but you can tell the brain is already running through the implications. ETA. Real IRA. Weapons that have gone missing.

"Arenaza disappeared on March 6, a little over three weeks ago." Without asking, I help myself to one of the dashboard cigarettes and push the lighter. "You didn't read about it in the papers?"

"Well, we've all been rather busy . . ."

"Rosalía was Arenaza's mistress. As far as I can tell, nobody else knows that piece of information. He was married and didn't want his wife finding out."

"Understandable in the circumstances. So why did he tell you?"

"Why does anybody tell anyone anything? Booze. Camaraderie. Mine's bigger than yours." The lighter pops and I take the first delicious draw on the cigarette. "Mikel and I were supposed to meet for a drink when he was in Madrid visiting Rosalía. Only he never showed up. I found out where she worked, followed her to the Irish Rover, and witnessed the conversation with Buscon. It looked important, so I followed him back to the hotel."

"Where you bribed Alfonso González."

"How do you know about that?"

"You're not the only one on his books, Alec." Kitson clears his throat to suffocate a smile. "Señor González has made enough money out of the pair of us in the past couple of weeks to buy himself a small villa in the Algarve."

"So you instructed him to make that call today? You set the whole thing up?"

"What can I say? Her Majesty had more leverage. Now tell me what you know about the girl."

I pause briefly, absorbing the fact that Alfonso betrayed me, but it makes no sense to get annoyed. Suddenly my doubts about Arenaza's disappearance, the long days and nights tailing Rosalía, the money spent on surveillance, all of it appears to have paid off. I am right back at the center of things. And the feeling is electrifying.

"Rosalía Dieste is thirty-four. She lives with her boyfriend in an apartment about half a mile east of the Bernabéu. . . ."

"We know that."

"She trained as an industrial engineer, specializing in nuclear energy."

"Nuclear energy?"

"You weren't aware of that?"

"No."

"You think it might be important?"

"Possibly. I'm going to need all of this on paper." Kitson checks his blind spot and coughs. What I'm telling him is clearly new and useful. "We're going to need you to come in and write everything down. Is that all right?"

So the conversation isn't being recorded. "That's fine." The M30 passes under a ruined stone bridge and we are briefly slowed in traffic. Up to the right I can see the outline of the Vicente Calderón. The night air above the stadium is floodlit; Atlético must be playing at home. "Rosalía left her job just a few days after Arenaza arrived in Madrid. There's no physical evidence linking the two of them, not even a record of any phone calls, but I'm convinced she's the girl Mikel was talking about."

"How do you know about phone records?"

"Because I paid somebody to look into her background." As if this was an entirely natural course of action, Kitson merely nods and accelerates into a faster lane. He seems to be adjusting to the pace of Spanish roads, growing in confidence even as our own journey progresses. "The investigators discovered that Rosalía's stepfather was murdered by ETA in a car-bomb attack in 1983. He was a policeman, she was very fond of him. It's obvious to me that she lured Arenaza to Madrid . . ."

". . . to avenge his death, yes." Kitson has made the link. "So what does that have to do with Buscon?"

"I haven't the faintest idea."

"What does your instinct tell you?"

"My instinct tells me not to trust my instinct." The man from SIS likes this remark and laughs quietly through his nose. "All I can assume is that she hired him to kill Arenaza."

"Very unlikely."

"Why?"

"Not the sort of thing Luis gets up to. Far too self-important to get his hands dirty. More likely there's a separate, unrelated link between the two of them, or she's part of a broader conspiracy. This is all very useful, Alec. I'm very grateful to you."

It sounds like the brush-off. We're going to circle back to Plaza de España and I'll never see him again.

"I don't want to be left out," I tell him, suddenly concerned that I have spilled too much information too quickly and may have nothing left with which to bargain. "I want to pursue this thing, Richard. I think I can help."

Kitson says nothing. He might be irritated that I have called him Richard.

"Where are you staying?"

"I'm here with a team of eight," he says.

"Tech-op boys? Locksmiths?"

I want to show him that I know the lingo. I want to prove my usefulness.

"Something like that. We've rented a property in Madrid for the duration of the op, an RV point well away from the action." As if the thought had just occurred to him, he adds, "How come the Spaniards don't know about Rosalía? If this man's been missing for three weeks, shouldn't you have gone to the police?"

It is an uncomfortable question, and one designed perhaps to turn the tables. Is he going to use that as a means of guaranteeing my silence?

"I only found out about the ETA connection on Thursday." Kitson appears to accept this, despite the fact that I have completely avoided the question. "On Monday a Basque journalist who's working on the disappearance is going to call me and I'm going to give him the whole story."

"I wouldn't recommend that." This is said very firmly. "I can't risk a hack digging around Buscon. Host governments don't take kindly to us lot carving up the local scenery. This journalist calls back, put him off the scent, stall him. The last thing I need is blowback."

It is the first time that I have sensed Kitson even remotely rattled. He takes an exit signed out to Badajoz and tucks in behind a red Transit van. Here is the stress of the spy, the variables, the constant threat of exposure. To lead a team on foreign soil in such circumstances must be exhausting.

"Point taken. But Zulaika is pushy, he sniffs around. Of all the newspapers in Spain, *Ahotsa* is the one that has kept the Arenaza story alive."

"Zulaika? That's his name?"

"Yes. Patxo Zulaika. Very young, very ambitious. Real tit."

Kitson smirks. "Then ignore him. Just give him denials. You're clearly a resourceful bloke, Alec. You'll think of something."

"Sure."

"Just keep me in the picture when he calls, OK? I'll leave you my number."

Thereafter the conversation turns to the affidavit. Kitson needs a written statement detailing my involvement with Arenaza, Buscon, and Rosalía. He asks me to type it up overnight and says we'll meet tomorrow for a handover at the McDonald's in Plaza de los Cubos.

"Nine o'clock too early for you? We can enjoy a hearty breakfast."

I say that will be fine and only as we are pulling into Plaza de España does he return to discussing the operation.

"There was just one thing, before you vanish into the night."

"Yes?"

I am standing outside the Citroën, leaning in through the passenger window. It is the middle of the paseo and there are seemingly hundreds of people passing through the western end of Gran Vía, families walking six wide on the pavements in order to show off their grandchildren.

"Does the name Francisco Sá Carneiro mean anything to you?"

"Francisco Sá Carneiro?"

"We think there's some sort of a connection with Buscon. We think he was going to meet him."

I can't prevent a smirk wriggling onto my face. To have caught out Six on such a simple technicality. This answer can only work in my favor.

"Buscon's not going to meet anybody," I tell him.

"He's not?"

"He's going to Porto. Sá Carneiro was a Portuguese politician. He died about twenty years ago. They named the airport after him. I'll see you tomorrow, Richard. Make mine an Egg McMuffin."

26

Sacrifice

As it turns out, we meet for only five minutes. Kitson shakes my hand near a lifesize cutout of Ronald McDonald, takes the brown manila envelope in which I have placed my affidavit, and leaves with the excuse that he has a "pressing engagement" in Huertas. It's obvious that Five and Six have warned him off me. I'm damaged goods, after all, persona non grata on a par with Rimington, Tomlinson, and Shayler. You get one chance with these guys and, if you blow it, there's no going back. It's club rules, the only way they know how to operate.

I eat breakfast at Cáscaras and wait all week for Zulaika's call. When he doesn't contact me, I begin to fear the worst. Either he has become another victim of Buscon, or Kitson panicked about his interest in the operation and arranged for half a dozen Bilbao heavies to put him off the scent. As the days go by, it begins to feel as though my encounter with the secret world has come to an abrupt end, like an old love affair briefly rekindled, then all too hurriedly snuffed out. But eventually Zulaika makes contact. At 8 A.M. sharp on the morning of Monday, April 7, ten days after I left my initial message, he rings the Nokia mobile. What is it about Zulaika and early mornings?

I am fast asleep in bed and reach across to retrieve the phone from my jacket pocket, straining my back in the process.

His name appears on the screen and I buy time by letting him leave a message:

Yes, this is Patxo Zulaika for Alec Milius, returning his call. I have been away on holiday and did not take my work phone with my family. Please call me at this number as soon as possible, your information could be important.

The voice is just as I remembered it—flat, smug, entitled—and acts as an immediate irritant. Interesting that he took a fortnight's holiday in the middle of the Arenaza disappearance. There have been extensive antiwar protests throughout the Basque country, which he would also have wanted to cover. Perhaps he has given up on the story, or been moved on to something new. I prepare my response, settle down on the sofa with a cup of strong black coffee, and call him just after ten o'clock.

"Mr. Zulaika?"

"Yes?"

"This is Alec Milius."

"I was hoping you would contact me sooner. You said that you had some information."

That same infuriating manner, devoid of even basic decency, every sentence managing to be both critical and pushy at the same time. I feel immediately predisposed to thwart him and experience a wave of gratitude to Kitson for providing me with the opportunity to do so.

"And good morning to you, too, Patxo."

He doesn't understand the sarcasm.

"*Qué?*"

"Nothing. I was just saying 'Good morning.' You always seem so keen to get down to business. Always in a hurry."

"Well fine, I am busy, perhaps this explains it. So what was it that you remembered?"

"Well, it may not be of any use, but let me see." I draw out the pause for effect, as if preparing to divulge information of over-whelming national importance. "At one point in the evening with Mr. Arenaza he started talking about Basque cuisine. I'd been to the Arzak restaurant just outside San Sebastián for a business lunch, you see, and eaten perhaps the finest food I'd tasted . . ."

"Yes, yes . . ."

"Anyway, I'm fairly sure that Arenaza said he was fond of a particular Basque restaurant in Madrid where one of his friends was the head chef. Trouble is, I can't for the life of me remember the name of the place. It may have been in Malasaña, something beginning with *D* or *B,* but that's just a hunch. I've walked around and looked in the *Páginas Amarillas* in an effort to save you time, but I just can't seem to find it. Is that any use to you? Does that tie in with any of your inquiries?"

There is a prolonged silence, one that I assume has been brought about by some frantic note taking at the other end of the line. It's going to be a pleasure to set Zulaika on a false trail. I hope he takes three weeks over it and gets fired for wasting *Ahotsa*'s time.

"Why didn't you mention this when we first met?" he asks eventually. "It doesn't sound like something you would forget."

"It doesn't?" He has always doubted my integrity, sensed that I have something to hide. "Well, I don't really know how to answer that, Patxo. You see, I *did* forget. But I thought I might be doing you a favor by letting you know."

"Perhaps you are," he says quietly, "perhaps you are." He might almost be talking to himself. "Was there anything else?"

"No, there wasn't anything else. Have you had any luck tracking Arenaza down?" While we're talking I might as well try to gauge the status of his investigation. "The story seems to have stopped in the papers."

"The assumption is that Mikel Arenaza is dead," Zulaika replies bluntly. "I have one other area that I'm working on, but it may not come to anything."

"Oh? And what's that?"

He appears to weigh up the good sense of telling me before concluding that no harm can come from doing so.

"There's a SIM card that we believe belonged to Arenaza. It was discovered by police inside a pair of shoes at his home in Donostia. A number of calls had been made to an engineering company in Madrid, and to an unidentified mobile phone, but so far we have not been able to find who it was he was talking to."

"It wasn't just for business?" My heart has started to race. The SIM card will link Arenaza to Rosalía within a matter of days. I remember Bonilla's words: *In my experience people use a secret mobile telephone that their partner knows nothing about.* "You think there's a more personal connection?"

"Perhaps." In the silence that follows I worry that Zulaika may have picked up on this phrase and interpreted it correctly. It was careless of me to use the word "personal," an implication that might easily suggest a relationship with another woman. "Did Mikel say anything about that?" Zulaika asks. "Did he ask anything about a company called Plettix?"

I play dumb. I have no choice. "No."

"What about Txema Otamendi?"

Last Tuesday, Otamendi, a former ETA commander, was shot dead at his home in southern France by an unidentified assailant. It is not known whether he was murdered as the result of an internal feud within ETA, or was simply the victim of a burglary that went wrong. I do not want to appear to have become overly interested in Basque affairs and ask Zulaika to repeat the name.

"I'm sorry, who?"

"Txema Otamendi was once a member of Euskadi ta Askatasuna," he replies. This is a pompous way of giving ETA its formal title. "He was killed last week. You did not know about this? Everybody knows about it."

"I don't really watch the news."

"Well, I am trying to establish a connection with Arenaza that goes beyond their formal political links. So if you have another of your delayed memories, Alec, perhaps you would think to call me again."

I cannot fathom why Zulaika would treat me with such condescension. Does he think I'm stupid? The lie about the Basque restaurant has clearly failed to ignite his interest and he must imagine that I am wasting his time. Let it be so. I say, "Of course, of course," and wish him "all the luck in the world," adding that it has been a pleasure to talk to him again.

"You too," he says, hanging up.

But now there's a problem. Do I tell Kitson about our conversation? This is certainly an opportunity to revive the SIS relationship, but the context is wrong. Never tell people bad news that they don't need to hear. Zulaika's interest in Arenaza won't affect Kitson's search for the weapons and will only harden his resolve not to involve me in any future dealings. There is no point, at this stage, in further weakening my standing with Six; I need to wait until I have something positive to give them, something that makes my involvement irreversible. Besides, they have displayed no interest in reestablishing contact since the handover of the affidavit. Why should I be loyal to an organization that has shown no loyalty to me?

27

Shallow Grave

The body of Mikel Arenaza is discovered six days later lying in a shallow grave about 130 kilometers northeast of Madrid. Julian calls me at home and asks if I am watching the news.

"They've found him," he says. His voice sounds cracked and shocked. I think that I can hear Sofía crying in the background.

Spanish television holds nothing back. Shots broadcast live just after 11 A.M. show what would appear to be Arenaza's arm, covered in clods of earth, protruding from waste ground at the foot of a low hill. His body is limp and very heavy, the skin so ghostly pale as it is pulled from the wet earth that I feel a dryness in my throat like a stain of guilt. Police are busy about the naked corpse with their black sacks and their stretches of tape, local villagers standing back to observe the scene, some sobbing, others merely curious. The broadcaster says that the body was found at dawn by a secretary on her morning jog. Though it was covered in quicklime, it was identified as that of missing Herri Batasuna councilor Mikel Arenaza, and the family informed in San Sebastián. Then the channel switches back to the everyday dross of daytime TV, to a chat-show host and a bearded chef making couscous with roasted vegetables. Life goes on.

The name of the nearest village was given as Valdelcubo and I go immediately to the car and drive north on the N1, reaching the outskirts sometime around two o'clock. En route I dial Kitson's mobile to tell him the bad news.

"Alec. I was just thinking about you. Was going to call later this afternoon."

This sounds like a lie and I ignore it. "Have you heard?"

"Heard what?"

"They've found Arenaza. They've found his body."

"Oh Christ. Where?"

I give him what details I learned from the TV and explain that I am on my way to the scene.

"You're going there yourself? Is that the right idea?"

I don't really understand the nature of the question and ask what he means.

"Well, it's pretty obvious. You're involved in this thing, Alec. You had information about Rosalía Dieste that you failed to give to the Spanish police. You turn up at the graveside, people might wonder who you are. There might be photographs in the press. The Guardia Civil will certainly want to ask questions."

Why would Kitson care about that? "I'll take my chances," I tell him.

"Look, I'm going to be frank. Buscon has gone to ground in Oporto and we're keeping an eye on him. Thanks to you, we've got people digging around in new areas of his background, trying to put the pieces together in relation to the girl. You could become essential in that task later on. London might need you. So I can't afford to have you as a visible presence at something as significant as Valdelcubo."

He uses the name of the village as though he were already familiar with it. I wonder if Kitson is hiding something. It's possible that he learned about the location of the body before I called him. In any event, what possible role could I play in any SIS investigation? I'm blown. London doesn't *need* me. Kitson is just worried that I'll spill the beans about his op if I start getting heat from local liaison.

"Richard, I don't really get this. I've told you what I know. I've written it all down. What else do you need me for? I just want to go to the village and see the situation for myself. Call it a personal quest. Call it closure."

There is a long silence while he gathers his thoughts. I pull the Audi over to the side of the motorway and switch on the hazard lights.

"OK," he says. "It's clearly time to spell this out." Over the roar of the traffic it is difficult to tell whether or not he is alone. "Everybody was very impressed by the quality of your product on Rosalía, Alec. *Very* impressed. Now there are people in London who don't want me to have anything to do with you, and I'm sure that doesn't come as much of a surprise. But at the same time there are those of us who feel we should let bygones be bygones and get you back on board as soon as possible. There aren't too many people of your age and experience who aren't working flat out on other projects. You understand me? We're stretched. You know the territory out here, you speak the language, you're coming at this thing from an angle that has already proved very useful. I'm anxious you shouldn't jeopardize that by doing something stupid."

It is certain that there are men working at Thames House and Vauxhall Cross who know exactly how Alec Milius thinks. John Lithiby, for one. Michael Hawkes, for another. They know that in order to cause me to abandon any misgivings I might have about working for Five and Six, and to secure my renewed loyalty to the Crown, it would be necessary to say more or less exactly what Richard Kitson has just said. *There are those of us who feel we should let bygones be bygones and get you back on board. Everybody was very impressed by the quality of your product, Alec.* Very *impressed.* These are the buttons that would need to be pushed. Flatter him, make him feel special. Cast out the lure of the secret game. Kitson performs the task so perfectly that I experience an almost giddy sense of excitement, something close to a miraculous feeling of relief at the possibility of being accepted back into the fold. It is no exaggeration to say that his words act as a balm that momentarily wipes out all feelings of despair and guilt that I might be feeling over Arenaza's death. But surely I have to be cautious; that is how they *want* me to feel. I have to hold on to my cynicism, to my memories of Kate and Saul. Don't let these guys crawl under your skin again. Don't let them back into your life.

"You want me to work for you? You're saying that you think I'd be useful again?"

"Yes, that's exactly what I'm saying." Kitson sounds quite disengaged by the whole thing. He might be telling me about a film he watched last night, a meal he ate. The notion of my rehabilitation is as logical and as predictable to him as the sun coming up tomorrow morning. "Don't you think so yourself? Wouldn't you like to see this thing through?"

"Well, you can understand that I'm a bit cynical when it comes to trusting people in your line of work. I have a problem with motive."

Kitson does that laugh again, the one through his nose, and says, "Of course." Then there's another pause before he adds, "Because of Kate?"

It's the smart question. He has already given me the formal position on Kate's accident. Either I accept his word or we have a fundamental breach of trust. If that is the case, then the relationship between us might as well be over before it has started. No officer will work with a source who doubts him. Skepticism is the cancer of spies.

"What happened to Kate was certainly the principal reason I lost the faith." A lorry passes close to my door at high speed and shakes the Audi in a sudden gust of wind. I think about Saul and imagine what he would say if he could hear me having this conversation. "Because of what happened, because of everything going wrong, I've had to live in exile for six years." I'm trying not to sound too pompous, too melodramatic. "That's had an effect on the way I see things, Richard. I'm sure you can understand."

"Absolutely," he says, and perhaps this reply is too quick, too easy. "Still, it would be dishonest of me not to say that I have some thoughts of my own on that."

"Meaning?"

"Meaning why don't we meet for lunch and talk it all out? I have to fly to Portugal this afternoon and won't be back in town for a couple of days."

He thinks I overreacted. Kitson thinks I've wasted six years of my life worrying about a problem that never existed. He's another Saul. I say, "That sounds like a good idea, let's have lunch," and let him end the conversation.

"Just turn your car around and head back to Madrid, OK? We'll catch up on Wednesday. Just sit tight until then."

He gives me an address in Tetuán, which I assume to be the SIS safe house, and a time—two o'clock on the afternoon of the sixteenth. Then we say good-bye and, against his express wishes, I pull the car back onto the motorway and continue into Castilla–La Mancha. The village lies about eight miles north of Sigüenza, a cathedral city that was once a front line for nationalist troops in the Civil War. This is Cervantes country, the bare plains and rolling hills and ruined forts of Quixote and Sancho Panza. Two thousand years ago there was a Roman presence here and the road runs in a pure straight line all the way to Valdelcubo, which turns out to be an archetype of the rural Spanish pueblo: crumbling, deserted, dusty. Boys are kicking a football against the wall of a pelota court in the center of the village, but so many strangers have passed through today that they no longer bother to look up when I drive past. At a café just off the main square, television crews from TVE, Telemadrid, and Euskal Telebista are eating *bocadillos* and slices of tortilla in the window and I worry that the Audi might draw their attention. Kitson's words are echoing in my ears, and he might have a source here who will report back if my car is sighted.

Driving out of the square I head down a narrow street barely wide enough for a single car and simply follow the scent of the story. A steady antlike stream of cops and hacks are funneling back and forth from the countryside, although by the time I reach the scene only a sprinkling of bystanders remains. Parking the Audi next to a pile of timber and encrusted manure, I walk to a high point from which it is possible to observe the entire area through 360 degrees. The landscape is breathtakingly beautiful and, before my gaze falls on the horror of

Mikel's impermanent grave, I find myself regretting the fact that I have spent so little time in this region over the past six years. Whatever happens, these will be my final weeks in Spain. When it's over, when Arenaza's killer has been jailed and Kitson moves on to pastures new, I will be obliged to leave, either to take up his offer of a renewed career with SIS, or to live in some as yet undisclosed location, there to rebuild the lies and the paranoia of Madrid, to discover new haunts and safe houses, to find another Sofía.

Arenaza's body has been completely removed. That much is immediately clear. A lone forensic scientist is examining the scene, planting her legs awkwardly as she encircles the grave, like someone walking through deep snow. When did they bring him here? Was Rosalía waiting nearby? It's hard to imagine that the woman I followed and observed day after day could have involved herself in something as diabolical as murder. Why jeopardize her career, her relationship, for vengeance? Why involve herself with a man like Luis Buscon? Perhaps Gael played a part in the entrapment. Perhaps that's where Kitson should be looking. An old man, clearly local, with age lines cut through his cheeks like scars from the sun, comes and stands beside me, muttering something about Batasuna being "the enemy." I move away from him with a nod and get back in the car.

One of the tracks leading back to the main road passes beside an old wall that is in the midst of being rebuilt. Fresh blocks of gray stone have been placed next to a hut in a small clearing, and there's a freshly constructed wooden cross planted at the top of a low summit looking out over the western side of the village. I click on my turn signal and wait for a car to pass before making the turn back into Valdelcubo. Just as I am preparing to pull out, Patxo Zulaika walks past the passenger window, holding a small baby in a harness attached to his chest. His eyes ignite. Peering through the window, he stares at my face, fingers raised to tap on the glass.

I manage to say, "Patxo, I thought I might see you here," before my throat blocks and dries up in panic.

"I cannot say the same about you," he replies. I slide the window down, erasing my reflection, trying as best I can to look relaxed.

"Well, I saw what happened on TV. Had the morning off so I drove up to see for myself."

He looks at me for a long time, drawing out the stare, as if to check the validity of my entire existence. Then his eyes scan the backseat and he purses his lips.

"So, you reporting for *Ahotsa*?" I ask, just to break the silence. Zulaika is the kind of man who obliges you to break silences.

"That is right. And you? You are leaving, Alec?"

I see that the top of his baby's head is chapped with cradle cap.

"Yes, I have to go back to work."

"Oh. Well I am also going to Madrid for the night. Perhaps you have time for a coffee?"

There's no getting out of it. If I make an excuse and drive off he will only force my hand at a later point. This is exactly what Kitson feared. This is what he was talking about on the motorway.

"Sure. But I can't be long. I have to drive down to Marbella later on for a few days. Where do you want to go?"

He suggests that I follow him onto the motorway. There's a busy roadside garage about fifteen kilometers south of Sigüenza where we can talk in private, away from the pricked ears of journalists and Guardia Civil. Now that he needs me, now that he wants some answers, Zulaika has added a courteousness, even a finesse, to his manner. He introduces his baby son—little Xavi—with a proud father's enthusiasm and excuses himself for five minutes while he retrieves his car. I'm going to have to play this one very carefully. He's on to me. Zulaika is very smart and very thorough and he will stop at nothing to get to the bottom of whatever it is that he believes I'm concealing.

He drives fast and we arrive at the petrol station just after 3:30. Inside he selects a table at the rear of the restaurant and obliges me to sit with my back to the room. Zulaika then announces that he's hungry and orders salad and *fabada* from the *menú del día*. That was sly: now we'll have to sit here talking until he has finished his food. With nothing to lose, I too order lunch and the first course arrives within three minutes. He has put Xavi in a rocker on the floor and the waitress keeps bending over to coo at him.

"I didn't know you had children."

"Well, we don't know each other," he says. "Why should you?"

Now that he has me where he wants me, normal service has resumed. The manner is once again curt and to the point.

"Did you drive down from Bilbao this morning?"

"That is right. My wife had to go to England last night so she left me looking after the baby."

"She went to England?"

"Yes. She has family there. Her grandmother is very sick."

It is illustrative of my incessant paranoia that I briefly forge links in my mind between Zulaika and SIS. The conspiracy goes something like this: Kitson knew that I would not be able to resist coming to Valdelcubo, so he tipped off Zulaika—who is a source for MI6—and hopes, in the long term, that the Spanish press will frame me for Arenaza's murder. The theory is completely absurd, and yet it is three or four minutes before I regain my composure, a period in which Zulaika has been talking in Basque on his mobile phone. He may have been checking his copy with the subeditors at *Ahotsa,* but it's impossible to tell.

"Do you understand Euskera?" he asks.

"Not a word." My salad has a lot of raw white onion in it and is otherwise composed of graying shreds of iceberg lettuce and some overripe olives. I set it to one side and watch as Zulaika eats his. "So what was it that you wanted to talk about?"

I time the question so that he has his mouth full of food; it's a good twenty seconds before he is able to respond.

"Well, I have to say that I was surprised to see you there today, Alec."

"You were?"

"I did not think the English were a morbid race."

On the basis that he would respond haughtily even to the mildest criticism of the Basque temperament, I feign annoyance.

"The English are not morbid. Not in the slightest. I simply became interested in Mikel's disappearance. It's not every day that you have a personal link to a man's murder."

"Of course. Don't be offended."

"Who's offended?"

He continues to eat in silence, pouring more vinegar on his salad as an articulated lorry parks outside the window, completely blocking out the sun. It immediately becomes colder at our table, like the chill between us, and little Xavi begins to cry. Zulaika has to pick him up off the floor and pat him on the back and, to judge by his slightly reddened cheeks, regards this as a loss of face. It's hard to play the toughened hack when you have dribbles of baby sick splattered on your shoulder.

"So where did you go on holiday?"

"To Morocco," he replies, putting Xavi back in the rocker and shoving a pacifier in his mouth. The waitress clears away the plates and says, "Such a beautiful boy," in Spanish before touching his cheek with her knuckles. Under her jeans she's wearing a red thong that rides up on her back as she crouches down.

"I haven't been to Morocco. Fez nice this time of year?"

"We traveled all over the country. Fez, yes. Also Tangier and Casablanca." He pours himself a glass of water. "I had no luck finding the Basque restaurant you were talking about in Madrid."

It takes me a beat to realize that Zulaika is referring to the lie I told him about Arenaza. I assume a look of disappointment and say, "You didn't?"

"No."

His eyes narrow to suspicious slits. To spite him I stare directly back, two kids in the playground. Zulaika blinks first.

"You know what I have been thinking?" he says.

"What's that, Patxo?"

"I think you rang to tell me something the other day. Something important. When you left your message, your voice it sounded tense. Then I think somebody got to you. I think you know what happened to Mikel Arenaza, but for some reason you don't want to reveal it."

I'll say this for Zulaika: he tests my skills as an actor. Moving my head slightly forward, I bounce my eyebrows into a look of utter consternation and do a Dizzy Gillespie with my cheeks. *"What?"*

"You have heard me," he says. "If you want to talk about it, then I will listen. If you don't, then I understand. I have my own theory about what is beginning to happen now in Spain."

He knows that I won't be able to resist this. As the *fabada* arrives, Patxo leans over, keeping his eyes on me for as long as he can, then wipes snot from Xavi's nose. The waitress spoons beans into my bowl and I dunk a hunk of bread into the sauce before rising to the bait.

"OK. What's your theory? What do you think is happening in Spain?"

He speaks through a mouthful of beans. "What do you know about the GAL?" he says.

At first I don't think that I have heard him correctly and ask him to repeat the question. He swallows his food, rests his spoon in the bowl, wipes his mouth with a napkin, and then, with the utter self-confidence of one who knows that he has stumbled on perhaps the biggest political story of his career, repeats the question with lazy understatement.

"I said, what do you know about the GAL?"

28

Dirty War

It is the autumn of 1983. Joxean Lasa and Joxi Zabala are two young men living in exile among the radical Basque community in southern France. Both are attached to the military wing of ETA and have participated some months earlier in a botched bank robbery in Spain. On the night of Saturday, October 15, they ask a friend if they can borrow his car in order to attend a fiesta in the village of Arrangoitze, on the French side of the border. The friend, Mariano Martínez Colomo, himself a refugee, agrees to the request. Thirty-six hours later, when Lasa and Zabala have failed to return the keys, Colomo notices that his car, a Renault 4, has not been moved all weekend. Nevertheless, two of the doors are unlocked, Zabala's anorak is on the backseat, and a hank of human hair, as if torn out in a struggle, is lying on the floor. When she opens the glove compartment, Colomo's wife discovers identification papers belonging to both men.

It later transpired that Lasa and Zabala had become the first victims of the Grupos Antiterroristas de Liberación, the GAL, a rogue group of vengeful Spanish security officials who would go on to murder twenty-seven people between 1983 and 1987. Most of their victims were exiled members of ETA living across the border in the area around Bayonne, protected by the Mitterrand government as political refugees. Seven, however, were innocent victims who had nothing whatsoever to do with Basque terror. The GAL had two simple objectives: to liquidate key figures in the ETA leadership and to change the French government's position on terrorist refugees. Subsequent investigations would prove that the GAL was set up and financed by senior figures in the Madrid government using covert funds diverted from the state. Other high-ranking police and military officers, as well as members of the Secret Service, were also implicated. The Socialist prime minister, Felipe González, escaped formal censure, yet his government fell, in large part due to the GAL scandal, in the elections of March 1996 that brought José María Aznar to power.

On the morning of October 16, 1983, Lasa and Zabala were driven from Bayonne to San Sebastián, where they were held for three months in an abandoned palace belonging to the Ministry of the Interior. They were gagged and blindfolded, almost certainly administered mind-altering drugs, beaten, and severely tortured. Some of the information gleaned during their interrogation would later lead to the deaths of other *etarras* at the hands of the GAL. Lasa and Zabala's bodies were eventually discovered two years later buried under fifty kilos of quicklime, 800 kilometers south of Bayonne outside the village of Bosot near Alicante. The men had been taken to an isolated location, stripped naked, placed before an open grave, and shot through the neck. It would be another ten years before their remains were formally identified, and five more before the men responsible— among them senior members of the Guardia Civil and the civil governor of Guipúzcoa himself—were brought to justice.

As Zulaika relates this story over beans and bread, his facial expression barely changes. He would have been no older than eight or nine when the GAL began its campaign of terror, yet subsequent events— the imprisonment of the interior minister, the implication that González himself may have orchestrated the dirty war—doubtless cemented in his young mind both the legitimacy of ETA's cause and the iniquity of the government in Madrid. The GAL may have succeeded in persuading the French authorities to take a tougher stance against ETA, but its enduring legacy was catastrophic. The GAL's bungled dirty war made martyrs of its victims and spawned an entirely new generation of young Basque activists dedicated to the use of violence as a legitimate political tactic.

"And you think this is happening again? You think Arenaza and Otamendi were murdered by the Guardia Civil? By the army? By mercenaries hired through Madrid?"

Zulaika pauses over a final mouthful of *fabada*. Xavi has fallen asleep, dribble at the sides of his pacifier. I have pushed my own bowl to the side of the table.

"It is something we in Euskal Herria have been anticipating for some time. Think about it. Aznar is committed to the destruction of ETA. This much we know. He has teamed up with Blair and Bush and they are united against terror, whatever that means. But how do you win a war of this kind? Not through negotiation, not through legitimate means, but through the state's own brand of terror. The dirty war. Spain in its democratic incarnation has a history of illegal tactics. From 1975 to 1981, that is, immediately after the death of Franco, when the country was supposed to have become a democracy, you have fascist groups avenging the death of figures like Carrero Blanco, responding in childish eye-for-eye fashion to the work of ETA. In 1980 alone, the Batalión Vasco Español, a collection of Madrid thugs, killed four people in a bar, then a pregnant woman, even a child in a playground. Two other women were raped before their murder by the BVE. The killers were well-known to local people, but no action was taken against them. Then the officer who is supposed to be in charge of the case is promoted to be the leader of the Spanish police intelligence service two years later. And you ask why people become angry. You ask why the dirty war is not possible."

"I didn't ask that. It just seems unlikely—"

Zulaika interrupts me, jutting forward, as if I have offended him. *"Unlikely?"* He's like a petulant teenager who hasn't got his way. I have the sense that this is the first time he has properly articulated his theory, and he won't like anyone testing it for flaws. "Last month a respected expert at the United Nations, the same United Nations that Spain and America chooses to ignore over Iraq, *proved* that our Basque prisoners have been subjected to torture and abuse in Spanish jails. It is still going on, Alec, to this day. The UN showed that those detained were beaten, that they were kept awake for long hours and forced to exhaust themselves with physical exercise, that they have plastic bags placed over their heads just to give the guards something to laugh about, that they are starved and beaten. It is Guantánamo on our own Spanish soil. You're naïve if you think that a dirty war is not being fought against ETA and al-Qaeda all the time. The ringleaders of the GAL are still treated as heroes by the majority in Spain. They walk into a restaurant and there is *applause.* But when a family from Euskal Herria wins compensation for the way they have been mistreated by the police, it can take *ten years* to receive the money. This is of course disgusting and the United Nations report also points this out. So what we are seeing now is just a scaling up of an already existing problem."

Zulaika shakes his head as if to deflect any potential rebuttal of his argument and leans back in his seat, draining another glass of water. The zealot at rest. What would be the point in drawing to his attention ETA's own record of more than eight hundred dead over a period of thirty years, the thousands injured, the families obliterated by terror? Isn't it time it all stopped? Too many lives have been taken for the sake of a line on a map that will never be drawn.

I manage to say only this: "Patxo, you have to agree that these are not good times for ETA. From what I read in the British newspapers, a lot of the leadership has been rounded up. The French have got their own antiterrorist police, they're working in conjunction with the Spanish, extradition is a lot easier than it used to be. Why would Aznar or his subordinates risk that by launching another GAL? It just doesn't make sense."

He pauses and calls the waitress over, requesting two cups of coffee. For once, she ignores Xavi, who sleeps. It has dawned on me that Zulaika must have knowledge of Buscon's role in the Arenaza abduction. A mercenary figure would validate his conspiracy. The masterminds behind both dirty wars disguised their links to the plot by hiring foreign extremists to do their dirty work for them. Kitson himself said that Buscon was a member of Portugal's Secret Service. Several right-wing figures from the Portuguese underworld were involved in the GAL.

"Let me answer that in two ways," he replies, following some truck drivers with his eyes as they exit the restaurant. "First, ETA is not finished. Not at all. It is like the serpent. You cut off its head and three more will grow in its place. The *gudaris* will simply bring the fight to France, and they will base themselves elsewhere: in Belgium, in more hospitable countries. Secondly, you must always remember that the Spanish are a vengeful people. Vengeance is in their blood. Perhaps as a tourist you do not see this. You see smiling families on the streets of Madrid and all the nice weather in Marbella and you think that nothing is wrong here. But they are cruel and morbid."

"I don't accept that at all. You said the same thing about the English." *And don't call me a fucking tourist, you prick.* "If nationalism shows us anything, it is that all human beings, of whatever creed or color, are capable of appalling acts of violence, of horrific cruelty. We all have it inside us, Patxo. You, me, the chef who made our beans. Madrid doesn't have the monopoly on inhuman behavior." His forehead creases up, as if he has failed to understand what I am saying. I don't bother to go back and translate. "Let's just stick to the facts. All you have are two dead bodies and no suspects and suddenly the entire Spanish state is involved in a third dirty war?"

The waitress has set down Zulaika's cup of coffee into which he pours two packets of sugar, stirring as he composes his response. She seems to flinch at mention of "dirty war" and looks worriedly into my eyes. Her face is white with fatigue and there is a slight pink rash on the underside of her chin. It has suddenly become very warm inside the restaurant and I take off my sweater, setting it on the seat beside me.

"Do you know the story of Segundo Marey?" Zulaika asks.

Marey was kidnapped by the GAL and held for ten days in 1983, despite having no discernible relationship with ETA. He was the most high-profile of the innocent victims caught up in the second dirty war. To see where Zulaika is going with this, and to keep up an impression of general ignorance about Basque history, I shake my head and say no.

"The Marey family are Basques. Like many people, they were forced to leave Euskal Herria in the Civil War because of the activities of the fascist troops under Franco. Segundo was four years old when he was brought across the border into France. As an adult, he lived a blameless life working at a furniture business. He played an instrument in a brass band and wrote about the bullfights for a small local newspaper. Then, at Christmas 1983, a thug from the French Foreign Legion comes to his door, knocks down his wife with tear gas, and takes him away. He had been kidnapped by the GAL on the orders of the civil governor of Vizcaya, a man who later became director of state security in all of Spain. The pimp had the phone number of the chief of police of Bilbao in his pocket. Do not forget these important connections. So they take Segundo to a shepherd's hut in the hills near Laredo where he is kept in conditions that you would not allow for a pig. Only they realize very quickly that they have made a mistake. A balding fifty-year-old furniture salesman who writes about the corrida is not the same thing as a thirty-seven-year-old *gudari* with a full head of hair who happens to live on the same street as Marey in Hendaye. But do they let him go? Of course they do not. They decide to take political advantage of the situation. They want to alarm the French and to bring to their attention the subject of so-called terrorism in France. Ten days later—*ten days later*—Marey was released and discovered by police, propped up against a tree in the woods near Dantxarinea. He was filthy and had not eaten. There was a note in his shirt pocket. I keep a copy of it with me in recent days. Would you like to see it, Alec?"

Before I have a chance to reply, Zulaika has reached into his briefcase and retrieved a single piece of paper, folded once and still relatively crisp and fresh. I would guess that it was printed out in the last three or four days.

Because of the increase in murders, kidnappings, and extortion committed by the terrorist organization ETA on Spanish soil, planned and directed from French territory, we have decided to eliminate this situation. The Grupos Antiterroristas de Liberación (GAL) founded with this object, put forward the following points:

1. Each murder by the terrorists will have the necessary reply, not a single victim will remain without a reply.

2. We will demonstrate our idea of attacking French interests in Europe, given that its government is responsible for permitting the terrorists to operate in its territory with impunity.

3. As a sign of goodwill and convinced of the proper evaluation of the gesture on the part of the French government, we are freeing Segundo Marey, arrested by our organization as a consequence of his collaboration with the terrorists of ETA.

You will receive news of the GAL.

I pass the note back to Zulaika and curl my napkin into a ball.

"What does this have to do with your theory?"

"Let me add something else," he says, holding up his hands as if I have spoken out of turn. At his feet, Xavi stirs. "The men who were responsible for this crime, and for two other GAL shootings, dined on lobster and roasted lamb in prison. They brought *putas* into their cells. The guards treated them as heroes."

"I didn't know that."

"No? Well now you do." Zulaika has raised his voice a fraction and appears to check his temper in a rare moment of self-awareness. "I am sorry. I did not mean to shout in front of my son." But Xavi picks up on the tenor of his father's anger and begins to kick in the rocker. When Zulaika removes the pacifier, the baby's screams fill the restaurant. He lifts him up, pats him on the back, says something consoling in Basque, and then looks at me as if he expects me to talk. I am still wondering what relevance the Marey kidnapping holds for his theory and can only stare blankly back.

"You know about the disappearance of another man in Bilbao? Juan Egileor?" he asks.

Egileor is not a name that I have heard before. I shake my head. Xavi is now screaming at such a pitch that we are drawing irritated stares from neighboring tables.

"He too works at a furniture company. Not with Sokoa, like Marey, but with ADN, the office supply company. Perhaps you know it. They have outlets in Euskal Herria, also in Granada, Marbella, Valencia."

"Yes, I've heard of ADN. A friend of mine bought a desk from them."

"He did?" Zulaika looks strangely pleased. "Well, Señor Egileor is one of three vice presidents of the company. He was taken from his home four days ago. No ransom note, no demands. The police have let it be known that they do not suspect the role of ETA in the kidnapping."

"Why not?"

"Because of the victim's links to the nationalist movement, because of his high regard for Herri Batasuna, his work for the party. No. If anything, Egileor would be considered a friend of ETA and therefore an enemy of the Spanish state."

"And you think he's been kidnapped by the men responsible for Arenaza's murder?"

Xavi is briefly silent. "It is certainly a possibility."

"But Otamendi was on his way out of the organization. That's what the papers are saying. Your theory might apply to Mikel and Egileor, but why kill a man who had turned his back on military action? A lot of stuff was stolen from his house. The television, jewelry, paintings. It looks like Otamendi just walked in on a burglary."

Zulaika has no response to this. The waitress has produced a bottle of warmed baby milk that he begins feeding to Xavi. I cannot recall Zulaika asking for her assistance, but he thanks her with a rare smile and stares back across the table, trying to trap me with his eyes.

"Look, I think you are the key, Alec Milius. I want to know what you are hiding. My newspaper can protect you if you are being threatened. But if somebody is trying to prevent you revealing what you know about this, understand that people will die as a result of your silence."

"Well, let's not be melodramatic." The fact that Zulaika has a slurping infant in his lap helps me to retain a moderately relaxed countenance in the face of this threat, but nonetheless it is difficult to deflect the question and maintain my composure. "Nobody is trying to keep me silent. All I know is that Mikel was abducted and murdered. There's nothing else."

"And what about Rosalía Dieste?"

It is too late to disguise my shock. I manage to say, "Who?" but Zulaika lets me swim in the lie. He knows that he took me by surprise. He timed the ace to perfection.

"Rosalía Dieste," he repeats.

"Never heard of her."

I must pursue this line at all costs and Zulaika knows that. He says, "*Claro,*" as I nod my head. In time, his face assumes the disappointment of a man who has been betrayed by one he trusts. It is an effective fatalism.

"When we spoke on the telephone after my vacation," he says, "you mentioned that Mikel had a personal connection with somebody in Madrid."

"I said that?"

"Yes. Because of the SIM card. That was your reaction. I have my notes if you want to read them. You said that the presence of so many calls to Plettix suggested that Mikel had a personal relationship with one of the company's employees. What did you mean by that, Alec?"

It is a constant effort to remain alert both to the possible limits of Zulaika's knowledge and to the content of our previous conversations. He could be making something up to trap me. He could be asking a question in a particular way in order to elicit an unguarded response.

"I don't recall saying that. You think I know this woman?"

Zulaika laughs quietly under his breath, as if I have insulted his intelligence. Placing Xavi back in the rocker he shakes his head and signals for the bill.

"You know very well who she is. Rosalía Dieste was Mikel Arenaza's mistress. Even his *wife* knows about her."

I feign further surprise. "Well, I wasn't married to him, was I? Mikel had a *mistress*? He didn't say anything about that to me."

"No, of course not." The waitress sets the bill down on the table and walks off. "Look. Dieste's stepfather was a Guardia Civil killed by a car bomb planted by ETA. So you have a family motive for revenge immediately. I think she trapped Arenaza in a love affair that was designed only to bring about his death."

"Seriously?" I assemble a brief sequence of baffled facial tics. "Surely that's a little far-fetched? A *honey trap*?"

Zulaika has not heard this term before and I have to explain it to him, using a mixture of Spanish and English. Once he understands, he nods and says, "Exactly. A honey trap," but I am shaking my head.

"Even if it's true, why does she have to be part of a larger conspiracy? Why couldn't she just have acted alone?"

The question is designed to draw out a vital piece of information. If Zulaika has knowledge of Buscon's role in the kidnapping, this is the moment at which he would be obliged to mention it.

"I do not think so." He places a twenty-euro note on the table. "You do not do something like this without help. Miss Dieste is an engineer. She is a woman. She could not kill a man of Arenaza's strength. The other killing, and the kidnapping of Juan Egileor, this indicates a plan involving several people."

"Then who are they?"

But Zulaika has no answer. I rise from the table. At least he knows nothing about Buscon. "You're paranoid, Patxo," I tell him. "You're a good journalist, but you're paranoid. You want to see things that aren't there. You're looking for a conspiracy where none exists. Why don't you just ask this woman in person? Why don't you just look up Rosalía Dieste and go to the police if she lies?"

Zulaika remains seated, watching my face intently for the reaction to what he is about to say.

"You think that I have not already tried this?" he says. "How can I? Señorita Dieste has disappeared."

29

Taken

We have parked our cars some distance from the restaurant. Zulaika waits outside while I go to the bathroom and then accompanies me around the back of the building, speaking for the second time to someone in Basque on his mobile phone. I am holding Xavi and use the child as a means of avoiding any further conversation about Rosalía or the dirty war. When Zulaika looks at me, I start to coo; when the baby kicks, I grip his little feet and wiggle them, telling Daddy that his son is going to be a striker for Athletic Bilbao. We cross a deserted expanse of dusty tarmac, passing behind a line of articulated lorries, and I am conscious of the roar of traffic on the motorway. Zulaika stares ahead, as if deep in thought, then opens the boot of his car. He piles his briefcase and Xavi's bags inside, places the baby in a chair on the backseat, and starts the engine.

"So, you are in a hurry, you have to go to Marbella," he says, "but remember what I tell you. If you want to talk about anything, if you think of something you might want to discuss in relation to the girl, you have my number. Day or night, Alec, day or night. Whatever you prefer."

I make the right noises and wave him off, saying, "Of course, Patxo, of course." I consider it something of a success that our meeting has ended without any serious capitulation on my part. Zulaika may suspect that I am concealing important information, but he was unable to break through the wall of my feigned innocence. I sing, "Bye-bye, Xavi, be a good boy now," in a light, easy voice and pat him on the head. Zulaika drives off, turns into an on-ramp up ahead, and has soon disappeared. I think he gave me one last glance as he left. It is warm and a helix of flies spirals wildly into the sky as I place my jacket in the boot of the Audi.

They must have come from behind me, from between the parked lorries. Their speed and their strength are overwhelming. I experience a sensation of weightlessness as I am lifted from the ground and bound by forearms of extraordinary power. There are at least two of them, both men. Something wet is pressed against my mouth and a panic fever surges through my body that quickly turns to sweat. I am aware of the sky and of the speed of things, of nobody talking, nobody saying a word. Very quickly, almost in one movement, I am bundled into the boot of a car, not my own, and slammed into darkness. There is an intense pain both in my shoulder and across the left side of my head, and my hands must have been tied because I cannot reach up to feel for blood. In the boot there is a smell like the burning odor of drilled teeth. I think that Zulaika did this to me. I blame Kitson and then I blame Buscon. We are moving off and I can hear voices coming from the inside of the vehicle. A woman is talking. The voices slip and fade.

It could be hours later, it could be days. I am lying on top of a bare, dusty mattress in what would appear to be an upstairs room. Something about the height of the sky through the window, the light. There is no furniture, no carpet or linoleum on the splintered wooden floor, no sink or toilet. And I am naked. It takes time to realize this but the sense of shame is powerful, like a child who has wet the bed. I cover myself briefly with my hands, sitting up and looking around for a sheet or piece of clothing, anything with which to recover my dignity. There is nothing. The pain at the side of my head, just above the left temple, returns with the rhythm of a heavy pulse. It is cold and I do not know where I am.

Outside, birdsong. A steady chorus. So it is either early in the morning or late in the afternoon. My watch has gone, my two phones, also my wallet and keys. I try the handle of the door but it is locked. There is no peephole, or any other way into the room. I cross toward the window. A stained, motheaten blanket has been tacked up with half a dozen nails to shut out the light, but it has fallen to one side, revealing fresh smears of white paint on cracked glass. The room would appear to be at the top of a two-story building looking out over a deserted field. Probably a farmhouse. There are no people in sight. The sky is damp and low and gray. The Basque country. I have been taken hostage by ETA.

After ten minutes I hear voices downstairs, then the scraping of a chair. They must know that I have woken up. My bones seem to contract and it is an effort to fight my own cowardice, to straighten up and to face them. Someone is walking up a flight of stairs. A man, judging by the weight of the footsteps. He places a key in the door, the handle rattles and turns, and I stand naked in the middle of the room, ready to face him. I will not be afraid. He is wearing a black balaclava and the sight of this is enough to push me a step back toward the window, as if sucked by fear. There is a mug of either black tea or coffee in his hand. Wisps of steam lick around his wrist. He is wearing a red sweatband and an old leather-strapped watch.

"Drink," he says in English.

For some reason I think it important not immediately to ask where I am, not to find out why I have been taken or who they are. I do not want to show fear to these people. He holds out the mug and encourages me to step toward him. And then I am screaming.

He has hurled the coffee into my face. The boiling liquid sears against my skin and in my eyes. The shock is so great that I cry out. I want to stop at nothing to hurt him, but a single punch as I move forward drops me to the ground and I vomit like a dog at his feet. He says three words in Basque and is gone. Voices echo up through the floorboards and I think that I hear a woman. She is angry. I can hear her shouting.

For five minutes I lie like this, no better than an animal, cold and humiliated. I lick my own arms to clean them. Please God, don't let me be scarred. My shoulders are red with the heat of the coffee, but they are neither raw nor burned. He must have waited until the drink cooled a little and then come upstairs to confront me. Planning. Why didn't they want to scar me? Why didn't he let me see his face?

An hour passes, perhaps two. The light outside does not change. I move away from the sick on the floor and lie back on the bed. There were beans in the contents of my stomach; the *fabada* was still in my system. This, at the very least, gives me a timescale. It must be the morning following the lunch with Zulaika. It will be another twenty-four hours before anybody realizes that I have disappeared. When I fail to materialize at the safe house tomorrow, Kitson will become suspicious. But what can he do? He will not jeopardize his operation by launching a search for Alec Milius. He may even have betrayed me himself.

Try to remain calm. Try to be logical. It is bewildering that after six years I have nobody in Madrid who will miss me, no woman or neighbor, no friend. It could be days before Sofía notices. I sit near the window for warmth and watch through the smears of paint for movement in the field. I do not want to shout out for clothing or for food. I do not want to give them that pleasure. Instead I will wait patiently and bear anything that they do to me. At the back of my mind is the persistent optimism that the guard covered his face with the balaclava. If they were going to kill me, he would not have taken that precaution.

But by the late afternoon I am cold and very hungry. I need to urinate and the blow to my stomach has left a welling bruise at the base of my ribs. A damp wind has started flowing through a narrow gap in the window and the sun has moved away. I try to sleep, but the smell of the sick near the bed is appalling and I can only lie with my eyes open, shivering, staring at the ceiling. Once or twice I hear movement downstairs, but I might otherwise be completely alone in the house.

As dusk approaches I tear the blanket down from the window with five hard tugs. It rips and falls over my head, scattering insects and dust. Moments later a car comes to the house, moving along a track that I cannot see. The sound of this is exhilarating; it proves the presence of life elsewhere. The car parks on the far side of the building and a single door slams. Boots on hard earth, then the faint murmur of a conversation. After no more than two or three minutes, the engine starts again and the vehicle moves away. The house is once again enveloped in silence. Unable to wait, I go into the corner of the room and piss against the wall.

It must be eight or nine o'clock when a different man comes back up the stairs. There is now very little light outside.

"Move away from the door," he says, and I crouch on the floor near the window, ready to spring if he attacks me. The lock clicks, the handle twists back, and a plate of food is pushed inside. I do not see a face, only a pale, hairless forearm. The voice says, "Fucking stinks here," and then is gone. He locks the door again and walks away.

There is no cutlery, nothing to drink, but I devour the food with my filthy hands, wrapped in the blanket that causes my skin to itch and catch. It is a tasteless stew, made with rice and carrots and old meat, full of fat and gristle, good for nothing but salt and energy. I make a spoon with the three middle fingers of my right hand and shovel the glutinous sauce into my mouth with demented speed. It appalls me how quickly I have been reduced to an animal state. Somehow a fly has made its way into the room and it buzzes around the food and the piss before settling in my encrusted vomit. Why don't they come for me? Why don't they ask me any questions?

With all that I have suffered, the anguish over Kate's death, all the years of solitude and the stupidity of exile, this is the absolute lowest point. I breathe and inhale an abject terror. The men and women of ETA are ruthless in the pursuit of their cause and they will not hesitate to harm me unless I give them what they want. But what is that? What has brought me here? In the numbed panic of capture I can assume only that Zulaika was responsible for this, that he is the creature of these people, their stooge and propaganda tool. He made two telephone calls, both in Basque, while we were eating. He must have been guiding them to me, setting me up. Zulaika ordered lunch not to prolong our interview but to give ETA more time to reach the garage.

It becomes a pitch-black night with no moon. The birds have stopped singing and there are no more cars. Very occasionally a dog will bark far in the distance, but I never hear any of my captors. The sense of isolation is compounded by the noise of airplanes flying high overhead, the last of which passes at perhaps eleven or twelve o'clock. I remember as a child at boarding school in England staring up at planes as they flew out of London and envying the passengers their freedom, their luxury. I imagined myself a prisoner, unable to escape and join them in far-off lands. All that seems ridiculous now. I cannot begin to conceive of the journey, of the decisions taken, which have led me to this terror, to this improbable end.

Then the woman comes. She waits on the other side of the door and instructs me to stand by the window with my back to the room.

"If you move toward me, we will kill you," she says in Spanish, and the threat is so commonplace, so stark and inhumane, that I have trouble associating it with a woman. She forces me to reply by saying, "Do you understand?" and I speak my first words to my captors.

"I understand. I'm standing beside the window."

The lock clicks and the handle turns, something is placed on the floor, and then she withdraws from the room. I think I heard her sniff and even choke at the stench. The door is locked again and, from the other side, she says, "Drink that if you want to sleep." But the sudden intrusion of light from the stairwell has bruised my eyes and it is some time before I can adjust to the darkness again. I almost kick over a glass of water on my way to the door and my toes land on a piece of cloth. They have left me a pair of ripped cotton shorts. I pull them on, swallow the water in two long gulps, and lie back on the bed. I dream of Mum and of Kate. I dream of home.

There must have been some kind of sedative in the water. I am woken in the black of Tuesday night by a turbulent noise. Two men are in the room with me and a bright light is being directed into my face. They are both wearing balaclavas and tear the blanket from my body, screaming, "Wake up! Get out of the fucking bed!" then lifting me, hooking my arms, and slapping my face. Just as quickly, they are gone. Darkness as the door is locked again and their footsteps fade. I can neither see nor hear anything now. My brain is dizzy and numb. Dimly, it occurs to me that these will be the first stages of a sleep deprivation. If that is the case, they will come again in half an hour, then again before dawn, and repeatedly into tomorrow. The idea is to disorientate and to terrify, to take the prisoner to the very edge of unconsciousness and then to wake him, so that he begins to fear even sleep itself.

I lie down and try to be strong. I have to fight this. But I am so disorientated that I can barely concentrate. How long did I sleep for? How many hours of rest will I need in order to keep my wits about me when the torture begins? For the first time I confront the possibility of my own death and almost welcome it. If I had stayed with Lithiby and Hawkes, if JUSTIFY had succeeded, would Five or Six have trained me for something like this? Would I have been better prepared? I catch the smell of piss and sick in the room and feel another desperate urge to urinate, lying still on the bed to try to make it pass. And then it must be another hour before they come again, the same two men, the same noise at the door so that this time I am ready for them, already awake when the torchlight is shone in my face. I reckon it a small triumph that I manage to sit up before they have the chance to manhandle me, and perhaps it is their revenge for this that they say something accusatory about tearing down the blanket, about my destroying the room, and one of them punches me hard, twice, around the kidneys. I am sick again, instantly. I drop my face over the side of the bed and must have hit their feet with the vomit because I am whipped, knuckle-hard, on the back of the head.

"Fucking spy," a voice says, but the meaning of this, the implication, does not immediately sink in. The vomiting has left me breathless and I hear quick and savage laughter in the stairwell. My nose stings, an acid link with the back of my throat. For some pathetic reason I crave the presence of the woman now and find myself on the edge of tears. Do not cry, Alec. Do not pity yourself for what has happened here. I make a point of sitting up again, of moving away from the bed toward the window, still wrapped in the blanket, trying to steady myself by taking deep fresh breaths of air.

But they have me. They have total control. Throughout all of the following day, through the appointed meeting with Kitson, the long hours of sunlight and a car coming again to the house, I am kept awake. I have to shit and piss in the same disgusting corner of the room where flies now swarm in numbers and buzz around my body. Where did they come from? The woman offers me food that I am too cowardly and hungry to refuse. Occasionally I will drink water, neither knowing nor caring where it came from or what it contains. In time, only one of them comes upstairs and keeps me awake simply by pounding on the door, rattling the handle, and shouting obscenities that evaporate in the squalor of my prison. Not once do I call out to them, not once do I reply. I retain at least this small dignity. But I am otherwise broken, an ended man. If Kitson does not come for me soon I fear that I will simply never leave this place.

It must be the third day, or the fourth, by the time they come in, all three of them, and lead me out into the light. A pale half-naked Englishman, a spy, stumbling into a muddy courtyard surrounded by farm buildings in the rain. We do not linger long and I see only fragments of the green surrounding hills. In their balaclavas they take me into a barn about fifty meters from the front door and order me to stand against the far wall with my hands above my head.

I know what's coming.

The freezing hosed water blitzes against my stomach and is then sprayed wildly in a narrow jet by the smaller of the two men. When I try to swallow it, to follow the liquid with my mouth, to taste the sublime fresh water, he shouts at me, "Not for drinking. Clean yourself," and I begin to wash my crotch, my ass and feet, then slowly under my arms, taking off the soiled cotton shorts because I long ago stopped caring about the embarrassment of nakedness. I have not slept in days, but these first moments are quite clear, the water tasting of rain and waking me up. A small pink bar of soap has been thrown onto the ground and I can smell the shit and the puke and the shame sluicing off me as I use it. The woman, who is thin and wears cheap leather boots and light blue jeans, has sat down in a metal chair in the center of the barn. The third man has slid the door shut and stands beside it holding a handgun. He too is wearing jeans, with a pair of white trainers, and is almost certainly the one who threw coffee in my face. All three of them have black, motionless eyes. There is straw and dried mud on the floor and a stale smell of manure, but it would appear that the farm has not been worked for years. Stained blue tarpaulins cover various rusted objects near the far wall, at least twenty meters from where I am standing. A single bright bulb is suspended from the ceiling, but slits and spots of light are still visible through the roof and the walls.

As soon as the hose is switched off I am shoved wet and naked into a small wooden chair to which my hands and feet are bound tightly by lines of electric cord. I do not struggle or complain. My body is covered in welts and bites and they start to itch now with the water. Then a burlap sack is jammed over my head and tied across my shoulders with what feels like a very narrow piece of string. When they bundled me into the boot, they knocked my left shoulder on the car and it is into this bruise that the string now bites like a cheese wire.

"What is your real name?"

The woman has spoken. She is clearly the leader. I hear the man who bound me moving back toward the door.

"My name is Alec Milius."

I can see nothing inside the sack, which is already very hot, yet these first moments are oddly calm. I know that my body is weak and pale, that my nakedness is emasculating, but somehow the intense tiredness and hunger I feel actually help me.

"Who do you work for?"

"I'm a private banker. I work for a bank. Endiom." It takes me a long time, perhaps too long, to spell out the letters. "E-N-D-I-O-M. It's a British company with an office in Madrid."

A fist tears into my stomach, doubling me over. I did not hear him there. The breath is ripped out of me, leaving a vacuum into which I choke and cough. There are particles of fine earth in the lining of the sack that catch in my throat. I cannot breathe. I try to speak but I cannot breathe. The woman says, "Stop lying. Who do you work for?" but I am unable to respond. The cord binding my hands is too tight and it feels as if all of my weight is being supported on my torn wrists.

Again: "Who do you work for?"

When I give the same response—the single word "Endiom"—I am punched a second time, and my assailant has to catch the weight of my head as I pitch forward. His hand covers my mouth through the sack and I want to bite at it, to return the pain. The woman says something in Basque that I do not understand. Then a great wave of nausea swells in me and I think that I might be sick. Again she asks the question, and when I do not reply I hear the grunt of the man beside me, as if he is readying himself for yet another strike. I try to tense my stomach muscles, to prepare for him, but I have lost all physical control over the lower part of my body. Then the click of a cigarette lighter just beside my ear. Oh Jesus, is he going to set fire to the sack? Summoning a desperate strength, I scream, "For Christ's sake, I'm not a fucking spy. You said that I was a spy. When he brought the food three days ago. When he kept me awake."

The lighter clicks off. I manage to scrape the chair away from the sound of it. There is silence. At the door the guard who threw the coffee clears his throat. I think that I hear him move toward me but I cannot trust my senses now. I am coughing again on the dust. I choke in the terrible darkness of the sack and shake my head, utterly disorientated.

"How long have you been a spy?" the woman asks.

This is the crazy, chopped logic of interrogation. Whatever I say, I say nothing.

"I told you, I'm not a spy. You are keeping the wrong man. I am not a spy. Please don't hit me when I tell you the truth. My name is Alec Milius. I am a British citizen. I came to Madrid six years ago. I work for a British company. You think that I'm a spy because of my link to Mikel Arenaza, but I had nothing to do with his death. I want to find his killer as much as you do. I think I know . . ."

But what I am saying is drowned out by the terrible screech of a heavy object being dragged across the ground. It is coming from the direction of the blue tarpaulins near the far wall. It sounds like a fridge, a chest, something large and cumbersome, the awful slide of fingernails being dragged along a blackboard. The woman was not interested in what I had to say. They were moving the object while I was talking.

"What is that?"

"Alec?"

Her voice is suddenly very soft and directly in front of me, just a few inches from my face. I could kick her if my legs were free. We could kiss. Even in this nightmare state, the thought arises that one should never strike a woman. I can hear the two men breathing hard as they come to a halt.

"Yes?"

"Have you listened to that?"

"Listened to what? To the noise? Yes, of course."

"And do you understand what I have told you?"

"What have you told me? You've told me nothing. I know that you're ETA. I am not a spy. . . ."

Another suffocating punch into my stomach. Who did that? Was that the woman? I scream something at her, aware that my private vow never to do so, never to grant them the satisfaction of hearing their punishment rewarded, has been easily broken. Then suddenly there is silence, long and quiet enough to hear a bird flap its wings in the rafters of the barn, until eventually the woman speaks again.

"Let me make things clear," she says. "There is a gas stove in front of you. This is what we have taken from the other side of the barn. Now I want you to listen to me very carefully."

Again, the awful static click of the cigarette lighter. One of the men is standing beside me. Someone turns what sounds like the dial on a cooker. I hear the hiss of gas escaping into nothing, followed by a hollow roar as it is lit. Oh, please God, no.

"If you refuse to cooperate with us, we will put you on this stove. We will burn you and you will be left to die. None of us cares about this. We have done it before and we can choose to do it again. So I want you to consider very carefully when you answer us."

I begin to weep. I cannot any longer hide my fear from them. My freezing body shakes with terror and cold and I feel a sort of madness welling up beneath the black horror of the sack. Let them do to me what they want. I have no more fight.

"Do it then," I scream. "*Venga. No soy un mentiroso.* Fuck you, you fucking animals. I am not who you think I am. I am not a spy. Fucking do it."

A wild slash across my head, the back of a hand, then something slamming into my knees, like a metal pole. My neck twists as tears cut across my eyes. I scream at them again.

"You are animals. You betray your cause." Where is this strength coming from? An extraordinary defiance has erupted within me and asserted control. "You do not know what is happening. There is another GAL. I know about the GAL. You kill me and burn me and you will all be finished."

I do not know whether my words have any effect. I do not care. I think that I pass out and then return to consciousness. I think that the gas is switched off. My knees throb with pain. It is as if my bones pulse. I cannot stop coughing. At last, eventually, the woman says, "What do you mean by that?" and her voice, for the first time, bears a trace of anxiety. "*Qué significa la otra GAL?* What do you mean, Alec?"

The use of my first name feels like a blessing. I have a chance to stop this nightmare. Sitting straighter, risking another blow from one of the men, I speak very slowly, with as much truth and care as I can summon.

"I was sent to San Sebastián. I was sent to Donostia by the bank. I met Mikel Arenaza and I interviewed him. I had to ask him questions for my work. He was kind to me. He said we should meet in Madrid and he telephoned me the day he disappeared. He called from the airport and we arranged to meet." Somebody moves away from the chair and leans up against the stove. I hear it shift very slightly on the stone floor. I try desperately to remember details and it helps that I do not have to lie. "Mr. Arenaza did not come to the meeting. I waited for him in a bar in Gran Vía. The Museo Chicote. It's a famous bar. I thought he was with his girlfriend and that's why he was in Madrid. He had a mistress. I want to make sense. You need to know this. Am I making sense?"

"Who?" the woman asks.

I pause, trying to get a clean, steadying breath under the hood. What is she referring to? Does she want to know about Rosalía? Why did the leader say "Who?" I have lost my train of thought. I want to ask one of the men to take off the hood and to give me a glass of water, but that would be to risk another blow.

"Her name is Rosalía Dieste. Her stepfather was murdered by ETA at Chamartín station. One of your operations a long time ago. She seduced him because he was Batasuna. She wanted him dead. It was revenge. I followed her because I liked Mikel. I was trying to find him."

Something happens. I feel the touch of metal on the skin of my biceps. A knife. The string tying the sack has been cut. Then they rip off the hood and immediately tie a blindfold very tightly around my eyes. I register nothing but a blast of light. I gasp at the air in the barn and cry out pathetically, as if freed from a black hole. Then the woman says, "Keep going."

"I am a banker, a private banker. I am not a spy. Please don't burn me. Please don't put me on the gas." It is so hard to think. "I followed her because I was interested. I knew about the girl and I didn't want to tell the police or the journalists who rang me because it was a secret. You see? Mikel told me not to tell anybody. He was my friend. Then I saw Rosalía with Luis Buscon. Do you know Luis Buscon? He is the GAL. I'm sure of it. There's a journalist, Patxo Zulaika, who knows all about this. Maybe you know him. I think you know him. He works for *Ahotsa*. He doesn't know about Buscon because I don't trust him. But he knows about the GAL. He told me at lunch. You need to believe me. You need to talk to him."

Nothing is said. There is absolute silence, a minute for the dead.

Then suddenly, heatedly, as if the volume had been turned up on a television, I hear them arguing in Basque. Even in my demented state I can tell that I have said something to unnerve them, something that might keep me alive. I may not have to tell them about Kitson. If they put me on the stove I would tell them about Kitson. I don't think I'd be able to stop myself. I like Richard. He is what I wanted to be. But if they put me on that stove and they light the gas under my naked thighs, God knows I do not know what I will tell them.

"Say that name again," she says. "Did you say the name Luis Buscon?"

"Yes, yes." I seize on this like food. "Luis Buscon. He is also called Abel Sellini. He was working with Dieste. He murdered Arenaza and took the body to Valdelcubo. That's why I was there today. Buscon is a Portuguese mercenary. Juan Egilan . . . I can't remember his name. The one who was kidnapped . . ."

"Juan Egileor."

"Yes. He has been kidnapped by the Spanish. And Otamendi too. He was shot because he is one of you. They hate you. They think you are terrorists. They are fascists who do not believe in the cause."

Again they go back to their conversation. All I want is half an hour to rest and gather my strength. I would give anything for that. I would give anything just to hold Sofía and to go back to our hotel in Santa Ana. If they stop hitting me, if they let me go, I will tell her that I love her. If they take away the gas, I will tell her that I love her.

"Luis Buscon is somebody that we know about. How did you know his name?"

"I bribed the concierge at the hotel."

"Which hotel?"

"The Villa Carta in Madrid."

"And how do you know that he is a Portuguese mercenary? How does a private English banker know something like that?"

How do I answer this? It is as if I can feel all three of them moving toward me, shutting down the space. It should be easier to lie because they cannot see my eyes, but I cannot think of what to say.

"The concierge told me. Alfonso told me." The found deceit is like a miracle. "He said Buscon always stays at the hotel and the staff had gone through his belongings. The hotel knows about fake passports, all the money he keeps in his safe. He books into the room under the name Abel Sellini. The police are keeping him under surveillance, but they don't arrest him because of what he is doing to ETA. Don't you see? They want him to carry on. He is leading the GAL."

"That is unlikely." The woman's reply is very abrupt and I feel the dread fear of another beating. If they do not believe me they will light the gas. Then it's over, all of this. They speak in Basque and one of them moves back to the stove. If I hear the click of the cigarette lighter again I think I will scream.

Say something. Do something. "Why is it unlikely?"

"Because we have known about Señor Buscon for a long time." The woman's voice is directed away from me, as if she is looking toward the door. I wonder if there is now somebody else, a fourth person, in the room. I wish that one of the men would say something. "He is an associate of the Interior Ministry. One of his oldest friends is second to the minister himself. Have you met these men?"

"No, of course I haven't. Of course not."

"Then why are you involved?"

"I've already told you. I am not involved."

"You do not know Javier de Francisco?"

"No." And this is the truth.

"If there is another GAL, it will be Francisco controlling it. He is the scum. You know that he was a soldier in the days of Franco?"

"I told you, I know nothing about him."

"Then let me educate you. A young Basque confronted him, a brave boy from Pamplona. And de Francisco took the boy, who had done nothing, and with two of his men they went into the country-side and they beat him with shovels until he was dead. So this man knows what it is to kill like a coward. He is the black viper of the government in Spain. And it has all been concealed by the corrupt government that you serve."

"That's not true." I do not understand the link she is making between Francisco and Buscon, between a murdered boy and soldiers of long ago. I know that I will get out of this place alive if I can just prove the authenticity of what Zulaika told me. And yet he must already have shared his theory with my captors. Great waves of pain pulse across the left side of my head, making it impossible to think. Is this what Kitson wanted all along? Did he set me up? I cannot work it out. If Julian walked in now, or Saul or Sofía, it would somehow make more sense. I cannot seem to reason. "I've told you. I'm a private banker. I live on my own in Madrid." I am saying things now that they have already heard, but there is nothing left. "I became interested in what happened to Mikel. I liked him, I really did. I shouldn't have followed Buscon. I shouldn't have followed the girl. I was just bored. I'm sorry. I'm so sorry. I am not a spy."

And then the beating starts again. After this I remember nothing. No more talk, no more questions, no fear or even pain. I remember nothing.

30

Out

There is a Dutch film, *The Vanishing,* in which a man wakes up inside his own coffin. He has been buried alive. In the final scene he is left alone to suffer this terrifying end, this nightmare suffocation, and the audience drifts out into the night bewildered by fear. And so it is in the aftermath of my own terror as I wake into the total blackout of a living death. I am lying on my side. When I reach out with my right hand it hits a wall. When I stretch it above my head it collides with a hard plastic panel that sends a numb pain through my fingers and wrist. My feet can push out no more than two or three inches before they too are stopped by a hard, fixed surface. Everything around me feels completely enclosed. Only when I reach above my face, as if to search for the lid of the coffin, do I encounter open clear space.

My senses gradually awaken. I am wearing clothes. It is warmer than I can remember for a long time. There are shoes on my feet and my eyes are gradually growing accustomed to the light. But when I lift my head, trying to sit up, a migraine sears across my skull, lifting vomit into the back of my throat. The pain is so intense that I have to lie down again in the darkness, breathing hard for release, swallowing.

I feel again with my right hand, slowly tapping along the panel above my head. There is an odd, recognizable smell, a mixture of alcohol and pine, that same acid sting in my throat. My fingers curl around what feels like the handle of a door. Lifting my head, risking the pain, I pull it and a bright light immediately flares into the space. When I open my eyes against it I see that I have been lying on the backseat of a car parked inside a tiny cinder-block garage. I am inside the Audi. What am I doing here?

The agony of asking my twisted body to move is worse perhaps than any pain that I can recall from the interrogation. Every part of me aches: feet, calves, thighs, arms, shoulders, neck, blending into a single conscious suffering. I am wretched with thirst. I have to sit with the door open and my feet on the ground for as much as thirty seconds while I gather the strength to stand. There is terrible bruising around my stomach, a scarlet map that appalls me when I lift my shirt to look at it. These are my clothes, the ones I wore to Valdelcubo; I am no longer wearing their rags. I try to put weight on my legs, but the pain makes it difficult to walk. After just two steps I open the passenger door and collapse into the seat.

The glove box is open. Inside I can see my wallet, the two mobile phones, and their chargers. It is bewildering. The SIM cards are inside and I switch the phones on, but they are drained of power. Why would they give them back to me? The *etarras* have taken all but twenty euros from my wallet, but the credit cards, the photographs of Kate and Mum and Dad, are all there. Dangling behind the wheel I can see my keys in the ignition. The keys to Calle Princesa, to the PO box, even to the bed-sit in Andalucía.

What is this place? A waiting room for death? My captors have clearly left, yet I have no idea where I am, of the time or date, of their reasons for doing so, or of my right to survive. I check my unshaved face in the rearview mirror for signs of bruising and cuts, but it appears to be mercifully unmarked. They would not have wanted the public to see my beaten face if I went in front of the press. That would be bad for ETA's support base. They were thinking all the time about the presentation.

Standing again, supporting myself on the open door, I walk very slowly, like an old and crippled man, toward the front of the garage. The air is stuffy and damp. I am aware of my own smell, of my sour breath and sweat. The door is not locked. When I turn the handle it slides up easily over my head, revealing a barren landscape of dust and low, pale hills. This is not the farmhouse. It is a different place. We have left the Basque country and come south into the desert. It looks like Aragón.

Finding more strength in the exhilaration of freedom, I walk round to the back of the garage where there are nothing but old plastic sacks and pools of muddy water. A dead bird lies on a pile of wood. I can hear cars passing, the tarmac whisper of engines and tires. A second, larger building is set back from the garage, ruined and open to the elements. I experience an overwhelming desire to leave this place and to be free. My stiff body is loosening up all the time, but if I do not drink something soon it will be almost impossible to drive. I have the presence of mind to bend down and to check under the car for a bomb, and my thighs and back and migraine roar with pain as I do so. Then I lower myself into the driver's seat, turn the key in the ignition, and head out slowly onto the muddy road.

My eyesight seems OK. I haven't checked the rest of my body for marks or scars yet, but I can do that as soon as I find a hotel. The radio works. Just to hear human voices again, to reconnect with the world, feels like a blessed second chance. It is several minutes before I learn the day and the date—Saturday, April 19—but the clock on the dashboard puts the time at 4:06 A.M. That must be wrong; they must have played around with it. Then the news comes on Cadena Ser at 11:00. The anchorman talks at length about the Egileor kidnapping and the invasion of Iraq. Saddam Hussein's statue has been torn down in the center of Baghdad and some idiot Yank tried raising the Stars and Stripes in its place. A colleague of Arenaza's has demanded a full investigation into the circumstances surrounding his death, but there is no mention of Dieste or Buscon, of Javier de Francisco or a dirty war. My own disappearance appears to have gone completely unnoticed.

Then, like a roadside miracle, I pass a stall selling drinks and fruit and swallow almost half a liter of water with unbroken, exhausted gulps. If my appearance or demeanor seems in any way unusual to the stallholder, she does not betray it. Taking my twenty-euro note, she merely frowns at the denomination, hands over a bundle of coins, and sits back down on a low stool. I ask her to locate our position on a map and she points to a section of road between Épila and Rueda de Jalón, a two-hour drive south from the Basque border. They must have brought me over in convoy in the boot of a car, dumped me in the backseat of the Audi, closed off the garage, and then headed back into Euskal Herria.

The road leads south to the NII *autovía*. If I turn right, I can be in Madrid by ten, but it's a long drive and my body, despite the fuel of water, will not withstand the journey. I need to rest and clean up. I need to think. My knees are stiffening up on the pedals and a nerve pain, like a small electric shock, shoots infrequently through the back of my thigh. I require the anonymity of a big city, somewhere I can disappear and gather my thoughts and decide what the hell I'm going to do. I'm not ready yet to face Kitson or Sofía, to go to the police or to confront Zulaika. So I make the decision to drive east toward Zaragoza, booking into a four-star hotel in the center of the city under my own name. Thank God I left the fake passports, the driving licenses, all the stupid paraphernalia of my secret existence back in Madrid. Had the *etarras* discovered those, they would almost certainly have killed me.

The phones start to chime as soon as I have plugged them in. Message after message from Sofía, two from Kitson and Julian, a single text from Saul. Even Mum has called, and to listen to the gentle, oblivious cadence of her voice is to experience once again the miracle of my survival. I had expected Kitson to be worried, but he rang on Tuesday to cancel our meeting in Tetuán. That would explain why his manner is so unperturbed. His second message, left at midday on the 16th, merely confirms this, citing "logistical difficulties in Porto." Only Sofía sounds upset, her messages growing in intensity to a point where she shuts down in frustration, convinced that I am ignoring her calls in order to "spend time back in England with that girl."

"Just be honest with me, Alec," she says. "Just tell me if you want it all to be over."

I draw a long, hot bath, drinking half a bottle of Scotch with too much Advil. The bruising around my stomach is very bad, and my knees, into which they slammed the metal pole, have almost locked up since the drive. There's an intense yellow-black bruise at the top of my left shin, a stain that I can never imagine eradicating. I'll need to see a doctor, to pay somebody privately to check me out and not ask too many awkward questions. There are also marks around my shoulders, more bruises on my back, even a clump of dried, sticky blood in my hair. When did that happen? I can book the appointment under a pseudonym and say that I got into a fight. Then I'll need blood work and X-rays. I'll need tests.

Just after nine I order a *sandwich mixto* from room service and make a series of calls on the hotel phone. Mum is out, so I leave a message on her answering machine telling her that I'm away on business and can be reached in my room. Saul is having dinner in a restaurant in London and it is difficult to hear what he is saying, but I feel a delirious homesickness just listening to his words, to the easy laughter of girls in the background. I worry that my voice is unstable and see that my fingers tremble on the bed when we are speaking. He says the divorce is going through with Heloise but does not elaborate, and promises to come back to Madrid before long. Then I call Sofía.

"Is it OK to talk?"

"What do you mean?" By her clipped, dismissive tone it is obvious that she is in a sour mood.

"I mean is Julian around?"

"He is out."

"Look, I'm sorry I've been out of touch. I can't explain now. It's not what you think."

"And what do I think, Alec?"

It sounds as though she has one eye on a television set or a magazine, just to irritate me. She knows I hate it when she doesn't concentrate on what I'm saying. I want to scream the truth at her, to weep, to ask for her help. I feel so utterly fragmented and alone in the hotel room and wish she were beside me, to care for me and to listen. But it is useless.

"I can imagine what you think. That I've been with another woman, that I've been in London or something. But it's not that. I had business, OK? That's all. Don't be angry."

"I am not angry. I am glad you are all right."

There is a long pause. She wants to bring the conversation to an end. I draw my knees up tight against my chest and find that I begin to shiver as I talk.

"Sofía?"

She moves the receiver away from her mouth and takes a deep, stagy breath.

"Yes?"

"Can you meet me? When I get back to Madrid? In two days? Can we go to the Reina Victoria?"

"On Monday? This is when you are coming back?"

There is mild criticism even in this simple question.

"Yes."

"And that's what I am to you now? Just hotels? You don't telephone me for more than a week and now you want to fuck me? Is that it?"

"You know that's not true. Don't do this. I've been through hell." My voice cracks here but she does not react.

"What do you mean, *you've* been through hell? *I* have been through hell. I am sick of this, Alec, I am *sick* of it."

"I got into a fight."

A tiny beat of shock. "What kind of a fight?"

It's strange. All I want now is to win the argument, to make her ashamed of her churlishness.

"I was beaten up. Here in Zaragoza. That's why I wasn't able to go south for Julian. He's left messages wondering where I am. I was unconscious for a while."

It is an awful lie, one of the worst I have ever told her, but necessary in that it works to bring her around. She is instantly distraught.

"*Unconscious?* You got into a fight? But you don't fight, Alec. Where did this happen? *Lo siento, cómo estás mi vida?*"

"Here in Zaragoza. I was looking at some property. Saul is thinking of buying a place up here. I said I'd help him while he was back in England. Some men attacked me when I went to my car."

"Saul was with you?"

"No. No. He was coming out from London later on. I just left the hospital today. Tell Julian, all right? I don't want him to be angry."

It feels bad to be doing this, but I don't have any choice.

"Alec," she says sweetly, touching my heart with her voice. I think of the barn, of that blackness under the hood, and squeeze my eyes tight to reply.

"I'm all right now. It's just some bruises. But I'm so angry, you know? I think if I saw those men again, I would kill them."

"I know, I know . . ." She is crying.

"I long to touch you," I tell her. "I miss you so much."

"Me too," she says. "I will book the hotel. We can talk about it then."

"Yes. But don't cry, OK? Don't be upset. I'm fine."

"I just feel so bad . . ."

There is a knock at the door. This startles me perhaps more than it might once have done, but it's just room service. Saying good-bye to Sofía I stand up slowly off the bed, securing my dressing gown as I look through the fish-eye lens in the door. There's a waitress on the other side, very pretty and alone. She seems struck by me when she walks in, a reaction that may be sexual, that may be shock. I cannot tell. She places a tray on the bed.

"*Buenas tardes, Señor Milius.*"

Out of nothing, a dream of sex pulses inside me. I would gladly lie down with this girl on my bed and sleep next to her for days. Anything just for the gentleness and peace of a woman's touch. I hand her a five-euro tip and wish she wouldn't leave.

"Thank you, it was my pleasure," she says, and I am on the point of asking her to stay when my head suddenly splits with pain. She has gone, closing the door behind her, and I drop like a stone on the bed, wondering how many more pills, how much more water and whiskey I will have to drink before this all goes away. I am angry as I look at my broken body, knowing that it was wrong to have arranged to meet Sofía so soon. The bruising on my legs and stomach will terrify her. I wish the girl had stayed. I wish I was not alone.

Like an invalid, I manage to eat only half of the sandwich before vomiting its contents into the toilet. Something is wrong with me, something more than just shock and exhaustion. It's as if they poisoned me back at the farmhouse, as if they put something into my blood. I fall into a hopeless sleep, waking up wired and distraught at four in the morning. I leave the lights on in the room for comfort and get dressed slowly, taking a walk around the center of Zaragoza for more than an hour. Then, back at the hotel, unable to sleep again, I check out at six, eat breakfast, and head back on the road to Madrid.

31

Plaza de Colón

Kitson is awake at seven when I call him from a petrol-station land-line. He does not sound surprised to hear from me.

"Been away, Alec?"

"Something like that."

I tell him that we need to get together as soon as I return to Madrid and suggest a two o'clock meeting under the waterfall at Plaza de Colón. He does not know the place, but I describe it to him in detail and ask him to come alone.

"Sounds intriguing."

The drive takes about seven hours. I have to rest repeatedly because my eyes ache with a persistent migraine. Painkillers have numbed my reflexes and I feel foggy with the consequences of what I am about to do. Back in the city, aware that ETA will now almost certainly know where I live, I drop the Audi in Plaza de España, take a quick shower at the flat, and follow the countersurveillance route around the *barrio* up to El Corte Inglés. It's vital that I am not observed meeting Kitson, who will demand assurances that I have not been followed. There's no visible tail at the bank on the corner of Martín de los

Heros, and nobody follows me into the trap on the first floor at the post office. At Corte Inglés I use the switchback escalators and try on several items of clothing while checking for surveillance. Again, nothing. As a final safeguard, I limp downstairs into the metro at Argüelles, get onto Line 4, and step off at the last moment at Bilbao station, waiting for a second train in case I was followed onto the first. For three minutes I have the platform to myself, then a schoolgirl of thirteen or fourteen comes down the stairs with a friend. Both of them are clutching satchels. ETA have either lost me or decided not to plant a tail. If they have put a tracer in the car it will lead them only as far as the garage. If they have triangulation on the mobiles, that will only pinpoint my apartment.

Plaza de Colón is a vast square on the eastern side of the Castellana about a kilometer north of the Museo del Prado. A vast Spanish flag flies in the center of the square beside a statue of Christopher Columbus. At its base, runoff from an elaborate fountain system forms a waterfall that pours down across the façade of a hidden, subterranean museum. The entrance to the museum can be reached only by walking beneath the waterfall via a set of stairs at either end. It is thus a natural environment for countersurveillance, a long, narrow corridor with a wall of water on one side and a public building on the other, invisible to outsiders. Our meeting can proceed unmolested.

When I appear at the bottom of the southern staircase, Kitson looks up but does not react. He is sitting toward the far end of the corridor on a low brick wall that runs beneath the waterfall. Water roars in a smooth arc behind his back, gathering in a shallow pool. Opposite his position is a map of Columbus's journey to America sculpted in high relief on the museum wall. I consult it for some time before turning around to join him. When I sit down he offers me a pellet of chewing gum from a packet of Orbit menthol.

"Do I need it?"

He laughs and apologizes for breaking last week's engagement.

"It didn't matter. I couldn't have come anyway."

"Now why was that?"

I take a deep breath. I have made a decision, against all my instincts for self-preservation, to tell Kitson the truth about what happened after Valdelcubo. It was a paralyzing choice. To lie to him might have worked in the short term, but if he were to discover at a later date that I had been tortured by ETA, all trust between us would break down. That would mean the end of any future career with Five or Six, not to mention the personal cost of failing our intelligence services a second time. And I need Kitson for what I have to do; I need Kitson for revenge. Yet if I confess what happened, he will be concerned that I might have told my captors about his operation in Spain. Buscon's name came up several times in the barn, where I was repeatedly accused of being a British spy. I am almost certain that I did not mention anything about Kitson or MI6, or the consignment of arms Buscon procured for the Real IRA in Croatia. Had I done so, they would surely have killed me. I cannot be certain about this. I may have told them everything; there are patches of the torture that I simply do not remember, as if they wiped my memory clean with some mind-warping chemical.

"I did what you asked me not to do."

"You went to Arenaza's grave," he says quietly.

"I'm afraid so."

The water behind us is like the roar of an applause that never dies. It almost drowns out his words. In a calm voice, he says, "And what happened? Why are you limping, Alec?"

So I tell him. I sit there for half an hour and describe the horror of the farmhouse. By the end I am shaking with anger and shame and Kitson rests a hand on my shoulder to try to calm me. This may be the first time that we have made actual physical contact. Not once does his face betray his true feelings; his eyes are as gentle and contemplative as a priest's. He is shocked, of course, and expresses his sympathy, but the professional reaction remains obscure. I have the sense that Richard Kitson understands exactly what I have been through because he has been unfortunate enough to have encountered it in his career many times before.

"And how do you feel now?"

"Tired. Angry."

"Have you been to see a doctor?"

"Not yet."

"Guardia Civil?"

"Do you think I should?"

This gives him pause. He lights a Lucky Strike and hesitates over his answer.

"You're still a private citizen, Alec, so you should do what you feel is right. I would expect you to go to the police. The men—the woman—who did this to you will be *waiting* for you to go to the police. In fact it might look suspicious if you don't. From a personal point of view, however, we would prefer it if you didn't go public. The blowback problem, et cetera. Yet the choice is absolutely yours. I don't want you to feel that we have any control over that decision."

"And if I don't go? What then?"

I want him to reassure me that his offer of cooperation still stands. I don't want what has happened to affect our professional relationship.

"The Office can certainly find you somewhere secure to live in the short term. We can relocate you."

"That's not going to be necessary. If ETA had wanted me dead, they would have killed me at the farm."

"Probably," he says, "but it'll be safer, nonetheless."

"I'll be careful. And what about my job?"

"With me or with Endiom?"

I was not expecting that. I was thinking purely about Julian. It may be that Kitson sees no reason that the kidnapping should affect my links with SIS; indeed, he may assume that it will motivate me to pursue Buscon and ETA with an even greater intensity. He is right about that.

"I was only thinking about Endiom. Why? Do you still think that I'll be useful to you?"

"Absolutely." He reacts as if the question were naïve, tilting back his head and blowing smoke up into the air. "But I need to know more about the dirty war. I need to know exactly what was said. The parameters within which my team are operating out here would be significantly widened by something like this. We need to get a full statement that I can telegram to London ASAP. You're going to have to try to remember everything that went on."

To that end, we go immediately to the nearest decent hotel—the Serrano on Marqués de Villamejor—booking a room using one of Kitson's passports. He sets up a digital voice recorder that he produces from his jacket. I give him names and theories, chief among them that Luis Buscon has a long-term association with a high-level figure in the Interior Ministry named Javier de Francisco. Kitson takes extensive notes and drinks Fanta Limón from the minibar. From time to time he asks if I'm all right and I always say, "I'm fine."

"So what's the long-term picture?"

"If there's another dirty war, if there are men in Aznar's government who are covertly funding attacks on ETA, that's catastrophic for Blair and Bush. How can you fight terror if it is the tactic of your allies to brandish terror themselves? Do you see? The whole relationship gets blown out of the water." These are the first heartening moments that I have known for days. It gives me a feeling of satisfaction that I should be able to articulate a view on the plot against ETA that will be listened to at Vauxhall Cross and perhaps even passed on to Downing Street and Washington. "The British and the Americans are either going to have to stop the conspiracy using covert means, or abandon Aznar as an ally. Now I don't know how they do that." Kitson exhales heavily. "The biggest problem, as far as I'm concerned, is Patxo Zulaika." My knees start to ache as I say this and I rub them, a movement that catches his eye. "He's a fervent Basque nationalist, he understands this dirty war as a hard fact. Before long he's going to have enough evidence to publish the whole story in *Ahotsa* and then the dam is going to burst."

"And how long before he does that?" For some reason Kitson thinks that I should know the answer to this question.

"Piece of string. But if Zulaika is controlled by the people who kidnapped me, he won't be interested in giving a balanced view. This is not a time to check facts and sources. He'll just run it."

Perhaps because the circumstances are almost identical to a similar debriefing that took place in 1997, I think back to Harry Cohen. It was in a hotel in Kensington that I told John Lithiby about Cohen cottoning on to JUSTIFY: a few days later, he was lying in a Baku hospital, beaten up by a bunch of Azeri thugs. In all honesty, if Kitson were to green-light a similar operation against Zulaika now, I would not object. I want him to suffer as I suffered. I want revenge for what he did.

"And you believe Zulaika? You think this is really what's going on? That Otamendi, Egileor, and Arenaza are victims of a third dirty war?"

"Look at the facts, Richard." That might sound patronizing on the tape. "There haven't been disappearances and murders of this kind in Spain and southern France for years, then three come along at once. Egileor's employer, ADN, is an office supply company. Segundo Marey, an innocent man who was kidnapped by the GAL in 1983, also worked for a furniture company that was accused of laundering funds for ETA. It's like a bad joke. Then there's Arenaza's body, found in quicklime in a shallow grave, identical circumstances to Joxean Lasa and Joxi Zabala. The parallels are deliberate. Whoever is doing this thing is taunting the Basques. The organizers of the first two dirty wars, and we're talking about individuals occupying some of the highest positions in the land, tried to protect themselves from disclosure by knowing very little about what was going on. To that end they hired right-wing foreign extremists to do their dirty work for them. Italian neofascists, French veterans of Organisation de l'Armée Secrète, Latina American exiles. These men were fiercely ideological, they hated Marxist groups like ETA, and almost all of them had a military background. Luis Buscon fits this mold precisely."

"He does," Kitson mutters. "Only in this case ETA are claiming that Buscon is a visible element in a conspiracy that goes as high as de Francisco."

"Why not higher?" I suggest.

"Who's Francisco's boss?"

"Only Félix Maldonado, the interior minister. Next stop, José María Aznar."

Kitson expels a low whistle and writes something down. Then, as if the observations are linked, adds, "We discovered evidence in Porto that Buscon hired mercenaries for the Croats during the Balkan war, hence his initial links to weapons smuggling."

"What's happened to those, by the way?"

He looks up from his notes. It's dark in the hotel room and the air is stuffy.

"The weapons?"

I nod. Tellingly, Kitson reaches across to shut off the digital recorder. He wants to protect his IRA product from ears in London.

"Situation pending. We have some of the weapons under observation, others appear to have taken flight. Of course, I've always thought it possible that the two investigations may be related. If what Zulaika told you is true, the Croat weapons may have fallen into the hands of the Spanish state for the purposes of fighting ETA. Buscon could have diverted them. That's certainly something I'll mention to London."

Something catches in my throat and I cough so violently that my ribs feel as if they will crack. Kitson frowns and offers me a bottle of water.

"And Rosalía Dieste?"

"What about her?" I ask, drinking it in slow, calming bursts. "Zulaika said she's disappeared. Implied she might have been liquidated. Your people have anything on that?"

Kitson switches the voice recorder back on and appears to hide a smirk, perhaps as a reaction to my choice of vocabulary. Then he tips back the last of his Fanta, crushes the can, and throws it in a perfect three-meter arc straight into the wastepaper bin.

"Rosalía Dieste is on holiday," he says. "Rome. She hasn't disappeared. Due back with loverboy this evening, no doubt with postcards of the pope, some fava beans, and a nice bottle of Chianti."

"Well, that's good to know."

"Your Mr. Zulaika must have been mistaken." I wonder if this is said for the benefit of Kitson's superiors in London: he has let me have a good run on the tape; now he wants to remind them who's boss. "Actually we have a different problem. A different problem with a different girl."

I stand up to relieve some of the stiffness in my body and my left shin sends a cord of searing pain directly under the kneecap. I fall against the wall near the door, gasping. Kitson sees this and almost knocks over the table in an effort to reach me. Taking most of my weight on his shoulders he then leads me into the bathroom and sets me down on the edge of the bath. He is surprisingly strong. I say that I am embarrassed by the sweat that has soaked through my shirt onto his arms.

"Don't worry about it," he says. "Don't worry."

I feel dizzy and take a towel down from a rack above the bath, wiping my neck and face. Only after a couple of minutes do I ask what he meant about the girl.

"What girl?"

"You said there was another woman, a new problem. With somebody other than Rosalía."

"Oh yes." He looks directly at me. "Buscon left a package at the Hotel Carta this morning."

"Buscon is back in Madrid?"

"Was. Checked out at eight. A woman came to pick it up about an hour later. Somebody we didn't recognize. You sure you're all right, Alec?"

"I'm fine."

He goes back into the bedroom and I hear him searching around in his jacket. I am still hot and out of breath, but the pain has mostly passed. "Careful," he says as he passes me what looks like a photograph that has been colorphotocopied onto a sheet of paper. "I had surveillance in the lobby and security faxed this through. Do you recognize her?"

I turn the paper over and it falls limp in my hand. I cannot believe what I am seeing.

"I'll take that as a yes," he says, registering my reaction. "So you know her?"

"I know her."

The woman in the photograph is Sofía.

32

Black Widow

"Sofía Church? Your boss's wife?"

A nod.

"You want to tell me more?"

I did not think it was possible to feel angrier and more unsettled than I already do, but Sofía's treachery is an all-new humiliation. I feel utterly bereft and strung out, as if my heart has been snapped and left for years to heal. Kitson is watching me all the time and I know, at the very least, that we cannot hold this conversation while I am sitting in the bathroom. I ask him to assist me and we walk slowly back into the bedroom. I have to stretch out flat on the nearer of the two beds and prop up my head with a pillow. It must be a pathetic sight. I do not even have the strength to lie about this.

"She's Spanish," I tell him, as if that's a start. "They've been married for five years. That's all I have, Richard. That's everything."

"You're sure?"

"I'm sure."

He knows. It's obvious. All about the affair with Sofía, all about Julian, all about the whole damn thing. They saw us together at the

Prado. Kitson's eyes are telling me to come clean before there's a breach of trust. *Don't let me down. Don't keep making the same mistake.*

"Look, switch off the tape."

"What?"

"Just do it."

He walks over to the table, sits down, and appears to shut off the mechanism. I do not have the guts to ask if I can double-check this.

"Sofía and I have been seeing each other for a while. We've been having an affair."

"OK."

In the bathroom, a tap drips.

"Are you married, Richard?"

"I'm married."

"Children?"

"Two."

"What does your wife do?"

"She does everything."

I like this answer. I am envious of it.

"It's not something that I'm particularly proud of."

"It's not something that I'm particularly here to judge." There is a beat of understanding between us. "And now you think that she might have played you?"

It is the spy's deepest fear, to be betrayed by those closest to him. Kitson's question is in itself a slight; an officer of his caliber would never have allowed himself to be so blatantly manipulated. I am trying to understand what the hell Sofía might have been doing at the Carta picking up an envelope left by Luis Buscon, but all I can think is that she has been using me all this time. It must have something to do with Julian's past in Colombia, with Nicole. Are they part of the dirty war? Sofía hates ETA, but no more or less than most Spaniards. She disapproved of Arenaza, but not enough to have him killed. Christ, I drank her, I made her come; there were times when we seemed to vanish into one another, so intense were the feelings between us. If all that was just a game to her, a woman's ploy, I do not

244

know what I will do. To lie within human intimacy is the greatest sin of all.

"Maybe it's not her in the picture," Kitson suggests, as if sensing my shame. It is embarrassing to hear him try to comfort me. "Maybe your eyes were playing tricks on you."

"Can I see it again?"

But it's her. The image is blurred and shows only the back of a woman's head, but the figure, the height, and posture are exactly Sofía's. She's even wearing clothes that I recognize: a knee-length tweed skirt, high-heeled leather boots. I am consumed by rage.

"Jesus Christ, what an idiot."

"You don't know that. There might be another explanation."

"Can you think of one?"

Kitson struggles to reply. He can't answer without knowing the facts. So, for the second time in a matter of hours, I have to strip myself of all obfuscation and tell him, in humiliating detail, all about my relationship with Sofía: the initial meetings; the endless lies to Julian; the stolen afternoons and the rows. God knows how I come across. And all the time I am trying to put the pieces together, trying to work out their long-term strategy. Why did they lure me in? Why would Buscon and ETA, Dieste, Julian and Sofía target an Englishman abroad if not to set him up as a patsy? But why me? Why Alec Milius? I tell Kitson about Nicole and Julian's life in Colombia, asking him to check their file, but can only conclude that this is an American operation, orchestrated by Katharine and Fortner as revenge for JUSTIFY. At the same time, it is impossible to see more of the trap that has been set for me. In spite of everything that I now know, I still can't sense what they might have in store.

33

Reina Victoria

I go back to Calle Princesa. Perhaps it would have been best to pack everything up, to find a new apartment in Madrid, even to move to a different city, but that would have felt too much like defeat. I would rather suffer the final humiliation of witnessing the plot's success, of seeing the look of triumph in Katharine's eyes, than give up now. It is more important to me to do my best for Kitson, to see this thing through, than to cut and run. In any case, he has said that he still needs me, and with our knowledge of Sofía's involvement in the conspiracy we now have a crucial advantage. We can turn the tables. I can start using *her*.

"See her, sleep with her, *habla con ella*," Kitson advised. "Act like nothing has changed. You haven't seen the photograph, you haven't any knowledge of any dirty war. And don't for God's sake start telling her about Patxo Zulaika and ETA. If she knows about them, she knows. If she's in on the conspiracy, she's in on the conspiracy. Far as you're concerned, the marks on your body came about as the result of a punch-up. Real estate deal turned sour. A bunch of Zaragoza estate agents taking the phrase 'two up, two down' a bit literally. Next thing you knew, you were in hospital."

So I keep to our meeting at the Reina Victoria. I did not sleep on Sunday night because the Danish boy upstairs began his banging, his toy hammering, just as I was dropping off at dawn. As a result, I feel obliterated by tiredness. I can no more pretend to Sofía's face that nothing has happened between us than I can make the bruises and the cuts on my body disappear. This is rage, as much as anything else: it is what Katharine must have felt when she discovered that I had lied to her for the best part of two years. In all probability, my deceit ruined her career, yet the knife in the back of her self-respect would have been far worse. In this sense, it's possible to see my pain as a kind of moral payback. Only I never kissed Katharine. I never slept with her.

Sofía is in a room on the third floor facing away from the square. It's too late to try to change it and, in any case, I don't want to make her suspicious about my motives.

Things seem wrong from the moment we first set eyes on one another. When I knock on the door, she answers it fully dressed. No negligee, no garter belt. No pigtails, no perfume. None of the visual paraphernalia of an affair. Instead, Sofía looks anxious and washed-out, a sheen of tears in her eyes. I feel immediately wrong-footed.

"What's the matter?"

I follow her into the room and sit down next to her on the bed. Straightaway she stands up and crosses to an armchair by the window. I worry that Julian has found out about us, even though such concerns are no longer plausible or even relevant. Christ, perhaps she is pregnant. Then she wipes her eyes on a Kleenex and stares at me. Can this be part of an act? She has not yet spoken, but I feel a wall between us that I cannot breach. She starts sobbing and, in spite of everything, there is still the desire to protect her.

"Sofía, what's going on? Why are you crying? Why are you upset?"

Her eyes are black as she looks back at me through the tears. Then she says, "Who are you, Alec?"

The question is like a curse.

"What?"

"Who *are* you?"

She stops sobbing. I do not know how to respond. Kitson didn't prepare me for this, nor could I have anticipated that she would be feeling this way. It has been so long since I played the professional game of lie and counterlie that I feel rusty and bewildered by what is happening. I can't see the angles. She must be playing me, but why the anger? I was expecting a routine evening of sex and champagne, of faked orgasms and room service, not the double bluff of a woman's tears.

"What do you mean, 'Who am I'? Why are you crying? Sofía, please . . ."

"I mean what I say." She discovers a new strength in her voice. "Who is Alec Milius?"

"Well, I could ask you the same question. Who is Sofía Church?"

Her neck seems to slip here, her face a desperate mask. "*What?*" Something is terribly wrong or I am simply not reading this correctly. "What do you *mean* by that?" she says.

"I mean I want you to tell me what's going on. Let me help you." I pass her a tissue from the box beside the bed but she swipes wildly at my arm. This angers me, perhaps because I am so tired, and I lose my temper. "Well, what then? What is it that you want?"

And she starts screaming at me, as crazed as I have ever seen her. The change in her mood is terrifying and I wonder if the frenzy is designed to cover something up. Standing out of the chair, she comes toward me and lands a pathetic fist on my chest, then slaps me repeatedly around the face. Words are blazing out of her mouth, few of which make any sense to me. It is as if she has lost her mind. I try to envelop her body in my arms in an attempt to control her physically, but she merely screams, "Let go of me, you fucking liar!" and the insults continue. A part of me worries that we will be heard in next-door rooms, but my hands are too busy up around my head, protecting my face from her rage. Then I lose all patience.

"Why the fuck are you hitting me?" I am on the point of pinning her against the wall. "Why are *you* angry with *me* when *you're* the one doing the lying? Why were you in the Hotel Carta this morning? Why?"

That stops her. I had not meant to betray Kitson, but it was necessary. Sofía is suddenly calm. In fact she looks stunned.

"You *know* about this? How? How do you know?"

Is this a confession of guilt on her part or more of the masquerade? If only I was not so exhausted. I took a triple shot of vodka before leaving the flat but it has done me no good. Are we being recorded? Is this little scene another element in Katharine and Fortner's grand plan?

"Of course I know about that. And I know about Luis Buscon. So I want to know why you were picking up packages from him. Are you working together?"

She steps farther away from me, shaking her head. She appears to lack the strength to cry again. Indeed she looks, to my eyes, like somebody who is going slowly mad. It is awful to see this in a woman whom I once cared about.

"Who is Luis Buscon?" she asks, trying to breathe deeply, trying to control herself. "Who is Luis Buscon?" I am about to answer her when she adds, "I get a phone call at work last night telling me to come to the Hotel Carta this morning to pick up a box of samples left by somebody called Abel Sellini. He says that he represents an Italian designer. I didn't know who he was. He said it was important. Who is Luis Buscon? Alec, what is this about?"

It starts to make sense. "What was in the package?" I ask. "Tell me. What was in it, Sofía?" I am hurrying her as she stares at me, desperate to have her betrayal disproved. She watches every tic of my face as she retrieves her handbag from the floor. Inside there is a letter that she takes out of an envelope, thrusting the single page into my hands like evidence of an adultery.

"What is this?"

"*Léelo,*" she says. Read it.

The letter is unsigned and badly typed. It consists of one simple sentence, written in Spanish:

Tell your boyfriend to stop what he is doing or your nice English husband will find out that he is married to a Spanish whore.

"There were photographs as well," Sofía says, beginning to cry again, and suddenly it all makes sense. None of what has happened has anything to do with Katharine or Fortner, with Nicole or Julian. Sofía hasn't betrayed me. But my immediate elation is checked by the knowledge that Buscon knew about our affair. He and his colleagues must have been following me for weeks. "I destroyed them," Sofía is saying. "There were pictures of you and me in Argüelles, Alec, photographs taken through the window of your apartment when we were kissing, pictures of me walking beside you in Princesa. Who *are* you? Who would blackmail us like this? Is it something to do with your work for Julian? How do you know that I went to the hotel this morning? Have you been following me?"

I have to construct a lie even as I am putting together the final pieces of the jigsaw. It has all been a terrible misunderstanding. I have to find a way of protecting Kitson's operation.

"It's to do with the men in Zaragoza," I tell her. "I can't tell you any more than that."

"The men that fought you?"

"The men that attacked me, yes."

"*Eres un mentiroso.*" She shakes her head and looks away toward the window. "You lie all the time. I want to know the truth."

"I am telling you the truth. This is something private that I'm involved in. It's a big real estate deal. I've saved a lot of money since my parents died and if I invest it in this project I could make hundreds of thousands of euros. But there are people who are trying to stop me."

"This Luis Buscon? This Abel Sellini?"

"*Exacto.*"

"Who are they?"

"They are businessmen, Sofía. Sellini and Buscon work for a Russian company in Marbella."

"For the *Mafia*?" She looks aghast, as if I have dragged her into a nightmare.

"I don't know if they're Mafia. I suppose they are. I met them as part of my work for Endiom. But Julian doesn't know anything about it. You can't tell him."

"I'm not going to *tell* him," she spits. "You think I am going to tell my husband about us? You think so, Alec? Is this what *you* would do? Show me what these men did to you. Show me the marks on your body."

"There are no marks."

But she is tearing at my clothes, tugging at the buttons so that one of them falls loose and flies free of my shirt. It is quite dark in the room and her reaction to the bruising on my chest is not as bad as it might have been. She just bites her lip and juts out her chin, eyes stung by shock.

"*Dios mío, qué te han hecho?*" Sofía arrives at an immediate decision, shaking her head. "You have to stop this thing now, Alec. These people are very serious. I do not want any more letters. I do not want any more photographs. I do not want them to hurt us. They will kill you next time, no? I want you to promise me that you will stop this."

"I promise you that I will stop this."

"And we are finished. It is over between us. I cannot see you anymore."

I suppose I am touched by the fact that she trips on these words, but a stubborn part of me won't let her leave. I need her now, more than I ever have, if only to be comforted by her. I cannot be alone any longer.

"Don't say that. Please don't overreact. If I pull out of the deal they'll leave us alone." I attempt to hug her, but she twists her body away from mine as if I am still hateful to her. "What's the matter?"

"Don't touch me!" She looks at me with such contempt. "You think I want to touch you after you involve me in this? You have never told me the truth about anything."

But in the same movement she returns to me, placing her arms around my back so that I can pull her toward me. She is suddenly beautifully still, exhausted, her face turned against my chest. Her hair smells so beautiful as she tries to find her breath. I kiss her head, breathing in the sweet caress of her forgiveness, saying, *"Lo siento, mi amor, lo siento. Por favor perdóname,"* but wondering all the time if this woman is still playing me for a fool. "I didn't mean to hurt you," I tell her. "I had no idea that they would threaten you."

And she says, "I need you, Alec. I hate you. I cannot leave," and tilts her head to kiss me.

34

House of Games

I sleep for thirteen hours straight, beyond Sofía's leaving, beyond check-out at the hotel. It is the middle of Tuesday afternoon by the time I wake up, as if from a coma, wrapped in a warm sweat of deep relaxation. For a long time I simply lie in bed staring at the bad paintings on the walls, enjoying a rare sensation of total restedness. Kitson asked me to call him with an update on the Sofía situation, but I run a bath first and order coffee and scrambled eggs from room service before dialing his number.

"Best if you come direct to the safe house," he says, "the flat in Tetuán." He texts the address to my mobile.

Kitson's team have set themselves up in a cramped apartment block in Barrio de la Ventilla, about two kilometers northwest of the Kia towers. I take the Line 10 metro two stops beyond Plaza de Castilla to Begoña, where I hail a cab and instruct the driver to loop counterclockwise around the Parque de la Paz en route to Vía Límite. There's no surveillance problem, but I walk the last two blocks just to be certain and arrive a short time after five o'clock.

"Sleep well?" Kitson asks as he greets me at the door.

"Like Sunny von Bülow," I reply, and he smiles, ushering me into the flat.

Four spooks—two men, two women—are gathered around a small Formica-topped table in the kitchen. I recognize two of them immediately: lead on, Macduff, and the woman from the tire garage near Moby Dick. All four look up from cups of tea and smile, as if at an old, familiar friend.

"You'll all recognize Alec Milius," Kitson says, and I'm not sure if this is just small talk or a dig at my countersurveillance technique. Either way, I'm irritated by it; it makes me look second-rate. Macduff is the first to respond, rising from his seat to shake my hand.

"Anthony," he says. "Good to meet you."

I was expecting something altogether different, a voice to match the bustling military gent encountered at the Prado, but that was obviously cover. Anthony has a scrambled accent—Borders, at a guess—and is dressed in stonewashed jeans with a black Meat Loaf T-shirt. Tire lady is next, too boxed in at her seat to be able to stand but honoring me with a look of real admiration as she stretches to shake my hand.

"Ellie," she says. "Ellie Cox."

The other man is Geoff, the woman, Michelle. The latter is under thirty and on secondment from the Canadian SIS. Kitson mentioned running a team of eight, so the other four must be out tracking Buscon. I am offered tea, which I accept, and sit down on a low pine bench at the head of the table. To my surprise all of them look a little bored and washed-out, and there's a strange end-of-term atmosphere to the gathering. If they are suspicious of me, they do not show it; if anything, they seem grateful to welcome a new face into their world, somebody unknown whom they can analyze and work out. Bottles of gin and mineral water and Cacique are lined up along a narrow shelf above Ellie's head, with cans of baked beans, some Hob Nobs, and a pot of Marmite peeking out of a cupboard near the cooker. Geoff has a British car magazine open on the table in front of him and spills a little milk on it as he pours my tea. Plates and mugs are drying on a metal rack beside the sink and behind me there's a clotheshorse swamped in laundry. It must be a tight squeeze living in here with four colleagues; they must get on each other's nerves.

"So you're the ones I've been seeing in my rearview mirror?" I ask, an unplanned joke that successfully breaks the ice.

"No. That was just Anthony and Michelle," Kitson replies, and we chat amicably together for five minutes until he says, "Alec, come with me next door," and one by one they nod and quietly go back to their cups of tea. Geoff opens the car magazine, Ellie sighs and plays with her mobile phone, Macduff picks at his ears. It's like the end of visiting hours in a hospital. I am led down a short corridor to a bedroom at the rear of the apartment with clear views over the distant Sierras. When we have both sat down in chairs next to a television by the window, Kitson takes out a pad and a piece of paper and asks what happened with Sofía.

"She has nothing to do with it."

He looks understandably suspicious, as if I'm protecting her. "Nothing?"

"Nothing. It was a misunderstanding."

"Enlighten me."

Once again I have to admit a professional failing to Kitson. This is becoming a habit.

"Buscon must have spotted me following him back from the Irish Rover. He put some of his government friends on my tail and threatened Sofía when they found out about our affair."

"What do you mean, 'government friends'?"

"I don't know for sure. Men involved in the dirty war. Guardia Civil, Military Intelligence, Mercenaries R Us. Buscon left the package for Sofía under the name Abel Sellini. She picked it up thinking it was connected to her work and found this inside."

I pass the note to Kitson. He has difficulty translating the Spanish, so I do it for him.

"Can you be sure this is from Buscon?"

"Who else could it be from?"

Kitson's expression hints at infinite possibilities. He looks faintly annoyed, as if I have let him down one too many times. "So there's a chance that they could still be following you?"

The logical sequence of events would certainly imply a serious threat to the integrity of his operation. If Buscon had me watched long term, there's a risk that one or more of my meetings with Kitson was compromised.

"They're not following me," I assure him, with as much force and sincerity as I can muster. "I've been clean every time we've come into contact." Thankfully, Kitson seems to accept this.

"And Sofía?"

"She was very upset. I told her that the note was from some Russian property developers."

"Mafia?"

"That's certainly what I was hinting at."

"And she believed you?"

"Yes."

At this point a phone rings in Kitson's pocket. He checks the readout and frowns.

"I have to take this," he says and leaves the room in order to do so. Ellie comes in after a minute, ostensibly to offer me more tea, although I suspect that she has been asked by Kitson to make sure that I don't snoop around. There's a framed photograph next to the bed, shot in middle-class black-and-white, a sharp-eyed woman whom I take to be Kitson's wife holding two small children. This must be where he sleeps. The shirt he wore to our last meeting at Colón has been dry-cleaned and is hanging near the window, and there's a carton of Lucky Strikes lying on the floor. I'm rubbing the bruise on my knee when he returns to the room and asks me to come back in the morning.

"Something's come up. I'm sorry, Alec. A lead on de Francisco. We'll have to finish this thing tomorrow."

But it's another seventy-two hours before we are able to meet again. I go back to the safe house the next day, only to be told that Kitson has been "unavoidably detained" in Lisbon. Geoff and Michelle are the only members of the team at home and we share a genial cup of instant coffee at the kitchen table while I recommend bars in La Latina and an Indian restaurant where they can get a half-decent chicken dhansak.

"Thank God for that," Geoff says. "Christ, I miss a good curry."

That night, doubtless while the two of them are flirting over *sag àloo* at the Taj Mahal, I join Julian in an Irish pub near Cibeles, at his invitation, to watch a football match between Real Madrid and Manchester United. United lose and I find that I am pleased for Real, consoling Julian with an expensive shellfish dinner at the Cervecería Santa Barbara in Alonso Martínez. Otherwise the time passes slowly. I try to rest as much as possible, to go to the cinema and relax, but my sleep is corrupted by nightmares of capture, vivid small-hour screenings of torture and abuse. A private doctor in Barrio Salamanca prescribes me some sleeping pills and I have blood work done for peace of mind, the results of which come through as clean. It's noticeable over this period that Zulaika has not published anything in *Ahotsa* about the dirty war and I wonder if SIS have silenced him, with either threats or a bribe. Nor is there news about Egileor, or any fresh developments in the killing of Txema Otamendi.

Finally Kitson calls and pulls me in at lunchtime on the 25th. We go immediately to his bedroom and it is just as if nothing has changed in three days. He is wearing the same clothes, sitting in the same chair, perhaps even smoking the same cigarette.

"I've been doing some thinking," he says. "You're not going to like it."

I see that his expression is very serious. This is the thing I have dreaded. He has brought me here to cut me out. SIS has reflected on events and decided that I have made too many mistakes.

"Go on."

"I think it would be best if you stopped seeing Sofía. Monday night was your last night together. OK? You work for us now. No more off-piste activities. It's just too dangerous."

I agree immediately. If that's all he wants, if that's all it takes to win this thing, I'll do it.

"It also makes sense in the light of what I'm about to discuss with you, but we need Anthony in here before I can do that."

Right on cue there's a knock at the door. Kitson says, "Yes," and Macduff enters the room. I had no idea he was even in the flat. When I came in, Geoff and Michelle were on their own in the sitting room eating bowls of cereal and watching *Friends* on DVD. How did Macduff know to come in at exactly that moment? Was he listening from another room?

"That's odd," Kitson tells him, voicing my own doubt. "I was just coming to get you. Been eavesdropping, Anthony?"

"No, sir."

He sits on the bed. He is slimmer than I thought, about five feet ten. Strange to hear a man in his late forties refer to Kitson as "sir." What are perceived as his weaknesses that he should have been overlooked for promotion?

"Have you seen the news?"

It takes me a beat to realize that Kitson is talking to me. "No," I reply, and he leans over and switches on the television. Macduff mutes the sound with a remote control that he has picked up off the floor. A game show is ending on Telemadrid.

"Two bars in the Basque country were shot up at dawn today," he says, "one in Bayonne, the other in Hendaye. On the French side."

I can feel Macduff's eyes studying me as he waits for my reply. In the absence of a specialist, am I regarded as the resident expert on ETA and the GAL? He wants to know how good I am, how quickly I can analyze and react to this new development. For the first time I feel a sense of pressure from one of Kitson's team and realize that I have something to prove.

"Bars used by ETA?"

"That's what they're saying," Kitson replies.

The link is obvious. "Then it's a new front in the dirty war. The GAL regularly shot up bars and restaurants on the French side in the 1980s, targeting terrorist exiles. They're employing the same tactics. Anybody hurt?"

"Nobody. It was prebreakfast." Kitson has one eye on the television, waiting for the evening news. "An old man drinking coffee got a shard of glass in his hand, the barman in Hendaye felt a bullet buzz past his head."

"Sounds nasty. Who speaks Spanish?"

Neither of them understands my question.

"I mean, where are you getting your information? Who speaks Spanish well enough to understand the news?"

"Geoff," Macduff replies. They both look a little sheepish, as if it's embarrassing that the two most experienced members of an SIS task force in Spain are not fluent in the local language. "A Basque journalist went on TV claiming that one of the cars involved in the shooting had Madrid license plates."

"Did you get his name?"

Kitson has to flick through the pad. He has trouble reading his own handwriting. "Larzabal," he says finally. "Eugenio Larzabal."

"And you say he was a Basque journalist?"

"For *Gara,* yes."

I say that I have never heard of him and take the name down in some notes of my own, trying to look professional. "What about Zulaika?"

"What about him?" Kitson asks.

"Have you been following him? Do you know if he plans to go into print with the dirty-war story?"

"Zulaika is going to keep his mouth shut for a week or two. That's been arranged." So they did get to him. "But he's not the only journalist in Euskal Herria. A kidnapping, a murder, a car with Madrid plates—it all starts to add up. Somebody somewhere is going to make the same sort of links. And once that happens, we'll be playing catch-up."

"You mean you'll have to tell the Spanish authorities what you know?"

"I mean they'll probably already know as much as we do."

I try to gauge the operation from a political perspective. How does SIS gain from failing to report the existence of the new GAL to the Aznar government right away? Perhaps Kitson's superiors care nothing for the legitimacy of the Spanish state, only for the terrorist networks that can be traced by pursuing Buscon. The dirty war is a sideshow in which I am a bit-part player. But then Kitson says something to challenge that assertion.

"Over the past few days we've been looking into Javier de Francisco's background, trying to get a fix on his motives. Anthony's come up with a plan."

This is Macduff's cue. He's more deferential in front of Kitson, less self-assured than he was on Tuesday with the others. Sitting up straighter on the bed, he gets the nod from his boss and embarks on a well-rehearsed monologue.

"As you know, Alec, Mr. de Francisco is the secretary of state for security here in Spain, to all intents and purposes the number two at the Interior Ministry under his old friend Félix Maldonado. Now if what you were saying last time is correct, senior figures in ETA believe he may be organizing this dirty war against them." Kitson sniffs and turns in his chair. "As I think was explained to you last time, we don't have the manpower here to embark on a full-scale investigation of whatever elements in the Spanish government may or may not be up to."

"Not yet, anyway," Kitson says, an interjection that would suggest that discussions are ongoing in London over the possibility of ramping up the size of his operation. That can only be good for my career.

"Now, it may come as a shock to you to learn that, as a result of their work at G8 summits, EU delegations, and so forth, SIS keep files on all senior government personnel with an impact on British affairs." Macduff lets this sink in and seems confused when I do not appear more surprised. "I've developed what I think is a good idea of how we might gain access to some of the information flowing into and out of the Interior Ministry."

"You mean blackmail? You mean you have biographical leverage with de Francisco?"

"Not as such."

There's a short pause while both men look at one another. I can feel myself being dragged into something amoral.

"How are you feeling, Alec?" Kitson asks. "What do you think you're capable of?"

The question annoys me. Why would Kitson ask something like that in front of a colleague? He must know that I'm still not properly recovered from the kidnapping.

"What do you mean?"

I look at Macduff. He looks at me. Kitson lights a Lucky Strike.

"Here's the situation. There are any number of ways we can find out information about an individual or group of individuals from an intelligence perspective. I don't need to list them for you. However, mounting an operation of any scale against a government minister is fraught with difficulty. As of this moment, not even our own station here in Madrid is aware of my team's presence on Spanish soil. In order to get comprehensive technical coverage of de Francisco we would have to alert the embassy in order to get the right kit smuggled out to us in a diplomatic bag."

"And you don't want to do that?"

"I don't want to do that."

It's obvious where this is going. They want to get me on the inside. But how? "So what are the alternatives?" I ask.

Kitson takes a long drag on the cigarette. "Well, if we had Francisco's phone numbers we could call Cheltenham and get them on a hot list, but that would alert GCHQ . . ."

". . . which you don't want to do . . ."

"Which we don't want to do. *Yet*. So that's where you come in. That's why I need to know how you're feeling."

"I feel fine, Richard."

Macduff looks at the floor.

"Really?"

"Fine."

This is not strictly true—how could it be, after what happened?— but I give my reply an ironic emphasis that effectively shuts down the discussion.

"OK then. The thing is, you speak Spanish. You know Madrid. And you've done this sort of work before."

"You mean JUSTIFY?"

"I do mean JUSTIFY, yes."

And there's the rub. Kitson has been very smart. He knows that after what happened with Katharine and Fortner I felt ashamed and ruined, as if nothing would ever wipe out the stain of treachery that led to Kate's and Will's deaths. He knows that all I have ever wanted was a second chance, to do it right, to prove to myself and to others that I was capable of success in the secret world. However, just in case I get cold feet, just in case he has read me wrong, he is going to pitch me in front of a colleague. That way it will be difficult to refuse. Kitson knows I won't want to look like a coward in front of Macduff. He grinds out the half-smoked cigarette.

"To get to the point, we wondered how you'd feel about becoming a raven." Macduff explains the term unnecessarily, perhaps because he has mistaken the look of surprise on my face for ignorance. "That is, somebody who sets out to seduce a target for the purposes of obtaining sensitive information."

"You want me to sleep with Javier de Francisco?"

This makes both of them laugh. "Not quite." Kitson scratches an arm and presses out of his seat. "Anthony is going to conduct some research of his own over the next ten days into the possible structure of the dirty war. We've already traced what looks like a link between secret Interior Ministry accounts and Luis Buscon. But meanwhile we'd like you to forge a relationship with one of de Francisco's personal assistants in an effort to discover how far up the food chain this operation against ETA really goes." He is standing by the window now, looking directly at me. "That will happen in tandem with our ongoing surveillance of Buscon, which we cannot ignore. Now if it's decided that the conspiracy has infected the upper levels of the Aznar government, then that obviously has an impact on our alliance with Spain. Any information you gather will go back to London and will be acted on. But without your help we don't have the resources to attack this thing."

It appears that I have no choice. A shallow part of me just wants to find out what the PA looks like.

"There's just one problem," I tell him.

"What's that?"

"You guys share a lot of intelligence with the CIA. I don't want them knowing where I am. If I come up with useful intel, I don't want my name on any reports that might find their way to Langley."

Macduff looks momentarily confused, but Kitson sees where I'm coming from.

"Alec, as you can imagine, bringing up your name with the Cousins isn't something we are in the habit of doing. JUSTIFY is an episode in the relationship between our two great nations that both of us, I am sure, would rather forget." A little grin here, almost a wink. "The CIA's contempt for you is certainly equal to, if not in excess of, your contempt for them. Neither Anthony nor myself nor anybody on my team has any intention of involving the agency in what's going on out here."

It's strange to hear Kitson speak so plainly of my reputation within the CIA.

"So this is why you wanted me to stop seeing Sofía? Because of this girl?"

"Part of the reason," he admits. "It would only complicate things if you continued to see her behind Julian's back."

The familiar use of Julian's Christian name makes me edgy, as if Kitson and Church have become friends. In my darker moments I still fear the revelation of a conspiracy between them. Nevertheless I remain light and cooperative.

"Well, I don't know whether to be flattered that you think I'd be capable of pulling off something like this, or offended that you see me as an amateur gigolo." There's an awkward pause while both of them work out whether or not they're supposed to laugh. Kitson does so; Macduff hedges his bets and produces a weak grin. "If she's de Francisco's PA, how do you know she's not involved in the dirty war herself?"

"We don't. They've certainly known each other long enough. And if she is, that's something that you'll need to find out."

I meet Kitson's eye. He's willing me to do this.

"Well, it's probably something I could look at."

I haven't begun to think through the consequences. Sex for information. Seduction for revenge. I can make jokes about gigolos in front of them, but the truth is that this is grim and seedy.

"Good," Kitson says. "Now for the bad news." From an envelope beside the bed he produces a series of photographs of the girl. My reservations intensify. "As you can see, we're not talking about Penelope Cruz."

The woman in the photographs is very tall and thin, with a long nose, limp, straight hair, and a pointed chin. Not ugly, exactly, but certainly not someone who would ordinarily draw my eye on Gran Vía. What am I letting myself in for? Is it too late to turn back? I should just abandon this whole thing and go back to my life with Endiom. The girl is past what most Spaniards would regard as marriageable age and dresses in a manner that can only be described as conservative. On gut instinct, however, I know that I'll be able to win her over. She looks unhappy. She looks insecure.

"What's her name?"

"Carmen Arroyo."

"And how much do you know about her?"

"We know a lot."

35

La Bufanda

Carmen Arroyo is thirty-five years old. She was born in Cantimpalos, a pueblo sixteen kilometers north of Segovia, on April 11, 1968, a daughter to José María Arroyo, a schoolteacher, and his Basque wife, Mitxelena, who is currently in hospital undergoing surgery for a small melanoma on her left shoulder. Carmen is an only child. She was educated at the Instituto Giner de los Ríos in Segovia and moved to Madrid at the age of eighteen, a typical *provinciana*. Having graduated from the Universidad Complutense in Moncloa with a mediocre degree in economics, she spent three years in Colombia working with underprivileged children at a hostel in Medellín, returning to Madrid in the winter of 1995. She passed the open competition for the Spanish civil service at Level D and has worked in both the Foreign and Agriculture ministries in a secretarial capacity, always for Javier de Francisco, who has become a close friend. She became his personal secretary in the spring of 2001, shortly after Aznar appointed him Secretario de Estado de Seguridad under Maldonado. Her appearance alongside both men at an EU conference on policing later that year was noted by SIS.

José María Arroyo owns a two-bedroom apartment in the neighborhood of La Latina on Calle de Toledo, right beside the metro station. Carmen has lived there for the past eight years. She shares the flat with an Argentinian actress, Laura de Rivera, who spends most of her time in Paris with a boyfriend, Tibaud, and is therefore rarely at home. Carmen has savings at the BBVA amounting to almost €17,000 and pays only a peppercorn rent to her father for use of the apartment. For the past five nights she has visited her mother's hospital bed at 7 P.M. sharp, taking fruit, flowers, or a woman's magazine on each occasion. She listens to a lot of classical music, attended a Schubert concert at the Círculo de Bellas Artes on Wednesday evening, and shops mostly at Zara for clothes. The take quality from the bug fitted by Macduff in her kitchen is good enough to ascertain that she watched a dubbed American movie—*Annie Hall*—on Thursday night while eating supper off her knees. Carmen talked to herself throughout the film, laughing regularly and making two phone calls in quick succession at around 11 P.M. The first was to her mother, to wish her good night, the second to her best friend, María Velasco, to arrange to meet for a drink at a bar in Calle Martín de los Heros tomorrow night. That's my opportunity. That's how we're going to start things off.

I wash my hair, shave, and put on a decent set of clothes, but orchestrating the meeting is even easier than anticipated. I wait in the foyer of the Alphaville cinema until Carmen shows up at around 11:30 P.M. wearing a dark jacket and narrow trousers in Thatcher blue. She's taller than I expected, thinner and more ungainly. She looks like the sort of girl I used to avoid in London: plain, shy, and unimaginative. Once inside she finds María and the two of them sit down at a table at the back of the bar, each nursing a bottle of Sol and a cigarette. I follow two minutes later, pick a table with an eyeline to Carmen's chair, and retrieve a crumpled copy of *Homage to Catalonia* from my back pocket. The flirting happens almost instantaneously; indeed, she initiates it, sliding the odd glance and smile in my direction, tentatively at first, as if she's not quite sure that it's really happening, and then gradually gaining in confidence as the minutes tick by. I steal looks only a couple of times early on, careful not to overplay my hand, but at one point she actually blushes when she looks up to find me staring directly at her. For half an hour we sit there, Carmen doing her best to concentrate on what María is telling her but finding it increasingly difficult not to be drawn away into a secret glance, a shy, blinking eye contact with her mystery admirer. María eventually cottons on and even turns around in her seat—much to Carmen's embarrassment—ostensibly to attract the waiter's attention but clearly to get a better fix on the stranger who has had such a remarkable effect on her friend. Then, at midnight, Macduff makes the call to my mobile and I pick up my book and leave.

She takes the bait. On the back of my chair I have left a scarf—a present from Sofía—and, sure enough, when I'm just a few meters down the street I hear footsteps behind me and turn to see Carmen looking anxious and out of breath.

"*Perdone,*" she says. "*Dejó la bufanda en el asiento. Aquí está.*"

She holds out the scarf and I pretend that I don't speak Spanish.

"Oh Christ. That's so kind of you. *Gracias.* I totally forgot. Thank you."

"You are American?"

By phoning Carmen at work and pretending to be a journalist, Macduff was able to establish that she speaks English. Her accent is half decent, but it's too early to tell if she's a linguist.

"Not American. Scottish."

"Ah, *escocés.*"

If we can communicate solely in English, that will play to my advantage. In the course of our relationship Carmen might say something to a friend or colleague in apparent confidence that I will be able to translate and understand.

"Yes. I'm just here in Madrid for a few months. You?"

"*Soy madrileña,*" she says, with evident pride. "*Me llamo Carmen.*"

"Alex. Nice to meet you."

We kiss in the traditional fashion and her cheeks feel dry and warm. It's already clear that the first part of the strategy is working well: Carmen has been bold enough to follow me outside and to strike up a conversation, and she clearly doesn't want me to leave. In time we'll exchange phone numbers, just as Kitson hoped, and the relationship will be up and running. Then all I need to do is work out a way of finding her attractive.

"You are enjoying yourself here?"

"Oh I love it. It's such a great city. I'd never been here before and everybody has just been so friendly."

"Like me?"

"Like you, Carmen."

A first tension-shifting laugh. It is a strange sensation, this falsified union, this charade, but as we exchange further pleasantries I find myself warming to her, if only out of a sense of guilt that my sole purpose here this evening is to take advantage of her decency and palpable loneliness. If I can bring a little happiness into her life, then where's the harm?

"So you're here on holiday?"

"No, not really. I'm supposed to be researching a PhD."

"You are student?"

"Sort of. I used to work on a newspaper in Glasgow but I'm taking two years out, with a view to becoming an academic."

The structure of this sentence is too complicated for her and she frowns. I rephrase it and tell her the title of my thesis—"The British Battalion of the International Brigades 1936–1939"–and she looks impressed.

"This sounds interesting." Then there is an awkward delay.

"It's cold and you're not wearing a coat," I tell her, just to fill the silence.

"Yes. Maybe I should get back inside."

Don't let her go just yet.

"But when am I going to see you again?"

Carmen's face twists with pleasure. This sort of thing rarely happens to her. "I don't know."

"Well, can I telephone you? Can I have your number? I'd love to see you again."

"*Claro.*"

And it's that simple. I scribble the number down on a blank page in the Orwell book and wonder if I should warn her, right here and now, that her life is about to be turned inside out by a bunch of scheming British spooks. Instead I say, "You should go inside. It's cold."

"*Sí*," she replies. "My friend is waiting. Who are you meeting?"

Kitson anticipated that Carmen would want to know if I have a girlfriend or wife, so I have a prepared response to the question. "Just somebody from my language class."

"*Vale.*" Something like disappointment, even a shiver of panic, runs through her eyes, although I may be reading too much into this. At the risk of exaggeration, it seems that she has already fallen for me.

"Thank you for this," I tell her.

"*Qué?*"

I hold up the scarf.

"Ah. *La bufanda.* This was nothing, Alex. It was nothing."

And we say good-bye. Two minutes later, when I have walked away from the bar and phoned Macduff to give him an update on the evening, a bus passes through the north end of Plaza de España. A banner is posted along one side advertising a new British film starring Rowan Atkinson. It looks like a Bond spoof—*Johnny English*. When I see the tagline beneath the predictably idiotic image of Atkinson wearing black tie, I have to smile:

"*Prepárate para la inteligencia británica.*"

Prepare yourself for British intelligence.

36

Blind Date

Carmen's conversation with María the following evening makes flattering listening. Macduff has isolated the relevant sections of dialogue, revealing the target's excitement at the prospect of meeting me again, married to an anxiety that I will fail to call. María counsels caution—it's in her nature to do so—but she shares Carmen's basic view that I am *"guapo."* Their only reservation, predictably, concerns my marital status, or the possible existence of a girlfriend back in Glasgow.

"You always have to be careful with men from the UK," María warns. "They're emotionally repressed. My cousin had a boyfriend from London once. He was very odd. Didn't wash properly, never spoke to his family, wore terrible clothes. They dress very scruffily, the English. And they drink. *Joder.* This boy was always in the pub, watching football, buying alcohol. Then he would eat kebabs on the way home. It was very strange."

I translate most of this for Kitson and Macduff, and it's no use pretending that I don't derive a significant amount of pleasure from Carmen's crush. It lifts my spirits after the farm, and I think Kitson understands this. He seems satisfied that our plan is on course and we discuss the next step.

The following morning—Monday—I call Carmen's mobile and leave a message expressing the hope that she will ring me back. When she does so, three hours later, she plays it cool but agrees to meet for a drink in Plaza Santa Ana on Wednesday evening. Kitson is not happy about the delay, but I assure him that things will move quickly once the two of us have spent some time together.

We meet beside the statue of Lorca at 9 P.M. under the watchful eye of the Hotel Reina Victoria, the façade of which acts as a physical reminder that I have yet to break off relations with Sofía. Carmen has dressed up for the occasion, as we expected she would, although her taste in clothes has not improved from Saturday night. She's also wearing a new perfume that I don't like, floral remnants of which linger in my nose long after I have kissed her hello.

"You look great," I tell her, and the compliment is returned as she suggests walking just a few meters to the Cervecería Alemana, an old Hemingway haunt where I took Saul on his second night.

"You have been here before?" she asks.

"Never."

Carmen is easy to talk to, intelligent and eager to please, and at first I ask a lot of questions, to set her at ease and to establish that I'm a good listener. It's what anyone would do on a first date, so the artifice feels natural and just. I hear about her work in Medellín, her friendship with María, and she speaks briefly about her job in the Interior Ministry. I deliberately let this slide and instead steer the conversation toward a discussion about the importance of the family in Spanish life, instigating a good ten minutes about Mitxelena's skin cancer. Looking suitably sympathetic, I tell her that my own mother had a malignant melanoma on her leg that was successfully removed, with no further complications, in 1998. Then I talk about my PhD, my job at the *Glasgow Herald* editing copy written by drunken Scottish hacks and she laughs when I make up a story about a crime reporter called Jimmy who was caught screwing a work-experience girl on the editor's sofa. She does not seem prudish or coy about sex but has an astonishingly conservative view of society and politics, even for a servant of the Aznar government. When, in a second tapas bar, I venture a mildly critical opinion of the Bush administration, Carmen frowns and argues with some force that America's mission in Iraq is not about oil or weapons of mass destruction, but a long-term crusade to create stable democracies right across the Middle East.

"If we are strong," she says, "if we have the courage to see that young men will no longer wish to become terrorists because they live in these new democratic environments, then the world will be a safer place. We cannot continue to be isolated, Alex. Spain must move into the rest of the world, and this is where Aznar is taking us."

Such an attitude is relevant to my operation inasmuch as it reveals something about Carmen's political affiliations. In due course, I will have to ask her for information that may help to bring down the government; her willingness to assist in that task will certainly be affected by her loyalty to the state. On this basis, it seems sensible to position myself in the same ideological neighborhood.

"I couldn't agree more," I tell her. "It's not naïve to suppose that once every family in the Arab world has a color TV, a microwave, and a vote, things will become a lot easier. I often think that Arab leaders *prefer* violence and poverty to democracy and freedom, don't you? If they could only share the Western values Bush and Aznar are trying to promote."

"What values do you mean?"

I have to scramble for answers. "You know. Honesty, tolerance, the desire for peace. There's nothing we want more than for these people to live civilized, peaceful lives as part of a civilized, peaceful global community. The idea that America would invade Iraq just to get its hands on some oil and a few construction contracts is cynical and counterproductive. It makes me really angry."

I may have gone a bit far here, because even Carmen looks astonished to have encountered a man under the age of forty espousing such views. Yet her perplexed expression gradually melts into one of intense relief. She has met a fellow believer. Assured now of both our physical and intellectual compatibility, she flirts with greater emphasis, and I feed off the energy of her desire, even as my own lies dormant. We order tapas and I pretend that I have eaten *jamón* on only two occasions in my life, a confession that cements her impression of me as a card-carrying *guiri*. For the rest of the night she makes a point of introducing me to the delights of Spanish cuisine— *boquerones en vinagre, pimientos de padrón*—and I play the role of the amazed tourist to perfection, marveling at the variety and sophistication of her nation's food. I am even mindful of María's warning about drunken Englishmen and match Carmen drink for drink despite longing for the fuel of vodka.

"You know what I like about Madrid?" I say at one point.

"No, Alex. Tell me."

We are sitting in La Venencia drinking *manzanilla* with a bowl of olives and a plate of *mojama*. The bar is itself an appropriately artificial environment, an old-style, spit-and-sawdust *bodega* in the heart of Huertas where the bullfight and flamenco posters have hung on the walls for decades, stained by years of smoke.

"I love it that the city is so relaxed and friendly. I love it that when I order a whiskey, the barman asks *me* when to stop pouring. I love the fact that the sun is shining virtually every day and that you can see small children running around in the Plaza Mayor at midnight. In Glasgow everything is so *gray*. People are drunk all the time and miserable. Madrid really lifts the spirits."

She falls for it.

"I like you, Alex, very much." It is a statement without any specific carnal inflection, largely because Carmen would surely be incapable of even the simplest eroticism. Nevertheless, her inference is clear: if I play my cards right, our relationship will quickly become sexual. Leaning across to touch her hand, I say that I like her too—very much—and both of us savor the moment with a mouthful of cured tuna.

"So, I have to ask now. Do you have a girlfriend back in Glasgow?"

I summon one of my consoling smiles. "Me? No. Used to, but we split up." She looks pleased. "And you?"

Macduff has not been able to ascertain anything about her previous relationships, although I would suspect that Carmen has been on the losing end of one or two disappointing encounters. There is something desperate, almost pleading in her nature, which a man might find initially sympathetic but increasingly tiresome. Her political views would also find few sympathetic ears, except possibly among those who still mourn the passing of General Franco.

"Not at the moment, no," she replies, a little fizz of spittle appearing at the side of her mouth. "For a while I was with somebody at work, but it did not go anywhere."

Now this is interesting. It might be possible to find out whom Carmen was seeing and to use that information against her. As soon as I get an e-mail address, Kitson might be able to persuade somebody back in London to look through her accounts on the sly. If either de Francisco or Maldonado was the boyfriend, that would certainly give us leverage. We talk for another half hour, mostly about Glasgow and the Scottish Highlands, but at around midnight Carmen yawns and says that she needs a good night's sleep.

This is it. The consummation. I offer to walk her the short distance from Calle Echegaray back to her apartment in La Latina.

"You English are so polite," she replies. I don't bother to remind her that Alex Miller is Scottish. "That is very kind of you. It will be nice to have you walk me home."

Yet things go wrong once we get there. Convinced that Carmen is both expectant of, even desperate for, a threshold kiss, I lean in, in full view of the customers at her local bar, only to be rebuffed by a slow, careful turn of the head.

"What's the matter?"

"Not now," she says. "Not here."

"Why?" For some reason I am intensely irritated. I had built myself up for this on the walk and her rejection is crushing. "What's the matter?"

A man is looking at us from across the street.

"I do not know if I want to kiss you yet. Please understand."

It is difficult to read her face. Is this a well brought-up, conservative girl playing hard to get, or a genuine expression of a sudden loss of interest? Was she worried that I would expect to be invited up-stairs, or simply embarrassed to indulge in a lengthy snog in front of her neighbors? Within a few seconds Carmen has kissed me all too briefly on the cheek and gone inside with a promise to "be in touch." I feel angry, but also embarrassed. The man across the street—who appears to be waiting for a cab—is still facing me and I look him full in the eye from twenty meters, staring him down. How dare she flirt with me all night and then duck home without a kiss? What the hell am I going to tell Kitson? Perhaps I was too self-confident. Perhaps I was too assertive and sure of success. In the shadow of my eyes, did she see the damage of the farm, of JUSTIFY and Kate? It is impossi-ble to know. Perhaps she decided, as long ago as the Alemana, that it was not in her best interests to make room in her life for a man who was so obviously damaged. But I thought that I had hidden that from her. I thought that I had played the game.

"How did it go?" Kitson asks when he calls at 1 A.M. "Anthony tells me you're not in the apartment. What happened?"

"Carmen Arroyo is a good Catholic girl is what happened." I strug-gle to sound composed. "We had a little kiss on the doorstep, nothing more, then she went inside. It was all very romantic, Richard. We're having dinner again on Friday."

"Did you set that up or did she?"

"The latter."

"You don't sound convinced."

"How does somebody sound convinced about something like that?"

There is a short pause. I have never been able to lie convincingly to Kitson.

"Then good," he says. "So you'll brief Anthony tomorrow?"

"I'll brief Anthony tomorrow."

37

The Raven

As it turns out, I needn't have worried. On Thursday morning Carmen sends me a text message apologizing if she seemed "strange" outside the apartment and promising to "make this up" to me if I am free for lunch on Saturday. I give Macduff the good news over coffee—explaining that our Friday dinner date has morphed into a weekend lunch—and he concurs with me that Carmen simply didn't want to seem cheap by sleeping with me on our first date. I run through my general impressions of the evening and then head home for a siesta. The vital question—concerning her willingness to betray de Francisco once she learns of the dirty war—is left unanswered. None of us can make an informed judgment about that until I have spoken to her at length both about her career and her views on Basque terror. Of course it's still possible that she herself might be part of the conspiracy. It's an implausible thesis, but the liar is always vulnerable to his own deceit.

When I have woken up, later than planned after a night of crippling dreams, I walk down Ventura Rodríguez and check e-mails at the Internet café. There's one from Saul, which reawakens all my old paranoia just at the point at which I was sure there was nothing left to worry about.

From: sricken1789@hotmail.com
To: almmlalam@aol.com

Subject: Enrique

So, what does a recently divorced man of 33 do with his time except sit around drinking Rioja and watching DVDs? And what does he do once he gets bored of doing that and of ringing up his old girlfriends, EVERY SINGLE ONE OF WHOM is now living in Queen's Park or Battersea with her "wonderful husband" and their little "bundle of joy" and their wedding list crockery and their David Gray albums? Well, a recently divorced man of 33 writes down a list of famous Spanish movie stars and translates their names into English.

Here's what I came up with:
Antonio Banderas = Anthony Flags
Penelope Cruz = Penelope Cross
Benicio del Toro = Ben of the Bull
Paz Vega = Peaceful Lowlands

Good game, isn't it? Only, I was doing this for quite a long time, got into singers and politicians, and guess what I discovered?

Julio Iglesias = Julian Church

He's a spook, Alec! It's a cover name! All your worst nightmares have been confirmed! Pack your bags! Sell your flat! Check your underwear for bugs!

Hope all well—

S

I cannot allow myself to react to this. If I am going to do my job properly there can be no doubt in my mind about the legitimacy of Kitson's operation, of Sofía's possible role in the dirty war or of Julian's double life as a spy. All these things have been ironed out. I have to blank out such conspiracies. In none of my initial research into Julian's background, nor in the more recent discoveries regarding Nicole and his life in Colombia, did I discover anything to make me remotely suspicious about his real identity. Julian Church is just who he appears to be—a private banker with an adulterous wife living out the expat dream in Spain. Saul is just winding me up.

Carmen and I meet for lunch on Saturday at a restaurant off Calle de Serrano, and it is from this point on that our relationship starts to become more serious. Barrio Salamanca is a more rarefied environment than La Latina, and one in which she seems a good deal more relaxed, at home with the expensive wives and moneyed twentysomethings gabbling into their mobile phones in branches of Gucci and Christian Dior. I glimpse, not for the first time, her secret dream of joining this elite urban middle class through marriage; they are, after all, the very people who voted her boss into office. Afterward we go for a walk in the Retiro and I hire a rowboat in a spirit of romantic endeavor and about fifteen meters from the concrete shore we share our first, surprisingly skillful, kiss. I spend the rest of the afternoon in abject terror of encountering Sofía walking hand in hand with Julian but disguise my apprehension with ease. Fortune-tellers, portrait painters, Peruvian puppeteers, even a poet from Chile have set up stalls along the western edge of the Estanque lake and we drift from group to group in the dense crowds with the permanent accompaniment of panpiped music. On a grass verge near the café a group of Chinese immigrants are selling head and shoulder massages for a couple of euros. Carmen offers to buy me one—giggling now, really enjoying herself—but just as I have sat on the low stool and felt a dry hand settling on my aching neck, two policemen appear on horseback, scattering every illegal immigrant in the vicinity to the four winds.

"Not very relaxing," I joke, struggling to my feet. Carmen laughs and we kiss again and she puts her arm around my waist.

"Why don't you come back to my apartment?" She says.

And that's where it all begins. The truth is that I do not compare her to Sofía, to Kate, or to any other woman I have been with. The time that we spend in bed together over the next two days feels almost natural, as if there were never anything false nor morally reprehensible in my pursuit of her. You get so far into a deceit, so entwined in a legend, that the life becomes your own. After the first time, for example, standing under the shower at her apartment on Saturday afternoon, I realized that it would be possible to continue seeing Carmen for as long as it took to obtain the information. Equally, if my task were suddenly completed, I could walk out of the door and never see her again, only to feel guilty about the damage to her self-esteem at some later date. JUSTIFY was exactly like this. The process of long-term deception against Katharine and Fortner became commonplace. In order to function effectively as a spy, it was necessary to forget that I was lying to them. It is a version of method acting, I suppose, although one with far more serious implications.

So I stay at her place all weekend, closing both the kitchen and the bedroom doors in order to muffle the sound of our lovemaking from Macduff's intrusive bug. I find physical characteristics to enjoy in Carmen—her flat stomach, the stone-smooth sweep of her back— and concentrate on these even as others—the smell of her hair, her chin, her childish laugh—conspire to repel me. There was only one thing that proved unnerving: her oddly muted reaction to the bruises on my body. Carmen barely commented on them. I had felt that they would be a barrier between us, even a clue to my true identity, yet it was almost as if she was expecting to find them, almost as if she had encountered violence in a relationship before.

On Sunday evening she has to visit her mother in the hospital and I take the opportunity to go through her personal belongings, making a visual record of any Interior Ministry documents and searching for evidence of love letters from her former boyfriend at work. There is, of course, the danger that Laura de Rivera might return at short notice from Paris, so Macduff is stationed in the window of the bar outside her apartment, watching the front door for visitors. At eight I leave a note explaining that I need to go home for a change of clothes and dead-drop Macduff the list of phone numbers drawn from Carmen's mobile while she was asleep. There were two for de Francisco and one for Maldonado, but as yet no information from her personal computer. A laptop is sitting on a chair in our bedroom, but I could not risk booting it up for fear of encountering a password.

Come Monday evening we meet for dinner again and drink a lot of good homemade red vermouth in Oliveros, an old family-run bar around the corner from her apartment. Over meatballs downstairs in a brick cellar we have our first serious conversation about ETA, but there's nothing in Carmen's unequivocal view of Basque terror to merit lengthy analysis.

"They are all fascists," she tells me, and I suppress a smile. "The only way to deal with ETA is to arrest their leaders and to make sure that there is no place for them to hide. This is the view of the Spanish government and it also happens to be the view of my family."

The vehemence of this last remark, given that her mother is Basque, surprises me a little, but I let it go. She is otherwise predictable company. She laughs at my jokes. She teaches me words and phrases in Spanish. We find out about each other's families—Alex's parents live in Edinburgh and have been happily married for over thirty years—and talk about music and films. I try to appear as smitten and sincere as possible and Carmen seems to be as enthusiastic about me as she ever was. Afterward we return to her apartment and I suppose that I start to miss Sofía at this point, if only for her intemperate moods and greater skills as a lover. The friction of adultery with a beautiful woman is different from the necessity of sex with a plain, if willing, target.

"What are you thinking about?" she asks, coming back into the bedroom afterward wearing just a pair of white cotton underpants. She picks the condom up off the floor, ties it quickly and skillfully into a knot, and places it in the wastebasket.

"Nothing. Just how nice it is to be here. Just how relaxed I feel. I didn't think I'd meet anyone in Spain so quickly. I can't believe you've just dropped into my life."

Her body is very thin and very pale. When she sits on the bed I can see the skeletal outline of her rib cage, her slightly fallen breasts, the nipples so tiny and almost shy. She lies beside me, on her front, and I stroke her back, thinking of Zulaika for some reason, wondering what Kitson did to shut him up.

"Would you like to meet my friend María?" she asks.

"Of course, if you'd like to introduce us." It does not seem odd that we have grown so close so quickly. These are the first heady days of a new relationship and anything within the masquerade seems possible.

"There's a party on Friday night, in Chueca. A friend of hers is having it. She asked us to come along."

"María knows about me?"

"Of course!"

Laughter now as Carmen turns over, meeting me with a wet kiss that soaks my neck. The back of her head smells oddly sour, like the skin under a watch strap.

"And what have you told her?"

I know exactly what she's told her. So does Kitson, for that matter. So does Macduff. That Alex is "so sexy" and "funny" and "not like the men we always meet in Madrid." Thankfully the pair of them have yet to discuss the intricacies of our sex life within earshot of the bug, but it can only be a matter of time. Eventually Carmen falls asleep beside me, but not before I have asked if I can surf the net on her computer. She readily agrees, booting up the laptop (password: segovia) before coming back to bed. At about one o'clock I roll away from her and creep out of the room, running a search on the laptop for "Sellini," "Buscon," "Dieste," "Church," "Sofía," "Kitson," "Vicente," even "Saul" and "Ricken." Nothing comes up, so I simply transfer files in bulk onto a 128 MB removable memory stick. Let SIS sort wheat from chaff: there's bound to be something in de Francisco's correspondence that will give Kitson a solid lead. To cover my tracks—and to make it look as though I spent the hour using Internet Explorer—I visit a random selection of sites (Hotmail, BBC, itsyourturn.com), shutting down the machine at around 2 A.M. Carmen keeps a bottle of cheap cooking brandy in the kitchen and I take a decent slug of that before trying to get to sleep.

Yet Tuesday throws everything into confusion. After she has left for work at 8 A.M., I walk back through Sol and buy copies of *ABC, El Mundo,* and *El País* from a newsstand at the eastern end of Arenal. All three carry front-page reports about a failed attempt on the life of an ETA commander outside his home in Bilbao. A twenty-two-year-old Moroccan immigrant, Mohammed Chakor, has been charged by local police. Details are sketchy, but it seems that Tomás Orbé, a veteran of ETA campaigns in the 1980s and early '90s, was washing his car outside his house when he saw Chakor approach, brandishing a gun. In the ensuing struggle the Moroccan let off a single shot that missed Orbé by several feet, embedding itself in the car. Orbé, who was himself armed, returned fire, seriously injuring Chakor in the neck. At the same time, Eugenio Larzabal, the *Gara* journalist who reported seeing a Madrid license plate on the car that fled the shootings last week in southern France, asks in a page-one story whether it is "more than coincidence" that the kidnap and murder of Mikel Arenaza, the disappearance of Juan Egileor, the killing of Txema Otamendi, the double shootings at the ETA bars, and the attempt on the life of Tomás Orbé have all taken place within the last two months. I notice that he is careful, perhaps for legal reasons, not to mention any individuals or government departments by name, yet the thrust of the piece is unmistakable: the shadow of a third dirty war hovers over it like a jackal.

By 10 A.M. the Orbé incident is being discussed by "Basque experts" on a Spanish radio program. Television stations do not appear to be overly interested, although footage of the Bilbao house and interviews with local residents are shown on morning news programs. I call Kitson and we arrange to meet at two at the branch of Starbucks on Plaza de los Cubos. He's late and looks tired, apologizing for the venue.

"Naomi Klein would doubtless disapprove," he says, perching next to me on a stool, "but I have a soft spot for their double tall lattes."

We are looking out over the concrete square, at Princesa on the far side, at McDonald's and Burger King to our right. "Could be bloody Frankfurt," he mutters, before asking for my "take on Bilbao."

"Bad news. It's obviously part of our wider problem. This guy was hired by Madrid and he messed up. The papers say he's unconscious in hospital, but once he wakes up he's going to start talking. Even if he doesn't make it, the press now have a hard lead. They've never had evidence like this before and *Gara* is already hinting at what we know. Larzabal has written a piece this morning that effectively accuses the government of running a dirty war. It's likely to be ignored in the short term, but ask yourself this. Why would a twenty-two-year-old North African want to shoot an *etarra* unless he was paid to do it?"

"Why indeed? You don't think it's linked to Letamendía and Rekalde?"

That's impressive. Last weekend, two veteran members of ETA, Raul Letamendía and José Rekalde, caused the first serious split within the organization for twenty years by renouncing the armed struggle. Kitson and I haven't talked about this, but it's possible that he read something in the British press.

"Not unless it's a case of mistaken identity. ETA don't like their members renouncing the cause. If you're in, you're in for life. It's not pony club camp. When Dolores Catarain deserted in 1986, they had her assassinated. And Orbé is hard-line."

"I see." Kitson runs a hand across his head. I enjoyed trumping him.

"The only thing that doesn't make sense in all this is the *logic* of a dirty war. ETA is on its knees. They arrested seven of its members last week. The French are cooperating. They have nowhere left to hide."

"But it *must* exist," Kitson says, and I find myself nodding in agreement. There is simply too much evidence to suggest otherwise. "How's it going with the girl?"

I reach into my jacket pocket and take out the memory stick. "Very well. I got some stuff out of her laptop last night. It's all in here."

I put it on the counter and he lets it sit there. He'll pick it up when we leave.

"And what about the relationship? How are you finding that?"

"Fine."

"Just fine?"

This is not a conversation I particularly want to have. I'd rather talk about the incident up north.

"Well, what can I tell you, Richard? It's Hepburn and Tracy. It's Hanks and Ryan. She's the love of my life. I can't thank you enough for introducing us because I really think she might be the one."

He is laughing. "That bad?"

I shrug it off. "No. She's a nice person, fanatically right-wing, but you can't have everything. It doesn't feel right to be taking advantage of her. But if some good comes of it . . ."

He takes out a Lucky Strike. "Exactly. If some good comes of it." I have a book of matches in my pocket and light the cigarette for him. In some ways, this simple act seems to cause Kitson more embarrassment than the intimate discussion of my sex life. "Thank you," he says, exhaling.

"Don't mention it."

And there is an odd, uncomfortable silence. Two loud American tourists come in behind us and fill it.

"I suppose it was always going to be the case," he says eventually.

"What was?"

"That it would be awkward."

Does he think less of me for agreeing to do it? I have worried about that.

"Yes."

"Still, as you say, if what she tells you and what you get on the disks help us to stop what's going on, then it'll all have been worthwhile."

Strange that of all the things we have ever discussed, this should be the subject to cause Kitson the most discomfort. An Englishman through and through. He looks thoroughly unsettled. I try a joke.

"Unless she gives me the clap, in which case I might sue the Foreign Office."

But he doesn't laugh. "I'm just sorry we've put you through it," he says, dragging an ashtray toward him. "Really sorry."

"Say no more."

For a while we sit in silence, watching the local Romanian beggar doing her Balkan moan outside. She works the crowds near Burger King and McDonald's, looking forlornly at the swaddled toddler in her arms. There's a VIPS restaurant next door and a regular flow of customers passing in front of the window. Inside Starbucks, a woman with a cup of hot chocolate looks to be moving within earshot of our conversation, so Kitson calls it a day.

"Look." He seems suddenly energized. "It's important that we get results from Arroyo as quickly as possible. If she can point a finger at the guilty parties we can arrange to have them taken out of the equation using our contacts in Spanish intelligence. A sex scandal, financial irregularities—these things are easy to arrange."

"A sex scandal won't do it."

"What?"

"Spaniards don't give a shit about that sort of thing. Aznar could be doing it sideways with Roberto Carlos and nobody would bat an eyelid. If you want to create a scandal in this country, stay away from the bedroom. They're a lot more enlightened than we are when it comes to things like that. More like the French."

"I see." Judging by his expression, Kitson doesn't necessarily regard this as a good thing. "Look, in order to create any sort of smokescreen, we're going to need hard evidence. SIS can't launch something with the collusion of the Spanish government without conclusive proof. It would be highly embarrassing if we've got our facts wrong. At the moment all we have is conjecture."

I dispute this. "You've got a lot more than that, Richard . . ."

"Fine." He has agreed, but it is as if he is about to lose patience. Why don't we just take the conversation outside and walk around for a bit? Why is he so keen to leave? "We don't have anything that would stand up in court." The hot chocolate woman has made her way to the counter and is now just a few feet away, but she takes out a mobile phone, dials a number, and begins chattering loudly in Spanish. That buys him time. "The vital thing to remember is that we're trying to preserve the dignity of the international relationship." Kitson puts on his coat, stubs out the cigarette, and lowers his voice. "Mr. Aznar is trying to drag this country, kicking and screaming, into the twenty-first century, and an illegal counterterrorism operation within one of his ministerial departments must not be allowed to get in the way of that."

"Richard, you're preaching to the converted. . . ."

"Fine."

I look down at the memory stick, annoyed now, taking Kitson's eyes with me.

"There might be something in there."

"Unlikely," he replies. "Anything state-sensitive will be on the Interior Ministry mainframe. Carmen wouldn't be allowed to take it home. Or at least she shouldn't be. You have to push it now, Alec. It's not just a question of snooping around a computer. You have to *run* her."

Behind us, the American couple are walking out of the door with takeaway cups of coffee. One of them says, "It was just like home," and waddles out into the square. The Romanian beggar blocks her exit.

"What about Anthony's investigations?" I ask, but it's clear Kitson just wants to leave. Perhaps he thinks we have been observed. "Hasn't he uncovered anything?"

"Not much." I don't really believe this response, but it's too late to start arguing. "Look." He is already at the door. "You're the prize catch here, Alec. You're the one who needs to deliver."

And with that he is gone, slipping the memory stick into the inside pocket of his coat. I watch him disappear into the lunchtime crowds, still wondering why he forced the issue so blatantly, so suddenly toward the end. Was it simply that his professional mask was disturbed by talk of sex and Carmen? Did that throw him? And how the hell am I going to find a moment in which to pitch her in the next twenty-four hours? My instincts tell me she'll simply throw me out into the street. Kitson should have listened to my concerns. That was bad tradecraft.

Then more confusion. Just as I am gathering up my belongings—a wallet, a mobile phone, a copy of the *Daily Telegraph*—Julian Church walks right past the window, deep in conversation with a beautiful black girl. I recognize her. It takes just a couple of seconds to remember where I have seen her before: in the hall of my apartment, standing naked, wearing a pair of bright yellow panties. She is the girl Saul was sleeping with on the morning that I came back from Euskal Herria. She was the student studying art at Columbia.

She was American.

38

Columbia

I follow them. They walk out of the square, still deep in conversation, and appear to be heading toward one of the southern entrances of the Cubos underground car park. At the last minute, however, the girl leads Julian off to the right into the foyer of an apartment block immediately behind the Torre de Madrid. She's wearing tight blue jeans and boots that accentuate her extraordinary figure. Their relaxed body language and physical proximity would suggest that they have met before. I am no more than six or seven meters behind them. There are two sets of glass swing doors leading into the building. They ignore the porter inside the entrance, moving along the L-shaped lobby toward a bank of lifts. I wait around the corner and hear only a snatch of their conversation.

"So this is where you live?" Julian asks in Spanish. It sounds as though the girl merely giggles as the lift doors close behind them. Two seconds later I come around the corner and try to discover which floor they were heading for. The lights are out on two of the six lift panels and another left the ground floor at more or less the same time.

It's not going to be possible to track them. There's only one thing for it: I'll just have to wait here until they come out.

"Is there another exit from this building?" I ask the porter, walking back up to the lobby entrance. He's an old man, at least midseventies, and it looks as though he hasn't had a conversation since the Spanish Civil War.

"*Qué?*"

"I said, is there another exit from this building? If two of my friends just went up in the lift, do they have to come out this way?"

"*Sí, señor.*"

In different circumstances, in the salad days before Mikel Arenaza, I would have played this differently. I would have followed the girl home and endeavored to discover the nature of her relationship with Saul and Julian by more subtle means. But the time for patience is over. If I am being used as a pawn in a CIA setup then I will confront my conspirators and let them know that the game is up.

It's exactly an hour before Julian comes back downstairs to the ground floor, alone and staring concentratedly at the ground. In that time I have worked through every possible variation of the situation, only to stumble at every turn. How does Saul fit into this? Was Sofía really telling the truth about the package at the Hotel Carta? Is Carmen herself a part of some sinister setup? My life has become a Rubik's Cube that it is simply impossible to solve. Standing up from the sofa, hungry and angry and ready for anything that Julian might throw at me, I walk quickly toward him until we are just a few feet apart. He is utterly startled when he looks up and sees me.

"Alec! Bloody hell!" A kind of public school bluster and charm instinctively kick in, an automatic reflex to protect him. "Fancy seeing you here."

"Who was the girl, Julian?"

"What?"

"The girl."

"What girl?" He's no good at this. He can't lie. He's even started blushing. "What are you talking about?"

"The girl I saw you with. Tight jeans, suede jacket, expensive tits. You got into the lift together, an hour ago."

He provides a snapshot of grace under pressure—"I'm not sure that's any of your business"—but the game is up. He walks away from me, stiff and straight, away from the lifts and out of the building. He knows, of course, that I will follow him and discover the truth. Perhaps he just doesn't want our conversation to be heard by other people in the lobby. It has occurred to me that this might be the CIA station in Madrid. Three or four floors above our heads packed with Yank spooks.

"You got into the lift together," I say again. "I saw you. You went upstairs with her."

By now we are between the glass doors. I notice that Julian smells clean and freshly soaped. Have they just slept together?

"She's a client, all right? Endiom business. I'm doing some work for her. What the hell are you doing here?"

"This isn't about me. It's about you. What's her name, Julian?"

"You're behaving incredibly strangely. I really think you ought to head home. We can discuss this another time."

"Is it Sasha?"

His face cannot disguise its fear. Julian stops at the top of the car park staircase and looks right at me.

"And?"

"And what's your relationship with her? What's her relationship with Saul?"

He appears to remember Saul's name but only vaguely. "I'm still struggling to work out why this is any of your business."

"It's my business because I've met her, Julian. I've seen her before. At my flat."

And this causes him to hesitate. You can almost see the wheels turning behind his eyes. I would have expected a more polished performance from a professional liar, but if Julian has a cover story, it isn't coming out. He just looks panicked and uncomfortable.

"Then you'll know what she does," he replies quietly, and suddenly it dawns on me. Sasha is not a CIA officer. Sasha is not a student studying art at Columbia University. Sasha is a Colombian hooker.

"Oh Jesus." It is difficult to work out which of us is the more embarrassed. Julian's expression has curdled into one of shame married to intense irritation. I am stuttering. "I've just put two and two together and got five, Jules, I'm really sorry. It all makes sense now."

"It does? Oh what a relief."

But of course he won't leave it. It is the final irony of our relationship, of my stupid, impulsive behavior, that he now proceeds to take me downstairs to a mock-German beer tavern where he all but begs me not to say anything to Sofía.

"It's just that it would *kill* her," he implores, nursing a tankard of *Weissbier*. "She's very old-fashioned," and I nod along, drink after drink, playing the friend and trusted confidant. *How many hookers have you seen, Julian? How long has this been going on? Does it feel good to talk about it?* We discuss the culture of prostitution in Spain—"an entirely different *ethic* over here"—and how hard it is "to maintain an interest in one's wife after one has been married for a few years." Julian says it was easy to find Sasha on the Internet and reckoned Saul must have found her the same way.

"Of course I regretted the whole thing instantly," he says, five minutes after confessing to at least three other adulteries. "It was all so . . . impersonal. You can't imagine being *intimate* with someone like that."

Finally, I try to placate him with a rapidly assembled medley of platitudes. I have work to do with Carmen and can't sit here all night trying to save my boss's marriage.

"The truth is I really don't care, Julian. I promise. Show me a beautiful woman and I'll show you a man who's tired of fucking her. What a person gets up to in his spare time is his own business. Human sexuality is a mystery, for God's sake. Who's to know what people like and don't like? It has no bearing on the sort of person they are. You've been really good to me. You gave me work when I needed a job, you've kept me in bread and water. I'm not going to pay you back by informing on you to your wife. Jesus, what do you take me for? Besides, I barely *know* Sofía. I'm hardly likely to go and tell her something like this."

"*Really?*"

"Really."

"You're a good bloke, Milius," he says. "You're a bloody good bloke."

39

Product

That night, Félix Rodríguez de Quirós Maldonado appears on national television in an advertisement for the Partido Popular. Carmen
is watching TVE on her sofa in Calle de Toledo and wriggles quickly
out of my embrace when her boss appears on screen. Watching his
performance, I am reminded of a line from Updike, heard years ago
on British radio: "Nixon, with his menacing, slipped-cog manner." It
is one of the more interesting characteristics of Spanish public life that
even the most mendacious-looking politicians—sharks with hooded
eyes and slicked-back hair—nevertheless find themselves in positions
of great authority. In the UK, a man of Maldonado's appearance
would struggle to make a living as a secondhand car salesman, yet
Spanish voters seem blind to his obvious corruption. This bully, this
suntan in a suit, has even been spoken of as a possible prime minister.
Not if I have anything to do with it. Not if Six blows his cover.

"What do you think?" Carmen asks, taking the book I was reading
out of my hands. I hate it when women do that, when they demand
your attention.

"Think about what?"

As I look up into her face I see that she has been disquieted by the advertisement, as if she knows something of the circumstances in which it was made. Her face looks drawn and a little worried and I struggle to think of something positive to say, even with the screen of deceit.

"Well, he seems very charismatic, very calm. It's hard to know without understanding what he's saying. I was reading my book. What was the advert about?"

"It's saying that the Interior Ministry has the best record on crime of any administration of the last twenty years."

"And is that true?"

Without humor or irony she replies, "Of course it is true." She still looks upset by something.

"What's the matter?"

I have come to realize that Carmen Arroyo is stubborn and thick-skinned, despite appearances to the contrary, and will not easily admit to weakness. Ignoring me, she turns the book over and flicks idly through its pages.

"You were reading this when I met you," she says. It is the same crumpled copy of *Homage to Catalonia* that I had in the bar. "Why have you not read it before?"

"I have read it before. I just wanted to read it again."

"And is it interesting?"

"Fascinating."

We speak briefly about Orwell being shot through the neck while fighting for the Marxists in Spain, but I want to get to the bottom of her feelings for Maldonado. In the back of my mind is the dream that they were once lovers. Should Carmen tell me that they were, I can move on her tonight, threatening to expose both of them if she refuses. This is cynical and cold, the worst part of our heartless trade, but in the circumstances it is my best chance of obtaining information quickly.

"Would you like me to cook for you tonight?" she asks.

"Sure. That would be great." I touch her arm and move my hand slowly toward her neck. "So what's he like to work for, as a boss?"

"As a *what?*"

"A boss. A manager." I am just about to say the Spanish word "*jefe*" when I stop myself, remembering Alex's legend. "Mr. Maldonado. How does he treat you? How much do you see of him?"

Carmen has a glass of Rueda on the go and she drinks from it before replying.

"Why do you want to know?"

"Because I've never really spoken to you about your job. Because I don't really know what you do all day."

"And you *care*?" She rises on this last word, as if nobody has ever cared, as if nobody has ever paid her the slightest bit of attention. Then she rolls into me and I smell that same unwashed staleness on her neck.

"Of course I care."

"Well, I do not like him particularly." This after a short pause. "I do not think he is a good man. But of course I support him."

"Because you have to?"

"No. Because of Javier. Because I am loyal to Javier. Félix is my boss's boss." She looks delighted to have mastered the word so quickly and I feel a warm hand escaping up my back. "And what about *your* boss, Alex? Tell me more about him."

"No, you first. Tell me what you do all day when we're not together, when I miss you."

There is that look on her face again, the slight sickness, but just as quickly it is gone, replaced by a grateful, loving smile. She is behaving very oddly, concealing something, a worry or an unhappiness. Sometimes I wonder if this is all just a game for her, and I suffer the quiet, paranoid nightmare that Carmen Arroyo is the one playing *me*.

"What's wrong?"

"What do you mean?" She drains her glass of wine and stands up from the sofa.

"I don't know. You've been acting strangely all night, not like I've seen you before. Ever since Félix appeared on television you've been uncomfortable."

"*Sí?*"

"Yes."

She shakes her head. "The wine is finished."

This is going to be more difficult than I thought. It will take time to break her down. But the one quality that a spy must always possess is patience; my time will come. I simply need to wait for the opportunity, a matador timing the kill. It's possible that Carmen is programmed never to discuss state business with nongovernment personnel. After all, she knows nothing about Alex Miller. There's no reason in the world that she should trust him at such an early stage in our relationship.

"Do you want me to go out and buy some more?" I ask, looking across at the empty bottle.

"That would be very kind," she replies. "And I will cook."

So I go outside. On the stairs I consider telephoning Kitson for advice on how to proceed, but I must be able to work this one out for myself. I'm convinced that either de Francisco or Maldonado has been romantically involved with Carmen at some point in the past. Both are married men, and the fingerprints of an adultery seem visible whenever Carmen speaks about them. How else to explain her sudden shift in mood tonight? How else to explain her evasiveness?

"Alex!"

She has opened the sitting-room window above me and is looking down from the first-floor balcony.

"Can you buy some spaghetti as well as wine? I have none in the cupboards. Laura must have eaten it."

"Sure."

It takes about twenty minutes to find a decent bottle of wine in the supermarket, as well as the pasta and some Häagen-Dazs. I need a drink after queueing at the checkout and duck into Oliveros for a vermouth. The owner, who remembers me as a friend of Carmen's, insists that I stay for a second glass, on the house, and attempts to involve me in a conversation about the war in Iraq. A middle-aged man smoking a cheap cigar says something complimentary about Donald Rumsfeld, but I can't challenge him without revealing a fluency in Spanish. It's close to 9:30 by the time I make it back to the apartment, but when I let myself in with Carmen's keys she is nowhere to be seen.

I check the sitting room and the kitchen, where sauce for spaghetti is bubbling gently on the stove, before it becomes clear that she is on the telephone in the bedroom, using her portable landline. The door is half closed and Carmen is talking rapidly, with a definite shiver of alarm in her voice. My first thought is that something has gone wrong with her mother in hospital and I wait in the hall to hear more.

"And you're sure about this? I just can't believe it."

I experience a moment of undiluted selfishness: if Mitxelena's condition has deteriorated, I will have to accompany Carmen on a long and tedious visit to the hospital. Any chance of recruiting her will be lost to my obligations as a boyfriend. But then I hear the single word "Félix."

"I'm only repeating to you what I said in the restaurant," she says. "All the time Javier has been asking me to send money to this account. He said it was something to do with his wife, a trust they were setting up for their children. Are you sure?"

I take a step backward and a floorboard creaks in the hall. Carmen must have heard me come in, so I go directly into the bedroom, smile an apology for being late, and dangle the bag of shopping at her. She barely looks up from the phone. Her face is blank with concentration. I gesture to see if she is all right, but she just waves me away.

"I don't believe this." She turns her back to face out toward the window. "No, it's just Alex. He doesn't understand Spanish. He doesn't know what's going on."

How can I hear the rest of their conversation? There's music on in the sitting room, but it'll look ridiculous if I linger here when I should be boiling spaghetti. But then Carmen walks past me, out into the hall, and turns the volume down on the hi-fi.

"If it's the same Sergio Vázquez then I don't know what to think," she says, sitting down on the sofa. *Si se trata del mismo Sergio Vázquez, entonces no sé qué pensar.* "But with everything that's happening around Chakor, I'm really worried, João. It looks like a connection. I don't know who to speak to about this."

There is a long pause in the conversation while "João" responds. It is as if I have walked into a perfect storm of information: this is raw product that appears to prove a financial irregularity within de Francisco's department, linked to the incident involving Mohammed Chakor, the Moroccan who was shot by Tomás Orbé. But who is Sergio Vázquez? Now that the music has been lowered, Macduff will be getting all of it loud and clear on the bug and may be able to recover those sections of the conversation that I missed while drinking in Oliveros. If we can find out more about João and Vázquez, the pieces should quickly start to fall into place. Rather than enter the kitchen, where it will be necessary to start removing pans and crockery from the cupboards, I go into the bathroom, pretending to examine my face in the mirror. It is still possible to hear Carmen's end of the conversation, even with the door slightly ajar.

"I understand that," she says. *Lo entiendo.* "But this is a man I admire. For God's sake, I was talking to Alex an hour ago about how much I like him, what he stands for . . ."

João interrupts again. If only Six had ears on Carmen's landline.

"I've been so stupid," she continues. "I tried to pretend that this was not going on, but there have been so many things, too many coincidences with Arenaza and Juan Egileor. I don't know what to do about it."

I step away from the sink, flush the loo, and go back into the kitchen. Hearing Mikel's name brings a pump of blood to my head. What does she mean about coincidences involving Arenaza and Egileor? That she suspects Maldonado and de Francisco of conspiracy in their disappearance?

Carmen now responds to something João has said: "I can't resign. What will I do? I've seen the e-mails with Chakor's name on them. You've seen the bank statements. We're talking about three-quarters of a million euros of public money, maybe more. God, maybe I shouldn't even be speaking on this phone. What happens when this man wakes up and starts saying that he was ordered to kill Orbé?"

Again João interrupts and Carmen's subsequent response—"Of course that's what happened"—would indicate that he questioned whether or not Mohammed Chakor was paid by elements in the Interior Ministry to assassinate Tomás Orbé.

"What if they trace it back . . ." But Carmen is unable to complete the thought. "What if . . . I don't even want to think about that. I can't believe that this is happening."

I have heard more than enough. On the evidence of this telephone call alone, Kitson must alert London and set in motion the SIS plan to disgrace de Francisco and Maldonado. How they do that, at this late stage, without the dirty war becoming public knowledge, I have no idea. But my work with Carmen is done. I now need to get out of her apartment as quickly as possible, to call an emergency meeting with Kitson, and to assist him as best I can. The last thing I hear her say, in Spanish, is, "I am a patriot, you know that. I believed in him. And now I feel so stupid. But I don't want to betray my friend," as I switch on the extractor fan above the stove, grating cheese onto a plate. Sixty seconds later Carmen goes into the bathroom, locks the door, and does not emerge for another ten minutes. I knock once, asking if she is all right, but she responds only to tell me to boil a pan of water for the pasta. When she comes out, I put my arm round her shoulder and she shrugs me off.

"What was that about?"

"What was what about?"

"The phone call. The argument you were having. Are you OK?"

"It wasn't an argument."

"It sounded like one from where I was standing."

She takes a corkscrew out of the drawer beside the stove and stabs it into the neck of the bottle of wine.

"And where were you standing?"

"In here. You sounded very upset."

"It's just a problem at the ministry, OK?" The cork pops. "Can we not talk about it?"

The escalating tension here might work in my favor. If I can manufacture a full-scale argument it may give me an opportunity to leave and to contact Kitson within the next thirty minutes.

"But I'd *like* to talk about it," I tell her, trying to sound patient and concerned.

"Well I would not," she spits. "Can you just stir the sauce, please?"

And here is my opportunity.

"Don't talk to me like that."

"*What?*"

"I said don't order me around. You said you were going to cook dinner for me tonight, so you stir the fucking sauce."

It is our first row. A sullen, intolerant sneer makes its way across Carmen's face as she leaves the room. She looks like a spoiled child.

"Oh, don't just storm out."

Under her breath she insults me, quite effectively—*Cerdo!*—and slams the bedroom door. I am so wired by the prospect of seeing Kitson that I experience only a momentary beat of sympathy for her wretched predicament. This lasts about as long as it takes me to collect my coat from the hall. Then I leave the apartment, slamming the door with my own brand of adolescent petulance, and hurry down the stairs to the metro.

40

Line 5

"This, as they say, had better be worth it."

I have pulled Kitson out of dinner at the Taj Mahal with Ellie, Michelle, and Macduff. He still looks exhausted, but his mood appears to have lightened considerably since Starbucks.

"Was just about to have my first mouthful of chicken *jalfrezi* when you called," he says. "Bottle of Cobra on its way, *sag aloo,* a nice *peshwari nan.* First normal food in weeks. Not bloody *jamón,* not bloody tortilla, not bloody chorizo. I've been running on a single *poppadum* since lunch, so make it snappy."

We have met in the ticket hall of the metro station at Callao. He clunks through the metal barriers and we head down the stairs to the southbound platform of Line 5.

"You wanted information out of Carmen," I tell him. "I've got it."

"Already?"

"Believe me, you won't be going back to finish your curry."

We find a bench at the far end of the platform and sit down beside one another, about ten meters from the closest passenger. Kitson is wearing hiking boots, a checked shirt with a frayed collar, a bottle-green V-neck pullover, and a badly patched tweed jacket. He looks like a sheep farmer who took a wrong turn at Dover. I tell him everything that I can recall from Carmen's phone conversation—that she suspects Maldonado and de Francisco of diverting public funds to bankroll a secret state operation against ETA—and he nods along, alerting me to the fact that he has triggered the digital voice recorder in the outer pocket of his jacket.

"This is dynamite," he keeps saying, "fantastic stuff," and I experience the exquisite high of a colleague's recognition and praise. "João's details were in the address book you lifted from Carmen's mobile. If it's the same guy, he's an old friend of hers from university who works at the Banco de Andalucía. She must have asked him to look into the money trail."

"Makes sense."

"And she said there was three-quarters of a million euros?" He lowers his voice slightly here. "Did she quote that exact figure?"

"That exact figure. Why?"

Kitson removes the jacket and places it across his lap. It's stuffy down on the platform and the air is hot with pollutants. "We have a separate confirmation of a slush fund controlled by de Francisco with around 765,000 euros in it, traceable to several Interior Ministry bank accounts."

"It's not a great deal of money."

"No." We have both arrived at the same conclusion. "A figure that small would suggest that we're either at the edge of a much bigger problem involving far larger sums of money or, more likely, that we're only dealing with a dozen or so individuals running a highly secret operation against ETA under the operational and financial control of Félix Maldonado."

"That's what your diligence is throwing up?"

He nods. "At the top you have Maldonado and de Francisco directing orders and covert funds, most of it diverted from government coffers, to three key individuals: Luis Buscon, Andy Moura, and Sergio Vázquez."

"Why haven't you mentioned those names before?"

Kitson looks at me, those calming, unchallengeable eyes. "Don't take it personally, Alec. Plenty of people were out of the loop on this one. That's just the way I like to run things. Believe me, after the work you've done on this, London is going to be cock-a-hoop. SIS has stepped into the breach and saved the day. The Spaniards have a problem in their own backyard and it took the Brits to solve it."

I don't respond to this and, in fact, my elation is no sharper than it was moments ago.

"Who's Andy Moura?"

"High-ranking Guardia Civil in Bilbao with a lifelong contempt for all things Basque. On record as saying that ETA could be destroyed within five years if only the police were allowed to do 'whatever they want.' Basque pressure groups have been after him for years. Cast-iron thug. Has survived three attempts on his life, two car bombs, and a shooting."

"Jesus."

"Yes, that's probably who he thanks every morning." A grin here. "Moura's fingerprints are all over the Otamendi kidnapping and possibly Egileor's disappearance as well. The Spanish authorities are keeping it quiet while they carry out an 'internal inquiry.' In other words, a cover-up."

"Speaking of which . . ."

"Hang on a minute." Kitson silences me with a flattened palm. This is not an aggressive gesture, more an expression of his desire to articulate a series of complex thoughts. "Now Vázquez has a similar sort of profile."

"You've heard of him before?"

A train is approaching, the sleek metal hum and vibration of engine on track.

"Oh, we've heard of him. He's CNI, Military Intelligence, an old right-wing friend of Maldonado who was caught on surveillance cameras beating up two ETA suspects in custody in 1999." The train punches into the station, a noise so loud that Kitson is forced to shout. "There was an internal stink within what was then called

CESID until Maldonado was promoted to interior minister and handed his old friend a pardon."

"On the quiet?"

"Precisely."

"And now Vázquez is returning the favor by helping to run the dirty war out of the CNI?"

The doors of the train slide open in a chorus of electronic beeps and we are surrounded by disembarking passengers. Kitson says, "Exactly," and plays with the material of his jacket. The pocket with the voice recorder in it is facing into his lap. "From what Carmen was saying tonight, it certainly looks that way." A small boy holding a toy gun has been staring at us from the carriage directly ahead. Kitson smiles at him and gets shot for his efforts. Once the doors have closed and the train has moved off, he resumes speaking. "As secretary of state for security, de Francisco has operational command of both the Guardia Civil and the police. Maldonado's reach extends even farther than that, into the heart of the intelligence community. As luck would have it we had a fairly decent file on Mohammed Chakor before the Orbé incident because he was wanted by Interpol in connection with some Ecstasy smuggling. There was an individual within CNI who was making contact with Chakor's mobile in Marseilles. We just didn't know who the hell that individual was until tonight."

"Vázquez?"

"Correct."

Toward us, walking very slowly along the broad platform, come two elderly ladies wearing fake fur coats and eating ice creams. Rather than licking them, they are uneasily chipping away at the cones with little plastic spoons. I suggest that we catch the next train and talk on the way south.

"Good idea." As if to give himself something to do in the interim, Kitson takes out a pack of Lucky Strikes and then appears to remember that it's illegal to smoke on the Madrid metro.

"It's all right. You can light up. People do it all the time."

"Not me," he says.

Ten minutes later we are on a train, passing back through La

Latina just after eleven o'clock. I think about Carmen and wonder what she is up to, how she must despise me for leaving in her hour of need. It is strange and probably unprofessional to feel these thoughts, but a small part of me does care for her. It is not possible to spend time like that with a woman, however ill suited to one's taste and preference, without forming at least the structure of an attachment.

"Alec?"

"Yes?"

"I was saying that if Carmen has linked the Interior Ministry to Arenaza and Egileor, it's only a matter of time before Maldonado and de Francisco are named specifically in press reports. There are going to be leaks, even if they only come from this friend of hers at the bank."

I had drifted off. Perhaps the strain of the Carmen seduction is finally taking its toll. We are sitting at the rear of an almost deserted train.

"If the people who tortured you had their suspicions about de Francisco and Buscon three weeks ago, it's a certainty they've passed them on to other Basque newspapers who will just be waiting for an opportunity to skewer the PP once they have hard evidence. The attempt on Orbé's life might have been the straw that breaks the camel's back."

"I know that, I know that . . ."

"So we've got to *anticipate* this. We've got to preempt it."

Kitson appears to be looking for my advice. "And you want my views on that?"

It feels strange to be asking such a question. Has the relationship turned full circle? In the past, before we spent time together, I tended to place all spies on a pedestal: John Lithiby, Katharine Simms, Michael Hawkes, even Fortner and Sinclair. Their work seemed more vivid, more essential to the smooth running of the planet than any vocation I could think of. I was in awe of them. Yet as I have come to know Kitson, the more I have realized that he is just like any other professional doing a difficult job: competent mostly, occasionally brilliant, from time to time merely rude and ineffectual. He is not, in other words, a special breed. He was simply spotted at a young age and taught a trade. That is not to say that I do not respect him. It is simply that, for perhaps the first time in my life, I feel the confidence to say that I could do Richard Kitson's job with equal efficiency. And after what has happened out here, that is probably what I will end up doing.

"What a lot of people don't understand about Spain is that it's still run by twenty or thirty big families," I tell him. "They control everything, from the newspapers to television, from commerce to banking, industry to agriculture. You find influence with the right families and you will find influence with the media. That's the way to organize a cover-up on this scale. The Partido Popular is like the Republican Party in the United States—it's the natural home of immense wealth. If the people of influence in Spain see that their position is in danger, they will circle the wagons. The money will be protected. The PP already control a lot of news content on domestic radio and television. Within two hours of you telling them that Maldonado and de Francisco had their fingers in the till, that scandal will be the story that runs and runs. It will completely short-circuit any rumors about a dirty war."

Kitson puts a hand on my shoulder. "I'm glad we got you on board," he says, rather oddly. "Couldn't have done this without you. I'll send a FLASH telegram to London tonight and we'll move on everything first thing tomorrow."

"So that's it?"

"What do you mean?"

"You're going with the financial scandal? That decision has already been made?"

"Well, it makes sense, doesn't it?" I have the oddest feeling that Kitson is lying to me, as if much of what we are talking about is moot or even irrelevant. "The Spanish authorities, in conjunction with SIS, will make it in Mr. Maldonado's interest to flee the country. I suspect that his old friend Javier will join him."

It's like we're talking about a game of Monopoly. "Hang on. What about the variables? What about blowback?"

"What do you mean?"

"Well, what if they stay? What if they want to fight it out in the courts?"

"Fight what? A financial scandal that doesn't exist? Run the risk of being vilified for starting another dirty war?"

I lean forward, turning to face him. "A lot of ordinary Spaniards might admire them for what they've done. There are guys from the days of the GAL who did time in prison and now get applauded every time they walk into a restaurant."

"We'll make it worth their while."

At the far end of the carriage, an inevitably South American accordion player has stepped on at Urgel station, four drunk students behind him. He strikes up some bars of a tango and they begin dancing in the space near the doors.

"What about Buscon? What about Dieste? Vázquez? Moura? They'll all need to be silenced, one way or another. And there are almost certainly others whom we know nothing about."

"True," Kitson admits, "true." He shuts his eyes and blinks rapidly, as if controlling a wild idea. "Well, Vázquez and Moura aren't going to talk to anyone. They're not stupid. They're not going to implicate themselves. And if the money trail finds its way to the CNI or the Guardia Civil in Bilbao, it can be explained away in terms of the war against terror."

This seems to me extraordinarily flimsy, but I let it go. "Then what about Mohammed Chakor?"

"Mohammed Chakor won't be talking to anyone. He died three hours ago in hospital. You can send flowers."

I shake my head. "And Buscon?"

"What about him?"

"Well, he hired Rosalía. He probably organized other operations. The shootings in France, maybe the kidnapping of Egileor. He certainly pulled the trigger on Mikel. Carmen has linked him directly to Javier de Francisco."

"We took Buscon into custody earlier this week. He's going to be tied up for a while. We're sending him to Guantánamo."

"Guantánamo?"

Kitson's face suddenly loses its characteristic equanimity. He has made a serious slip.

"The Yanks have been after Buscon for ages," he explains. "Weapons smuggling, narcotics, we just handed him over . . ."

I jump on this. "Oh, come on, Richard. Since when were the CIA involved in your operation? You told me you hadn't even alerted our embassy in Madrid." Then it dawns on me, a shaming feeling. "Fuck. SIS can't organize the cover-up on its own, can it? London doesn't have enough leverage. They need the bloody CIA to hold their hand."

"Not so. We had finished our debriefing of Buscon, resolved the Croatian issue, and then alerted the Cousins to the fact that we were holding a wanted man. It's what allies do for each other."

"So he just gets dragged off to Guantánamo to share a cell with some Afghan peasant farmer who got mistaken for an international terrorist?"

"What do you care?"

"I'm just not a big fan of the Yanks. I told you that it was a pre-condition of my cooperation that the CIA wasn't told of my where-abouts."

"Nor has it been," Kitson replies, this time with more venom. Once again, our little spat is being recorded for the benefit of ears in London, and he wants to be seen to get tough. "Try to forget about Luis Buscon. He's a separate issue."

"And when you questioned him about his role in the dirty war, in the Arenaza killing, what did he tell you?"

"Alec, I'm afraid I can't divulge any more. You don't at this point have clearance. Suffice to say that he proved a less than cooperative prisoner. Categorically denied any links to Dieste or any involvement in the abduction of Mikel Arenaza. Was only prepared to talk about Croatia. Maybe the Yanks can get more out of him. They're not as sensitive as our lot. Use different methods, if you follow my meaning . . ."

I stare ahead at the black tunnel flashing by, at the plastic seats and the floor. It's sickening.

"So my work is just done? That's it? You have what you wanted?"

"It looks like it. More or less." This comes off as cold and matter-of-fact, so he tries to console me. "Look. There's talk of John Lithiby coming out here next week. To oversee things. You can meet him and discuss your future. He wants to thank you in person. This doesn't end here, Alec. This is still your triumph."

The train is pulling in to Carabanchel. Kitson puts on his jacket and prepares to leave. One final question stops him. "What about Carmen?" he says. It's no more than an afterthought.

"What about her?"

"Will she talk?"

A mischievous part of me feels like misleading him, but duty overrides this.

"Carmen is loyal to the PP. She's having a crisis of conscience, but she'll keep quiet about it for the greater good. You'll just need to have a word with her."

Kitson nods. "And you're going to keep seeing her?"

"What do you think?"

And with that he is gone. The doors of the train slam shut and a lone British spy vanishes into the white light of a suburban metro station. A moment of intense and sudden regret comes over me and I wonder if any of it was worthwhile. Sleeping with Carmen when Kitson knew so much already. Demeaning myself to save Blair and Bush and Aznar. What was I *thinking?*

An hour later, returning home, I see that an envelope has been pushed under the door of my apartment. Inside there is a letter, handwritten in Spanish. It is from Sofía.

My darling Alec

Julian came home tonight and said that he had seen you to-day. More than this, he said that you had spoken for a long time and that he had seen a side of you that he had never noticed before. He said that for the first time you had revealed yourself. And I found that I was jealous of this. He spoke very highly of you, said that he regarded you as a true friend. He said that he was glad to have another Englishman with him here in Madrid. I began to wonder if you had arranged to meet him so that you could laugh about me. I began to think that I was your little private joke.

We have moved away from each other, my love. You never used to care about the things you seem to care about now. About money, about ambition. You never used to care about the future. I loved that about you. You were so settled, you were so much *lighter*. Then I do not know what happened to Alec Milius. I think something in his past found him and darkness fell across his face. There is no place for me under this darkness. I have been crying for days and Julian does not know that my tears are for you.

We are not lovers anymore. It seems that we are not even friends. You have not chosen me. In the end, you did not even fight.

When I have read the letter I have to sit down on a stool in the kitchen and breathe slowly and deeply for a long time, as if to carry on would release sobs of despair. Where is this coming from? It is like the farm again, a near breakdown, all the shame and the regret suddenly catching up with me. I did nothing for Sofía. I used her solely for my own pleasure. I took no responsibility for my actions and ignored her in her hour of need. And now she is gone. I have thrown her away, just as I threw away the others.

41

Sleeper

And so the cover-up moves into place, and for five days the terrible, invisible, inevitable power of the secret state envelops Spain. How many of the players in this Establishment fix know the truth about the dirty war? Aznar? The proprietors of *El País* and TVE? A few house-trained executives and editors? It is impossible to know. I acknowledge the brilliance of SIS—with, quite probably, an American input—yet find that I am dejected by the speed with which the press have been duped and cajoled. Sofía's letter has much to do with my somber mood: a sense of intense regret overcomes me as I realize that the aftermath of my sick little game was just another fix and sham. I question time and again whether it was the right thing to do. Saul's words haunt me: "What are you doing to make *amends*, Alec?"

As Kitson predicted, both Félix Maldonado and Javier de Francisco flee to Colombia—on the same airplane—where they both go to ground, despite the best efforts of the republic's finest journalists to track them down. Three days later their wives and children follow unmolested. Carmen and three other women from the secretarial pool, as well as numerous individuals from the Interior Ministry, were taken into custody at the weekend for questioning. I have heard nothing from her, despite attempting to make contact on four separate occasions.

In *Gara,* the ETA-sympathetic newspaper printed in San Sebastián, Eugenio Larzabal runs a story on May 12 in which he attempts to link the kidnap and murder of Mikel Arenaza and the disappearance of Juan Egileor to de Francisco's sudden flight to Colombia "in the teeth of the Interior Ministry finance scandals." *Ahotsa* is more reserved—and Zulaika's byline nowhere to be seen— yet the paper claims to have traced the car seen at the shootings in southern France to "an associate of Andy Moura." Extensive research has also been conducted into Mohammed Chakor's background, and an editorial urges the Madrid government to investigate why a known drug smuggler was photographed in February of this year talking to Sergio Vázquez, the disgraced CNI officer pardoned by Félix Maldonado. In *El Mundo* there is a similarly tantalizing but ultimately inconclusive op-ed about a possible third GAL. When I read these stories, I fear that the entire edifice of the cover-up will crumble in a matter of hours, but on Tuesday there is not a single article or letter or news story dedicated to the suggestion of a third dirty war in any outlet of the mainstream Spanish media. Again I marvel at the extent of the cover-up yet lament its efficacy. Why, at the very least, have there not been demonstrations on the streets of Bilbao? Has the government done a deal with Batasuna, promising prisoner releases or leverage in votes against the Basque Nationalist Party? It has all come down to trade-offs. It has all come down to politics.

Kitson rings on the morning of the 14th. I am surprised to hear from him; a part of me was resigned to the fact that we would never meet again. And I had grown used to that. It didn't bother me as much as I thought it would.

"So what do you think?" he asks.

"What do I think about what?"

"The press reports. The angle on the financial scandal?"

"It looks to me like a dam that is waiting to break." This may sound like I'm baiting him, but it is an honest assessment of the situation now that several days have passed. "For the moment, Aznar seems safe. He moved quickly, he distanced himself from the culprits, he assumed a presidential air on the White House lawn. But how long can it last? This is Spain's Watergate. You can't bury a story of this magnitude for long, regardless of how much money or influence the Americans think they have. *El País* has been told to keep its mouth shut, but when smaller left-wing outlets get hold of the story they're not going to pass up an opportunity to hammer the PP. Then it's just a question of who gets the exclusives, who can track down the main players. Open season. They say that Maldonado and de Francisco were squirreling away millions of euros in secret bank accounts, but nobody has heard their side of the story."

"Upbeat as ever, Alec," he replies, "upbeat as ever. Look, if the Aznar government falls, it falls because of bad management at the top. Better that than an illegal state-funded war against ETA."

"True." That's what all of this boils down to.

"Anyway, I have news."

He sounds chirpy. I am sitting alone in Cáscaras eating my breakfast and looking out the window. As we talk I keep thinking about what Kitson said in Starbucks: "Aznar is trying to drag this country, kicking and screaming, into the twenty-first century. Nothing must be allowed to get in the way of that." But does Spain *want* to be dragged? Isn't it the beauty of this country that she is fine just the way she is?

"What news?"

"Lithiby is in town. He wants to see you tonight. What are you doing for dinner, Alec?"

I experience only a small pulse of excitement, nothing more. In truth I no longer care whether or not he offers me a job. How can that be? For weeks it was all that I could think of. All of the risks and hard work were justified if they moved me toward the reconciliation I craved. Yet I find that I am exhausted and strung out; I have learned nothing about myself except the clear impossibility of changing my nature. I would happily spend the rest of my days living on a beach in Goa if it would keep me out of people's way. It turns out that all I ever wanted was approbation and, now that I have it, it proves worthless. And what of the human cost? Both Sofía and Carmen have been destroyed by my craven behavior.

"Nothing," I tell Kitson. "I'm not doing anything for dinner."

I had planned to go over to Carmen's apartment, to try to talk to her, perhaps even to explain, and I might still do that before any meeting with Lithiby.

"Good. What about Bocaito. Do you know it?"

"Of course I know it. I was the one who told you about it."

"So you did, so you did. Well, nine o'clock suit? He'll be on British dinnertime."

"Nine o'clock will be fine." So this is to be my crowning ceremony, the spy who came in from the cold. A pretty girl walks past the window and I look at her through the glass, getting nothing back. "What hotel is he staying at?"

Kitson hesitates and says, "I haven't the slightest idea."

"And are you coming?"

"Me? No. I'm going back to London."

"Already?"

"On the next plane. Most of the team were called home at the weekend." Kitson puts on a voice, a comic affectation that I've not heard him try before, imitating a bureaucratic mandarin. "Insufficient numbers back home to exploit leads indicating active preparations for terrorist attacks on UK soil. Manning the pumps, in other words."

"Well, good luck. I hope we'll catch up one day." It feels like a strange thing to say, an abrupt good-bye. Kitson doesn't respond, just ventures an upbeat, "Oh, guess what?"

"What?"

"They found Juan Egileor an hour ago."

"Who did?"

"SIS. In Thailand."

"What the fuck was he doing in Thailand?"

"Good question. Resort in Koh Samui. No sign of a kidnapper, no sign of mistreatment. Just a Spanish translation of *The Beach* on his hotel bed beside a teenage boy from Bangkok with a sore ass and a sheepish grin on his face."

"Jesus. So he wasn't abducted? He just took off of his own accord?"

"It would appear so."

And we leave it at that. Kitson tells me that Egileor is being questioned in the Thai capital and will be flown home within the week. The press, he says, have yet to be informed about his reappearance, but an absence of foul play "will certainly assist in quashing rumors of government interference."

It's not until later that evening, at Carmen's apartment, that I realize quite how misguided that assumption is.

"So take care," Kitson tells me. "And remember. Bocaito. Nine o'clock."

"Nine o'clock."

42

La Víbora Negra

At 7:30, after lunch and a long afternoon tidying my flat, I go around to Carmen's apartment. The lights are on in the first-floor windows and I can see a shadow moving between the rooms. This could be Laura de Rivera, but when I ring the buzzer there's no answer and I assume that Carmen just wants to be left alone. An elderly couple emerge at a quarter to eight and I step forward, holding the door for them as they offer muffled thanks. They don't seem to notice or care as I slip into the building behind them. There's a smell of garlic in the stairwell. I decide to try to talk to Carmen through the door of her apartment.

"Carmen!"

A shuffle of socked feet on wooden floors.

"Quién es?"

"It's Alex. I need to talk to you."

"Go away, Alex."

"I'm not going to go away."

"I can't see you anymore."

"Well, at least open the door. At least let me see your face."

"What did you tell them?" she asks. She is speaking Spanish, as if she knows that I understand every word.

"What?"

"You heard me. What did you tell them?"

"Just open up. I don't understand what you're asking."

The security chain rattles and there's a twist on the latch. Carmen opens the door ajar and holds my gaze through the gap. Her face has been obliterated by worry and fatigue, black gothic shadows beneath her eyes. It is a depressing sight.

"You think I don't know who you are?" she asks, again in Spanish.

"What?"

Frustration gets the better of her. She closes the door, frees the chain, and invites me inside with a grand, sweeping gesture of contempt. *"Pasa!"* There is alcohol on her breath.

"Carmen, what the fuck are you on? Are you drunk?" I move past her. "You haven't answered your phone for days. You won't return any of my messages. I've been worried sick about you."

She turns and smiles, a poisonous leer. "I have a question for you."

"Go ahead. Ask anything you want."

"What was significant about the Naftali Botwin company on the Aragon front in 1937?"

"What?" I am utterly bewildered until I realize that she is testing my legend. It is a question about the PhD.

"What? Why the fuck do you want to know that?"

"Don't ignore the question." She slams the front door and heads into the kitchen, where she pours herself a large tumbler of red wine.

"I'm not ignoring the question. I just don't think it's very important at this stage in our relationship for us to be discussing the political idiosyncrasies of the Spanish Civil War."

She laughs, a spat of contempt, and little spittles of wine settle on my cheeks and lips. *"Que mentiroso eres!"* What a liar you are.

"Carmen, you're clearly very upset. You've been drinking. Do you want to tell me what's going on?"

"Do you want to tell me what's going on?" She imitates my voice with a shrill, clipped accent. "I will tell you what is going on. I will tell you.

Alex Miller is a spy. A spy who has ruined my life. I have been told never to speak to him again. Alex Miller, who put his dick inside me for the sake of his career and said that we would be together forever. Alex Miller, who kisses me and speaks perfect Spanish"—I interrupt with a brisk "no," which she ignores—"and who betrayed me to the CIA." She switches to Spanish, her face so twisted with the disfigurement of betrayal that it is sickening to witness. "You've known all along about what Félix was doing. You have known all along that he was paying murderers to kill and torture the men of ETA and Herri Batasuna. And you came to me because you knew that I could find you information. And when you got it, by listening to my private conversations like the coward you are, you went running to your fucking American government and they covered everything up."

On no account, no matter what the circumstances, ever break cover. It does not matter if your identity has been exposed as an utter sham. Maintain the spy's composure. Give them nothing.

"Carmen, please speak in English. I don't understand what you're saying."

"Hijo de puta!"

She hurls her glass across the room toward my face, the tumbler smashing against the door behind me and sending red streaks of staining wine across the walls and floor. I back away.

"They arrested me," she says. "They took me in. They told me everything. They told me that Javier, a man I loved and trusted, had run away because he had been stealing money from the government." She is speaking in rushed, drunken English but manages a kind of throat noise here, a guttural insult to those who interrogated her. If anything, this seems false, in some way overdone, and I feel uneasy. "As if that is what happened! I told them what I knew, and I told the other staff what I knew, but they would not listen to me. They did not want to know the truth. That Javier had organized a dirty war against ETA, that Mikel Arenaza and Txema Otamendi and Juan Egileor and Tomás Orbé were all connected to the crimes of one man—Félix Maldonado."

"Now that doesn't sound right," I tell her. "Who are these men you're talking about? You need to calm down . . ."

"Calm down?" She insults me again—"*Cerdo!*"— and sweeps her arm across the kitchen table. Yet as I watch the pieces of fruit and the biscuits and a plastic bottle of water falling to the floor, I feel that there is something not quite right here. Carmen's anger seems contrived, as if she has learned her lines by rote. Why did she list those names so precisely, with such melodramatized conviction? Does she want to convince me of something that is beyond logic? "Do you not know about Félix?" she screams, and again it sounds as though she is overplaying her hand. "Do you not know what he has done? Let me tell you, Alex Miller. As a soldier in the army of General Franco, his men took a teenage boy in Pamplona who had insulted them and beat him to death with *shovels*. With *shovels*. He is a murderer. Félix Maldonado is the black viper of the Interior Ministry and it is time that the world knew."

My blood runs absolutely cold.

That final phrase, the description. I have heard it used before, to describe de Francisco, just as I have heard the story of the murdered boy. At the farm, in the mouth of the woman who tortured me. Both of them used an absolutely specific translation from a mother tongue into English: *la víbora negra.* The black viper. In my consternation I back up farther against the wall, my mind inverted by doubt. Surely it isn't possible that Carmen is one of them? In the same instant, and I have no idea how this mental process takes place, Egileor's appearance in Thailand makes perfect sense. ETA faked his kidnapping. We were led to believe that he was a victim of the dirty war, but his safety was never in doubt.

I try to maintain my composure, but Carmen has detected the doubt in my eyes. I say, "That may be the case, sweetheart, that may be the case . . ." but her expression has tightened. It is as if she realizes that she has made a critical mistake. Does she know that I know? Think, Alec. *Think.* This cannot be happening. You could be wrong. You could just be paranoid and confused. But it is as if scales have fallen from my eyes. I have been used. We have all been used.

Too soon, perhaps, because it risks everything, I move toward the stove and prepare to seize a knife from the block beside the fridge. Carmen follows my eyeline and does not seem surprised. Is that a smile at the edge of her mouth? She says, "What are you doing, Alex? Listen to me!" but the rage in her performance, the authenticity of it, has been replaced by something like cunning. She blocks my approach to the knives with a physical intensity that is quite unlike her, as if she would be capable of committing an act of violence without any thought to its consequence. Then I hear another person moving through the flat. This noise is a moment to compare with anything in the barn, the same sense of powerlessness, the same terror. Carmen frowns as I say, "Who the fuck is that? Is there somebody else here?" and in an instant every tic and nuance that I associate with her face seems to completely fall away, like an actor dropping out of character. It is as if she ceases to be Carmen Arroyo and assumes an entirely new personality. I feel physically sick.

Simultaneously a man comes into the kitchen, my height, compact, and athletic. He looks first at Carmen, then at me, and I look down at his right hand where he is holding a knife. I think I say, absurdly, "Now hang on a minute," but everything has moved into a different sphere. Then I see that he is wearing a red sweatband on his wrist, and an old leather-strapped watch, and I am right back in the nightmare of the farm faced by the man who treated me like a worthless animal. Anger and terror and panic rise in me with the force of a fever.

What happens now happens very fast. Carmen moves toward me and I reach for the knife block, seizing an empty wine bottle from the counter, which I swing at the man, connecting instantly with his head. He drops to the ground so suddenly that I am actually taken by surprise. There is no noise. I have never struck a person like that before and it was so easy, so simple. He did not even speak. Then Carmen tries to seize my arms, kicking precisely at the agony of my knees. We struggle briefly and I find that I punch, without doubt or hesitation, at her face, at a woman's face, throwing blow after blow at her feeble, corrupted, treacherous body, each enraged strike a savage revenge for the farm. I don't know how long this goes on. Eventually both of them are on the ground, the man still unconscious, Carmen groaning as blood curls from her lips. I'm not proud of this, but I drive my shoe into the Basque's mouth two or three times, smashing teeth, almost crying with the pure adrenaline pleasure of revenge. I land a kick into his stomach so that he groans in pain. Carmen tries to reach for my legs to stop me but I am exhilarated by the opportunity to hurt them. It is even in my mind, a terrible thing, to sink the knife deep into his heart, to be revenged for the torture, for Mikel, for Chakor and Otamendi, for every loyal minion ETA betrayed so that their plan could reach fruition.

But I am exhausted. I move toward the kitchen door and walk out into the hall. How much noise did we make? Outside, perhaps from one of the apartments on the third or fourth floor, I can hear somebody shouting, "What's going on down there?" as I look back at their still bodies. Carmen is facing the floor, the Basque groaning and drifting in and out of consciousness. They are touching each other.

Noise on the staircase. I have to get out of here. Closing the front door behind me I hurry down the stairs and step out onto the street, turning quickly in the direction of Plaza Mayor.

43

Counterplay

There's a bar at the southern end of the square with a sign outside, in English, saying HEMINGWAY NEVER ATE HERE. I've never been inside before, but it feels safe, crowded with oblivious Brits, a place far enough away from the apartment where I can clean up and gather my thoughts.

Nobody looks at me as I make my way toward the bathroom. I wash my face in cold water for a long time and check my shoes for blood. My right fist hurts from the fight but my hands are unmarked and there seem to be no visible signs of the struggle in my appearance. At the bar I order a whiskey and sink it in three successive gulps, the sweat cooling on my body all the time, my heart rate coming down. I keep checking the door for police, for Carmen, but there are just tourists coming in, bar staff, locals.

I can sit here. I can hide. I can work it all out.

The evidence, the tip-offs, were staring us in the face. We were just too stupid to see them.

Carmen's muted reaction to the marks and bruises on my legs, for example. I had assumed that she was either disgusted by them or simply being polite in an awkward situation. It never occurred to me that she was *expecting* to find them. It never crossed my mind that Carmen Arroyo already knew about what had happened at the farm.

Then there was her enthusiasm for all things American. That was wildly overplayed. In the two years since 9/11, I have rarely met a Spaniard under the age of forty with a single complimentary thing to say about George W. Bush, yet Carmen was borderline neoconservative. Her enthusiasm wasn't born of loyalty to the PP; it was all an exaggerated bluff.

Then, of course, there was the most obvious clue of all. Why would the Spanish government bother to launch a secret campaign of violence against ETA when ETA is on its last legs? Kitson and I talked about this, at length, but we never thought simply to turn everything around.

Outside, perhaps a block away, a police siren flashes by on the street. In my mind's eye there is a clear and precise image of Carmen and the man slumped on the floor and for the first time I wonder if their injuries will be serious. The fight was a frenzy of rage; I seemed to lose all sense of myself in the quest for revenge. Christ, perhaps I even killed a man tonight, left him brain damaged, paralyzed. Yet there must still be some salvageable sense of decency inside me because I feel terrible about having done this.

It's not possible to get a mobile reception at the bar so I make my way toward the entrance and dial Kitson's number. His phone has been switched off and I leave as clear and concise a message as I can.

"Richard, you have to call me." Behind me, a customer laughs at just the wrong moment. "Something very serious has happened. Did Anthony hear what went on in the flat? Did you get it on the bug?"

Macduff has a number, too, but that is also on voice mail. They're both probably in the air on their way back to London. They both think that the job is done.

Back inside I order a second whiskey, get a cigarette off a girl, and begin to piece everything together. It all goes back to the farm. Why didn't they kill me when they had the chance? Why did they set me free and plant the idea of de Francisco's involvement in the dirty war in my head? There was no way that ETA could have known, at that stage, that a dirty war was being organized out of the Interior Ministry. In any event, if they had had information of that kind, they would have gone straight to the press.

It's obvious, too, that Carmen always knew I spoke Spanish. I was *meant* to overhear her conversation with João last week. Right from the start she knew who I was, why I was coming to her, who was playing whom. I was being used by ETA to feed information back to SIS, which they hoped would accelerate the destruction of the Aznar government. Only they didn't count on the cover-up. They didn't think it would be possible to obscure a conspiracy of that size. And Carmen shouldn't have told me the story about the boy from Pamplona. That was her one mistake. Otherwise the simplicity of it was breathtaking. Look at the victims they chose: Mikel Arenaza was, by his own admission, on his way out of politics. He had grown weary of the armed struggle and was looking to start a new life with Rosalía, away from the duplicity and double standards of terror. Txema Otamendi had also turned his back on the organization. He tried to question the moral and political good sense of military action and paid the price. The others, the two men who survived the so-called dirty war, were the only individuals still of use to ETA: Juan Egileor, a millionaire businessman who had made massive financial contributions to the revolutionary cause, disappeared of his own volition, and took a two-month holiday in Southeast Asia in the company of a Bangkok rent boy. Tomás Orbé, a functioning *etarra,* was most probably tipped off that Mohammed Chakor was coming to get him. Why else was he carrying a gun? Only he wasn't meant to kill him. The wound to the neck was too severe. Had he survived, Chakor would doubtless have sung like a canary, telling the world's press that he had been hired to shoot a leading *etarra* on the orders of Sergio Vázquez and his old friend, Félix Maldonado.

Eventually I pay my bill and head out onto the street, sticking to the shadows under the colonnade of the square until I'm out on Calle Mayor. A cab glides past and I hail it, giving directions to Calle de la Libertad. It has occurred to me that I am running late for the meeting at Bocaito, although in Kitson's absence John Lithiby will be a more than capable replacement. Numbed by whiskey, I sit in the backseat, scribbling down notes as my pen jumps with each spring of the suspension. To turn up at the meeting in such a condition is far from ideal, but I have no choice. SIS needs to know about these new developments as soon as possible. Lithiby is my sole remaining contact.

There's only one thing I'm not sure about: the precise nature of the relationship between Maldonado and Javier de Francisco. What seems most likely is that they were simply Basque sympathizers who gradually worked their way up the political ladder, concealing themselves for—what?—fifteen or twenty years while they fed information back to their ideological masters in ETA. It's Burgess and Maclean, Philby and Blunt all over again, a nest of spies at the heart of the Spanish state. And now they must live out the rest of their lives in a pointless Colombian exile. Two high-level ETA operatives gone to ground after waiting years for their chance to strike from the immaculate camouflage of office. I feel almost sorry for them. Francisco probably recruited Carmen during their love affair, or she was turned during the four-year stint in Colombia. She seemed to confess to a relationship back at the flat. *A man I loved,* she said. And of course her mother, the ailing Mitxelena, is a Basque married to a man whose father fought against Franco in the Civil War. I was very dumb about that. I should have put two and two together.

As the cab accelerates through Puerta del Sol, I try Kitson again. There's no answer, so I just hang up, wondering how long it will be before the neighbors break into Carmen's flat and alert the police. If they track me down, I can always plead self-defense. Christ, if the worst comes to the worst I can probably claim diplomatic immunity. That's the least SIS can do after what I've pulled off tonight. When Lithiby hears about this, about what I've done for the service, everything in my past will be forgotten.

44

The Vanishing Englishman

Bocaito is packed. It's ten minutes past nine when I push through the door toward the seating area at the rear of the restaurant. Waiters in aprons and white jackets are preparing canapés at the crowded bar. There's a smattering of tourists eating an early dinner in the restaurant, but no sign of Lithiby. I'm given a reserved table near the kitchen and listen to the constant clatter and sizzle of plates and pans as my mind races once again through the thesis. Is there a flaw? Is there still something I'm missing?

By half past nine Lithiby has still not shown. I order a second glass of wine and rub my right hand under the table, trying to soothe the intense pain in my fist. I go to the bathroom again and check my face for marks. A small scratch has appeared, unnoticed before, within the two-day stubble on my jaw. Kitson is still not answering his phone and it feels like Museo Chicote all over again, waiting for Arenaza to show even as Buscon was digging his grave. A British couple—*The Rough Guide to Spain* on their table next to a bottle of Vichy Catalán—have been arguing for twenty minutes about a flight back home in the morning. The man, bald and tired, keeps checking his watch, drinking the water constantly as his wife suggests over and over again that they "*must* order the cab for six o'clock." Beside them, at a table tucked in the far corner, three quieter Americans are grazing on steaks and fish. Then the mobile phone pulses in my jacket pocket and I tear it out.

"Richard?"

"This is not Richard."

It is as if the room tilts and makes strange, the cold air of shock enveloping me in a dizzy confusion. For an instant I can barely breathe as my body revolts at the sound of her voice. It can't be. Not now. Not after everything that has happened tonight.

"Katharine?"

"Hello, Alec."

I take the phone away from my ear and check the readout. *Número Privado.* Then she speaks again.

"John Lithiby's not coming tonight. No doubt he sends his warmest regards. Last I heard John was earning $450,000 a year working for Shell out in Nigeria. So how have *you* been?"

She doesn't let me answer. The voice doesn't let me respond. It's part of a script I haven't read, words in a hideous scheme. I am on the point of challenging her, trying to find out how or why this could be happening, when Katharine Lanchester says, "The Central Intelligence Agency would just really like to take this opportunity to thank you for all of the hard work that you've done on our behalf over the course of the last few months. We really couldn't have pulled this thing off without you. You've gotten so *good*, Alec. What happened?"

"Kitson is CIA? Richard is an *American*?"

"Well, Brown University out of Charterhouse, but we like to think of him as one of our own. His mom's American, after all. You were mirror-imaging, Alec. Seeing yourself in him, just as we knew you would."

Katharine is laughing under this, contempt and delight in each revelation. I want to lash out at her. I feel more humiliation in this single instant than I have ever known in my life. I have been played for a fool by all of them, one after the other.

"But how did you . . . What . . . I don't . . ."

I cannot get the words out. The British couple are staring at me, as if sensing that something is not right. When I look at them their eyes flick away and there's an instant realization that Michelle wasn't Canadian SIS; she was American all along. Did Geoff and Ellie smother their accents? Did Macduff?

"How did we know about you?" Katharine asks, picking up on my question. "How did you fall for such a dumb trick?" I look at my left hand and it is gripping the edge of the table so hard that I can see the white bones of my knuckles bulging like pearls. "Well, what can I tell you? It was all just such a coincidence. You dropped right out of the sky. There we were in Spain, just a small-time operation tracking Buscon, and who do we find on his tail? None other than Mr. Alec Milius. As you can imagine, one or two people at Langley were kind of interested to see you, so we cooked up a little revenge."

They weren't tailing Buscon because of a consignment of Croat weapons. They were tailing him for something else. That explains why Kitson slipped up about Guantánamo. I try to maintain a physical dignity in this public place, but my body has cooked to a sweat. It feels as if every part of me is shaking.

"You see what happened, Alec? Is it starting to make sense? Luis was connected to A. Q. Khan, the Pakistani nuclear scientist. A big player, in other words. Tried to sell uranium-enrichment equipment to the Libyans. Now we can't have guys like that roaming the quiet European countryside, can we? He wasn't looking out for a box of rifles for the Real IRA. Christ, you were so *gullible.*"

Her voice is exactly how I remember it, not a note change, not a day gone by. America's seductive trap. Where is she speaking from?

"You had no idea about the dirty war until I told you?"

"Oh, that was *such* a bonus." Somebody laughs in the background. Fortner? "We must confess that without your help we would never have established a link between Luis and the Spanish government. The war would have gone right ahead and chances are that democratic Spain would now be on its knees." She pauses. "And we want to thank you for giving us that golden opportunity, Alec. Really we do. I needed a break. The *agency* needed a break. You see how *invaluable* we are now to the Europeans? You guys can't live without us."

Questions start forming in my mind. Do they know about Carmen? I cannot work it out while Katharine is still talking; every one of her sentences seems to noose and tighten around my rage. Does the CIA know that Maldonado and de Francisco were Basque spies? Does that theory even hold anymore? Again the British couple look up at me and I realize that I am breathing so loudly it must be audible to the nearby tables.

"So here's the deal." Katharine has cleared a slight catch in her throat. I can sense the coup de grâce and she delivers it with bitter precision. "There's no job for you with MI6, OK? No precious work and no future for Alec Milius. Nobody has forgiven you for what you did and John Lithiby does not offer redemption. It was all for nothing. You suffered for nothing."

With this my mood subsides in a switch to pure hatred. "I don't care about the job," I spit. It is like the torture again, the same defiance in the face of my tormentors, as if I have been freed by the shame of defeat. There is nothing left to lose.

"Yes you do," she replies, startled. "You care about the job. It's all you've ever cared about—"

"You killed Kate," I tell her.

She stops talking. There's silence on the line, as if we have been cut off by poor reception, a glitch of technology. Then, very quietly, "I don't ever want to hear that accusation repeated. We are not murderers. You believe what you want."

She's still angry about what happened, even after all these years. That gives me strength now. Later, when I am alone and going back over Kitson memories, the jar of Marmite at the safe house, the Hob Nobs and the car magazines, then I will feel humiliated. But at the moment it is enough to deny Katharine the triumph of her plan, just as Carmen and her accomplices were ruined by the failure of theirs. "You killed Kate," I repeat. "You killed two innocent young people with their whole lives ahead of them."

"Let me tell you something about that, Alec." There is a hiss of stubborn control, a tone I remember from our final conversation in London, all those years ago. "Let me tell you about your girlfriends. Right now Sofía Church is looking at photographs of you and Carmen Arroyo rowing your nice little boat in the Parque Retiro. Right now, Sofía Church is looking at shots of her boyfriend kissing another woman. . . ."

This flattens me. Why would they hurt Sofía? The CIA has tapes of me in bed with Carmen. What will it do with them? I will never be free of this foul trade.

"You fucking bitch. You didn't need Carmen, did you?" This, too, has occurred to me in the last few seconds, a subconscious realization beneath the raw shock of Sofía's pain. It explains why Kitson was so laissez-faire about the cover-up. The intel I brought him was always secondhand; the CIA had eyes and ears in every orifice of the Interior Ministry. "Why did you make me do that?"

"To humiliate you," she says. The frank admission, so coldly stated, is sickening. "To show you how low you could sink. Why else?"

"Is it because I didn't fuck you in London? Is that what this is about?" I am losing control. I have to maintain my dignity. The bald Englishman again looks at me, but his warning glance does nothing to settle my rage. "Did you never get over the fact that I wouldn't fuck you, Katharine? Did you leave the note for Sofía at the hotel so that you could break her heart as well?"

Now both of them fire disapproving stares at me and I suddenly find that I am embarrassed to have spoken like this, to a woman, in public. The strange, civilizing reflex again kicks in. So that I can speak my mind, I put a ten-euro note on the table and walk out of the restaurant, past the distracted waiters and the legs of *jamón*, holding the phone by my side as if the Americans' triumph might somehow drop onto the floor.

"What about Anthony?" I ask, out on Calle Libertad in a freezing wind. If I turned through 180 degrees it feels as though they would all be standing behind me.

"What about him?" she asks.

"He was British. They were all British. . . ."

"It was a house of mirrors."

A car comes quickly up the narrow street, making me jump. For a moment it's hard to hear what Katharine is saying. I hold the phone tight against my ear, cold and alone, bitterly angry. She says something about Macduff working in the private sector, being "a chameleon, a freelance." It was a long con, a Spanish prisoner.

"You spent all that money, all that time, just to get *back* at me?"

"It wasn't so difficult. It wasn't so expensive." Her voice is calm, matter-of-fact. "You were a luxury, a convenience. It was just like swatting a fly. And the ends more than justified the means."

She seems to laugh as I ask about ETA. "Did you do that? Did you make the farm happen?"

"Oh no. We're not *inhumane,* Alec." Again, a commotion in the background, the sound of a man savoring revenge. "Our intel at the time pointed to Zulaika, for what it's worth. Matter of fact we used that to silence him." She lets this sink in, the easy cruelty of American power. "Like I said, you just dropped into our laps. You were a bonus. We didn't have plans for you. Matter of fact, after Milan a lot of us felt you'd gotten away. And then it was just like a miracle. Let's just say that you were a guilty pleasure that none of us in these difficult times could resist."

I do not reply. I have heard enough. The events of the last two hours have turned me completely inside out, a switchback of unimaginable complexity, and there is now nothing that I can say to Katharine, no further taunt I can deliver that would improve my situation one bit. Best just to be done with it. Best just to admit defeat and move on.

"Well, it looks like you've got some thinking to do," she says, as if going back to the script. Are they watching me, even now? Were the couple in the restaurant part of her team? "You should observe the sight of all your hard work gone to waste. You should think about the two innocent women who are suffering tonight because you put your own personal satisfaction before theirs."

"Go fuck yourself, Katharine."

And I hang up before she has a chance to reply. Two more cars come toward me on the street and I step aside, bewildered as a drunk, walking down the hill as they pass. I need a bar. I have to drink. It dawns on me as an irreversible fact that I must now leave Madrid. I have no choice. I will have to abandon my furniture and my belongings and start a new life away from Spain, away from England, with just a bag of money hidden behind a fridge. It is what I have always dreaded. I did not know what it was to love a city until I lived in this place. What an idiot I have been. What an *amateur.* The first thing you should know about people is that you don't know the first thing about them.

45

Endgame

Two innocent women.

Two.

I am on a third glass of Bushmills in a bar in Chueca when this phrase begins to repeat. I can't shake it. It feels like the clue to the game, the counterplay.

Two innocent women.

The Americans don't know about Carmen. The Yanks stopped looking. The subtlety of ETA's plan defeated them. As we all did, they chose to see only what was in front of them. The CIA has no idea that the dirty war wasn't real.

The barman must see the light of hope in my eyes because he smiles at me, drying glasses with a white cloth. Half an hour ago he poured a whiskey for this dejected, sad-sack foreigner and now things are looking up.

"You OK?" he asks in English, and I even manage a smile.

"I think I might be," I tell him. "I think I might be."

It isn't clear if he has understood. Another customer has come into the bar and he has to serve him. I buy a pack of cigarettes—Lucky

Strikes, in honor of the brilliant, deceiving Kitson—and light one as the hope of an unlikely redemption glows in my heart. For a British intelligence officer to have uncovered a network of Basque spies in the Spanish government represents a major coup for SIS. Madrid would owe London for years. At the same time, the CIA's apparent triumph would be rendered meaningless.

So I still have a move, an opportunity to recover. I still have a chance for a mate.

The British embassy is on Calle de Fernando el Santo, about half a mile north of Bocaito. It would take longer in late-night traffic to hail a cab, so I walk through Chueca and arrive outside the entrance within thirty minutes, checking my tail for watchers and dumping any possible surveillance using two bars on Alonso Martínez. There's a small red buzzer beside a metal door and I push it. Seconds later a uniformed man emerges from a guardhouse inside the gates, walking down a short flight of steps to address me. He is tall and well built, speaking through the bottle-green bars.

"*Sí?*"

"I am a British citizen. I need to speak to a senior member of the embassy staff as a matter of urgency."

He juts out his thick lips and chin. He doesn't understand English. I repeat my request in Spanish and he shakes his head.

"The embassy is closed until tomorrow." He has a low, flat voice and this is his moment of power. "Come back at nine."

"You don't understand. It is a matter of great importance. I haven't had my passport stolen, I'm not looking for a visa. I am talking about something far more serious. Now you need to go into your cabin and contact the ambassador or first secretary."

The guard, perhaps unconsciously, touches the sidearm attached to his belt. An elderly couple walk behind me on the street and I see a light switching off about fifty meters away inside the building.

"As I told you, we are closed for the night. You will have to come back in the morning. Otherwise, read the sign."

He indicates a board above my head listing a telephone number to call in the event of an emergency. Perhaps it's the whiskey, perhaps it's the anger engendered by Kitson's betrayal, but I lose my temper now. I start shouting at the guard, demanding that he let me in. There is a bouncer's contempt in his manner and the strong physical grace of a trained, bored soldier. He looks primed to strike.

"I advise you to go home and sleep," he says, doubtless catching the smell of alcohol on my breath. "If you remain here I will call the police. You have been warned now."

Then, a miracle. A moat of light as a door opens in the concrete building behind him. A young diplomat, no older than twenty-eight or twenty-nine, emerges into the forecourt. He seems to sense the commotion at the gate and looks up, meeting my gaze. He has brown, uncombed hair, intelligent eyes, and a way of moving that's so relaxed it's as if his whole body is chewing gum. He comes toward us. Dark suit trousers, brogues, a long, antique British overcoat.

"Algún problema, Vicente?"

"Sí, señor."

"There's no problem," I interrupt, and he looks almost startled to hear the language of the old country. "I apologize. I've been standing out here shouting because I have something of great importance to tell the ambassador. I'm not a madman, I am not a fake. But you need to take me very seriously. You need to let me in."

Very cool, very reserved, the diplomat conducts a rapid up-and-down analysis of my appearance. Shoes to face. Lunatic or messiah?

"Can it not wait until the morning?" he says. "I'm the last to leave."

"No, it can't wait. That's what I'm trying to tell you. It's about the government here, the financial scandal." The guard takes a step back, letting the diplomat get closer. "My name is Alec Milius. I am a British citizen. I am a former support agent of the Secret Intelligence Service and I have lived here for a number of years. I can't tell you anything more than that without breaking the Official Secrets Act. But I need to speak to a senior member of the embassy staff as a matter of urgency."

"Do you have any form of identification?"

With that simple question I know that he is taking me seriously. I reach into my jacket pocket and take out the Paris-issued Lithuanian passport. It's not ideal, but it will do. The diplomat pulls it through the bars as the guard scuffs his feet.

"This is a Lithuanian passport. It says here that you were born in Vilnius."

"That part of it is fake," I tell him, and it looks as though this seemingly crazy revelation serves only to cement his belief in my authenticity. "I haven't been to the United Kingdom since 1997. My situation is complicated. I have information for the Foreign and Commonwealth Office, which will be of immense importance to—"

He interrupts. "You'd better come inside."

I feel a great surge of affection, of victory. The diplomat turns to the guard and instructs him to buzz the metal door on the right of the fence. I walk toward it and step onto British soil for the first time in seven years.

"And you said your name is Alec Milius?" he says, offering me a hand to shake.

"Alec Milius, yes."

It is a sort of homecoming.

Acknowledgments

Paddy Woodworth's superb book *Dirty War, Clean Hands* (Yale University Press, 2002) offers a comprehensive history of ETA and the GAL, and was indispensable in the writing of *The Spanish Game*. My thanks also to the incomparable Isambard Wilkinson, who guided me through the complexities of Basque politics on an eye-opening visit to Alava and Guipúzcoa. Lucy Wadham, author of the fine novel *Castro's Dream,* helped to inspire the character of Luis Buscon. Jamie Maitland Hume played a crucial role in the development of the plot. Nothing, however, would have been written without the love and support of my wife, Melissa, who makes everything possible.

I am also very grateful to everybody at *The Week,* to Joshua Levitt, Juan Pablo Rodríguez, C. Hunter Wright, Liz Nash, Ken Creighton, Bathurst's of Savile Row, Mercedes Baptista de Ybarra, Kim Martina, Bill Lyon, Ana-María Rivera, Trevor Horwood, David Sharrock, Lourdes García Sánchez-Cervera, Juliane von Reppert-Bismarck, Jamie Owen, Emily Garner, Gonzalo Serrano, Carolyn Hanbury, the Petrie family, the Mills family, Alexa de Ferranti, Ian Cumming, Richard Nazarewicz, Laura, and all the Johns at Finbar's.

Samuel Loewenberg, Rupert Harris, Smriti Belbase, Sid Lowe, Henry Wilks, Boris Starling, and Natalia Velasco read early drafts of the novel and offered invaluable comments and observations. My baby son, Stanley, ate several pages of the manuscript. Then the usual suspects took over: Tif Loehnis at Janklow and Nesbit; Rowland White at Michael Joseph. My thanks also to Luke Janklow, Claire Dippel, Rebecca Folland, Kirsty Gordon, and to Frances Sayers, Diane Reverand, Kathleen Conn, and Keith Kahla at St. Martin's Press.

As I was putting the finishing touches to the manuscript, I learned that my close friend Pierce Loughran, who had helped so much in the creation of both *The Hidden Man* and *The Spanish Game,* had died suddenly. He was thirty-six. Pierce was a man of great kindness and astonishing erudition, and I was lucky to have known him. He is greatly missed.

C.C.

London, June 2008